W9-DHX-004

Winner of a Holt Medallion for Southern Themed Fiction, and the *Houston Chronicle*'s Best Christian Fiction Author of 1999, **Annie Jones** grew up in a family that loved to laugh, eat and talk—often all at the same time. They instilled in her the gift of sharing through words and humor, and the confidence to go after her heart's desire (and to act fast if she wanted the last chicken leg). A former social worker, she feels called to be a "voice for the voiceless" and has carried that calling into her writing by creating characters often overlooked in our fast-paced culture—from seventysomethings who still have a zest for life to women over thirty with big mouths and hearts to match. Having moved thirteen times during her marriage, she is currently living in rural Kentucky with her husband and two children.

## Books by Annie Jones

### Love Inspired

*April in Bloom*

*Somebody's Baby*

*Somebody's Santa*

*Somebody's Hero*

*Marrying Minister Right*

*Blessings of the Season*

*"The Holiday Husband"*

*Their First Noel*

*Home to Stay*

*Triplets Find a Mom*

*Bundle of Joy*

### Steeple Hill Café

*Sadie-in-Waiting*

*Mom Over Miami*

*The Sisterhood of the Queen Mamas*

Annie Jones

# SOMEBODY'S BABY
## and
# SOMEBODY'S SANTA

**H** HARLEQUIN® LOVE INSPIRED® CLASSICS

Recycling programs
for this product may
not exist in your area.

ISBN-13: 978-0-373-60973-4

Somebody's Baby and Somebody's Santa

Copyright © 2014 by Harlequin Books S.A.

The publisher acknowledges the copyright holder
of the individual works as follows:

Somebody's Baby
Copyright © 2007 by Luanne Jones

Somebody's Santa
Copyright © 2008 by Luanne Jones

www.Harlequin.com

**Printed in U.S.A.**

# CONTENTS

What do you think? If a man owns a hundred sheep, and one of them wanders away, will he not leave the ninety-nine on the hills and go to look for the one that wandered off? And if he finds it, I tell you the truth, he is happier about that one sheep than about the ninety-nine that did not wander off. In the same way your Father in heaven is not willing that any of these little ones should be lost.

—*Matthew* 18:12–14

# SOMEBODY'S BABY

For Elijah Dobben and Riley Davis, the two newest babies in the Jones family tree. You already have the blessing of wonderful parents who love you so dearly, but also a legacy of faith that will serve you all your days.

And remember when they speak of your "Great" Aunt Annie, that's not just a label, it's a promise! Really. I already have toys in my closet for when you come to visit.

# Prologue

"What is your secret, Miss Josie?"

"Secret?" Josie Redmond wiped her hands on the long white bib-apron covering her pink T-shirt and black jeans. She swallowed hard to push down a bitter lump of anxiety. Her gaze darted from the face of the man sitting at the counter to the huge glass window with the swirling red lettering spelling out the name of her business—Josie's Home Cookin' Kitchen.

Did her customers know she hadn't taken in enough money this month to pay her business loan to the Mt. Knott First National Bank? That the bleak downturn in business for the Carolina Crumble Pattie Factory had taken its toll on not only her customer base but also threatened to rob her of a very essential ingredient to her success? Or had someone gotten wind of the fact that her twin sister had been trying to contact her?

Just thinking of what her sister wanted left Josie feeling jumpy as a cat, fearing for everything she held dear.

Her eyes went to the far wall of her diner, the one she had painted with special black paint, virtually turning the whole side of the room into a giant chalkboard. She had meant it to keep young people from carving their initials on the tables and to allow children something to busy themselves with while their parents lingered over the last bites of dessert. But somewhere along the line, it had turned into a town message board. A place where people left notes to friends, reminders of upcoming events and, in a segment sectioned off by vines drawn in pink and green chalk, a prayer request list.

"Please remember Millie Tillson's oldest girl— baby due any day."

"Traveling mercies for Agnes and Virgil."

"For our children and teachers as the new school year begins."

Some farmer in the midst of a dry summer spell had simply scrawled in an earnest, oversize script: "RAIN."

And of course: "Pray for the Burdetts. Our jobs. The whole of Mt. Knott."

All summer Josie had been praying about all the things that got posted on her wall, as well as for the welfare of all the people she cared about in her adopted hometown of Mt. Knott, South Carolina. But her deepest concerns remained between her and the Lord, not something she wanted thrown out to feed the small-town rumor mill.

"Secret?" She laughed and tossed her head, knowing it would make her strawberry-blond ponytail bounce and give her an even younger appearance than her twenty-four years. "What secret?"

The older of the two long-past-middle-age regulars sitting on the stools at the lunch counter lifted his fork with the last bite of cherry pie for his answer. "Go-oo-od stuff."

The other man leaned in on his elbows, his deep-set eyes twinkling. "When you going to marry me, Sweetie Pie?"

All the men over a certain age in town called Josie Sweetie Pie. They said it was because she was sweeter than a baby's kiss and cuter than a bug's ear and whatever other cornpone phrase they could toss out to make her laugh. But really, they called her that because Josie Redmond, who otherwise thought herself a most unremarkable young woman, made the best pies in seven counties.

Everybody said so. In fact, more than one person just passing through town had told her that if she could ever figure out a way to market the unique pastry to the masses, she'd make a mint. Right now, Josie couldn't even afford to *buy* a mint, she thought, letting her eyes trail to the empty candy dish by the cash register.

"You? You're not her type, Warren." The more rough-around-the-edges of the two men looked into his coffee mug and grinned. "It's *me* she's going to marry."

"And spend the rest of my life trying to stay ahead of your appetite for pie, Jed? No, thanks." Josie teased the white-haired man in striped overalls and a short-sleeved plaid shirt. "I am on to you two. Always proposing and slopping sugar all over me like that when I know all you really want is to sweet talk your way to a second slice on the house."

The older men laughed.

"Best pie I ever tasted," Warren pushed his plate forward, the fork rattling over the streaks of cherry pie filling adding to the simple pattern. "But don't go and tell my wife."

"About you proposing?" Josie took the plate away.

"Naw, she knows all about that. Don't tell her what I said about your pie. She thinks I only come here to eat it because her new job keeps her too busy to bake."

At the mention of someone having a new job heads turned and the room got real still.

"Part-time at the bowling alley over in Loganville. And no, they ain't looking to hire anyone else." Jed raised his head and hollered to everyone all at once. He lowered his head a bit and gave it a slow shake.

"Rents shoes to snotty teenagers who don't know they're smarting off to a woman who probably did quality assurance on every Crumble they stuffed into their rude little mouths growing up."

Warren huffed.

*Crumble.* What an apt word for both the dessert cake and for the condition that the poor management at the factory—which everyone also called "the Crumble"—had left the town in. All those hopes, all those plans, all those lives, crumbled like the crisp brown-sugar topping of the "coffee cake with the coffee right in it."

Josie stared at the empty plates in her hands. "You know, y'all, I think I might have shortchanged you a bit on the size of your pie slices this morning, let me get you a second sliver on the house."

She would never make her bank payment doing business like this, but Josie couldn't help it. The whole town had felt the sting since the Burdett family had had to make cuts at the factory. Nineteen jobs gone already and another half dozen on the line. It might not seem like a lot but in a town of less than two thousand, counting kids and retirees, it made a palpable impact.

What a great time to try to open a business, Josie thought as she picked up the clear plastic lid on the pie stand. But then, timing had never been her strong suit.

Josephine Sunshine Redmond had been born almost a half hour after her identical twin sister, Ophelia Rainbow. That led their free spirit of a mother to announce, often and all their lives, that this meant Ophelia embraced life, chased it, was unstoppable in going after what she wanted while Josie was a plodding, methodical, reluctant old soul.

All their lives her sister had rushed headlong into one, uh, *adventure* after another while Josie tried to find comfort and like-minded people wherever the family's lifestyle landed them. Whenever they had arrived in a new place, chasing anything from freedom of expression—meaning a place where their mother could sell her art at local shops and craft fairs—to seeking out new experiences, which could mean *anything,* Josie had looked around for a nice, friendly church.

That was one new experience her mother just couldn't understand. So when Josie announced she had given her life to Christ at seventeen, the family had left her behind with her grandmother right here in Mt. Knott to finish her senior year of high school and find her own way in life. Josie had done just that. She had gone to work for the Burdetts and used their college-payback program to get an associate's degree in business administration. Then, at the beginning of this summer, when she knew her job was about to be phased out, she'd used the general goodwill toward her in the community to open the diner. It was early August now. They'd been open a full three months. Josie still had the community's goodwill but not their financial support. No one had any money to spare!

Her sister had had her own set of new experiences, mostly involving men and substance abuse. She came to visit Josie from time to time, and Josie tried to influence her for the good, but it never lasted. A day or two of saying she was going to change was always followed by nights of partying and the inevitable taking off for parts unknown. The visits had stopped entirely a year ago when Ophelia had dropped a bombshell—well, a baby boy, actually— on her sister's doorstep. She asked Josie to care for the child for a few weeks while she got herself together, then disappeared.

Now Ophelia was trying to get in touch. After a year of loving the little boy she had named Nathan, a Biblical name that meant gift, Josie was now afraid that her rotten timing had reared its head again and she was about to lose her son forever.

*Beep. Beep.*

The familiar bleating of their local mailman's scooter horn jerked Josie out of her worried state.

She looked up and blinked, then looked at the two pieces of pie in her hands. She must have sliced them and plopped them on plates without even thinking about what she was doing.

"Here you go, boys." She plunked the free food

down on the counter and rushed toward the door and out onto the sidewalk in front of the diner.

"Got a letter for you, Miss Josie." Bob "Bingo" Barnes waved a large white envelope. "Looks important."

"From a lawyer?" Josie asked. Her fingers trembled as she reached for the suspect packet.

Bingo, a big man with bad knees who always delivered the mail on a small red scooter with an orange flag sticking out of the back, blinked at her. "I don't think it's from a lawyer."

But now that Josie had suggested it, the man clearly wanted to hang around and make sure.

Josie fingered the name on the return label, then glanced over her shoulder trying to calculate which would draw more attention. Should she stand here on the street in full view of everyone, take the bad news and have the whole town know her business in a matter of minutes? Or rush inside past all her regulars and hide in the kitchen and raise all kinds of concerns and speculations that would follow her for days, maybe years to come?

"Better to just get it over with," she muttered.

"Ma'am?" Bingo leaned forward, his eyes peering at her and his frown overemphasizing the fullness of his jowls.

*R-r-r-rip.* Josie worked her finger under the flap. She held her breath and slowly slid the papers out.

"Everything all right, Miss Josie?"

She was a struggling single mom, abandoned by her own family. Her business was teetering on the brink. Her town's economic base was literally crumbling beneath it. And yet…

She stared in disbelief at the papers in her hands. The paperwork signed by Ophelia relinquished parental rights and included a birth certificate naming his biological father so Josie could find the man and secure his approval for her to go forward with Nathan's legal adoption.

To the rest of the world Josie Redmond was just a plain little pie maker in a pickle, but when she saw the contents of that envelope she knew she was blessed beyond all belief. And all she could say was, "You know, Bingo, God is so good. And thanks for asking, because, yes, everything is going to be just fine now."

# Chapter One

*Two Weeks Later*

The South Carolina sky was black. His boots, jeans, T-shirt, all black. They matched Adam Burdett's silent, gleaming Harley—and his mood.

He narrowed his eyes at the simple frame house before him. Though he had grown up around Mt. Knott, this part of the small town was unfamiliar to him. His family had tended to keep to their fancy homes outside of town and didn't interact much with others.

"Bad for business," his father had said. Better to draw a distinct line between employees or potential employees—which is how they saw everyone in town—and friends. Never ask a personal question. Never commit anything more than a name and face to memory. Never offer more than the job description spelled out on paper.

"You do those things," the old man had warned his sons while they stood in the office of his snack food factory, "and it makes it a lot harder to have to fire a person later. And you will have to fire one of them, maybe a lot of them at some point."

According to the letters to the editor in the *Mt. Knott Mountain Laurel and Morning News* that Adam had read when he hit town a few hours ago, the old man had known what he was talking about. A lot of people in town were out of work. Even more were out of patience with the lack of a solution to their plight. A few were pretty close to being thrown out of their homes.

He gritted his teeth and forced the mixed-up emotions in his gut to quiet. On one hand the failure of his father's factory was just what Adam had wanted. On the other...

He gazed at the humble home again and exhaled, long and low. On the other hand, maybe there was something to be said for making connections, for caring about what happened to people once they walked out the factory door. He never had, and look where his callous attitude toward others had led him.

The empty matchbook in his hand rasped against his thumb as he flicked it open to check the address scrawled there. This was it. In this house, illuminated only by the pulsating light of a small-screen TV, Adam would find his son.

*His son.* The words tripped over his ragged nerves like a fingernail strummed over taut barbwire. Adam Burdett had a son.

He hadn't even known it until yesterday morning when a slick-haired private investigator had weaseled his way into Adam's office with the news and an unthinkable demand—that Adam sign away all rights to his child, sight unseen. There was about as much chance of that happening as there was of that P.I. ever suggesting such a notion again in this lifetime.

Adam hadn't belted the guy. But then again, he hadn't needed to.

Adam might look like nothing more than a good ol' boy, redneck rodeo rider with beef for brains, but looks, like too many other things in life, could be deceiving. Raised in a family of wealth and influence by a mother who treasured the value of an education, none of the Burdett boys were dummies. They could put thoughts and words together as well as they could fists and flesh.

And Adam had proven as much and then some to that paper-waving P.I. Give up his son for adoption and never look back? Adam huffed out a hard breath. Uh-uh. He'd never do to any child what had been done to him.

He folded his arms over his chest, fit one well-worn cowboy boot over the other at the ankle and leaned back against his parked Harley. Everything Adam had become in this life—and everything he had failed to become—he owed first to his adoptive mother, who had never treated him like anything but her own child and next to his own father. Whoever that was.

He knew who it *wasn't*. It wasn't his adoptive father, Conner Burdett, the father of Adam's three brothers. *Adopted* brothers. It shouldn't have been important to add the "adopted" part. Adam had never felt it mattered to his mother, but to the others?

The long-legged and fair-haired Burdett boys claimed Adam as their own even though Adam's broad, muscular build, dark eyes and angular features told differently. The family never spoke of it outright, but Adam sensed the subtle differences. He knew the gnawing ache of never feeling sure that he truly belonged.

To the outside world, at least, Adam was just one of the wolf pack of Burdett boys. A picture flashed in his mind of the four of them standing on the porch of the huge Burdett home in T-shirts they'd had made with their family nicknames emblazoned on them. Those names not only told of each boy as an individual, but said a lot about the real nature of their relationship in the family.

The oldest son, Burke, was born to the title "Top Dawg" and he lived up to the designation. "Lucky Dawg," Adam's next younger brother, Jason, got his name after a near miss that could have cost him his life, or at least a limb, at the factory. The youngest of the Burdett boys, Cody, earned the name "Hound Dawg" for his notorious talent for trailing girls. It had hung with the kid even now that he had become the only Burdett son to marry. It even clung to him when he became a minister.

All three grown men now shared Conner's lean build and eyes, which some called blue green, others green blue. They had straight noses and golden tan complexions.

Adam glanced at his reflection in the Harley's side mirror. Dark-brown, hooded eyes stared back from a face the color of baked red Georgia clay. He swiped a knuckle at the small bump on the bridge of his nose and sneered.

If his looks didn't give anyone doubts as to where Adam honestly fit into the Burdett family they would have only to hear *his* nickname to figure it all out. His mother said they'd tagged him with it young because they could never keep him in one place, that he shared her wanderlust. Her story rang true enough, he supposed, but that didn't ease the twinge of pain he felt every time the man they all knew was not his father called him by his nickname—"Stray Dawg."

All the old feelings twisted in Adam's gut. He refused to let a child of his become another stray, raised by someone who could never fully call the boy his own. No way. Not possible. And he'd do anything within his power to keep it from happening—even go crawling back to the scene of his greatest bravado and worst behavior. Back to Mt. Knott, if not back to his family.

Not that they'd have him back.

Adam had roared out of Mt. Knott a week after his mother's funeral, with an inheritance in hand, all ties to the family business severed and a hangover that had all but erased the events of his last nights in town.

He hadn't heard from or seen his family now in a year and a half but they had surely heard of him. His new position with a competitor had all but run the Burdett boys out of business. Now in order to do the right thing by his baby, he'd had to come home to a place where he knew he would not be welcome. But he would do it. He'd do anything for this baby he had not yet seen.

He scuffed his boot heel on the pocked driveway as he straightened away from his treasured Harley. He'd waited long enough. It was time to go and claim his heir.

Josie hadn't even bothered to lock up the diner. She had just tossed the keys to the young man who did the dishes and asked him to see to it. The message from the young girl who watched Nathan on Thursday evenings, when Josie stayed open until nine, had been muddled by panic. But two words stood out that had caused Josie to tear off her apron and all but run the two blocks from her business to her small rental house.

"Baby's father."

A shudder worked its way through her body. The man who had the power to grant her the one thing she wanted most in life—the chance to adopt the baby boy she'd loved as her own since his birth—was in her home.

She drew in the smell of coffee and day-old pie clinging to her pale-blue T-shirt and the fluffy white scrunchie holding back her curly hair. She'd had to wait a week to get up the nerve and the funds to hire a private detective to contact the man on the birth certificate. Not that she couldn't have tracked him down herself but, well, just looking at the name made her anxious. Adam Burdett!

She hadn't known him but she certainly knew of him. And in a funny way, what she knew had filled her with what now seemed false confidence.

After all, he was the one who had turned his back on his own family and a whole town. How serious could he be about wanting to play a part in his son's life when he had done that? He was Mr. One-Night Stand. According to her sister, he hadn't even called the next day to say…whatever it is a guy says after an encounter like that.

Josie wouldn't know that kind of thing. She and her sister might be identical twins, but their lifestyles were as different as their personalities. Yin and yang. Their mother, a "freethinker" who couldn't keep a job, didn't want a marriage and seemed always in pursuit of the latest trend in spiritual enlightenment, called them that. Light and dark. Day and night.

Josephine and Ophelia.

Josie snorted out a laugh. Even their names said it all. Josephine sounded sturdy, practical. She worked hard and wanted nothing more than to serve the Lord, make a permanent place to call home, to create a family with a man she could trust and depend upon. And to be the kind of woman he could depend upon in return.

"He's in your bedroom," the sitter whispered the last word as Josie hit the front door of her house.

Josie gave the girl a reassuring nod and headed down the hallway. If she could afford a house with more than one bedroom, he'd be in the nursery, but since the crib was in her room, she had expected to find him there. She pulled in one long breath, peered into the dim room, illuminated by only a soft glowing light on her dresser. She stole a quick peek at her sleeping baby, then pushed open her door with one hand, ready to do battle. "I don't know what you think you're doing. But if you value your life, you'll get your hands out of my drawers."

He looked as if he was about to swear, but he didn't, though Josie suspected it was more from shock than good manners or morality. He shut the small drawer he'd been peeking into. He peered at her, instead, then his whole face changed. His eyes narrowed. He smirked a bit. "I didn't expect to run into *you* here."

The deep gravel-throated whisper made her shiver. She froze in the shaft of light pouring in from the hallway. Her stomach clenched.

"I'd say you're looking good, but then, you know that, don't you? You always look good." He did not move into the light, remaining just a silhouette against the mirror above her chest of drawers. "Even after all this time and after…everything you've been through. You look as good as the last time I saw you, Ophelia."

Josie blinked in the darkness, hoping her eyes would adjust to sharpen his image. At the same time, she wanted to clear up a few things for him, as well. "Listen, pal, you've made a mistake. I'm not—"

He stepped from the shadows into the muted light.

Josie's mouth hung open, her every sense in that one instant focused on the man who held her future in his big, calloused hands.

He wasn't huge, though he seemed larger than life in presence. His shoulders angled up from a trim waist and western-cut jeans that bunched in furrows over his traditional-style cowboy boots. What she saw of his face, his strong jaw, determined mouth and slightly crooked nose made a compelling, if not classically handsome, image.

He moved in on her, like something powerful and wild sizing up his prey. His eyes glittered.

She pressed her lips together, too angry at his supposition and his presumptive presence to trust herself to speak.

He began to slowly circle her so close that his soft shirtsleeve rasped against her bare elbow.

The man was playing games with her—or more to the point, with Ophelia.

Ophelia liked games. They were her stock and trade. The man was no fool to go on the offensive to try to beat Ophelia at her own impressive bag of tricks. A sucker for excitement and danger, this predatory act might have been just the thing to get Josie's twin to go all liquid and make her easier to negotiate with.

But she wasn't Ophelia. She was smart, practical Josie. The dull one. The mom with a child to protect. This man's act was totally lost on her.

His boots scuffed lightly at the floor.

She tossed her head back, lifted her chin in her best attempt at regal composure. If he wanted to deal with her, it would be as two mature adults, no games, no stooping to base animal attraction to put her at a disadvantage. "Listen, cowboy, I know what you're up to."

His shoulder brushed against the curls trailing down her neck from the knot of hair atop her head.

A wolf, that's what he reminded her of, she decided. "I am not the same woman you shared a bed with a couple years ago."

"Yes, I can see that now."

About time. He'd spent at least one night in tangled passion with her sister, after all. Obviously, that was enough to help him see how very different they were, how very un-Ophelia-like and unappealing to a man like him Josie was.

"Yes, you've made a mistake, all right," she said. "A big one. I am not—"

"I got it. Not the same woman. You think I don't see that?" He slid his gaze over her, quick and businesslike, as if he were sizing up the marbling on a slab of pot roast before he tossed it in his shopping cart.

*Marbling. As in fat.* She shook her head at where her mind had immediately gone. Of the many ways she had been made to feel inferior to her sister, being a full size larger than Ophelia, was one Josie couldn't shake. And all local jokes about never trusting a skinny cook didn't really ease her discomfort over it, either. Now she couldn't help feeling self-conscious under this man's scrutiny. She found herself folding her arms over a stubborn pout of a tummy no amount of killer crunches had ever diminished.

He put his hand lightly on her back.

Josie gasped. She raised her hand to push him away and found muscles tight as steel beneath her fingertips.

His touch, warm and gentle, almost a reverent caress, belied the strength within the man. She lifted her gaze to his.

"How could I have not seen it? It was clear the moment I laid eyes on you," he murmured. "You aren't the same woman."

"No, I'm not." It sounded almost like an apology, she realized too late. This time she did push his arm away from her.

He let it fall easily to his own side as if she had had no effect on him whatsoever. "And you sure don't look as good as the last time I saw you."

Accustomed as she was to unfavorable comparisons to her sister in the attractiveness department, this man's assessment stung like a backhanded slap to her self-esteem.

She hung her head. "I'm not surprised you'd think—"

He dipped his head and his eyes searched her face. "You look better."

"Better?" she squeaked, cleared her throat, then matched his smoky whisper in depth and volume. "Better?"

"Mmm-hmm." He nodded. "Motherhood becomes you."

She smiled. Maybe this guy wasn't a total jerk after all. He knew who she was and had picked up on the one thing in which she had outshone her vivacious twin. Motherhood did become Josie.

She managed a modest smile. "Thank you for noticing. I know we have a lot to deal with, but it's good to know you can see how important being a mom is to me."

"Oh, yeah, I can just guess how 'important' motherhood is to a girl like you—" a sudden change came over his features; a hardness rang in his tone as he wrung out the rest "—Ophelia."

*Yeeoow.* Now she knew how those football coaches felt when the player dumped a tub of ice on them to celebrate a victory! She peeked to make sure that the baby was still sleeping, then turned with a flourish to face this cowboy-biker-Burdett creep. "How can you not know who I am?"

"I could ask the same of you. Do you know who I am?"

"Of course I know who you are," she whispered back, closing in on him to keep her voice from disturbing her child. "You are the man who, if he doesn't get out of my bedroom this instant, will be explaining himself to the whole Mt. Knott Police Department, every last one of them a close personal friend of mine."

His mouth lifted in a one-sided sneer. "I'll just bet."

She spun quietly around to snatch the only picture she had of herself and her twin from on top of her dresser. "I know them all from going to school here. From working year after year alongside their moms and sisters and wives and friends at *your* family's factory. I know them from serving them meals at my own diner."

Confusion registered in his ominous expression. His gaze flicked downward to the framed photo, then up to her face as if asking if she expected him to understand what she wanted to show him.

She tugged it up higher for his inspection. "That's Ophelia." She jabbed her finger at the girl in the forefront of the photo with her hands up and her hair in her counterpart's face. "That's me. Josie."

"Josie?" He shook his head. "Who is Josie?"

"Josie is me, pal. The woman who is kicking you out of here before we wake my baby." She shoved at his shoulder to prompt him to get moving.

"For the baby's sake, I'll go, but just so we can sort this whole mess through somewhere else."

"Agreed." She ushered him into the hallway, pulling the bedroom door firmly shut after them.

"And for the record, ma'am," he said, stopping short in front of her so that she could neither move past him or retreat.

"What?" she asked, trying to sound as brave as she had felt while defending her son.

"For the record…" He leaned down close until his face loomed before hers, his eyes demanding her total focus. "That little boy asleep in that crib in there—"

She held her breath.

"—is *my* baby."

## Chapter Two

"Go on home. I'll be all right." This woman, this spitting image of Ophelia Redmond only…softer, gave the babysitter a comforting pat as she nudged the wide-eyed gal out the front door.

Adam stuffed two fingers of each hand into his back jeans pockets and shifted his weight to one leg. Softer or not, that tangle of red-blond curls with the honest eyes and mama-tiger-protecting-her-cub ferocity stood between him and his son. He didn't like that. Did not like that one bit.

And Adam was determined he would not like her, either. He'd come for his son and that left no room for anything but cold indifference toward the woman who wanted him to relinquish his parental rights.

Josie shut the door and turned to him, a smug expression on her pretty face. "I'd ask you if you wanted some coffee, but seeing as you're not staying long enough to—"

"I take it black," he told her. "The coffee, that is. In a mug, not some wimpy little teacup."

Her eyes cut straight through him like two burning coals. They shone with emotion and life that he'd never seen in her twin's gaze. Not that it mattered, of course. As far as he was concerned, Josie Redmond was the enemy.

"And piping hot," he added, enjoying tweaking her anger a bit more than he really should have allowed himself.

She took in one long, deep breath, held it, then let it out, slow—real slow. "Anything else?"

"With sugar."

"Do tell."

"Yep."

"Well, I like mine decaf. Instant decaf." She jerked her head toward the open door to his left. "You'll find everything you need on the counter."

"Me?" He jammed his thumb into his breastbone.

"You want coffee, you make coffee." She put her hand to the wall and kicked her thick white shoes off. "I'm officially off duty, Mr. Burdett."

"Adam," he drawled, hoping it hid his grudging admiration for her unflappable response and her no-nonsense approach.

She reached up and snagged the white hair-holding thingy loose. Spiral curls clung to it as she dragged it downward. She shook her head, her hair tumbling down to brush her straight shoulders. She put her hand behind her neck. "What did you say?"

"Huh?"

"Maybe *I* should make the coffee after all." She narrowed one eye on him. "Wouldn't want to tax you too much, you know, by expecting you to talk *and* handle a kitchen appliance at the same time. Could get tricky."

Adam huffed a hard laugh, more amused than he wanted to admit. "Bet you get a lot of tips with that winning attitude of yours."

"I do all right." She turned and padded into the kitchen.

"I'll just bet you do," he muttered.

"What'd you say?"

"Adam." He strolled into the glaring light of the kitchen and leaned against the cabinet where she was pulling out two coffee mugs. "I asked you to call me Adam. Mr. Burdett is my father."

"I know." She clunked one cup down on the counter.

"Yeah. Of course. Everyone around here knows the Burdetts." He watched her for some sign that she shared his opinion of his family. Why he wanted to find that commonality with her, he didn't know. It just seemed, standing here in this small space with her, that it sure would be nice to have a girl like her on his side. "You know which one I am, right?"

*Somebody's Baby*

She placed the second cup down as though it were as delicate as an eggshell, then stretched her hand out for a jar of instant coffee. She wrenched the lid off the jar, then yanked open a stubborn drawer, making the silverware clatter as she pawed around inside it.

He tried to will her to answer. He wanted to hear firsthand from someone who didn't share his last name, just what people in Mt. Knott thought of him and what he had done to his family's business. He wanted to hear it from *her*.

"I know which one you are." Her fingers curled around a spoon, and the room grew very quiet. Finally she said so softly that a draft from the nearby window might have blown the words away, "You're the man whose name is on my baby's birth certificate."

She did not look up. She went right on making the coffee. But it didn't escape Adam's attention that as she scooped the dark-brown powder into each cup, her hand trembled. With one sentence she shifted from a smart, sassy woman in control to one scared little lady.

That's just what he had wanted when he had first shown up tonight.

Then why didn't he feel better about it?

"What am I doing?" The spoon clinked against the inner lip of the cup. She shut her eyes and shook her head. "I should have heated the water first."

"Never mind." He straightened away from the cabinet.

"No. I'll fix this." She lifted both cups. They rattled against each other, tipping one and sending instant coffee spilling over the counter. "Now look what I've done, I—"

"Look, forget it." He stepped forward, feeling every inch the heel for having reduced her to this. "I don't need any coffee."

"No, I said I'd make it and there's one thing you ought to know about me, Mr. Burdett. If I say I'm going to do something, I do it." She set both cups down, then began to scoop up the dark dust in her palm. It sifted through her fingers like sand. "I can fix this. I can—"

"Josie." He took her by the wrist and turned her to face him. That's when he saw the tears rimming her eyes. They seemed held in place only by the sheer force of her will not to cry. He cupped her fisted hand in his palm. "I didn't come here for coffee."

"I know," she rasped. "You came here to take my son."

A few minutes ago he'd not only have agreed with her, he'd have thrown in a crude adjective to seal the deal. Now? All he could do was clear his throat and say, softly, "Then maybe we should just talk—"

She jerked her head up. "I'm not anything like my sister, you know."

He smiled then. "I can see that."

"You can?"

When she looked confused, Adam noticed, a small crease appeared between her eyebrows.

"How can you possibly see I'm not like Ophelia? We only just met."

"I can see it—" he rubbed one knuckle along her cheek as gently as he could manage "—because you're the one who's here with my son, not her."

"That's because…" Her voice failed. She blinked. A single tear dampened her cheek. She pushed out a shuddering breath. "I love him. He's mine."

It killed him to hear that, and at the same time it made him proud and elated to know his boy had been loved and wanted by somebody. Adam studied her with a series of brushing glances.

Not just *somebody,* he realized when his gaze searched hers. The baby's aunt. His birth mother's identical twin. Someone with a blood bond and a heart with the capacity to put her needs aside to care for a helpless infant.

And grit. Josie had to have grit, he decided on the spot. How else could a woman choose to bear the burden of single motherhood? How else could she stay in Mt. Knott and watch the jobs and opportunities ebb away, partly because of his own actions, and even begin her own business because she knew she had to provide the sole support for a child?

"You can say that? After Ophelia just dumped him on you?"

"I never said she—"

"But that's what she did, right?"

The woman lowered her gaze to the floor. "It doesn't change how I feel about him."

Adam swallowed, and it felt like forcing a boulder through a straw. Everything he'd determined about this lady flew right out the window when he considered all he'd learned in just a few moments with her. He liked her plenty, in all manner of ways, most he didn't even understand yet—and he reckoned she was plenty good for his boy, as well.

"Please, Mr. Burdett," she whispered, her chin angled up and her eyes bright with unshed tears. "Please tell me you haven't come to take away my baby."

"Actually, ma'am, I…" Adam sighed.

Who was he kidding? He couldn't take his son away from the only mother the baby had ever known. He wouldn't.

"I haven't come to take him away, Josie."

She shut her eyes and mouthed the words *thank you*.

Adam didn't know if she spoke to him or to heaven—maybe both. He took one step back. So he'd wimped out of doing what he'd come here to do. That didn't mean he'd called a complete surrender…and he respected this woman enough to make sure she understood that without question.

"But I think you should understand, ma'am." He

stuck his thumb through his belt loop and anchored his boots wide on the gleaming vinyl floor. "I won't simply sign some papers and walk away, either. He's my boy and I'll do whatever it takes to make sure I stay involved in his life. *Whatever* it takes."

Joy and apprehension battled within Josie, and in the end joy won. He said he wasn't going to take her baby. Knowing that, she figured she could handle anything else thrown at her by this biker/cowboy with a voice that poured over her nerves like honey over sandpaper.

"Then let's talk, Mr. Burdett." She extended her hand toward the small kitchen table, her hope renewed that this could still work out in her favor. "If you still want some coffee, I can—"

The sputtered coughing cry of the baby halted her offer and Adam Burdett's movement toward the table at the same time.

He gave her a quick, panicked look. "That him?"

"Unless my cat's become a ventriloquist, I'd say yes." She laughed but couldn't make it sound real, not knowing that if the baby awakened she'd have to let this…this…*father* person see him. The very notion made her heart race.

She cocked her head to listen, praying that the baby was merely restless and would quiet and go back to sleep on his own.

"You got a cat?" Burdett leaned into the doorway to stare down the hall in the direction of the bedroom.

"What?" She blinked, moving to the door to lean out just a bit farther than he did.

"A cat." He slouched forward, his face a mask of concentration all focused on any sound that might arise from the child. "I heard it said that it's not good to have a cat around a baby."

"That's an old wives' tale." Josie rolled her eyes.

No other sound came from the baby's room. She relaxed enough to appreciate the level of confusion and worry on Burdett's face over the routine sounds the baby had just made and some silly superstition.

The baby was quiet. Maybe the fact that she'd dodged the letting-him-see-his-son-for-the-first-time bullet made her warm a little to the man. Or maybe it was the tenderness in those eyes that allowed her to loosen up a bit and say, "You don't know much about babies, do you, Mr. B— I mean, Adam?"

"This is my first," he said softly.

"Mine, too," she said, even softer.

She bet no other new parents had ever shared such an awkward or awkwardly sweet moment. Josie found within herself the power to actually smile. Maybe after a few meetings, a few long talks about parenting philosophy, visitation expectations, some practical lessons in the care and feeding of a one-year-old, she'd be ready to allow this man to see their son. Then later, maybe, after he'd proved himself capable, he could hold the baby and—

Just then the baby broke out in a howling lament. Josie froze.

"I don't know much about babies, ma'am." Burdett glanced at her and then down the hallway, his whole body tense. "But I do know that means someone needs to go check on him."

She took off before he finished the sentence. Josie heard his big old boots clomping along the hallway right behind her stocking feet and it irritated her.

"So then, you're saying it's okay—your cat and the baby?"

"What cat?" She spun around, placing one hand and one shoulder to the bedroom door. He practically loomed over her as she glowered up at his concern-filled face and snapped, "I don't have a cat."

"You don't?"

"No."

The baby wailed again.

"But I do have a child who needs my attention. Now if you'll just go wait in the kitchen and excuse me, I'll take care of my baby." She started to slip inside the room without opening the door to any unnecessary invitation.

His arm shot past her head, his palm flattened to the door just inches from her eye level. "Whoa, there, sweetheart."

She twisted her head to peer over her shoulder.

"I promised I wouldn't take the baby from you." His dark eyes went almost completely black. She saw the heat in his cheeks and felt it on his breath as he lowered his voice to a raw-edged whisper. "But I double-dog promise you something else, as well, I won't take *this* from you, either."

"What?" A corkscrew curl snagged on her eyelash and bobbed up and down as she batted her eyes in feigned innocence.

"I won't take this game of trying to shut me out of my baby's life. I want to make that very clear."

It was. And despite the anxiety it unleashed in her, Josie realized, she respected and admired his attitude. For a year now she had painted the baby's father as some sleazy party animal who hadn't even cared enough to find out what had become of Ophelia. It gave her some curious comfort now to know that wasn't the case. Her son had a decent man as a father.

A decent, gorgeous, Harley-riding, Mt. Knott-deserting rich man who could change from rapt preoccupation over his child and some imaginary cat to issuing hard-nosed mandates about the boy in a matter of seconds, she reminded herself.

"Do you understand that, Josie?"

She understood that and so much more. Like her problems with the diner and the simple existence she had known before she took in Nathan, from this point forward the life she had planned was going to take a different turn, and, like it or not, it was going to have to include Adam Burdett.

## Chapter Three

They both shuffled quietly inside the room, using only the stream of light from the hallway to guide them.

"Hush, now, Nathan, shhh. Quiet down. It's all right." Josie, standing in profile to Adam, cooed some kind of magical, maternal comfort to the lumpy blue blanket she pulled from the crib.

"Nathan?" He turned the name over and over in his mind. He liked it. "Is what you named him?"

"Yes. It means…" She snagged her breath and held it a moment. "It's Biblical. It means gift."

"I like it." He found himself nodding slowly to show his approval.

"I'm glad," she whispered, but nothing in her body language underscored her claim. She cuddled the baby close and spread the blanket out over the two of them so that Adam could not even see a tiny finger or a lock of fine baby hair.

He longed to lay eyes on his boy for the first time, show himself and say, "Hello, Nathan. I'm your father. I'm here now. I won't allow you to grow up feeling as if the people who should have done anything within their power to keep you, gave you away and didn't care."

Adam knew most adopted children did not feel this way. But he had. He had been *made* to feel that way. And now that he had returned to Mt. Knott, he would not only shield his child from those emotions, Adam would make his remaining family pay for having treated him so callously. He had the means and the motivation. The news of his unexpected fatherhood had hastened his plan but had not quashed it. If anything, it gave him new passion for the battle that lay ahead. He would do this not just for the child he had been, but for the child lying in this small, dark room before him.

Adam strained to get a good look at the kid without getting too close. Deep in his gut, he truly wished to step forward and scoop his son up in his arms. But somehow his body would not cooperate. He hung back, his back stiff, his legs like lead, folding then unfolding his arms across his chest, then letting them dangle limp at his sides.

"Is he..." He craned his neck to peer around a

tossed-back flap of the blanket that draped from Josie's shoulder to her midthigh. "Is he okay?"

"Well, he's not wet or…otherwise." She rocked her body back and forth, and the crying died to gurgles and gasps.

"Maybe he's hungry." Just saying it made Adam feel all fatherly. Maybe this wasn't such a hard thing after all, to take care of a baby.

"I doubt that." She patted the bundle gently, still rocking.

"He would have had a bottle before bed."

"But babies eat at all hours." He spoke like a veritable authority on the subject even though, deep down, he felt like a complete dolt. Him! Adam Burdett, one of five highly valued and overpaid vice presidents of acquisitions and mergers for Wholesome Hearth Country Fresh Bakery, a division of Cynergetic GlobalCom Limited. How could one small, totally dependent creature reduce him to such uncertainty and ineptitude? "Don't they need to, um, refuel, during the night?"

"Refuel?" For the first time she laughed faintly.

But still, something in the sound of it made Adam long to hear it again.

"Yeah, you know. Like a minijet with diapers?" He pressed his lips together and made the sound of a sputtering engine. "Or a rechargeable battery."

"If they ever find a way to channel this kid's energy into a battery or an engine, I'll have to give up my job and chase him around full-time."

"Yeah, you wouldn't want that."

"Are you kidding? I'd love to give up worrying about how I'm going to keep the Home Cookin' Kitchen open and be a full-time mom to Nathan." Her eyes grew wide suddenly. "Not that I want my business to fail. I love what I do. I love providing a service to Mt. Knott and seeing everyone, and I love cooking. Especially…well, my specialty is not important beyond, you know, being a mother being my specialty."

She was babbling. Not in a ridiculous, silly way. She was just nervous. And relieved. Nervous and relieved all at once. He could sense that in the way her words all ran together, then stopped suddenly. He didn't learn much from what she said, of course, but it did help him see her inner conflict over her roles as a woman business-owner and a mother to his son.

"But if I could somehow not have to keep the crazy hours at my Home Cookin' Kitchen and could just spend all my time with Nathan, at least in these early years, I'd do it in a heartbeat. No regrets. No complaints." She stopped abruptly again, and this time her eyes grew wide before she added, in a little slower and more pronounced voice, "Not that I'm hinting that's what I expect you to provide."

She'd babbled until she had spoken the truth. In doing so, she'd given Adam a glimpse into her desires and perhaps some future negotiating power. He filed the information away and, on the surface, let it go. "So, he's not hungry?"

"No. I don't think he's hungry." She kept swaying back and forth and jiggling the baby, who had begun to fret and grunt quietly beneath the blanket. "He's been sleeping through the night for a couple of months now."

"He has?" Adam was rocking now, too. He couldn't seem to help himself. Though he wasn't sure, he figured this was how it felt to carry on a conversation on a boat. "Well, maybe he's sick, or needs some—"

"Maybe…" she interrupted in the same soothing murmur she used with the baby "…he just had a bad dream."

"Dream?" He stopped rocking long enough to consider that. "What on earth does an itty-bitty baby like that have to dream about?"

"He's not so itty-bitty. He's got plenty of things to dream about, a whole lifetime of experiences. *His* lifetime." She shot him a look that even in the dim light Adam interpreted as a challenge. *I have been this child's mother for his entire life. Where have you been?* "He'll have his first birthday in two weeks, won't you, tiger?"

"He will?" Adam stretched out his fingers, needing a kind of visual cue to help him do some lightning-fast math. "That means he was born in September, so August, July, June—"

"January."

"What?"

"He was conceived in January, one year, eight months and two weeks ago." She faced him, her mouth set in grim accusation. "Don't tell me that doesn't even ring a bell. Maybe you've just been with so many women that it's all a blur."

"Oh, it's a blur all right, but not for the reasons you think." He scratched at his cheek while his mind struggled to force all the pieces together. "Maybe you don't recall this, but…"

Adam faced a choice. Speak the truth and risk having it sound like a plea for pity or at least leniency for his behavior or skim over it. He could stand here and own up to that bad behavior without any preface or attempt to put it in context.

His mother had died. He felt he had not only lost the only one who'd seen him truly as her own but that he had also lost his place in his family. When his suggestions to take the Carolina Crumble Pattie to a wider market had been ridiculed by his father and brothers, Adam felt he had lost his reason for staying in Mt. Knott as well. By the time he met Ophelia, a beautiful woman who shared his disdain for the small town, he had not been thinking about right and wrong.

He had been in pain. He needed to feel he wasn't

a lost cause, just a stray that nobody wanted. He felt worthless and figured he didn't matter to anyone, not even God. It became easier to fall into sin, he had learned, when you take your eyes off the Lord and start looking at the mess you have made of your life and the mess life has made of the world around you.

He had long prided himself on being a man who told the truth. It was one of the things, he felt, which set him apart from his father.

While Conner Burdett was not a dishonest man, he had built his business on the belief that knowledge was power. And Conner protected his own power by controlling what knowledge he allowed others to have.

On the other hand, telling her about all the years of pain and loneliness that led up to those few wild nights that January would probably just sound like an excuse.

Adam didn't like people who made excuses. Besides, he had no way of knowing if he could trust Josie with an emotional truth that could cut him to his core. She may yet prove herself the enemy in a bitter custody case. He decided to tell the truth, but not all of it. It twisted low in his gut that he would follow his father's path but if she listened, really listened, she would hear the message beneath the words and have an inkling of what had fueled his angry rebellion.

"If you recall, I came into my inheritance in January." *I lost my mom. My only ally.*

Her determined jawline eased a bit.

"I found myself with a totally new status." *Finally, officially, on my own. Alone.*

Her gaze dipped downward.

"I didn't handle it particularly well." *I'm not making any excuses.*

She nodded, her brow furrowed. "I'm sorry about the loss of your mother."

"Thanks." He'd struck a chord, he supposed.

"She was a remarkable lady. A real force in the community. A good Christian who supported so many social causes and cared about people. She really put her faith in action."

"More than you probably know." He thought not only of how his mother had taken him in as a child and raised him as her very own, but also of the ways she devoted her own inherited fortune to help those in need. It tugged at Adam's heart to realize that back then he'd been so fixated on striking back at his father and brothers that he had done nothing to honor his mother and the things she had taught him. That did not alter his plan for revenge, however.

He was a Christian. He just wasn't *that* kind of Christian. He fought back a twinge of shame over having even thought that, much less allowed it to stand as his justification. "If it helps, I am not proud of what I did."

"I'm not the one you owe an apology to." Josie poked her chin up, fidgeted with the folds of the blanket that still concealed his son from him.

"An apology? I wasn't aware I owed an *apology* to anyone." It was what it *was*. He felt bad that it had gone so wrong. Felt some shame that his grief and resentment had uncovered his weaknesses instead of revealed his inner strength. But getting all touchy-feely about it now wouldn't change the past or set things right today.

He had come to town with only two indisputable responsibilities, to claim his son and ruin his so-called family. Neither Josie nor Ophelia Redmond figured prominently in his designs. "Your sister was a willing partner in what happened between us. Don't forget that she was the one who failed to notify me about the baby. It's not as if I haven't paid a price for my poor choices."

"I don't doubt that." She gave him a look of sympathy that did not sink to the level of pity.

He hadn't known anyone who had ever managed that with him and appreciated it in a way he could not for the world have articulated. His whole life, people had given with one hand and taken away with two. Encounters with even the most sincerely empathetic often left him undermined and exposed. He wondered if Josie would finally be the exception.

"However…"

"I should have known," he muttered under his breath.

"Hmm?" she asked over the wriggling and almost inaudible fussing of the baby in her arm.

"Give with one hand, take with two," was all he felt compelled to say.

*"However..."* She patted the blanket and adjusted the form beneath it, raising it higher against her own small frame. The legs kicked and a tiny hand flailed out to grab a strand of her hair. She ignored it and forged on. "Your *choices* have resulted in this small life. And whether you have suffered enough or who is to blame for how the two of us arrived in this situation no longer matters. When you are a parent, it's not about you and your feelings anymore, it's about what's best for your child."

"My child," he echoed softly. "Thank you."

"You're welcome." She batted her eyes in a show of seeming disbelief, then leaned back to look under the blanket and the wriggling infant in her arms. "I don't usually yell at strangers like that, but..."

"I'm not thanking you for yelling at me." He chuckled at the very notion. He could go just about anywhere in this town and get yelled at, and by people a lot more experienced and colorful at it than Miss Josie Redmond.

"Then, I don't—" She hook her head.

"When," he explained as softly as the baby's gentle stirring.

"What?"

"You said *when* you are a parent. Not *if.* Your intention with that little speech was to put me in my place. And with that small distinction, you did." He reached out and brushed the blanket from atop the child's head.

The baby squirmed and made a sound that went something like "ya-ya-ya," then laughed.

Neither music nor birds nor even the grandest of majestic choirs could ever sound as sweet as the sound of his baby laughing.

"Anyway," he explained, knowing he'd have to appease Josie in some way before she'd even think of allowing him to hold his son, "I admit to my part, my shortcomings in all of this. I did spend time with your sister, obviously, and—"

"And it didn't mean a thing to you."

He lowered his head and his tone and took one step toward the woman holding his son. "You will never understand what it meant to me, lady."

She cupped the baby's head and took a step back from him. "Then why didn't you call her? Why didn't you try to find out what happened to her?"

"Because…" Again a choice loomed before him. Tell the whole truth and risk losing some of his power in the situation or say just enough to get what he wanted now. He looked long and deep into Josie's defiant yet anxious eyes and knew he only had one real course of action. The truth. "Because I was only thinking of myself. I acted like a wounded dog, snarling and mean and willing to do anything to protect myself. I spent a night with your sister, drunk most of the time but aware of what I was doing, and then I walked away and never looked back. Because that's what suited me."

There he'd said it. He'd given her plenty of ammunition to take a potshot at him and do some emotional damage. He did not deserve this child. But, as he hoped both his words and tone made quite clear, he would do whatever it took to be a part of young Nathan's life. *Because it suited him.*

"Oh." Clearly she did not know what to make of that. But she did not seem even remotely willing to use his confession against him. "Are you saying that if you had known sooner, you'd have returned sooner?"

"No." Again he spit the hard truth out. He had worked diligently this past year and a half to put himself in a position to do the most damage to…or good for, depending on one's vantage point, the Carolina Crumble Pattie Factory. If he had learned about his son sooner, he would have come for the child, but not until the time was right. "No, I can't say I'd have come back sooner. But I can say I am here now and that's what we have to deal with."

They stood in silence for a long, anxious moment.

Adam could practically see the thought process playing out over Josie's features. He wanted to say something to tip her confidence in his favor, but in the end he could only say straight-out what was on his mind. "You asked me earlier tonight not to take your son away, Josie, and I agreed. I won't. I can't do that to him—or to you."

He focused on her, standing in the shaft of light from the open door.

She seemed so small and alone in the otherwise dark room, that he felt drawn to her and the child cradled against her body.

He moved in, so near that he could see the fearful questioning in her eyes. He knew how it felt to wonder if anyone was on your side. To pray not to lose the person you loved most in the world and wonder how you would survive if the worst came to pass. He had prayed that prayer the night his mom died. But he had not come to destroy *this* little family. He had it within his power to prevent his son from losing the only mother he had ever known. He would not fail little Nathan in that regard.

Because, even though he had only known about him for a short while and had yet to even properly see him, Adam already loved the little guy. He supposed that among all his many faults and flaws, this redeemed him just a little. That in this feeling he knew a small taste of the greatest love of all, the love of God.

He placed one hand upon his baby's head and one protectively on Josie's tense shoulder. "Since you know I'm not going to take the boy, Josie. Why don't you just let me…hold him?"

She wet her lips. Hesitated.

"Please."

In one fluid movement Josie swept her hand beneath the child legs and then carefully laid him in his father's arms.

*His son.* Adam caught his breath. For all his good intentions and promises, holding his child for the very first time made him wonder if he'd spoken too soon. He did not want to tear this baby from the only mother it had ever known, but this was his son. His flesh and blood. And Adam would not settle for weekends and every other Christmas, just experiencing bits and pieces of his childhood.

He felt Josie tense at his side, but he didn't focus on her discomfort. Adam had always made his own rules in life—or figured a way around the ones he didn't like. That's exactly what he was going to do now.

He gazed into the baby's bright blue eyes and found just enough voice to whisper, "Hello, son. Daddy's here now. Daddy's here—and nothing is going to come between us ever again."

## Chapter Four

*"Nothing's going to come between us again."*

Adam's words to Nathan still rang in Josie's ears twelve hours later as she rushed about the diner trying to get ready for the morning coffee crowd.

Yes, *crowd.*

Large cities and fancy coffee shops and cafés with big noisy machines were not the only places that people liked to gather to chat on their way to work in the mornings. There had always been the usual fellows, the retirees who liked to do a little of what locals lovingly called, "pickin' and grinnin', laughin' and scratchin'." They met every day but Sunday, of course, to solve the problems of the world, tell jokes and stories they had all heard a hundred times, and reward their long-suffering wives with a little bit of "me" time.

Then there were the commuters. Ever since the

layoffs had started at the Crumble, more and more folks began their drives to workplaces in other nearby towns with what Josie had listed on tent cards on the tabletops as "Cup O'Joe To Go." It wasn't the kind of thing you could get at those fancy places. No *grande* or *venti* size disposable cups with insulated wrappers to keep the drinker from burning his or her hands or fancy tops that looked like Nathan's sippy cup. No, this was a bank of coffeepots, sweetener options and creamers where people walked in, filled up the coffee conveyance brought from home, dropped a dollar or two in an old pickle jar and headed off to face the day.

Often stopping to share a word of encouragement with one another or to check the chalkboard for messages or new prayer requests. Always with a sense of community that one couldn't find anywhere else.

This was, to Josie, the essence of why she lived in Mt. Knott. It was also one of the reasons she had brought Nathan to work with her this morning. She felt safe here and felt her son would be safe here, as well.

Not that she thought Adam would do any harm to Nathan or even break his word about taking the child but…

But in her whole life she could not recall ever having felt so vulnerable.

A product, she suspected, of more than just Adam's introduction into Nathan's life. This emotion was also a byproduct of her realization that the man would be a presence in *her* life for a long time to come, as well.

She went up on tiptoe to peer over the cash register at the baby playing quietly in the bright blue portable playpen in the corner of the café.

She had promised herself she wouldn't make a habit of bringing Nathan to work. Maybe when he was older, she had thought, she would have him come by after school. He could do his homework in one of the booths and she would serve him a snack and whatever advice she could spare until he got into calculus or something else she knew nothing about. But until then she had determined she would have him at work as little as possible.

Josie didn't need to bring him here, really. She had been blessed with a network of moms and grandmothers around town who had taken turns watching her son since Ophelia left him in her care. The original plan was to depend on this patchwork safety net just until the newborn was old enough for day care. Well, that had been the plan, but then when the jobs began to dry up, so had the town's only daycare center.

She wondered if Adam Burdett would see that as unacceptable and use it as a wedge to take Nathan from her. He had promised he wouldn't do that, but then, what did she really know about him?

"Adam Burdett?" The first person she had asked,

not giving the particulars behind her sudden interest in the man, had pondered it a moment. "Oh, Stray Dawg! Yeah. Yeah, I know which one he was, uh, is. The one who cashed out. Cut and run."

"Heard he went through that cash in nothing flat." The woman at the cash register took her change from Josie and, as she dropped the quarters and nickels into her coin purse, she elaborated, "Gambling." *Clink.* "Drinking." *Clink.* "Women." *Clink. Clink.*

"Gambling?" Josie shoved the cash drawer shut. "Drinking?"

"And women!" Warren and Jed confirmed in unison as they broke off from the morning gathering of curmudgeons to take their usual seats at the counter.

Of course Adam had women. A wealthy, handsome man like that probably had all kinds of girlfriends. She blushed at her own lack of sophistication and what many people would *tsk-tsk* as simple, out-of-date values. To hide her chagrin, she ducked back into the kitchen to check on the morning's first offering of pies still cooling on the racks beside the oven. *Girlfriends?* She doubted very much that a man like that thought of his conquests as girlfriends.

The aroma of apple and cinnamon and other spices filled the air. The tart sweetness of cherries bubbling in deep-red juices stung her nose. All buffered by the homey smell of flaky crust and Josie's specialty topping.

She went to the back door and cracked it open a

tiny bit, to allow some fresh air into the hot, almost steamy kitchen. She paused only a moment, lifting her ponytail and turning her head to cool the back of her neck before hurrying back to her tasks, and to talk of Adam. She peered through the door and shut out the noise and views of the room around her.

"Ended up with a factory job, they say." A man took a wad of bills from his wallet, showed them to some fellow coffee-bar patrons as if to say "this one's on me" then stuffed them into the pickle jar. "Ironic, huh?"

"Reap what you sow." One of his cohorts raised his mug in grateful salute for the freebie. "Bible says."

Josie glanced around for one of the silicon gloves she used to handle hot pie plates and the like. When she didn't find it immediately, she grabbed the nearest dish towel and used it to cover her hand as she picked up one of the cherry pies. She didn't want to miss a word of the conversation in the dining room.

"I spotted that Adam at a hotel in Raleigh a year ago. Back when my husband went to that International Snack Cake Expo deal, remember?" spoke up Elvie Maloney, who had just started coming in after she went back to work when her husband lost his middle-management job at the Crumble. "Kept to the outskirts of the show. Didn't interact with the old gang, not at all."

"Well, can you blame him?" Micah Applebee

scoffed. Micah had worked out at the Crumble for even longer than Elvie's husband. "After the mean-spirited way the Burdetts treated him?"

"The way they treated him was to make him a millionaire," Elvie shot back.

"Wish they'd up and treat me like that. I wouldn't even care if it was mean-spirited," Warren joked.

"You say that now but you'd come in here blubbering like a baby," Jed teased.

"Yeah, and using hundred-dollar bills to dry my tears," Warren said right back. They both laughed.

"Well, that Stray Dawg Burdett boy might have done better using money for hankies. It might have got it soggy but at least he'd have some of it left." Elvie whirled her spoon through her coffee.

"How do you know he doesn't?" Jed asked.

Elvie tapped the spoon on the edge of her cup, making everybody look her way. "Because he was at that conference working for somebody else. If I had millions, the last thing I'd want to do is work in a snack-cake factory all week and go to conferences on snack cakes on the weekend. Real suspicious if you ask me."

"Suspicious don't begin to tell it when you're talking about that one." A man wedging himself between two other people at the coffee bar snatched up a decaf pot and poured two cups worth into a thermal travel mug as he called out. "He's a wild one."

"The *smart* one, you mean," someone else at a

nearby table chimed in. "Got out while the getting was good."

"Really?" Josie tried to fit the pieces of information together. That wasn't as easy as it seemed. While she sincerely wanted to believe the best of the man, she didn't dare allow herself to dismiss words like *suspicious, cut and run, gambling*...and *women*. As in multiples. *Many*.

The man who wanted to claim his place as her son's father had been up to something since he'd left town, and Josie needed to know what. And why he had come back, if it wasn't for Nathan's sake alone. She stole a peek at her boy and exhaled in relief to see him happily laughing over a game of peekaboo with Jed. She'd done the right thing by bringing Nathan with her today. She simply could not risk letting that wild one, that stray, that Adam Burdett get his hands on her son.

Not until she knew more about the man.

She set the pie down, wiped a blob of cherry filling on her starched white apron and asked, as she headed back toward the kitchen, "Is that when things soured at the factory? When Adam left?"

"Die was cast long before that." Jed paused with his red bandanna kerchief held up between him and Nathan.

"Oh?" Josie tried to sound as if she didn't care, but deep down it gave her some solace to know Adam hadn't been involved in the downward spiral of her beloved Mt. Knott. "I worked there for years, part-time most of it, but still, I never once saw any signs of the place heading for disaster."

"What's the Bible say? Pride goes before the fall? I reckon that place ran on pride, mostly, the last few years. When the mama died, that really tore things, though." Jed made a show of inhaling the scent of pie, sighed then jerked the kerchief back down and made a face at the baby, much to Nathan's delight. "Can't say how many times my wife came home after a quarterly meeting worried for her job. Hear her tell it, the son that took off was the only one bold enough to stand up to his daddy and say things had to change or they'd go under."

Josie's heart swelled a little at that. It warmed her to know her son's father had once shown true concern about the business that supported so much of her hometown.

She took up another pie, using only the dish towel as a hot pad and whirled around to peer into the front room from the kitchen. "So then, Adam Burdett is basically a good guy?"

"Yes he is," came the whispered response from behind her. "And I'd appreciate it if you didn't talk about me behind my back."

*Splat.*

"Awww." Came the collective groan from the patrons.

The damp smell of pie, apple this time, rose

around her. The heat from a stray piece of fruit burned Josie's toe through her discount-store tennis shoe. Bits of crust lay smashed to smithereens all over the brown-red tile.

"Can you salvage any of it, honey?" either Jed or Warren asked.

She didn't try to distinguish between them as the other one quickly followed up with, "I had my mouth all set for a slice of that."

Josie walked farther back into the kitchen, shut out all the comments from her sympathetic customers and fixed her attention on the man who had slipped in through the open back door.

"I wasn't talking about you behind your back."

"No? Well, you sure were *listening* about me behind my back." He managed to sum up the situation without coming off arrogant or angry.

She smiled. "Then come on out in the open. I'm sure people here will be more than happy to talk about you right to your face."

He did not look amused.

Josie felt bad. She hadn't meant to hurt his feelings. She'd only tried to lighten the mood, to distract the man a bit after he'd caught her trying to find out more about him. And…and she wanted to show him her diner.

There. That was it. For some reason she wanted her baby's father to see what she had accomplished this last eight months since the first round of factory layoffs. She wanted him to know his son was being cared for by someone with drive, ambition, good sense and…and her very own pie carousel.

"I was just kidding, Ad—"

He put his index finger to his lips to cut her off. "Please. Don't say my name."

She glanced over her shoulder toward the dining room, which had gone uncharacteristically quiet. "Why not?"

"I don't want anyone to know I'm here. Not yet. I'm staying at a hotel on the highway and being very careful about the streets I take. Please don't undo all that now."

"I have to ask again, why not?"

He glanced toward the dinning room as well, then lowered his head and his voice. "Look, I just came by to see the kid. Went by your house and your neighbor told me you had to take him to work with you today."

Wanted to, not had to, she thought. To keep him safe from you. And she was wise to do it, apparently, since the man had already been by her home and it wasn't even 9:00 a.m. yet.

As if he sensed her trouble, the small boy in the playpen in the corner of the café shouted and threw a toy in the direction of his mother.

And on the heels of that, Jed, who had been playing with the child, stood up and called out, "Everything all right in there, Sweetie Pie?"

"Sweetie Pie?" Adam stood just inside the door of the kitchen.

Josie rolled her eyes then began pushing at the mess on the floor with the toe of her already pie-plopped shoe. "That's what everyone around here calls me."

"Oh?" Adam squatted down and used the pie pan to scoop up the mess. Unlike the spoiled, rich, suspicious-acting man she had been warned about, he didn't seem to mind getting his hands dirty. Josie could not say the same for his sense of humor. "I thought that your sister was more the everybody's sweetie type."

"Leave my sister out of this," she snapped.

He dropped the pie—pan and all—in the trash, then wiped his hands off on a towel.

Josie rushed over and snatched the pan out again. "I already lost the cost of ingredients on that. I can't afford the price of a perfectly good pan, as well."

"Sorry," he said, and seemed to actually mean it. "My mind was on other things... Sweetie Pie."

Josie heaved an exaggerated sigh, then went to the cherry pie that had been cooling all this time, cut a healthy slice, slapped it on a plate, then pressed that into his hand. "They call me that because of this."

He gave her a wary look.

"What's the matter? You too good to eat small-town-diner, homemade pie?"

"No one ever accused me of being too good for

anything, ma'am." He dipped his head, his eyes glinting. "But my mama did manage to instill enough manners in me that I try not to eat pie with my fingers. At least not in front of a lady."

Josie blushed at her oversight and hurried to get him a fork.

He dug in, taking as big a bite as the fork would hold. He tasted. He paused. He swallowed. "Mmm."

"Does that mean you like it?" Why it was important for this man to like her pie, Josie didn't want to think about. But it was. Very important.

"So good it gives me an idea."

"I thought we'd already established I am nothing like my sister."

"Leave your sister out of this." He wagged his fork at her in warning.

She blushed again. Guilty of the same thing she had just nailed him over.

Jed called out, "Sweetie Pie? You having trouble with that clean-up in there?"

"No." Josie would not lie but she didn't want to just disregard Adam's request totally. "I'll be out in a minute."

"Thanks." He took another bite, set the plate aside and began looking around. "I don't want people to know I'm in town."

"How could you possibly keep a thing like that a secret?" Josie tugged up the corner of her apron to wipe his hands on. "Your father or brothers will be sure to make a big deal about your being back in town."

Using the hem of her offered apron, he pulled her close to him and dabbed a bit of pie filling and crust from the corner of his mouth.

The crisp cotton of her apron looked stark against the darker tone of his hands and face. Just as the whites of his eyes and teeth did. The contrast might have put her in mind of a wolf or some other predator, but when she let her gaze sink deeply into his eyes she felt just the opposite. She felt protected.

He let the apron drop.

Josie stepped away.

Adam put his hands in the back pockets of his black jeans and began looking around the kitchen as he said, "My father and brothers are the last people I want to know I'm here."

Josie did not have a suspicious nature but that did not sound good. She plunked her hand on her hip. "Well, forgive me for this, but…why?"

He said it along with her, his smile playful.

She folded her arms and did not laugh.

"I can't say, Josie." He took her by the upper arms as if he wanted to fix her in time and space so that his message could not go awry. "But I can tell you this—if people start talking about me, someone will remember I was with Ophelia."

"So?"

"So, then they will start putting the pieces together. They'll talk. Speculate. They buzz and carry tales back and forth, building them up, getting half the details wrong. That's the way it is in an anthill of a town this size, right?"

He was right about the nature of small towns, but he was wrong in assuming it was automatically a bad thing. "I heard it said once that a good neighbor is the best family some people ever have. That's how I feel about the people in this anthill. Outside of my grandmother and Nathan they are the only family I have. I don't plan to keep any secrets from them."

"Okay. I'm not asking you to keep secrets so much as to not volunteer anything for as long as possible. Not yet. To everything there is a season, right?"

Josie raised an eyebrow at his ease with scripture. She wondered if she should be impressed or insulted that he could pull it out so readily for his use.

"I'm not suggesting you never tell anyone that I'm Nathan's father. Just that when you do, the timing should be right."

"Right? Timing?" Josie shook her head. Her stomach churned. "That certainly sounds a lot like keeping secrets to me, Ad—" she shifted her eyes to the bustle that had resumed in the outer room "—uh, mister."

"Fine, then think how this sounds. How do you think Conner Burdett will react to the news that he has a grandson right under his nose? One living in a small house with a single mom who sometimes takes the kid to work with her?"

The churning in her stomach turned ice-cold. She wanted to run out into the dinning room, snatch up her child, take him home and hide. Instead she reined in her fears and asked, "He wouldn't…could he… challenge me for custody?'

"I don't know what he would do, but if he wanted to, he could. Especially with me not firmly established in the boy's life."

"No. No. Adam. Don't let that happen." Josie went to him and placed a hand on his chest. She had no business making such a forward move. Only it was not a move. It was an act of desperation. "Please."

He put his hand on hers and held her in place before him so that he could gaze directly into her eyes. "I won't, Josie. I will do everything in my power to protect you and Nathan and to keep you together, always."

"Always," she murmured. She had no reason to believe the man, but she did.

"Hey, Bingo!"

Josie's heart skipped, but it wasn't because of Adam's promise. Or his nearness.

At least, she told herself those weren't the reasons.

She'd just been startled. She had been in the kitchen so long she hadn't heard Bingo beeping for her to come out and collect her mail. Now he'd had to climb down off his scooter and come inside to deliver the mail.

Talk about reasons to get the anthill buzzing!

"You know everyone, Bingo," called out a woman Josie did not recognize—not Elvie or one of the commuters—which only drove home Adam's point about how quickly all sorts of folks would be talking about him…and Nathan…and Ophelia. "Maybe you can help us out here. Remember the second Burdett boy?"

"Huh? Oh, yeah. Yeah. The Stray Dawg!"

Adam flinched.

Josie hesitated only a moment before putting her hand on Adam's sleeve and giving a squeeze.

"What do you know about him?" the strange woman asked again.

"Who's asking?"

"Josie was…where is that girl?"

"I'm still in the kitchen." She nabbed the pie pan with one slice missing and headed for the door, leaving Adam to finish clearing away the crumbs of the pie she had dropped.

"Hey, Sweetie Pie." Bingo waved to her with the stack of mail in his hand. "Interesting y'all should bring up that Burdett now. Didn't your sister spend some time with that Stray Dawg last time she were in town, Josie?"

"I, uh…" Josie would not lie but she couldn't bring

herself to jog the memories of people who might unknowingly threaten her relationship with Nathan.

"That's how I remember it." Bingo placed the mail down on the counter. "Not long after his mama's death. The pair of them tore around on that motorcycle of his, then they both up and disappeared."

"That's right," someone muttered.

"How could we forget that?" came another comment.

Bingo paused long enough to stretch his legs, being extra-careful of his bum knees. "Until that Ophelia came back to give Josie her baby..."

*Grrr-eeee.* It went so quiet in the room they could hear Bingo's joints creak.

Everyone in the room turned at once to look at Nathan.

Josie plopped the pie pan on the counter in front of Jed.

"Go get him," Adam whispered.

She did not need a second urging.

In a couple of steps she had the baby in her arms. "Oh, y'all, what imaginations."

Not a lie. Just an observation. *An observation intended to distract from the truth.* And it left Josie feeling guilty and uncomfortable.

"Now excuse me." She slipped into the kitchen without further explanation.

Adam met her with his hands open to accept Nathan.

Josie hesitated for a moment.

"You are going to have to trust me sometime, Josie. I am this baby's father and I am not going to just go away. If we hope to raise him together, we have to trust each other."

"To everything there is a season," she murmured back at him.

"Josie, hon? What's going on?" From the sound of Jed's voice, he had come around the counter and was headed for the door.

Adam looked at her.

"What will you do with him?" she asked.

"Take him to your house for now."

"You can't take him on your motorcycle!"

He smiled. "I'll walk. I can slip through the back alleys and side streets."

She pressed her lips together. She was about to let this man she had only just met, a man with the only claim to her son—until his father learned about the connection—just walk away with him.

"Sweetie Pie?"

What choice did she have?

"Go," she said. She gave her son a kiss on the temple, trying not to allow herself to imagine it might be the very last time she could ever do that. "I'll slip away and get home after lunch."

"We'll be there, Josie."

"I want to believe you," she said so softly that she knew the man retreating through the back door could not possibly have heard her.

## Chapter Five

"Poor baby." Josie looked at her grinning son with his T-shirt on backward and inside out, only one sock on and wearing a cereal bowl on his head like a hat.

"Hey!" Adam, sitting on the floor in front of the couch beside the baby, fooled with the waistband of the clean but haphazard diaper, trying to get it to look right. He stood up and surveyed his work. "I think he's in pretty great shape considering I've never taken care of anything more demanding than my career or my Harley."

Nathan waved a wooden spoon like a regal scepter and babbled his favorite "ya-ya-ya."

"I didn't mean Nathan. I meant you." She laughed and trailed her gaze over the man.

Barefoot, baby powder smudged up and down his jeans, his once crisp business shirt had a row of tape—the kind Josie kept handy for when the disposable diapers came unstuck—down the front placard. His neck and the hollows of his cheeks were ruddy. The side of his hair that wasn't jutting straight up was globbed down by a blob of orange baby food.

"What?" He held his arms out.

"Nothing." She put her hand to the tip of her nose to hide her laughter, then added. "I like the new look. Takes business casual to a whole new level."

"Guess I could use a little…" He whisked the back of his hand down his jeans, creating a cloud of baby powder. Clearly pleased with that, he yanked the tape off, muttering, "Kid kept trying to eat the buttons, so I improvised a safety measure."

"Nice." She nodded. "And the reason for the mashed carrots in your hair?"

"The…" He thrust his fingers alongside his temple and raked them straight back. He winced. He withdrew his hand, stared at the orange goo there and exhaled in one exhausted groan. "I had no idea what I was getting into, obviously."

"You did fine, I'm sure." Better than Josie had suspected he would do. Her house was not in disarray. Her child was happy. "You hungry?"

"Am I ever." He reached down and picked up the baby, who promptly whapped him on the head with the wooden spoon. He didn't even miss a beat as he followed Josie from the room. "I didn't want to rummage around in your kitchen. But I did steal a taste of Nathan's baby food."

"You didn't!"

"I did." He made a face then backed up a few steps and slid Nathan into his high chair.

"How was it?"

"You know how some dishes—exotic food, delicacies, specialty dishes—a lot of times are better than they look?"

"Uh-huh."

"Well, baby food isn't one of those dishes." He worked his tongue around as if he was still trying to get the taste off. "When does he start eating real food?"

She laughed then bent to place a kiss on her son's cheek. "His diet is designed to help him grow healthy and strong."

"That's fine for him, but I'm already healthy and strong."

He certainly was. "Well, lucky for you I didn't take that into account when I made this plate up for you. I had taste in mind." She held up the "to go" box and flipped up the lid. The aroma of meat loaf and hot rolls and green beans and fried okra filled the room. The collection of some of her specialties was probably not the usual rich man's meal, but if the gossip proved true, Adam was no longer a rich man. Surely he'd appreciate the effort if not the flavor.

"Mmm. That smells wonderful." He took the container and inhaled deeply. "Fried okra? I love fried okra. My mom used to make that."

"Really?" Josie took a step, slid open a drawer and retrieved a fork to hand him, all the time managing to keep the plastic grocery-style bag over her arm from swinging about and making a mess. "Did she ever make pie?"

"No, but she made cake—a few thousand a day."

Josie stilled. "Are you saying the Carolina Crumble Pattie was your mom's creation?"

"Yep. Well, it was an old family recipe that she perfected."

The idea her pies relied on an old Burdett family recipe improved upon by Adam's own mother warmed Josie all over. She opened her mouth to tell Adam so, but he stopped her by closing his eyes, lifting his chin, stretching up his whole body and taking a larger-than-life sniff of the air around them.

"I'll take care of Nathan for a week if you brought me a slice of pie."

"Then I guess you'll be taking care of him the rest of the summer and into the fall, because I brought you a whole pie." She let the bag rustle. "Sit. I'll get you a plate."

"Don't go to any trouble." He took a seat at the kitchen table. "This won't be the first meal I've eaten straight out of a take-out box."

"Nonsense." She grabbed a plate, then shut the cabinet door quickly so he wouldn't see that she only owned two decent place settings and one of them was chipped. "Food always tastes better when you eat it off a proper plate."

"Thanks." He transferred his lunch from the box, then grinned up at her when she put the whole browned-to-perfection pie to his left. "Must say, your pie certainly looks a lot better on a plate than on the floor."

"It's not the only thing that takes on a different appearance when viewed in a more welcoming context."

"Welcoming." He said it slowly, his gaze fixed in the distance. He waited a moment and she wondered if he expected to hear an echo or something. Finally he pulled his chair up close to the table and said, "I like that word."

"I mean it."

"I believe you do."

"And you don't believe your family would feel the same way toward you?"

"If they are smart they won't."

Josie didn't know what to make of that. Was his sentiment sad or sinister?

He dug in, unselfconsciously humming his approval with every bite.

Sad, she decided, and set about trying to change his perception. If you scratched the surface of his stoic, stone-faced, wounded-stray image, many things about Adam were just plain sad. "It all reminds me of the story of the prodigal son."

"No, Josie." He stabbed a bite of meat loaf. "This is nothing like that."

"It certainly seems—"

"No. The prodigal son came crawling back, willing to live as a servant or to eat with the animals." He gestured with the meat loaf still on his fork. "That is not the case with me. No."

"Adam…"

"I've returned to Mt. Knott with a plan, and humbling myself before my father is not part of it." He took the bite, chewed, then struggled to swallow.

Josie couldn't decide if the food or the feelings were responsible for that. Just in case, she jumped up and got the gallon of milk from the fridge, poured him a big glass, then plunked it down in front of him. "If you don't hope to reconcile with your family, then just why did you come to Mt. Knott?"

He froze with the glass of milk halfway between the plate and his mouth. He shifted his eyes quite pointedly in Nathan's direction.

"Don't give me some noble story about coming for your son." She beat him to the punch.

By the look on his face he didn't know whether to respond with indignation or by being impressed.

"If all you wanted was to claim Nathan, then you could have sent a lawyer or the sheriff or, more logically, shown up on my doorstep with both of those." That's how she'd envisioned it happening when she had nightmares about it. "You needn't have bothered ruffling your hair with a long, nighttime Harley ride for that."

"I would do far more than inconvenience myself for my son." He touched his hair where the orange baby food had been. "But I would never send a stranger to take him from his mother."

"His mother," she murmured.

No matter how many times she heard it from his lips, it still took her breath away. Ophelia had signed the proper papers and this man saw her, *Josie*—not her sister—as Nathan's mother. The thought of it caused a rush of hope to flood her being and she said a quick prayer that the Lord would bring to pass legally what she and Adam knew in their hearts to be true.

Then she went back on the defensive. Where her son was concerned, she could not afford to let down her guard for anyone. And she had to make sure Adam knew that, knew just what kind of person he was dealing with. "I'm saying I may not be one of those worldly, sophisticated women you are accustomed to—"

"What women?" he asked around a mouthful of okra.

She did not stop to answer his question, but just plowed right on with her thought. "But don't make the mistake of thinking I'm so naive I can't understand what's going on."

"I can assure you, I don't think of you that way at

all." Another swig of milk. His dark brows angled down, he leaned forward on his elbow. "That said, I just have to ask—what *is* going on, Josie?"

"I have no idea," she admitted freely. "There. Now you know exactly who you are dealing with. A lunatic."

He laughed, then helped himself to a thick slab of pie.

She conceded her humility with a soft chuckle, then she sat back in the chair. "But you've told me this trip home, the timing, your plans are not just about Nathan. If not specifically, then by the things you *don't* say and the way you say them."

He set his fork down and allowed what she had just said to sink in.

He made her nervous. "See? A lunatic. But not one that's entirely off base on this. I know things are not what they seem on the surface. And I know that I would be foolish not to be wary about that. I also know that—"

"What *I* know is this is very good pie."

"Don't change the subject," she warned, then watched him stuff down a whopping bite, she went all mushy inside and had to ask, "Do you really think so?"

"I do." He laughed over her response and took another bite. "I've certainly tasted a lot of pastry products in my lifetime. Desserts and more than one person's share of snack foods, but this…this is special. Old family recipe?"

"I don't even have an old family." She shook her head and hoped that hadn't come off too pathetic. To try to counteract that, she scooted her seat in close and decided to share what she had discovered today, "I've got a secret ingredient that comes from an old family recipe, though."

"I bet you have a lot of secrets, Josie."

"No." She sat back. "I'm pretty much an open book."

"And me without my library card." He touched her hand.

She blushed. "My grandmother taught me how to cook. I lived with her from the time I…"

Became a Christian. She wasn't embarrassed to talk about her faith, but she didn't know any way of doing that without bringing up how her mother and sister had rejected her. And in doing so remind him that she was not Nathan's mother by birth. She wondered if that was a weakness of faith on her part? "From the time I moved to Mt. Knott in high school until she died a few years later, when I already had a job at the Crumble."

"You worked at my family's factory?"

"I told you that. Didn't I tell you that?"

Neither of them seemed to recall. That should have sent up a red flag to Josie that either the man wasn't listening to her or she wasn't paying attention to what all she said to him. Or perhaps that when they were together they were too…sidetracked to bother with the small details of a conversation.

She stared at her hands, determined not to look into his eyes in hopes she would remember this exchange in detail. "I didn't survive the first round of job cuts."

"I'm sorry."

"Thanks. But in a way it was a good thing. It put me in motion to open the diner."

"Yeah. Sure. What seems like a disaster can often provide people with the push they need to take control of matters, to make bold moves, to better their lives." He sounded as if he needed convincing.

Josie found this odd as he hadn't been a part of the mess at his family's factory.

"I had Nathan to support after all."

"You must have been terrified."

"Not really. I had my faith."

"In yourself?"

"In God."

"I can't…that is, I wish…"

"Your mother was such a strong woman of faith. Your brother has a wonderful, growing ministry. Don't you share their beliefs?" There. She asked it outright. She had to. The man was not just Nathan's father, it seemed that he was a seeker.

"It's not my mother, it's that…well, God is portrayed as a loving father, isn't He?"

"Yes."

"I don't know how to relate to that."

"Was your father really that bad?" Conner Burdett had always scared her. A powerful man, he tended to storm about not speaking, especially to an insignificant worker like her.

"Bad?" He cocked his head to the right and chewed slowly. "Wrong word."

"What's the right word?"

"Hard," he said quietly.

"He was hard on you?"

"He was hard on everybody, including himself, I think."

"Your mom balanced that out for him some."

"Yes, she did."

"But that didn't make him any less hard, I suppose."

"Hard?" He shook his head. "Maybe that's not it, either. Because, as you say, my mother had some influence over that. And he wasn't hard on any one person. There was a kind of fairness to it all. I think maybe the word I should have used is...unyielding."

"That is different. Subtly, but..."

"Like your secret ingredient, it can change everything."

She nodded. "I appreciate your being so honest with me."

"Don't kid yourself, Josie. Just because we've

shared these few moments, you don't really know me. You don't really know what made me who I am."

"Who are you?"

"Haven't you heard? I'm the Stray Dawg."

"But if you have a hundred sheep and you lose one, that's the one that's on your mind. That's the one you worry about and go out and seek so that you can bring him home."

"You had Sunday school with Miss Minerva, too?"

"No. I told you, I didn't grow up here. I never had a home or a family or a regular church where I went to Sunday school each week. But I've always had a Bible. And last night I looked up Luke 15, the story of the prodigal son."

Adam pushed his plate away, his mouth set in a grim line. "Maybe I made a mistake. Coming here, coming to you first before…"

"Before what?"

He did not look as if he felt any inclination to answer her, just took another bite of pie and stared at Nathan.

"Before what, Adam? What is it that you came to Mt. Knott to do?"

Even if he had decided to tell her, which Josie doubted very much, he did not get the chance.

A thunderous pounding on the front door made her jump. "Hello?"

She looked at Adam. Her heartbeat had gone completely awry. "Is that…"

"I guess we didn't get out of the diner fast enough to outrun the speculation."

"What are we going to do?"

Adam pushed away from the table, stood and reached for Nathan. "I am going to keep my son out of sight and you are going to go and get rid of my father."

# Chapter Six

Adam stood behind the door of the bathroom, holding Nathan in his arms. In the split second he'd had to duck out of sight, it just seemed more prudent to do this rather than head to the door at the end of the hall. Josie's bedroom.

Yeah, Nathan's crib waited in that room, but so did every private thing about Josie. Her clothes. The pillow where she rested her head at night. The picture of her and Ophelia.

Adam had enough problems dealing with her without confronting those kinds of things right now. Besides, the bathroom was closer to the front door. Better situated to hear what Conner Burdett had to say.

"Hello?" the masculine voice boomed. The knocking did not relent. "Hello in there."

"Just a…" Josie put her finger to her lips to remind him to stay quiet, then waved her hand to order Adam to close the door. "Just a moment, please."

"I know you're in there, young lady. Don't think you can hide from me."

"Hide? Me? Hide from…him?" Adam looked his son in the eye. "This is *not* hiding."

"Ya-ya-ya."

"No, really. That is *not* who I am. It's important to me that you know that, kid. I'm not hiding. I'm exercising discretion. Control. Got that?"

"Ya-ya-ya." Nathan waggled his head, his dark hair floating back and forth like down.

"Don't buy that, huh?" What Adam had intended as a joke left him uncomfortable and defensive. He met his own eyes in the bathroom mirror and frowned. "How about this? I'm protecting your mother. *Both* of your mothers."

"Hello?" Josie's voice was steady but tentative as the front door creaked open. "May I, um, may I help you?"

"Josephine Redmond?" Conner got right to the point.

The door creaked even louder.

Adam could imagine his father blustering in past Josie as if she wasn't even there. He clenched his jaw.

"Yes." Hesitation and anxiety colored Josie's usually warm, friendly tone.

"Good." Heavy footsteps thudded farther into the front room.

"Mr. Burdett, I didn't expect anyone to drop by today. Sir, if you don't mind…" She let her voice trail off, leaving her uninvited visitor to do what anyone with even the most basic good manners would do— apologize and offer to return when it was convenient.

Poor naive Josie. She must not have known that not only did Conner not mind that he'd inconvenienced her, he had counted on doing just that.

*Keep 'em off balance. Always maintain the upper hand. Hold business meetings in your own office and if you can't, then never take a seat before your adversary.* Conner had whole lists of edicts about interacting with others.

Adam had once asked, "What about people who are not your adversaries?"

"There are no such creatures, boy," Conner had replied with a look bent on driving home the point that the man included his own sons in that sweeping generalization.

"You didn't expect company," Conner's voice grew louder, a sure indication he had barged right into the house and had headed straight for the kitchen. "Yet here you just happened to bring a pie home from your restaurant in the middle of the day?"

Adam tensed. The last time he had heard that tone, that cadence of speech, that calculating manner, was the day he'd gotten a check, the lump-sum payment to buy him out of his share of the family business and the money his mother had left him in her will. He thought the next time he heard it, the man would be begging him to save the business. Now to hear him toying with Josie like this…

Adam flexed one hand over the doorknob. He wanted to go out there to rescue Josie.

Nathan squirmed.

He studied his son's face. Despite having only recently become aware the child existed, much less knowing him, just looking at him filled Adam with so much emotion. And he knew he would do anything to keep him safe. He knew Josie would feel the same way.

"Is that your way of asking for a piece of pie, sir?"

Silence. Conner hadn't seen that coming.

He wouldn't. Kindness and hospitality were foreign concepts to the old man.

"Good for you, Josie," Adam whispered.

"Uh, uh-huh. Pie would be nice." The tone shifted slightly. "Thank you."

Adam didn't know what to make of it.

"But what I'd rather have—" the old bluster returned "—is to get my hands on my grandson."

"Get your hands on?" Josie repeated the demand with hushed anxiety.

Adam hated this. Hated having to stand by and make her endure his father. He should be the one facing the old man down, bearing the brunt of the old man's belligerence.

"Just to hold him for a moment, you understand."

It was the quietest, most humble sentence Adam believed he'd ever heard his father speak to anybody but Maggie Burdett. Where did that come from? Who was this person standing in Josie's kitchen insisting…no, merely asking in humility and faltering hope…to see his only grandchild?"

"Where is the little fellow?"

"I…I don't think I should tell you that, sir."

Something between a wheeze and a chuckle answered her. "You've already told me more than you realize."

And just that fast the man Adam readily recognized as Conner Burdett resurfaced. He'd been a fool to think the seasoned bully could have changed. It had all been an act. An act to manipulate Josie and unearth answers.

"I haven't told you anything," Josie said.

"Oh, yes you have. For starters you didn't deny he was my grandson. Nor did you say you didn't know where he is, just that you didn't think you should tell *me*."

Adam drew in his breath and held it until his lungs ached. The Burdett offensive has just begun. Conner would go after Josie, hammer away at her with every tool in his considerable arsenal until he'd gotten every bit of information from her and left her in tears and fearing for her son's future.

"I know you have my flesh and blood." The words came slowly, though Adam did not know if that was for effect or because Conner was choosing them so carefully. Either way they made the bile rise in Adam's throat. "The child is a Burdett and I have rights."

"Please, Mr. Burdett..." Josie's voice disappeared into a sob.

That was it. Adam could no longer stay out of this.

"This is my family, the son of my son," Conner boomed.

"Wrong." Adam stepped fully from the bathroom and reached the kitchen in just a few steps. "This child is *my* son. That makes him nothing to you but the child of some stray you took in and never really loved as your own."

*You can know a man a lifetime and still not know everything that he is capable of, good and bad. That is not the kind of thing you can gauge in a matter of a few seconds. Unfortunately, sometimes a few seconds is all you have—so make them count.*

Conner had taught Adam that a long time ago. Start with the details and work your way out. Listen to what a man tells you, but don't dismiss what your own gut has to say. Adam applied those skills now to quickly size up the old man.

Eighteen months ago, Conner Burdett made an imposing figure. Though in his sixties, the tall, raw-boned man had still sported a full head of mostly brown hair, keen eyes that sparked with grit and vigor and the ever-present authority that came from knowing no matter what, he still owned fifty-four percent interest in the family business.

As far as Adam could see today, that controlling interest in the company was all he still possessed. He made a fleeting study of the man before him.

The elder Burdett had lost weight. His hair had faded to white and thinned considerably. The newly developed stoop of Conner's shoulders had taken inches from his height. The man who had once seemed a veritable pillar of confidence to a younger Adam now stood almost eye-to-eye with him. And in those eyes Adam saw a weariness and remorse that had never been there before.

Adam clenched his jaw and reminded himself to listen to his own feelings. His son's future could well be at stake and he wouldn't risk it to something as deceptive as appearances or sentimentality. Conner Burdett was still capable of anything. *Anything.*

Adam braced himself to bear the full brunt of his father's wrath.

"Adam? Son?" Conner reached out. His hand shook. He took one step forward and then another as if he couldn't quite believe what he saw before him.

"Yeah?" Adam shifted his weight, pulling Nathan more to one side so that he could hand him off to Josie if he should need to.

"Thank you," Conner whispered and it was clear he meant it as heartfelt gratitude to God.

That humbled Adam but did not reassure him.

Then Conner placed his hand on Adam's sleeve, balled the fabric in his fist then pulled both Adam and Nathan into a tight embrace. "My prayers are answered. You've come home."

Adam stiffened.

*Come home?* Is that what he had done? He sought Josie. When their eyes met, he tried in one look to convey his confusion, his uncertainty, his panic.

She smiled. A wonderful smile that spoke of long longed-for reunions, at the joy of homecoming, of hope.

Conner took a deep breath and exhaled in short huffs as if he were...*sobbing?*

Adam tried to swallow. He had no idea how to respond to this. Anger, bitterness, rejection, even hatred—he had steeled himself well for any of those. But *this?*

"I, uh, I don't—" He started to pat the old man's back but couldn't bring himself to do it. Again he fixed his eyes on Josie's.

"You know what, Mr. Burdett? Why don't you come into the kitchen and have a seat while I dish you up a big old slice of that pie I promised?"

Adam had charged out ready to come to Josie's defense no matter what it took and here she had ended up rescuing him. And with nothing more substantial or less significant than pie.

"Hmm?" Conner pulled away at last.

"Pie?" She laid her delicate hand on the curve of

his shoulder to draw his attention toward her. "It's cherry. And if you'll have a seat, I'd be honored to serve you up a piece."

"Thank you, my dear." He gave her a nod. "But first, give me a moment. I want to…" He raised his hand.

Without thinking, Adam shied away, caught himself and forced his body to go perfectly still.

Conner's dry, trembling palm brushed along the side of Adam's face.

"I just…" Conner touched Adam's cheek, his jaw, then dropped his hand to his shoulder. "I just want to look at my boy."

*My boy?* Even commanding up every ounce of anger and disappointment he had ever felt toward this man, Adam could not make those words sound pejorative or hard-hearted. There was just so much yearning in them, so much peace and pride.

*Don't you mean your stray?* Adam wanted to say. Yes, wanted to say it with all his being. Not because it seemed appropriate but because he wanted to push the old man away.

He wanted to throw a barrier up between them. One that had existed there for so long. Adam had based his every decision the last eighteen months on the belief that that barrier justified his contemptible plan. And now…

And now Conner Burdett was standing before him, a shell of his former self, wiping a tear from under his eye with one gnarled knuckle. "I didn't think I'd ever see you again, Adam. Not before… well, not before we met again in heaven."

"Oh." The softest, saddest sound ever escaped Josie's lips.

Adam looked at her, knowing she was thinking not just about him and his father but also about what she would have given to have heard such conciliatory words from her own mother or even her sister. The sweetness of her sorrow penetrated Adam's life-hardened exterior and opened something up in him that had been closed off for far too long.

"And this little fellow." Conner gave Nathan's plump leg a shake. "Hey! I know who you are. Do you know who I am?"

"Ya-ya-ya."

"Um, uh…" Adam had no idea what to say.

Conner didn't wait for him to come up with something. He lifted Nathan's small body from the crook of Adam's arm. "You know who I am, little man? I am *your* daddy's daddy."

*"Since when?"* Adam muttered, needing to put things back in perspective. He stepped forward to take the child away.

"Since the first time I held you in my arms. You were about the same age as this young fellow." Conner patted the small boy's belly. "Looked a lot like him, except you were a skinny thing, with big, sad eyes, and your hands always in tight little fists."

Adam froze.

Josie's gaze dropped from his face to his side.

He shook his hand to release the tension as he un-fisted his fingers.

"And I felt about your daddy the way I bet he feels about you," Conner said to the baby.

Adam straightened, ready to deny that.

"That even though you two just met and the way things are in life, you may never really feel as though you are much more than strangers with a shared history, he would walk through fire for you." Conner did not look at Adam.

Which was a relief because Adam could not have looked at Conner then if his life depended on it.

Had he heard right? His father acknowledged that they were virtual strangers and yet he would walk through fire for him?

Walk through fire but not walk into a bar or cheap hotel in Mt. Knott in those days when Adam needed him to come and ask him to return to the fold. To say one-tenth of the handful of healing words he'd just uttered and pave the way for Stray Dawg to find his way home while it still meant something.

He couldn't accept that. Would not accept it. It was just talk, after all, from a man who made his living negotiating to get the better end of every deal.

Adam pushed his shoulders back. Conner wanted something. Adam could not be fool enough to let that slip from sight because the suddenly frail man had tugged at a few heartstrings.

"Why don't we sit down and have that pie?" Adam pulled Nathan from Conner's grasp, then went into the kitchen, settled the child in the high chair and pointed out a seat at the small oak table for Conner.

Josie frowned. Clearly she had expected more from Adam. Expected compassion, gratitude and mercy. Well, if that's what she thought she'd find in him, she had better get used to being disappointed.

But if, as Conner had put it, she expected nothing less of him than that he would walk through fire for her and their son, then he would never let her down. "Once you taste Josie's pie and spend a few minutes around Nathan you'll find yourself as proud as I am that she is the one raising my son."

Josie stilled with a knife posed over the pie. She blinked a few times and sniffled.

He tipped his head to her, affirming that was, indeed, how he felt. He hoped she knew, too, that he had just laid down the gauntlet. He had asserted his position and confirmed hers. He would brook no interference, no custody battle, no questioning of his decision from his powerful father or family.

She smiled and lifted her chin, making her soft, lovely ponytail bounce against her back. Then with a sidelong glance at Conner to make sure he wasn't watching, she served Adam the larger slice of the two pieces of pie.

He winked to show his thanks, then as soon as she set the plates down before the two men, he pulled the old switcheroo. Slid the larger slice right under Conner's nose and accepted the smaller portion for himself.

"You're going to want to have as much of this pie as you can hold," he told the old man, then leaned back and muttered to Josie, "and if his mouth is full it will give us more time to do the talking."

"Can I get you anything else? Some milk to drink? If you'd like some coffee you'll have to wait a minute while I brew up a fresh pot."

Adam thought of how she had told him to make his own instant the night he had come to claim his son and so he took her offer to make a pot for them as a compliment. Pie. Coffee. Kid. That should mollify the old guy just fine.

They'd show him what a fine home environment Nathan had. They'd get his assurance, for what it was worth, that he would not try to override their judgments about what was best for Nathan. They would send him on his way.

Then Adam's real work would begin.

Josie pulled a foil bag of coffee beans from a canister on the counter. The whir of her grinding them in a small electric appliance made it impossible to carry on a conversation for a minute or so. That, coupled with the time Conner was devoting to savoring his first bite of pie, gave Adam time to think things through.

He'd have to act fast. Make his move before the rest of the family found out how long he'd been in town without telling anyone. That fact would arouse suspicions. He loved his brothers but he would never make the mistake of underestimating them. Conner might have loved them more, but he certainly had not gone easier on them.

Burke, older than Adam by four years and known by all as Top Dawg, would be the first one to start putting the clues together. A few phone calls to contacts in the business would tell him plenty—*contacts,* not friends. Top Dawg had many things in life, money, looks, power, brains and the fawning adoration of most of the town of Mt. Knott, but the one thing he did not have was friends. Jason and Cody would neither know nor care about what Adam had in mind. They had long ago given up looking upon the lowly Carolina Crumble Pattie as their livelihood. According to Adam's sources, they each still held their small percentage of the company stock but did little else except show up for meetings and rubber stamp whatever Burke and Conner asked for. They would be no problem.

That left Conner.

The aroma of freshly ground coffee beans filled the air and Adam fixed his attention on the man sitting to his right. "Great pie, isn't it?"

"Very good." Conner jabbed his fork toward the half-eaten slab of golden crust and red, juicy cherries dripping in a thick syrup. "You know we could use something like this down at the Crumble. Your brothers keep telling me we need to try new things. Expand the line. Innovate. Burke says we have to do something or—"

"I'm glad you like it, sir." Josie finished loading the coffeemaker and pressed a button to start the brewing. It gurgled and grumbled and she turned her back on it to let it do its work. "But I don't think it would do you much good as a new product because I used—"

"Because she used to work for you already and you fired her. She has moved on." Adam lifted a bite of pie up as if offering a toast before he poked it in his mouth.

Josie gulped in some air. Her eyes got big. The room grew so quiet they could hear the coffee drip, drip, drip into the carafe. She shook her head. "Mr. Burdett, that's Adam talking, not me. I never said—"

"I'm sorry about your job, Ms. Redmond. We did what we had to do. Greater good and all. Been a regular struggle to keep the doors open these past few years, even though I haven't taken a cent out of the company myself, sunk everything right back in hopes of…not that it's made a difference."

Adam frowned. Had his father just apologized?

And admitted weakness? And said he hadn't taken any money out of the company for *how* long?

"I absolutely do understand, Mr. Burdett. I am trying to keep my business afloat, as well." She poured a cup of coffee for Conner. Only Conner.

"Our layoffs can't have made that easier."

"No, sir." She pushed the sugar shaker and a bowl of creamer packets toward him. Still offering nothing to Adam.

"But that's going to change." Conner dumped two teaspoons of sugar into the rich dark liquid in his cup.

"It is?" Josie stood up, still not making a move to get anything for Adam to drink.

Frustrated, Adam considered getting up to fetch his own coffee, then decided to wait it out, and defiantly broke off a big piece of pie crust and ate it.

"Of course," Conner took a sip then beamed a huge smile. "Adam is back. Things are going to turn around now."

Adam coughed and covered his mouth to keep pie crust crumbs from spewing everywhere.

Conner forged ahead without the slightest response to Adam's reaction. "And to celebrate we're going to host a barbecue and invite the whole town."

"Oh, Mr. Burdett, I think that's exactly what Mt. Knott needs." Josie knelt down by Conner's chair, her whole face transformed with delight.

"Good. Then you can make the pies and, uh, side dishes, at your usual prices, of course."

Adam struggled to force down the dry bits of crust but it wouldn't cooperate. His fist came down on the table but not hard enough to bring a halt to the conversation. And this conversation needed to halt. His father had it all wrong. Adam had his own plans and he wouldn't let anyone or anything interfere with them.

"Mr. Burdett, you may have just provided me with a way to keep my doors open at least a little while longer!"

Adam gulped. He wouldn't let anyone or anything interfere with his plans, except Josie.

He had thought just moments ago that if she wanted him to walk through fire for her, he would never let her down.

He was about to prove that. Obviously he was about to walk through fire for her—and that fire would be in the form of a barbecue with his family.

## Chapter Seven

Conner Burdett had gobbled up the last of his pie after he had offered Nathan a small taste, which the child smeared on his ear, his chin, his eyebrow, everywhere but his mouth. When Josie had come back from cleaning the child up, Conner had gone.

"He wanted me to give you this." Adam offered her a business card held between two fingers, the way she'd seen boys fling playing cards into hats.

She took if from him and, reading the words imprinted on it, understood why the stray Burdett brother might have wanted to send the card sailing as far away as possible.

"Burke Burdett," she read the name softly, scanned his official title and then studied the number handwritten beneath it. His private line. Not the kind of thing the average citizen of Mt. Knott was privy to. Josie turned the card over in her hand. On the back were the words, "Timetable. Menu. Payment" in shaky handwriting.

"I guess I'm supposed to call your brother about these things?"

Adam only nodded before he slipped Nathan from Josie's hold and turned the child so they could look each other in the eye. Of course, Nathan did not cooperate fully with that eye-to-eye plan, which made the picture of the father and son all the more endearing.

Adam sniffed the air. "One of us doesn't smell so good, buddy. Now, I'm always fresh as a mountain meadow myself, so I suspect it's *you*."

Nathan giggled.

"I'll handle diaper duty, Adam."

"No. I can do it. I've gotten pretty good at it over the course of the day." He actually sounded pleased with his newly acquired skill. "Let's go, kid."

He draped the baby over one arm. The position made it look like Nathan was flying through the air, and loving it from the pleasant sounds he was making.

Good for Adam to get a little taste of what his own parents must have gone through with a headstrong, handful of energy in an adorable package. Looking at the two of them together now, she couldn't deny that Adam not only was Nathan's father but that he belonged in her son's life.

Her two fellas disappeared into the back room.

Adam entertained the baby, alternating between making funny sounds and acting properly disgusted with the task at hand.

Josie leaned against the doorway and slid the card into her T-shirt pocket, knowing she'd forget where she'd put it if she put it in her jeans, and it would probably get washed with her aprons and other work clothes this evening. Then she stood back and waited for Adam to finish with Nathan. That first night she hadn't even wanted him to see the boy, now he was doing the dad thing as if he'd done it all along.

She couldn't help thinking of her own family. Not of the family made up of her mother and Ophelia, but the one she had always dreamed she would make for herself.

When she was a young girl, being hauled from town to town as her mother chased everything from dreams to men, that family meant a mom and dad, Ophelia and Josie. Also a baby brother or sister, or maybe a calico cat with a bell on its collar.

During her early years of living in Mt. Knott, when her grandmother was alive, she had been content to think of the two of them as their own special little family. Lately, though, being a single mother and running a business on her own sometimes had her daydreaming about what it would be like to have a husband as a helpmate. Not just to shoulder the chores and responsibilities but also to hold her hand in church and take her in his arms while they sat on the porch on warm summer evenings.

"Well, you may want to call in the toxic-waste disposal team to take care of that *diaper,* but I can sound the all's clear for the kid." He moved Nathan on his arm down the hallway again making a siren-type *waaa-ooo, waaa-ooo* before he reached the kitchen and said, "The kitchen is now safe for noses everywhere!"

She gazed at Adam holding Nathan. It was too soon to allow herself to wonder about Adam as potential husband material. In fact, his history with Ophelia made that prospect a bit…strained. Then again, when had anything with her sister been anything *but* strained?

That thought only made Josie feel more isolated. More adrift in the world. More wistful for her own home, family and husband, one who shared her values and would not disappear on a whim.

"Okay, you little rug rat. I've enjoyed spending the day with you but I've got to go now. You be good for your mom and no more wasting any of her delicious pie as face paint."

He covered the boy's rounded belly with one large, tanned hand.

Nathan kicked and laughed.

That made Adam do likewise. Laugh, not kick.

They had the same laugh, Josie noted. Soft and deep at first with a sort of raspy quality as it played itself out, growing quieter and quieter even though their faces remained bright and their bodies still shook. Finally it ended with a satisfied sigh.

"You don't have to run off on my account. If you want to spend more time with Nathan, that's all right with me. I have to get back to the café and set up for the dinner rush."

"Rush?" He cocked an eyebrow.

"Okay, trickle," she confessed. It was true that she did most of her business before one o'clock, but she did get a small flurry of activity around six when commuters stopped in to pick up take-home orders they had called in earlier in the day. Later another cluster of people would come in after their suppers to have pie for dessert. On really hot days she kept even busier because many thought it was worth the extra expense of eating out to avoid heating up their own homes.

Josie knew the people of this community. She knew their habits and their tastes, and it had paid off as much as it could. "But I can't afford to miss even a dribble of business these days."

"I realize that." He nodded. "Which is why I have to get moving."

"Moving?" The word made her shiver.

"Have a lot to get done, and now that my family knows I'm here, I don't have much time to do it."

"What's the supposed to mean?"

"It's not *supposed* to mean anything, Josie." His

dark eyes fixed on her. His expression remained calm, but she could see the storm beneath the surface—as if what he felt and what he thought did not match up and he was going to have to reconcile them or choose. "I don't skirt around issues or try to pretty up the ugly truth. You know I came here for a reason, a reason I am not inclined to discuss with anyone." He handed Nathan back to her. "I will tell you this, though."

Josie pulled Nathan close. "What?"

"One of the reasons I don't want to tell you details about my plans is that, having met you now, having seen how you and Nathan fit into the fabric of Mt. Knott, I am not as sure of my intentions as I once was."

"That's a lot of words, Adam, but hardly any information."

He smiled, not too much and not with any joy in his eyes. "Maybe all you need to know, Josie, is that no matter what, from this point on I am not going to make a decision without taking you and Nathan into account first."

"Taking us into account is one thing. Taking us, um, that is, me into your confidence is quite another." She settled Nathan onto the floor in the front room to let him crawl around and play. As she bent forward the business card slid from her pocket and fell onto the ragged gold carpet. She snatched it up and went on with her point. "Taking us into account sounds nice, but really, it just means you are going to do what you decide anyway without asking me what I think."

He did not deny it or offer to do anything differently. He just brushed her cheek with his thumb and asked, "Did anyone ever tell you you're very wise for your age?"

She tapped the card against her open palm. "I've had to be to get by."

He nodded. "And now you have to do the wise thing and take the job cooking for this barbecue deal."

"You'd rather I not do this, wouldn't you?" She couldn't look down her nose at his not confiding in her if she didn't speak honestly with him.

"If it's just the money—"

"It's not." She held her hand up to cut him off, noticed the card in her fingers and folded her arms.

"If that's even a part of it, though, I could help you out on that score."

She took a step backward. "I can't take your money."

He looked down at Nathan, who had crawled to the couch and was trying to pull himself up into a standing position. "A case could be made that I owe you a year's worth of back child support."

"No. I don't see it that way." Josie shuffled one foot in Nathan's direction, ready to lunge out and nab him if he should fall. "You didn't know about him."

Adam shifted to the side, as well, only he seemed to be doing it in response to Josie, not a gut reaction to protect his child. "That doesn't change the fact that you had expenses."

"No. If we are going to start 'making cases'—" she paused and made quotation marks in the air "—in order to ease our guilt, then I should make one for the fact that I didn't track you down sooner to tell you about Nathan."

"I thought you didn't know about me until Ophelia sent you the adoption paperwork."

"I didn't. But I didn't make that effort either." She scanned the business card, the worn carpet, the baby who had just succeeded in pulling himself up onto his own two feet then promptly plopped back down onto his well-padded bottom. "And deep down I often thought that I should have made that effort. I may be naive about a lot of things. Innocent, even. But I do know it takes two people to make a baby, and I never once really tried to seek out Nathan's father."

"You are not just wise, Josie." He cocked his head. He studied her in much the same way he had on the first night they had met, but this time there was something more in his eyes. Respect. He didn't bother to conceal it when he said, with quiet conviction, "You are...amazing."

"Nope. Just someone trying to do the best I can, to be a good person and a good Christian."

"I know. You are."

"I try." She turned to watch Nathan again.

The baby grunted and groped at the couch cushion. He dug his tiny fingers into the fabric. His chubby legs bounced once, twice then his body jutted upward and he stood. "Ya-ya-ya!"

She smiled at her son. "Like everyone, I fail sometimes but I never stop trying."

"That's what makes you so wonderful."

Josie wished she could scoop her son up to take the attention away from herself. But she didn't want to take anything away from his hard-won accomplishment.

"You have to stop saying things like that or my head will swell up so big that I won't be able to get my café apron over it." She pantomimed putting on the apron that covered her from neck to knees.

"Ahh, you've caught on to my plan, to keep you from cooking for that barbecue."

They stood there in silence. Josie didn't know what to say or do.

Nathan lurched sideways for one step then another, his fingers curled into the soft cushion for support as he cruised toward the armrest.

Josie raised her head and now commanded Adam's gaze. She wanted to please this man but she was not ready to surrender that kind of trust to him. He had plans he would not tell her about and she had rent to pay.

"I won't take money from you." She laid it out as plainly as possible. "Not when I have a terrific way to earn it for myself. It's the right thing to do and won't cause you any hardship."

"I don't know about…" He stopped, looked down at Nathan, then back at her. "Wait. You think me paying your back child support would create a financial hardship for me?"

"Everyone in town knows you went through your inheritance right away."

"Oh, *everybody* knows that, do they?"

"You don't have to be ashamed. Like I said, we all fail. The important thing is to keep trying to do better."

He opened his mouth and raised his hand, like a man about to launch into a speech. Then his eyes shifted. His brow crinkled. He exhaled in a quick, hard huff. "I can't stand here and talk about this now, Josie. Just believe me when I say that if you should decide not to take the job, I will support you emotionally and financially in that choice."

*Thump.*

Nathan reached the end of the couch and sat down on the carpet, hard. He did not cry or fuss about it, just plunked down and sat there.

"It's not *just* about money, Adam." Now Josie did go to her child and pick him up. "It's also about me giving something back to the people who have been so kind to me."

His brow furrowed. "My family?"

"The people of Mt. Knott."

"Even if you have to take money from the people who have let the whole town down to do it?"

"I don't see them as having let the town down. They certainly did not want their business to flounder. I don't understand your animosity toward your father. As a father yourself now, it just seems that you'd be more forgiving."

He hung his head. "Maybe I haven't been a father long enough."

"But you've been a son for most of your life, a brother and a—"

"And a stray."

*You don't have to be a stray,* she wanted to say. *You have Nathan now. Nathan and me.* "Why can't you let go of that?"

He paused.

For a moment she thought he might break down, then he gathered himself, squared his shoulders and shook his head. "I have to go."

She could have offered to walk with him. He'd left his motorcycle behind the Home Cookin' Kitchen, after all, but she knew he wouldn't want to be seen with her and Nathan. A protective move, he'd say, but Josie could not make herself accept that without some reservation. So she watched Adam leave the house via the back door and disappear into the night without anything more demonstrative than a mumbled goodbye.

Ten minutes later she shut her front door behind her, not knowing what to do first about all this. Should she panic or praise the Lord?

Praise. Definitely praise.

Once she had spent a little time in prayer and thanksgiving, she would surely not feel so over-whelmed by everything and underequipped to deal with it. She had to stop and marvel at that notion. She had lived from one crisis to the next for so long, hung on by her virtual fingertips to survive from her childhood to her son's infancy.

But now she wasn't quite sure how to act when so much good news came her way. One thing after another, each brighter and more positive than the last. Who knew that even that would carry its own kind of stress? Have its own unique way of needing to lean on the Lord?

Josie hummed a hymn and walked toward the Home Cookin' Kitchen with a spring in her step that had not been there in a long, long time. She carried Nathan in her arms and from time to time he would lay his chubby cheek against hers as he gnawed his fist and "sang" along with her.

"Ya-ya-ya."

It wasn't exactly to the tune of "Blessed Be the Tie that Binds" but the child did manage to keep the right rhythm. Of course, every mother thought her own child was some kind of genius. And while Josie didn't see a musical career in Nathan's future, she did think he might have an affinity for listening and repeating.

"Ya-ya-ya."

"No. Not ya-ya. Try this, ma-ma."

"Ya-ya."

"No. No. Listen—" Josie pressed her lips together to sound it out. "Mmmma-mmma."

"Na-na-na."

"Mama." She hadn't encouraged the child to call her that before now. She couldn't. Not until…

Josie could not dismiss Ophelia's fickleness and that, until now, she had to be aware of the fact that there was an unknown father who could show up and take Nathan away. Now she had Adam's word, knew that his father was a sweet gentleman willing to welcome her into the family—if only on the fringes—and Ophelia's signature on the proper legal documents that meant that Nathan would soon be hers forever.

The only thing that could make this day better was to hear him form the name she hoped he'd call her for the rest of his life. "C'mon, Nath. Mama. Ma-ma-ma. Mama."

"Na-na-na."

"Mmmmmama. Ma-ma." She pointed to herself.

"Mmmmmya-ya." He pointed to himself.

"No, Nathan, that's me. Mama." Just saying it

lifted her heart. So she pressed her fingertip more emphatically to her chest and said it again. "I'm your mama."

The child touched one finger to her face. "Ya-ya. Na-na. Da-da!"

"D-dada? Where did that come from?" Why was she asking him that? Even if he could have responded, Josie already knew the answer. "I have had you since the day you came home from the hospital. Walked the floors with you, prayed over you, spent every possible moment I could with you, and you call me the same thing you call your boo-boo bear and your big toe. He *has* you for a morning and a few hours in the afternoon and already you know the name, Da-da."

She hugged her boy close, not minding one bit that he had formed an instant and irrepressible bond with his father. Josie couldn't help noticing the man's charms herself.

"Dada. Da-da-da." He waved is hand around.

"Okay, I got it. Save it for when you see—" She followed the line of her son's finger and gasped. "Adam?"

Across the street from the Home Cookin' Kitchen and down about half a block was the unmistakable shape of a man in black standing by a gleaming Harley. He had his back to them and showed no probability of turning around, not when he was leaning

with his forearm on a sleek silver car, talking to...
someone. She couldn't see who.

"Not that it matters," she murmured to Nathan,
thinking that even a one-year-old had to know she
had really been talking to herself. "What the man
does is his own business. Though...that doesn't *look*
like business. Unless it's funny business."

Josie pulled Nathan close and stepped into the
doorway of the vacant building next to the Home
Cookin' Kitchen. She needed a moment to gather
herself. She did not know what Adam was up to,
though he'd made it clear he had no intention of telling her, so she couldn't be hurt by his need for privacy.

But the fact that it was *not* privacy that the man
wanted but *secrecy,* that's what needled her.

She recognized the signs of it from all her years
dealing with her mother and Ophelia. Master ma-
nipulators, they always had schemes and small sub-
terfuges working behind the scenes. Always had to
be someplace, meet a person here or there, never in
the open. Never on the up and up.

Josie's heart sank. She would not condemn Adam
or write him off based on what little she did know.
But she also could not simply believe in him blindly.

Adam had asked her to trust him and said he
would take her into account when making decisions.
But judging from his effort to get her not to cook
for the barbecue and this sneaky behavior, the only

thing he was taking into account was his own clandestine plans.

If it were just her, she might…but it wasn't just her. And if the adoption plans went well it would never be just her again.

Adam could promise to take her into account, but Josie didn't have a choice, she had to think of Nathan first and do what was best for him. That meant keeping both the doors of her business and the lines of communication between herself and the Burdetts open. And if Adam didn't like it, then…

A pang of guilt made her look in his direction just in time to see him point the way out of town, then step away from the silver car to reveal he had been speaking to a woman. A pretty woman. Poised. Even from this vantage point she gave off a sense of power and professionalism that Josie could never posses.

The woman started her car and pulled away from the curb.

"Dada."

"Shh. Nathan," she snapped.

The baby silenced.

"Mama's not mad at you, honey, it's just that…"

Adam got onto this Harley and took off, right behind the woman in the sleek sedan, without so much as a backward glance.

"I need to think." She tucked the child close and

hurried to the front door of her well-lit diner, mumbling as she did, "Now, where did I put Burke Burdett's business card?"

## Chapter Eight

"Thank you for meeting me out here on such short notice." Adam extended his hand to Dora Hoag. A compact, athletic woman with short black hair and the kind of personality that made people around her feel as if they were always running behind the power-walking, Bluetooth talking, multitasking, no-quarter-asking executive.

"It's just that once people know I'm in town it would only take a web search to connect me to Global…"

"I understand your personal issues in all of this, Burdett." She didn't look at him when she spoke, so he was glad she'd used his name.

Dora tended not to look people in the eye unless they were her superiors or somebody she could get some good business out of. More than once Adam had almost commented on something she had said only to realize in the nick of time she was carrying on an electronic conversation and was hardly even aware of his presence.

She took only a moment to sweep her gaze over their surroundings.

Adam did the same.

He scowled that the half asphalt, half gravel parking lot that Adam had promised employees time and again they would finish off—only to have his father say it was fine the way it was—had not been fixed. And the long, low building painted buttery yellow and…well, the color had originally been called café au lait meant to evoke one of the flavors in their famed Crumble Pattie, had not been repainted in years. Now the butter color looked more like someone had mixed mud into vanilla ice cream, and the café au lait had sun-faded to a pinkish color not unlike the pancake makeup he'd seen elderly ladies wear to church. Separating the two colors was a border of bright blue-and-white checks and what was supposed to be an image of their lone product stamped like a large seal of approval to one side.

Corporate logos were supposed to be so easily identifiable that even without the red script "Carolina Crumble Pattie" emblazoned next to it, everyone who had ever seen the product would immediately recognize it. Adam had grown up making and eating that product and he still had no idea what the image on the building was supposed to be.

Luckily they had not used it in packaging or anything official. One of the ongoing battles Adam had had with his father was about that very image. Adam had suggested they tap a fresh-faced local girl for the image of "Carolina Pattie"—and as he recalled that, Josie came to mind. But his father had flatly refused, not because Conner believed in the power of the disproportioned artwork but because he loved the artist, his wife, Maggie Burdett.

Adam had to force down the lump in his throat then. He looked away from the facade of the building and narrowed his eyes on the hills in the distance.

"But to me there is nothing personal at all here." Dora gave a sniff, frowned, then brought her full attention to bear on Adam, or as much of her attention as she gave to anyone in his position. "It's just business."

"But it won't be to my family." He motioned toward the back door marked Employees Only and pulled a key from his pocket. He unlocked the door, feeling a twinge of guilt about it. Dora didn't want to recognize the personal connection but she had no problem using it to give her a slight edge in her decision-making process. "My older brother and father would rather drive this business into the ground than to have to admit they needed me to broker the deal that would keep them afloat."

"That's why they are in the shape they are in."

She crossed the threshold into the dimly lit hallway. "Can't run a successful business like that, right?"

Adam assumed she didn't actually expect him to answer. Surely Dora had her own business opinions and theories.

He reached out and even in the darkness knew just where to find the light switch. It was a little like coming home to be here now. The comforting whirr of the fluorescent lights. The echo of their footsteps on the concrete floor. The familiar smell of the day's baking still lingered in the air.

Adam looked at the key in his hand, then down the length of the hallway with office doors on both sides. Then he searched beyond to the factory proper at the far end. Whether Dora wanted a response or not, he felt he had to say one thing. "They made a success of it for a lot of years."

"I know." There was an uncharacteristic kindness to her voice. Then she cleared her throat and took a step down the hall. "I've seen the profit-and-loss statements for the last decade. Mostly loss the last few years."

Adam squared his shoulders. "We can change all that."

"*Global* can change all that." She did not snap or come off defensive. If anything, Adam picked up a note of weariness, perhaps resignation in her reply. "And I know perfectly well what Global is capable of doing."

So did Adam, which was why he wanted to hear what Dora had in mind before Global went after the Crumble. They couldn't buy the company out if they didn't want to sell. Since the company was privately held, they could not force a hostile takeover.

What they could do was look at the company from every angle and see how they could make their own Crumble Pattie, bypassing the Burdetts altogether and undercutting their sales. That could put them out of business a full six months to a year sooner than the family would have managed to close the doors themselves. Or Global could come in, make a nice offer to take over the factory, let them keep their good name and take the Crumble Pattie to a national market as "one of the Global family of fine foods." They could save the company.

Except Adam suspected his father and brothers would not see it that way.

"On the up side of things, the Carolina Crumble Pattie Factory turns out a very good product." She walked to the first office door and stopped to face it. Adam did not have to share her line of vision to know what name was painted in gold and black on the frosted glass: Conner Burdett—President. "They are a widely recognized brand in the region and a ready and loyal workforce."

"That hasn't changed," he reminded her.

"You don't have to sell me on this company, Burdett." A few more steps and a half turn put her in front of Burke's office door. She reached out to brush her fingertips over the name there. "I just needed to clap eyes on the physical locality before I make a recommendation to the higher-ups."

"And that recommendation will be?" Burke's deep voice startled Adam but seemed to have little effect on Dora.

Adam turned around and planted his feet shoulder width apart. He supposed the two of them looked a bit like old-time cowboys calling one another out in the street. Adam, who felt his features probably seemed darker and more menacing in the narrow hallway, stood six inches shorter than Burke, the tall fair-haired man with broad shoulders and unblinking blue eyes.

Adam did not react to his brother's looming presence with anything more than a quiet, "I suppose you want my key back?"

Burke let the door fall shut behind him. "I'd settle for an explanation for why you are here."

"I'd rather give you my key." Adam started to tug it off the key ring.

"Don't bother. If I had been worried about keeping you out I'd have changed the locks." That could mean more than one thing: the most likely being that Burke already knew about Adam's connection to Global and had prepared himself to handle it; or he was just toying with his younger brother, letting Adam know he would never be intimidated by a stray like him.

"I assumed you came here because *you* were worried," Adam challenged. "Somebody call and report seeing Dora's car and my Harley in the lot?"

Burke shook his head. "I came out to meet with Josie Redmond about this fool barbecue deal Dad wants to throw."

Adam stepped back. "Josie?"

"She should be out here after she closes up."

"So, she is going through with that, then?"

"Was there ever any doubt?"

*Yes.* Adam had hoped she would turn his father down. Not just because he did not like the idea of her being in the middle of it all. Also since his brothers clearly had no inclination to organize the meal if Josie didn't pitch in, the whole event might just fall quietly by the wayside. "When is this barbecue?"

"Saturday," Burke said sounding more like a bull snorting than a man discussing a party.

"*This* Saturday?" Dora tipped her head and looked directly at the taller of the two brothers.

Burke nodded. Then he cocked his own head at the same angle as Dora's and said, "*You're* welcome to come."

Adam had not introduced Dora on purpose. He didn't plan on changing that now. "She won't—"

"I might just do that," Dora cut Adam off and held her hand out to Burke. "Dora Hoag."

"Burke Burdett."

Neither of them gave their business titles or bothered to share what relationship they had to the man they had in common, Adam. He couldn't help but feel a little left out over that.

She held Burke's hand longer than she'd ever held a handshake, or even eye contact with Adam. "Does your company do this kind of thing for the community regularly?"

"Never," Adam muttered.

Burke did not let go of Dora's hand but waited for her to slip it away. Then he added, "And the old man isn't doing this for the *community*."

Dora looked from the older brother to the younger. "Oh?"

Burke squinted Adam's way. "It's a big party to honor the return of the favored son."

Adam pressed his lips together to spew out a curse. He caught a glimpse of his boss standing by watching with undisguised interest. Then he looked to Burke, who had spent a lifetime provoking all of the younger brothers and enjoying it far too much when Adam, inevitably, rose to the bait. He decided to forgo any gut reaction and respond with calm honesty. "*Me? The favored* son? Hardly."

"These days you are."

"No." He refused to believe that. "Being the singled-out son is not the same as being favored. I've never been favored in this town for anything, unless it was to let everyone down."

"That's not how I recall it. The old man and I

have always butted heads. Lucky tries to stay below his radar. And the Hound…" Even though they had outgrown and/or rejected the designations long ago, Burke still called each of them by their old nicknames.

"Cody," Adam corrected quietly. "The old man has to be proud of Cody."

"Yeah. Sure. Pleased that the Hound found his calling and that he married a really nice girl. But less pleased that they are waiting to start a family until they have a church and anything but pleased that his preacher son is trying to influence him to apply Christian values to running the business."

"What's wrong with that?" Dora asked.

Adam and Burke both looked her way.

Her expression had changed, brightened while at the same time appeared more relaxed than Adam ever recalled her looking in the past. "Global sprang from a family business founded on Biblical principles."

Adam hadn't known that. It certainly didn't show in their current business model. Or did it? He had to admit to himself that he'd been so focused on his own goal he hadn't given that much thought.

"Interesting." Burke eyed her, sizing her up.

Burke sized everyone up. Adam had always had the impression that nobody ever measured up to his brother's standards.

"Maybe you can tell me how that has worked

out for—" he gave her an almost admiring smile "—Global, did you say?"

Adam cleared his throat to take the heat off Dora. "Okay, so the old man is on the outs with Cody. That doesn't automatically move me up to the top of the heap."

Top of the dog pile was Burke's spot, and Adam concluded he wouldn't be able to resist making sure everyone, especially the woman who had caught the older brother's interest, knew it.

"No, that doesn't place you on top in Dad's eyes. But being the first of his boys to produce a grand-child *does*."

Once again his family proved him wrong.

Adam shut his eyes and rubbed the bridge of his nose. Every disclaimer he could dredge up, from Nathan not being a Burdett by blood to wondering how their father could accept a child born out of wedlock, faltered unsaid when Burke leveled his gaze on Adam and added, "You don't know what it means to him to hold at least one member of the next generation before he dies."

"He's too tough to die," Adam blurted out, all cavalier and full of bluster. But the bluster came not from the well of anger that had sustained him for far too long. Just acknowledging that his father had any weakness, much less that he would not be with them for years to come, left Adam feeling like a six-year-old kid, lost and afraid. "He's not…he's not sick is he?"

"Yeah. Heartsick," Burke said.

"Because of Mom?" Adam asked.

"Mom. You. The business. The town." Burke did not look Adam in the eye as he went down the list. "Your coming back and that baby are the first bright spots he's had in a very long while."

Adam swallowed hard and clenched his jaw to force back the emotion rising from his chest.

"Maybe I shouldn't be hearing this," Dora said softly, but she made no attempt to leave.

"Maybe you *should*." Burke did not say that he knew what she was up to, that he understood that she saw everything that mattered to him as a property, a product, an investment or a loss. "Maybe it wouldn't be such a bad thing if you knew a little about my father."

Adam stepped up. "Burke, that's not—"

Burke ignored him. "Everything that old man did, he did for this family. His family is still what matters most to him."

"Easy for you to say," Adam muttered, only, for once he felt no anger or animosity behind it.

"Maybe it is. Maybe it is easier for someone outside a situation to see it for what it really is. With that kid, you gave him the one thing no spreadsheet or year-end report or bank balance could ever provide—a glimpse into the future."

Adam did not know what to say to that. He knew Burke was right about his father and the family, yet he seriously doubted his own role in that family. How could he and a child he had produced, not from love and commitment and honor, but in a thoughtless run of sinful self-indulgence, mean anything to Adam's adoptive father? He meant the world to Adam already, of course, but to Conner Burdett? The child didn't even carry the name.

Yet.

*Yet?* Adam had never had a genuine "lightbulb" moment—where his dim view of the world suddenly became bright and clear as daylight in an instant— until now. Now standing in this building where he had literally grown up, where he had played with his brothers as a child and fought with them as a young adult, and torn away from them as a determined business man with his own ideas, Adam understood.

He owed it to Nathan to give him not just a name but a place in this family. Nathan deserved his part of the legacy that was the Burdett family and the Carolina Crumble Pattie Factory. The good, the bad… and the delicious.

He chuckled to himself at that.

"What?" Burke demanded, probably feeling defensive over the idea that Adam might be laughing at him.

Adam shook his head. "Nothing. You just opened my eyes a little bit, big brother." Adam slapped a hand on Burke's broad shoulder, and slapped it hard. He cared for the big lug but he hadn't turned to emotional mush. "I realize I have a lot more to accomplish while I'm in town than I had originally planned on."

"Then get out of here and get to it." He brushed Adam's hand off, but he did it with respect in his eyes.

That was new, Adam noted. He decided to test the depths of that respect. "I will. But I have to finish the job I came here to do."

Adam held his hand out to indicate Dora should accompany him down the hallway. "Ms. Hoag?"

"Hold it." Burke put his hand on Dora's arm. "You sold your shares in this place eighteen months ago. It's not yours to show to anyone."

"You plan to call security for your own brother?" Dora asked. She sounded more curious than concerned.

"No, ma'am."

Adam tucked his thumb into the waistband of his favorite pair of broken-in black jeans. He stood his ground.

"I don't need to call security to deal with my brother. I *am* the security that deals with him." Burke managed somehow to take up the whole breadth and height of the section of narrow hallway where he stood. "He'd do well to remember that."

"You haven't bested me since we got into it right

after I graduated high school. And may I remind you, you always had a few years and five inches, and—" Adam stopped to look his brother over, taking a moment to show he'd noticed the way age had thickened the older man's midsection. He'd not gotten fat, by any means, but he wasn't the lean kid he'd once been. "And a few pounds on me."

"Not to mention a lot more smart." Burke tapped his finger to his temple and grinned.

"What's that supposed to mean?"

"It means I have enough sense to offer to spend my evening with this lovely lady, showing her around the place and to tell you to get your tail out of here and go see how you can be of help to your son and Josie instead of hanging around where you don't belong like some—"

"Watch it," Adam warned.

"Stray dog," Burke concluded. "Be a man, Adam."

The knot in Adam's gut rivaled his fist for size and tension. If his boss hadn't been standing there calmly watching his every reaction, Adam might just have decked his brother then.

He eyed the bigger, beefier man head to toe and corrected himself. He'd have taken a swing at him. Made contact, even, then probably gotten the fire whipped out of him. Two years ago, even a week ago, Adam would have thought it would have been worth the pain and humiliation of defeat just to show his brother, or anyone, that he would back down to no one. Now?

Now Adam held his hand out to the man, not clenched in a fist but open and in a show of deference and gratitude. "I think I'll just do that. In fact, why don't we both be men and conduct ourselves and our business with one another the best way we know how. As Christians."

Burke eyed the hand. He scratched his chin. Clearly he knew that if he took Adam's hand now he was not just making an overture of reconciliation, he was pledging to act according to the principles they had both learned from their mother about morality, forgiveness and trust, among other things.

He hesitated, looked at Dora Hoag, who was studying him not unlike the way a scientist eyes a test subject, then he exhaled loud and gruff.

"Yeah." He grabbed Adam's hand and clamped down hard. "Okay."

"You all right with this, Ms. Hoag?" Adam asked.

"He's your brother. You tell me. Will I be all right?"

Adam chuckled. "If you can stand him, you'll be fine."

Dora Hoag *had* come to see the facilities. Adam knew she would reveal nothing about their business plans to Burke. Likewise, Burke would not tell Dora any secrets that might throw the deal in either direction. It would, in fact, be either a quiet tour or one that veered off into more personal territory. Who knew where that might lead? Maybe a year from now Adam would be in Mt. Knott running the plant and Burke would be traveling the country in charge of acquisitions.

Besides, Burke would be within his rights to throw them both off the premises. Leaving her here with his brother actually seemed the best solution.

"If you hurry you can get to Josie before she closes up." Burke reached into his jeans pocket and pulled a folded piece of yellow legal paper out. "Give this to Josie. It's more budget, cost-per-guest type of thing, than a menu. All I care about is, is there is enough food out here by noon Saturday to feed every hungry mouth that shows up. I'll leave the actual food part up to her."

Dora looked at him as if that had told her something significant about the man.

"What can I say?" Burke shifted his shoulders and settled his thumbs in his belt loops in an "aw shucks" manner that belied the hardened business acumen lurking beneath the surface. "I'm a number cruncher not a chef."

"Don't buy that act," Adam told Dora with a smile.

She shook her head. "Don't you worry about me."

Adam laughed, quietly. "Yeah, he may be Top Dawg around here but I've seen you in action, Ms. Hoag. You are the Alpha Shark in a sea full of circling man-eaters."

For half an instant it dawned on Adam that Ms. Hoag, not the savvy businesswoman, but the just plain old smitten woman, might not have wanted that kind of image put before Burke.

But she laughed, gave Burke a look that promised Adam meant every word then turned to the younger brother and looked him in the eye for the first time maybe ever. She said, "I will see you at the barbecue, Burdett. And I can make you this promise. I'll give you my recommendation there, before I turn it official."

It was a courtesy Adam had not earned by rank or familiarity, so he appreciated it all the more. Despite her claims of it not being personal, she was granting him the chance to know what she would say, what Global would most likely do, before anyone else knew.

Once that would have made him so proud, given him a sense of power over his family. Now it felt like a heavy burden to bear. Not because anything had changed about his father or his family or how they felt toward him. He was still the outsider. The one who no longer had a stake in their livelihood and who had never had a place in their hearts, the stray.

But Adam had changed, just a little.

He *wasn't* a stray.

He was a father now, and he had to start acting like it, starting with going to Josie and supporting her in doing what she thought was right for herself, the people she cared about and her son. Even if what she thought was right meant catering to and collaborating with his family.

## Chapter Nine

Josie stood back from the blackboard wall. She pulled the scrunchie from her ponytail and sighed in relief as the curls fell around her shoulders and the tightness eased from her scalp. She replayed her earlier phone conversation with Burke Burdett.

She had to whip up every last ounce of courage to make the call, partly because she knew Adam hadn't wanted her to do it. But mostly because, of all the Burdett brothers, whose reputations were considerable in this town, Burke was the most…the biggest… the…well, he didn't just *like* the nickname Top Dawg, the man *lived* it. He had to take the lead in every situation, every conversation and he had to come out on top of every transaction, deal or exchange. What chance did a girl like Josie stand with a man like that?

Pretty good, it turned out, once he'd learned that

Adam had offered her money to not take the job. She hadn't meant to tell him that. It had just slipped out. But after it had, the man had gone to great lengths to accommodate her.

She would have liked to tell him she had never known that kind of rivalry for a sibling who, while you worked and followed the narrow path, chased after their own interests and still ended up your parent's darling while you went unnoticed. But she understood the feeling exactly and he knew it.

That fact had gone far to forming an unspoken bond between them. Burke wanted to get every last detail of this party right, and when she thought of Adam with that polished and poised businesswoman, she wanted that, too. It might be a party to commemorate Adam's return, but it was going to give Josie and Burke each a chance to shine. Whatever good it would do them.

So Burke had been particularly open to her suggestions when she explained her plan to use her suppliers for the food and sundries and enlist the help of the locals to get the "fixin's" to the tables.

Burke had told her he didn't care how she did it. As their official caterer she just needed to get it done right. Still, she felt bad about not cooking everything herself. However, given the short notice and the number of pies they would need to feed the crowd, it was the only realistic solution. Besides, Josie loved the idea of the community showing the Burdetts just what they could do when they all pulled together.

"This just might work." She studied the complex maze of columns, lines and arrows charting out how to supply enough food for the celebration.

"Oh, good. You're not closed yet." Adam came striding in with such confidence that she knew he couldn't have imagined for one second that he'd find that door locked.

"Just sorting out some details before…" Somehow admitting where she was headed after closing felt like a bit of a betrayal. Only, Josie couldn't say exactly who it was she thought she'd be letting down—Adam or Burke. Or herself. "Give me your honest opinion."

"Always."

"Do you think potato salad is a salad or a side?"

"What?"

Josie rolled her eyes at her own feeble attempt at diversion. She'd never been any good at anything that required her to be socially adept or coy. That was Ophelia's area of expertise. Josie had admired that about her sister, except for how her sister sometimes used it to take advantage of others.

She looked at the square-shouldered man who had obviously found much to appreciate about Ophelia, as well.

Still, she'd started this, so she had to stumble through it.

"Um, you know, potato salad?" She pantomimed eating as if she thought the man spoke another language, or perhaps had once been seen using globs of potatoes and mayonnaise as a hat and needed to know she meant the *other* kind of potato salad. "Would you classify it as a salad or a side dish?"

"Why would I want to do either?"

"Well, *you* wouldn't but *I* have to." She stepped back and showed him the convoluted columns on the wall. "See, I've just about worked this all out." She waved her hand like a game-show model. "But there is sort of a…hiccup in the division of salads-versus-side-dishes. We're heavily weighted toward side dishes."

He squinted at the board and made a noncommittal, "Hmmm."

"It's probably fine. I think we'll have enough food if everyone brings what they are assigned."

"Looks like you've got it all figured out." He turned toward the wall.

She stared at the squiggles and notations, waiting for him to say something about it all. To point out that if she had been ethical enough not to take money from him for something she didn't deserve, she shouldn't take it from his family for the same reason. She wasn't doing the majority of the cooking, after all.

Maybe he'd find some other fault with her decision.

Or maybe he didn't care at all, especially since he had a real lady friend in town.

The longer they went without speaking, the more the situation, or the nonsituation, built up in her mind. If she let it go on much longer who knew what wild story she would concoct? A potato-salad conspiracy? Bank loans being called in before the barbecue check arrived? Adam choosing the woman in a silver sedan to step in as Nathan's stepmother?

"I had to do it, Adam." The words rushed out. "It was just good business. The way things are in Mt. Knott, turning down this amount of business just wouldn't be smart."

He looked at her at last, a twinkle in his eyes. "Well, no one ever accused me of being smart,"

"Don't feel bad. Some folks have to be content to be just another pretty face," she teased him right back. As soon as the words left her mouth she felt the heat rise in her face like some silly schoolgirl. Socially adept as Ophelia, she was not. "Uh, you'd better go. I have to lock up and see if I can get someone to watch Nathan before I go out to discuss all this with your brother."

"All this?" He held his hand out. "Salads and hiccups and all?"

"Uh-huh."

"As has been pointed out not that long ago, I am not the smart one 'round these parts, but wouldn't it have been smoother to have him come here and see this for himself?"

She gave a shrug. "He's the boss."

Adam's mouth tightened. "Fair enough," he relented. "But right now your boss is busy with my boss."

"Your...does she happen to be a very well-put-together lady?"

"Well, I've never checked her for patches or busted seams—"

"I'm glad to hear that!" Josie slapped her hand over her mouth before her ineptitude got her into further trouble.

Adam grinned. "But, yes, Ms. Hoag comes off as very well pulled together."

"Comes off as? Meaning looks can be deceiving?"

"Lots of things can be deceiving," he said enigmatically. "But this 'look' is on the up-and-up."

Josie nodded. "So, what does that mean for me?"

She forced herself not to put her hand over her mouth again. She was asking what Adam's boss being with *her* boss meant for her, not what Ms. Hoag's "look" and association with Adam meant to her. If he didn't gather that then...then maybe she'd have some of her most burning questions answered.

"It means I get to bring you this." He held out a piece of folded paper. "It's the budget for the party that Burke worked up on your preliminary information."

"Oh?" She took the paper and unfolded it slowly.

"If it's not right, if you need more money or autonomy, leave it to me. I'll fix it. I'll make sure my family does right by you, Josie."

*But who will make sure* you *do right by me?* Never a slow learner, Josie had managed to keep that remark entirely to herself. Still, she did wonder…

"What do you think?"

"Think?" She had kept the remark silent, right?

"About Burke's figures."

"Oh." She took a minute to read over the paper. Burke had been quite generous with her, but not so much that she would have felt compelled to argue the money. "I think I can work with this."

"Really? And get it all done by Saturday at noon?"

"I'm closing down after the coffee rush tomorrow, and I'm going to make pies into the wee hours of the night."

"You poor kid."

"No! I can't wait. I'm looking forward to it. The chance to do what I love and the one thing I know I am good at."

"One thing? No way." He moved closer to her. So close he could brush the freshly undone curls off one shoulder as he said with quiet intensity, "Josie you're great at so many things…"

"How would you know?"

"I just do. You're a good mom, I know that and…"

"And that's enough for now." She held up her hand

and retreated from him. "It really means a lot to hear you say that, though."

He only nodded, his hand still in the air at shoulder level for a moment before he let it fall to his side.

"That's one reason I'm so excited about tomorrow." She took a chatty tone, hoping to take control of things again. She walked briskly toward the front door, hoping Adam would follow and be on his way. "I get to do the work I love, knowing it will be enjoyed by the people I love, plus I get to have Nathan nearby all day."

He did follow, a bit too closely.

When she turned around, she found herself just inches away from the man. "What…could be… better?"

"What indeed?"

"What indeed?" she murmured. Then, coming to her senses before she gave in to the deep, soothing masculinity of his voice, she gave the door a push and cool air rushed in around them. "I know. It sounds completely corny to a man like you."

"A man like me?"

"A man of the world."

"Harsh words."

"Harsh? That you're educated, well-spoken, well traveled, experienced and sophisticated?"

"That I am 'of the world' when *you* so clearly need a man willing to come out of the world and separate himself from its ways."

She smiled slightly to hear him paraphrase the Biblical admonition that Christians should be apart from the world. "I was thinking more that you're worldly and I'm...Mt. Knotty."

"You're the last person I'd consider naughty," he teased. "In fact, I'd vote you Most Likely to be Nice."

"Knottish, then." She gave him a good-humored scowl.

"Knottish or not at all, I'm in the very same boat as you there." He put his hand on the door and raised his face to the summer breeze. "I grew up right here in Carolina countryside. Except for this last year and a half in Atlanta I haven't lived anywhere else. I spent my holidays here, my summer vacations and made this my home after college."

"I guess I never thought of that." Josie stared out into the fading light of evening. "I always pictured the Burdetts as having a different kind of lifestyle than the rest of us."

"We did. Still do, I suspect." His arm still braced to prop the door open, he narrowed his eyes at the blackboard wall. "Where the rest of you got to clock out and leave the factory behind you, we all carried the responsibilities with us all the time. As a kid I used to ride my bike straight to the Crumble, did my homework in my dad's office, then went home with my mom for dinner then back to help my dad lock up."

"Oh, Adam, that is so sad."

"Sad? How so?"

"Sort of missed out on your childhood, didn't you?"

"And your childhood, Josie?"

She shook her head. "I sort of missed out on my childhood, too. Though I don't know that Ophelia would say she missed out on hers."

"Personally, I think she may still be living hers."

"Adam!" Josie had thought the exact same thing, but it was the age-old conundrum about brothers and sisters. You can say whatever you feel about them, but just let someone else try it and suddenly you'll defend your loved one. "Ophelia must have matured some. Otherwise why would she have signed the papers allowing me to adopt Nathan and finally shared the information about his father?"

"About *me*," he corrected.

She pressed her lips together.

He bowed his head for a moment, then looked again out into the serene small-town setting.

Josie put her back against the other side of the door frame and crossed her ankles. "At least when you were doing all those things, you were doing them here, in a safe home, a nice town and with your family. I was dropped off in Mt. Knott and only saw my mother now and then, and Ophelia almost never."

"I guess I do have *that* to be thankful for."

Ophelia wasn't the only one showing more maturity, Josie thought. Two days ago Adam would have used that opportunity to lambaste his family or make a joke about their rocky relationships.

"It's not that bad, now that I have—" her gaze met his "—now that I have Nathan. And I hope that Ophelia will come around in time. I wrote her a nice long thank-you letter when she signed those papers and told her she was welcome to visit us anytime."

"And you think she will take you up on that?" His eyes grew dark. His back went straight.

Josie wasn't sure if it was hope or horror in his voice.

"She's my sister, Adam. I can't forget that."

"Neither can I," he said softly. "You may think of me as a man of the world, but I'm just as humbled and confused by all of this as you are, Josie."

"So if we're not worldly what does that make us?" she asked.

"A couple of Mt. Knott-heads?" Laughter mingled with the more somber emotions in his expression.

"A couple of workaholics." She checked her watch. They'd both put in more than a full day's duty and it wasn't even dark yet. Realizing he wasn't going to take the hint and walk out, Josie headed inside. Full day's work or not, she still had to close down.

"So what do we do about that?" he asked.

"Do?" She flipped the lock shut and turned the Open sign to the Sorry, We're Closed side. "About what?"

"About all work and no play making us dull folks."

She headed for the cash register, wondering if she could just pull the drawer, lock it in the vault and count the money in the morning. "I don't think anyone has ever described you as dull, Adam Burdett."

"Would it shock you to say that sometimes I wish they would?"

*Ching.*

She stood with her hand hovering above the register key that had just opened the drawer. "Yes. I can think of a lot of other words I'd use for you, but *dull?* I just can't see it."

"What words?"

"Hmm?" She wrestled the money compartment free and clunked it on the counter.

He stood at her side now. "What words would you use for me?"

She gave the stacks of bills, all ones and fives, a quick reckoning. "*Strong. Decent.* Maybe a little bit—" she lifted the top half of the compartment to check underneath for checks and twenties and found one of each *"—dangerous."*

He did not contest that.

She started to turn to take the drawer to the back, then her curiosity got the better of her. She had to know. "What words would you use to describe me?"

"You? Hmmm. That's tough."

"Oh, yeah?"

"Ex-peshully for a pretty-faced country dawg like me, ma'am, who ain't got a very big vol-cab-ulurry."

"Maybe if I held up a treat and commanded you to speak?" She sank her teeth into her lower lip.

"Do I get to choose what you use for a treat?"

"Okay. I get it. I'm too...*me* for words." She spun around and headed into the kitchen, intent on putting the money in the back room, gathering up her sleeping child, getting home and putting this day—and this man—behind her.

*"Capable."*

"What?" She looked up as her shoulder touched the office door and found him right beside her.

"One of the words I'd use is *capable.*"

"Well, isn't that...utilitarian?" She stepped into the small room and set the money on the desk.

"And *smart,*" he added, following her inside.

"Better," she plucked the key to the vault off the hook, then turned and found she couldn't take another step.

"And—" he leaned in *"—kissable."*

Moments before he could put his lips to hers she had to whisper. "But I'm not Ophelia."

"What?"

"I may be the things you described me as, but the one thing I am not...is Ophelia."

"I know that."

"Then you will understand why I can't let you kiss me now."

"I will?"

"If you'll excuse me I have got to finish up in here and take Nathan home."

"Now?"

"Yes, now. He's already asleep, and I'd like to get him to his crib."

"No. You said you can't let me kiss you *now*. Does that mean you can let me kiss you eventually?"

Josie hesitated.

"Ah, c'mon, give a guy some hope."

"Adam," she whispered. "It's too fast. It's too… much. We have to think about Nathan and his custody." *Then there is the whole Ophelia issue.* "We can't just give in to our feelings for each other without taking things like that into account. It's too soon."

She marched to the door. "If you don't mind. I have to lock up before I leave."

"Let me see you home."

"I can manage the short walk." She shoved him out the office door. "But if you want to spend some time with your son, come by here tomorrow afternoon. There might even be something sweet in it for you."

"Ahh, hope springs eternal." He put his hand to his heart.

"I'm talking baked goods," she called after him.

But he didn't seem to hear a word of it.

# Chapter Ten

Adam belted out his own version of "That's Amore" with a tribute to "Josie's apple pie" as he swung open the front door of the Home Cookin' Kitchen.

Everyone in the whole room, including Nathan in his portable playpen in the corner, fixed their eyes on him. Mouths gaped open.

He paused in the open doorway. "What? Can't a man face the day with a song in his heart?"

"If it stays in his heart," Jed grumbled.

"Once it starts spilling out past his teeth and starts getting stuck into the ears of innocent bystanders, them innocent bystanders got a right to make a comment."

"And your comment is?" Adam asked.

The two older fellows exchanged glances before they spoke as one, saying, "Shut your piehole!"

"Aw, leave him alone. I like this side of him. Better than that strong, silent type skulking about on that noisy motorcycle," said a woman standing at the table of coffeepots, pouring cream into a steaming thermal cup.

"I like the *other* side of him," Warren gruffly proclaimed.

"The other…" Adam looked over his shoulder at his supposed "other" side.

Now all eyes moved to Warren.

"What are you talking about?" Jed shifted his weight to one stool away from his regular spot at the counter.

Warren coughed. "I'm talking about the side of him we all see when he's heading out the door."

Jed grunted to show his disbelief.

"Seems that's what them Burdetts do the best, anyway. When things get tough they turn tail and save themselves."

"That's not fair, Warren." Josie came through the kitchen door wiping her hands on her apron.

"Ain't fair that after twenty years at the Crumble my wife now has to work all hours catering to teenagers in a bowling alley in another town, either."

"Have you ever stopped to think how much time each of the Burdetts has spent trying to keep the business afloat?" she asked. Her gaze flicked up to meet Adam's, then just as quickly she looked away.

"Afloat? That explains a lot." Jed snorted and retook his regular seat. "We thought they was making snack food, *they* thought they was building bass boats!"

"Hey, hey! Paychecks from that factory paid for most of the bass boats sitting in driveways around this town. They didn't plan for things to go sour out there." Josie threw the towel down.

"Maybe they should have." Warren swiveled around to look at Adam head-on at last. "Sour snacks were a big trend for a time. Maybe if the Burdetts had just once considered adding to the line of products..."

"Well, I have heard of backseat drivers and armchair quarterbacks, Warren, but never diner-stool businessmen. You haven't even taken into account—"

"No, Josie, don't feel you have to defend us." Adam held his hand up. "I agree with the man. The Burdetts could have done better by this community."

Adam could have gone on about how he felt the Burdetts had treated him personally or taken this opportunity to tell the townspeople about his hopes for turning things around. But since he could not, in his own heart, untangle the two, he did not trust his motives for saying anything.

Funny, a few days ago, before meeting Josie and seeing the way she tried so earnestly to live her faith, Adam would never have questioned that. He'd have spoken his mind, no matter who it hurt or why he said it. "I guess if that means y'all would rather not have me around while you have your breakfast, I'd understand."

"Naw. I've had to stomach Jed's ugly mug all these years." Warren jerked his thumb toward his old friend. "I can stand a Burdett for a few minutes, I reckon."

"That's his indirect way of saying he appreciates your honesty," Jed translated.

"Thank you very much." Adam gave a nod, then launched into his song again.

"I appreciate your honesty, pal, but not your singing," Warren tacked on good and loud.

Everyone laughed.

Josie put her hands over her ears. "Would you stop making all that racket?"

She caught his eye and smiled.

He did not know if the redness of her cheeks came from their gazes meeting or from the heat of her defending his family name or from her work in the kitchen where she had just been baking. She cocked her head, and her topknot of curls wobbled. She batted away a loose strand of hair and left a smudge of flour on her nose.

Adam had never seen a more beautiful woman in his life.

She stooped to pick up Nathan and settled the fat baby on her hip.

No, Adam amended his original conclusion, *now* she was the most beautiful woman he'd ever seen.

"Assistant pie chef reporting for duty." Adam gave her a snappy salute.

"You?" Jed scoffed.

"Yeah. Me." He lowered his hand slowly.

"But this is baking." Josie waved her hand, scattering a fine puff of flour through the air. "It's not something I associate with a Harley-riding bad-boy type."

"Bad boy?" On one hand he wanted to point out neither adjective fit him. On the other, he found it kind of cool that she saw him that way. Women loved bad boys, right? "Does that mean you want to tame me?"

"Hmmm." She put her hand on her hip and cocked her head. Her curls bounced against her head. "Maybe if you traded that motorcycle in for a minivan."

"Hold the phone, Sweetie Pie. What goes on here?" Jed swiveled around on his stool. "Most women wait until they've got a fellow's ring on their finger before they go trying to change him."

*Minivan?*

*Ring?*

*Whoa!*

He'd come back to Mt. Knott to claim his kid and show his detractors exactly what he was capable of—succeeding where they had failed. Not to go the home-and-hearth route with...

Adam looked to the woman setting his son down.

Yeah, he had wanted to show everyone just what he was capable of. Why did he suddenly think he might be capable of so much more than he himself had ever suspected?

"I grew up in a food-prep industry." He approached the counter, spotted Nathan standing in his playpen, bent down and said to his son, "Explain to your mom, please, that I can manage to turn out a few edible pies."

"Edible? I hope my pies are a little better than just edible."

"You notice they never touched the marriage and man-changing issue?" Warren stroked his chin.

"Completely tap-danced all the way around it." Jed waggled two downward-pointing fingers to demonstrate the deftness of the pair's maneuvering.

Adam held both hands up. "Hey, I came here and volunteered to handle freshly baked pies, not hot potatoes."

Warren laughed. "You're all right, Burdett."

Jed joined him. "He has our stamp of approval, Sweetie Pie."

"Great. Then why don't y'all stick that stamp on real tight, take him down to the post office and see if you can send it off to parts unknown for a while. Because nobody gets in my kitchen while I make pies."

"She's afraid you'll learn her secret ingredient," came the jovial voice of an older woman at Adam's back. The aroma of coffee curled up in the steam from her mug.

"If I was her I'd be afraid he'd steal more than that," a younger woman pouring sweetener from a pink packet chimed in.

Josie's face went a deeper shade of red.

Adam chuckled.

Neither of them denied her statement.

"I think we'd better add Josie's name to the prayer list, then." The older woman clamped the lid down on her thermal cup and headed toward the wall.

Adam turned to look at the column on the blackboard wall. He opened his mouth to make a joke. Then closed it, humbled, and simply read the requests in silence.

"Please, please, pray that my mom keeps her job. Kyle."

"Remember those who have lost health insurance, that we all stay well. Elvie."

"Please pray I find work." That followed by not one but an entire list of names.

After so many selfish and anger-blinded years, the problems of the Burdetts and Mt. Knott suddenly felt bigger than Adam's pain. That was Josie's doing, he decided. No, that was so much bigger than Josie.

He scanned the list again, and found something that made his breath still.

"Please pray for Adam Burdett." No signature.

Yes, he had felt lonely and rejected, ignored and

unloved. Well, welcome to the world. So many hearts bore those burdens and yet they stopped and took the time to pray for others, to come together, to help each other.

"You don't have to add our Sweetie Pie to any list," Jed said softly. "She's always in our prayers."

The rough older men narrowed their eyes at Adam.

He twisted around to meet their silent admonition with a somber look. He got it. And he wanted them to know it.

Jed nodded in acknowledgment first.

Warren took longer but when he raised his cup to recognize the promise that had passed between them, it warmed Adam to his gut.

Then Josie clapped her hands together. "All right. That's enough of that. Everyone fill your cups, add your sugar and cream and settle up your bills, please. I'm ready to lock up for the rest of the day."

"Which side of the door do you want me on when the lock slides into place?" Adam asked quietly.

Josie frowned, well, as much as she ever frowned. It was more a cross between a pout and a playfully sour face.

Adam grinned at her.

She sighed and shut her eyes.

He didn't know if she was saying a prayer, gathering her strength to do what she had to do or blocking him from view so she could think straight. Maybe all three. But when she finally opened her eyes again, she was smiling.

"I want you on this side." She pointed to the spot beside her.

"Fantastic! Get me an apron and call me the Mt. Knott doughboy!"

"Oh, you can have an apron but you aren't getting anywhere near my dough."

Josie hit a button on the cash register, and the drawer popped open with a *ding!*

"So what job do you have in mind for me? Cherry picker? Apple slicer? Peach peeler?'

"I was thinking more gopher."

"I know this is the South but I don't think even here that anyone will want gopher pie."

"The gopher won't be in the pie—the gopher will be in your apron."

"Won't that make it more difficult for me to get any work done?"

"Going for things that I need will be your job. That and watching Nathan."

"Never thought I'd see the day," Jed laid down his payment plus a little extra. He made a sign to Josie to indicate she should keep the change. "Nope. Never thought I'd see the day when a Burdett would do the bidding and get ordered around by one of their own laid-off workers."

"Sorta gets a guy right here." Warren pounded his chest as he headed out onto the street.

"So does indigestion," Adam called as he held the door open for the departing customers.

"Yeah. But there's a tonic for indigestion," Warren said. "For what you've got, son…?"

He and Jed both shook their heads.

"…ain't no remedy on Earth for that," Jed concluded. "Nothing to take for it."

"Oh, I don't know. He could try taking some vows." Warren laughed.

Adam gulped. *Vows?* He cared about Josie, even having only recently gotten to know her. But vows? "Look, I admire Josie's pluck and appreciate the job she's done with Nathan, but…"

"Don't underestimate what it means to find a woman who is a good mother to your child."

"And your child ain't actually *her* child."

"It don't hurt when she's prettier than a speckled pup."

"And cooks better than your own mama."

"Josie's a good woman."

"And we expect you to be good to her."

"I will. But I'm not ready for marriage."

"Apparently you wasn't ready to be a daddy, neither, but here you are."

"Here I am."

"Maybe you ought to take a good long look at yourself before you settle your mind on what you are and are not ready for."

Adam turned and looked at himself reflected in the glass door.

Apron.

Baby.

Giving up an entire day to spend time with a woman giving him orders and turning up the heat and turning away his advances.

And he didn't mind any of it.

Well, he would have liked it better if she'd let him kiss her. But he understood and respected her choices.

That fact alone gave him pause. Maybe those older fellows had a point. Maybe he did need to take a good long look at himself before he made up his mind about himself and Josie.

## Chapter Eleven

"Do me a favor?" Josie stepped to the doorway, the first of many freshly baked pies in her silicon-mitted hand.

Adam looked up from a rousing round of a game that might be called "see Daddy scramble after every toy Nathan throws on the floor" and made the bug-eyed bear in his hand squeal with one well-timed squeeze. "Anything."

"First, stop chasing down everything he throws."

"Just trying to make myself useful."

"As what? A Labrador retriever?"

Adam looked at the bear then back at Josie. "Woof."

She laughed. "You're supposed to be the one in charge. Do you really think that if you go after everything the instant he tosses it overboard you are teaching him the way things work in the real world?"

"The *real* world?" Adam scowled. "He's a baby. Why does he need to know about the real world?"

"Because that's the world we are all born into. We have so little time to get his feet on the right path, with so many things trying to get him to stray…"

"What if straying comes naturally to him?" Adam flipped the bear over and over in his hands.

Adam was testing her and she knew it. Just as Nathan might push something away or even throw it aside.

"Straying comes naturally to all of us." She glanced around her at the tables and chairs that would, on a normal Friday, be just now filling up with the lunch crowd.

She had served her friends, her fellow townspeople and strangers day in and day out. She had sat next to many of these same people in town meetings and church services. But here, where they had not always been on their best behavior, they had taught her something more precious than any of them knew.

Her eyes went to the prayer list and she managed a slight smile. "Isn't that why Jesus is known as the Good Shepherd? We need Him to watch over us and bring us back into the fold when we lose our way."

"Why, Miss Josie, I didn't expect a Sunday school lesson from you today." His mouth quirked up on one side, half in humor, half in challenge to her. Another test.

Would she pass it? Would she stand up to him? And, more important, stand up for her beliefs?

"Didn't expect a lesson, but I notice you didn't say you didn't *appreciate* getting one."

"You are a wonder, Josie." He laughed.

"Takes one to know one," she joked.

"Me? A wonder?" He dropped the toy into the playpen with the baby, then took a few steps toward the counter. "Only if by that you mean I *wonder* if I'll ever get the hang of this Daddy stuff."

"I think you will."

"Do ya?" he asked softly, his eyes dark and his smile a very masculine mix of smug and wistful.

"Yeah, maybe by the time he goes off to college," she teased.

Adam opened his mouth, probably to protest or to at least boldly proclaim his belief in his own parenting abilities when Nathan let out a *"Ph-th-th-th-ppp-ttt"* and sent the bear sailing right at the side of Adam's head.

The bear hit its mark then slid to the floor.

He gazed down at the thing then at the baby, who stood with his pudgy fingers flexed and wriggling in the direction of the bear.

"Sorry, kiddo. Game over."

Nathan grunted in anger and stretched up on his toes, his arms rigid and his cheeks red.

Adam plopped the bear on the counter. "Next time maybe you'll realize that if you really want something you have to hang on to it. Don't let it go. And certainly don't throw it away and assume you can have it back whenever you want."

Nathan shrieked.

Adam did not budge. "Listen to your ol' dad. This is a subject he knows something about."

Josie froze. What exactly had Adam thrown away, then wished he could get back again? Not Nathan, as he had never known about the child. Ophelia? She held her breath to think of it.

"Okay, got that." Adam now turned his full attention on her. "What else can I do for you? You just name it."

*Fall in love with me and become Nathan's father in every sense of the word forever and ever.* She leaned against the door frame and sighed over her indulgent little fantasy. Her and Adam and Nathan. Their own patchwork of a family. Visiting with the other brothers and their families, if any of them ever had any, on holidays. Watching Nathan grow and perhaps giving him a sister or brother or both. Sharing a home and a future. Going to church together. Going to…

The smell of pies ready to be taken from the oven brought her back to reality. "Um, if you don't mind, would you taste this pie?"

"I don't mind. But I have tasted your pie before. It's delicious."

"When I bake a few at a time, it's delicious. But

trying to make enough for this barbecue? I've never tried to mix up that much pie crust before. I'm not sure I got the right ratio of flour to—"

"Yes?" He arched an eyebrow.

"Oh, no. You are not getting my secret recipe out of me that easily." She slid the pie pan onto the counter, then turned around to retrieve a knife and a pie server. "Not unless you can figure it out for yourself."

"If I do—" he sat himself at the counter and picked up a fork "—will you finally tell me your secret, Josie?"

"I'll tell you mine if you'll tell me yours." It came out before she could stop herself. And then she was glad she had *not* stopped herself. Because of all the things she wanted from Adam, knowing his secrets, knowing the undeniable truths upon which he based his decisions was right up there.

"Let me have a taste of that pie." He did not promise to share anything with her.

She slid the stainless steel server in under the crust of the small triangular piece she had cut from the whole. Slowly she lifted it up, then lowered it slowly, then lifted it again. It had the right heft.

She closed one eye and peered at it with the other eye narrowed as if scanning the thing with a laser beam. It had the right look.

She closed both eyes now, pulled back her shoulders and inhaled. It had the right aroma.

The top and bottom crust broke into delicate flakes just as they should. The filling clung to the chunky upper crust that was her trademark, in the way it always did, with the fruit still firm and plump, not watery or crushed under the weight of the top. Still, Josie would not be satisfied that she had done her best until she heard it from someone whose opinion mattered to her.

That thought made her take a sharp right turn with the pie plate still in hand. "Here, Nathan, you take the first bite."

"Hey! What about me?"

"This is your chance to show your son how to practice patience by example," she returned, aiming to appear witty when, in fact, she was terrified.

She was a mother. A mother who had lived the past year in fear that at any moment her child could be taken from her. Now, just when it seemed she could put that fear behind her and move on to build a life for herself and her child, this man comes along. Yes, Nathan's father, but also a virtual stranger to Josie. A stranger, by his own admission, with a secret.

She could not afford to take that lightly. Nor could she allow her own feelings alone to dictate her actions. She had to get her priorities right and keep them right. No matter how she felt about this man, she was first and foremost Nathan's mother.

She pinched off a bite just right for a one-year-old and poked it into Nathan's mouth.

He worked it around with his tongue more than with his tiny front teeth. Some of the red dribbled onto his chin, and he rubbed his fist over it and began to gnaw at his balled-up fingers. "Mmmm-nnnnm-mmm-nop-nah-nnop."

"Does that mean he likes it or not?" Adam moved in close behind her and then leaned forward to peer at the child, bringing him closer still.

"I don't know," she confessed, her eyes glued on the boy's reaction in a gargantuan effort not to sense how close Adam was standing. Not to smell the still-fresh line-dried scent of his apron or hear the jingle of his change and keys when he put his hand in his pocket.

"Ya-ya-ya!" Another shriek, then Nathan went on tiptoe and stretched his arms out for the plate in Josie's hand.

"I think he likes it." Adam laughed

Josie laughed, too, and offered her son another infant-size piece on her finger. "I think he does."

"Now how about you let me have a taste and see what I do?"

She spun around, the pie filling still clinging to her hand and found herself nose to nose with the man. "A...a taste?"

"Of pie." He slipped the plate away, moved to the counter and found the fork he had left lying there.

"Don't worry, Josie. I won't press you for anything you're not ready to share. Not your secrets. Not your kisses. And most especially not your—"

*Beep. Beep. Beep.*

"What's that?"

"Bingo!"

"I didn't even know we were playing."

"Not the game, the mailman."

"We have a beeping mailman?"

"He has a little horn on his scooter to warn people to clear the path or let them know he's making a delivery. He has bad knees."

"When did Mt. Knott get a beeping mailman?"

"He's always been the mailman in this part of town as far as I know." She hurried across the room. "I can't believe you don't at least know about him. He certainly knows plenty about you."

"He does?"

Josie winced. She probably shouldn't have reminded him of how she had gotten people talking about Adam right after he came to town, which probably was how his father found out about Nathan, which led to the barbecue that Adam did not want to attend, which—

"So, who else have you talked to about me besides the bad-kneed beeper?"

"Bad-kneed beeper." Josie laughed. "I'll have to tell him that."

"Josie?"

She twisted the lock and pulled open the front door.

"Wouldn't have bothered you. I know you had big plans for today." Bingo eyed Adam.

Adam eyed him right back.

"But this looked important. Didn't want to take a chance of you not seeing it."

"He reads the mail?" Adam moved through the dining room in a few long strides. "You read her mail?"

"Just what's on the outside." The big man looked hurt and just a wee bit defensive. "Gotta read what's on the outside or else I wouldn't know what to deliver to where."

"Yeah, he's gotta read what's on the—" Josie turned the letter over and what was on the outside of the envelope hit her like a slap in the face. "It's the letter I sent to Ophelia to thank her for signing the papers to allow Nathan's adoption." Josie's hand trembled. "Marked 'Return to Sender.'"

"Really? I didn't know people actually did that." Adam moved in behind her, his hand out, but he did not try to take the envelope from her.

"Oh, yeah. All the time. Or they put 'not at the address.' The real creative ones sometimes send their own messages. Don't think I can say what they write on the envelopes, not in front of Josie." Bingo reached into his bag then and retrieved a stack of bills and advertising flyers. He thrust them toward her. "All means the same, the person on the address didn't get the mail."

She ignored the other mail and rubbed her fingertips over the blocky words beside her delicate-scrolled lettering. "Doesn't look like Ophelia's handwriting."

Adam took the mail from Bingo, his eyes always trained on her. "That good or bad?"

"Well, if it were in her own hand, I'd know she was there and just didn't, for whatever reason, want to hear from me." She looked up and blinked, half expecting tears to flood over her eyelashes, but they did not come.

"Family can be tough on each other." Adam brushed his hand over her shoulder.

"Some more than others," Bingo observed.

Adam smacked the mail in one hand against his open palm. "Don't you have mail to deliver?"

"Miss Josie?" Bingo looked to her to send him on his way.

She nodded.

"Now don't go fretting too much about that. Could be any number of things behind it, not all bad." He limped out the door, got onto his red scooter and gave a beep goodbye.

"You think that's true?" she asked Adam as they walked back to the counter. "That there are a lot of reasons mail gets returned and it doesn't mean that something bad has happened?"

"What do you think?"

"I think this means that Ophelia isn't at this address anymore."

"Then where is she?"

Where indeed? *You have a baby with her, why don't you know?* Josie pressed her lips together to keep her questions and quasi-accusations from exploding into the open. She rubbed the space between her eyebrows. At last she fought to keep from bursting into tears.

"Maybe you can contact your mother. She might know how to find Ophelia."

"She might. But in order to ask her, I'd have to first know where my *mother* is." That did it. The tears flowed, though less like a dam bursting and more in sobbing fits and starts.

Adam slapped the mail down and came to her. He started to touch her arms, then thought better of it. He tried to put his arm around her shoulders, but their shaking made that difficult. Finally he crooked one finger under her chin and lifted her face so he could look her in the eye as he said, "I don't understand."

"I haven't seen my mother since my grandmother's funeral." And at the mention of that, Josie felt completely and utterly alone all over again, just as she had the day of that funeral when her mother had driven off with her grandmother's car loaded down with anything of value from the house she and Josie had shared. "I spoke to her a time or two, but she called *me*. I don't have a number to call her. She stays on the move most of the time."

"On the move?" He dropped his hand and reached out to get a napkin from the dispenser on the counter. He handed it to her.

"Not running from the law or anything like that. At least not that I know of." She wiped her eyes, blew her nose, then grimaced. "Seems like Nathan might come by that tendency to stray from both sides of the family. You can't be too shocked by that, I mean, you and Ophelia…"

"I know." He hung his head. "I have no excuse for my behavior, Josie. I was hurt and angry and acting like a…a—"

"Like a toddler trying to get the people around him to stop everything and do his bidding?"

Adam chuckled softly at his own expense, then his expression went somber. He shook his head. "It was wrong. *I* was wrong. Doubly so to involve your sister. I didn't care that what we were doing would take its toll on her, the drinking, the carelessness of that temporary…relationship."

He struggled to get the words out without offending her, without embarrassing her.

For that Josie was grateful. And she showed it by trying to lift some of Adam's guilt. "You can't blame yourself for my sister. She was…*careless* and prone to the *temporary* for a long time before she met you."

"I know." He nodded. "She has her own pain. Her own deep-seated fears. Her own longing to make the people she loves notice her, to love her in return."

"Ophelia?" Josie had never thought of her sister that way.

Willful. Selfish. Haughty. Wild.

All of those things she had ascribed to the woman who shared her physical attributes but none of her spiritual convictions. But hurting? Fearful? Longing to be loved?

Josie had thought she alone had those feelings, that she alone deserved them. Had she really misjudged Ophelia so harshly?

The very notion rattled her to the core of her being.

"I never thought of her in that way. To me she was always Ophelia, the inspired. Ophelia, the nonconformist. Ophelia, Mom's favorite."

"Favorite?" Adam's whole expression clouded. "Burke said that about me today. Called me the favored son because I came back and because I gave my father a grandchild. But if you ask me there is no reason to favor me. I've handled so many things so poorly. The fact that Nathan is here and healthy, that's all you, Josie."

"Not *all* me," she spoke deliberately as the full measure of what her sister had done dawned on her. "Ophelia had Nathan. She carried him and chose not just to give him life but to give him a chance by bringing him to me and letting me care for him, be his mother."

"She knew you could do it."

Josie shook her head in awe. "That was a selfless act of pure faith, Adam. I never saw it until now. I never saw the real Ophelia until you showed her to me today."

"Me? I can barely see beyond the tip of my own nose, Josie."

"I don't believe that."

"How could you not? The whole time I've been in Mt. Knott I never once tried to find out about you and your family, just whined about my own."

"You've been so focused on your own issues… and rightly so. I'm nothing to you…"

"That's not true—about you being nothing to me, not about me being focused on my own issues. That, I hate to admit, is completely true." He took her by the arms and pulled her around so that he could look her in the eyes. "But I'm here now and I'm not going anywhere."

"Actually, I think you should."

"What?"

"Go," she said.

"But I—"

"Please, Adam. Just give me some time to myself. I have a lot to think about *and* a lot to do."

"I wanted to help you."

"If you want to help me, then pray for me."

"Okay."

"And for Nathan," she called as she watched him make his way to the door.

"Of course."

"And…" She folded her hands together, knowing she had to say one more thing and yet selfishly wishing she could just leave things as they were. To ask Adam to make his priorities that simple, her and Nathan.

But now she knew there was another person out there who needed God's love and compassion. And nothing would ever be right in their family until they faced that. "And pray for Ophelia, too."

# *Chapter Twelve*

"**Y**ou're too young to know this, Nathan, but there is an old saying. 'Today is the first day of the rest of your life.'" Josie lifted the baby from his crib.

She'd gotten up early. Even after staying up late into the night baking, she'd been too excited to sleep in. "This is not just the first day of the rest of my life. Except for the day that I knew for sure that I was going to be your momma, this is going to be the *best* day of the rest of my life."

She'd made up her mind about that as she'd baked and prayed and baked and prayed some more. The more she put her situation before the Lord—Ophelia, their mother, her feelings for Adam—the more she had come to appreciate the promise of the future. And that future started with this wonderful day.

"Dada."

"Yeah. Dada is going to be there right alongside

you and me at the family barbecue. And for the first time ever I am going to be part of a family."

Her whole life she'd wanted this. She'd dreamed of it. She'd prayed for it. Now, if only for a few sunny hours, she would know what that felt like.

"A family. I know I've always told you how everyone in this town, all the members of our church and all my customers who so kindly keep us in their prayers are our family, but it's not the same."

"Ya-ya-ya."

"And who knows? Maybe after the Burdetts see the community the way I do, they will see that the Crumble and the Crumble Pattie are a part of *our* family as well. And together we can…" Josie raised her head half expecting to hear fife-and-drum music playing the "Battle Hymn of the Republic" or some such patriotic and inspiring tune to accompany her homage to the power of people all working for a common good. Instead she saw her baby happily making spit bubbles and motor noises.

She sighed.

"It could happen. Especially with Adam back in town and you here to stay. Those both seem like reasons enough to make it work."

"Ya-ya-ya."

"And then with everyone working again, my business will pick up and I'll have enough money to finish up the adoption once and for all. *All* being me—"

she poked him in the tummy to make him giggle "—you. Our own little family."

"Dada."

"And Dad, too, but not exactly…that is…" Josie considered not saying anymore about it.

Nathan didn't understand, after all, and she had started the day out in such a great frame of mind. Why muddy things up trying to wade through the complexities of their family dynamic?

One day Nathan would be old enough to understand and she needed to have practiced this speech often enough that she did not botch it up when it counted the most. "Okay, here's the deal, sweetheart. I have no idea what the deal is."

Nathan laughed.

Josie exhaled, her shoulders slumping forward. If she were Nathan's birth mother, if she were Ophelia, it would be different. Not easier, she realized, thinking back to the day before and her newfound empathy for her sister's situation. If she were Ophelia, she would still have to account for her behavior.

Josie might be well on her way to a new understanding of her sister, but Ophelia still had to be accountable for her past and for the things she had done to bring Nathan into the world. Among other things, she'd have to explain to her son about not being married and about keeping Nathan's existence a secret from his own natural father.

But from the legal end of things, if Josie *were* Nathan's birth mother, there wouldn't be lawyer fees and court costs to worry about. Unless Adam or his family had wanted to fight her for custody.

"If I were your birth mother, things wouldn't really be easier, would they?" She kissed her son's cheek. "They might be cheaper, but I can't even say that for sure. The only thing that would be different would be that I would know that Adam was not confusing his emotions for me with his emotions for the mother of his child, because I'd be both! But as things stand now, I have no idea how to know if he really cares about me, or—"

*Ding-dong.*

"Pack mule at your service!" Adam nudged the front door and presented himself for her inspection.

He wore jeans with holes in the knees. Sported a faded orange-and-blue T-shirt with the old Carolina Crumble Pattie logo on it from back in the days when they had enough workers to sponsor a softball team. And squashing down his dark, gorgeous hair was a bright-green John Deere baseball cap.

"I want you to know I don't do this for just anybody," he said.

"Do? Do what?" She tried not to laugh outright. "Dress up like a scarecrow?"

"Haul pies. I mean it, Josie, not only am I going to a place I had wanted to avoid, and to spend time with people I had wanted to ignore, I got up early on a Saturday morning to take *pastry* to a *bakery*.

If that's not a sign of blind devotion, then I don't know what is."

"Blind devotion? Well, that certainly explains the way you're dressed. No one with 20/20 vision could have put that outfit together."

"I think I look adorable. What do you think, son?"

"Dada." A squeal. More spit bubbles. A laugh.

"I have half a mind—"

Josie opened her mouth to second that, jokingly.

He held one finger up to silence her. "Half a mind, but a full heart."

She sank her teeth into her bottom lip to let him know she wasn't going to try to best that.

"Half a mind, full heart and an empty bakery truck. All of them at your disposal."

Were his mind and heart really hers? Josie didn't dare dwell on that question. So she asked about the safest offering. "A bakery truck?"

"Unless you have a better idea for how to transport to the Crumble enough pie to feed all of Mt. Knott."

Josie went to the door and peered out at the truck usually seen making deliveries throughout the county, including the occasional, stealthy stop at Josie's Home Cookin' Kitchen.

"I had Jed and Warren and some moms in mini-vans each going to take as many pies as they thought they could safely transport."

"Jed and Warren? When you counted how many

pies they could 'safely' transport I hope you allowed for the ones that would not be 'safe' in their hands." He smiled.

Josie smiled, too. She actually had planned on having a pie or two go missing during the short trip to the Crumble. Josie smiled because Adam had thought of it, too. For a guy who had only just returned to a town he purported to have held in contempt, he sure had gotten a feel for—and a good-natured regard for—the locals awfully fast.

That spoke well of the man, she thought. As someone who had moved often and under questionable circumstances, Josie had learned that often what you got out of new relationships was directly proportionate to what you put into them. That is, if you bothered to put anything into them at all. Adam *had* bothered.

Not only that, he had made connections. Clearly, he liked Warren and Jed, and they liked him. She just knew that if Adam gave everyone in Mt. Knott the same chance, they would have the same results. And then…

The rabbit-fast thumping of her heart made her nip any kind of further speculation in the bud. She narrowed her eyes at the bakery truck Adam had so sweetly put at her disposal.

"It's not an elegant horse charging to your rescue, but then I'm more black sheep than white knight." He gave a shallow bow followed by a brazen wink.

*Sheep. Not stray dog.* Josie tried not to read too

much into that, but given their talk about the Lord as a shepherd and what it meant to bring the lost lambs home, she couldn't help but stare at the old truck and murmur, "This is better. This is much better."

On sheer impulse she went up on tiptoe and kissed his cheek.

"Much better," he murmured, his dark eyes glittering as she stood with her face just inches from his. "Much, much better."

"Much, much," she whispered, lost in his eyes, not exactly sure what she had just agreed with.

He gave her an answer by returning her kiss—right on the front porch where everyone in Mt. Knott could see.

And Josie didn't care.

The kiss was sweet and brief, but it took Josie's breath away and left her knees wobbling. Just the way a real first kiss was supposed to.

When it ended she realized she had her hands on Adam's shoulders. She jerked them away as if he had suddenly become hot to her touch.

He snagged her by the wrist. "Josie, I, this…this has all happened so fast for me."

"Me, too."

"Yeah, I know but you've had a little more time to get used to some of it. Suddenly I'm a father, or at least I have a child."

"Da-da-da." Nathan, who had been cruising around the furniture in the living room while his parents stood in the open doorway, dropped down and banged a spoon on the floor.

"You're a father," she assured him.

"And I'm back in Mt. Knott."

"Believe me, I've noticed that."

"And suddenly my family is having this big shindig in my honor." He scoffed at the last word to show he felt he either did not have any honor or did not deserve for his family to treat him with it.

"It will be fun, just wait and see."

"I've never been any good at waiting," he said, stepping close.

"Think of yourself as setting a good example for your son."

"You've used that on me before."

"Parenting is a job that knows no hours and never ends. Nathan learns from us all the time. We don't just teach him through our words but also through our actions."

"Is that your way of saying I shouldn't grab you up and kiss you on the spot."

"On *this* spot," she touched her cheek. "That's okay, I suppose. For anything else, I think we'd better wait until after the barbecue when we can be alone to talk things through."

"What if you don't feel like talking to—or kissing—me after the barbecue?"

"Why wouldn't I?"

"I don't know."

Josie's stomach tightened just a little. All these things she had been thinking of Adam, had she just come up with them because she wanted them so badly to be true? She had lived in dreams—dreams of being in a family, of having a family, of having a real home—had she lost track of the harsh realities surrounding this man?

She looked deep into his eyes.

Naw. What she saw there was no fantasy.

She shook her head. "Sometimes I think you take this man-of-mystery persona a little too seriously, Adam."

"Me? A mystery? Why, I'm the easiest guy in the world to figure out."

Josie sputtered out a laugh.

"I'm just a man who isn't afraid to ask for what he wants."

"Like you asked for your inheritance for example?"

"I was thinking more like asking for another kiss."

She wagged her finger at him and shook her head. "Asking for what you want might work when you're asking for a kiss that doesn't mean anything. But when you ask for a kiss from *me,* and especially in our situation, I think you had better *ask* if you want everything that comes with it."

"I'm…I'm not completely certain what that is."

Josie raised an eyebrow. "Oh?"

"Look, Josie, I don't know exactly what will happen between us after today. That's just flat-out reality. I do know that I would very much like for there to be an 'after today' for the two of us, however."

"That's part of the problem, Adam. There is no 'two of us.'"

"Not yet." He inched closer still.

"Not ever." She gave him a light but firm shove. "There will never just be the two of us. We have Nathan to think of."

"I don't see how our having a good relationship can be a bad thing for Nathan."

"It's not, *if* we have a *good* relationship, a solid one. Those can't be built on shaky ground."

"Then we may be in trouble, because every time I'm near you the earth moves and I can hardly keep my footing." He grinned.

"We have not known each other long enough for you to make a judgment like that," she warned, even though she felt exactly the same way.

"Haven't we? I feel as if I've known you a long time."

"But you haven't." She held her breath a moment and considered holding back her opinion about what Adam was experiencing. But she couldn't. He had kissed her once already and awakened all sorts of doubts in her. If they ever hoped to work through her apprehensions, they had to deal with them out in the open. "Are you sure you don't have me confused with someone you have known longer and with much more intimacy?"

"You mean Ophelia?"

"Of course I mean Ophelia. I *am* her identical twin."

"Her twin, sure, but identical? Not by a long shot."

"We have the same build, basically. The same hair color, complexion and face. I suspect if you saw us together you wouldn't be able to tell us apart."

"Oh, yes I would. You two may *look* alike. That doesn't mean you are alike."

"Of course not. But given the short time you've known either of us…" She let him draw his own conclusions.

"I realized who you were once I saw you holding my son, Josie. Protecting him. You are his mother." Adam brushed her hair back. He bent in close, but instead of trying to kiss her lips, he planted a kiss on her forehead. "And I can't thank you enough for that."

"Really?"

"And for the record I know the difference between you and your sister. I know you, Josie. I don't know Ophelia. I'm ashamed to have to admit it but I never really knew her, any more than I think she knew me. That's one of those things people who ridicule Christian values never get around to mentioning when they make it seem that satisfying every animal urge is normal and healthy."

"What?"

"They don't tell you how lonely that kind of encounter can leave you, how empty. How like a wounded animal, a—"

"A stray?"

He nodded.

"I know you are applying that to Ophelia, Adam, but you might want to take a look at how it applies to your family."

"My family?"

"Sure. You give in to the easy urge to feel sorry for yourself. To snap at the people you had to rely upon, to foster distrust of them. Those are not the acts of a man who is trying to live like Christ."

It took him a moment and a few long, slow breaths, but finally he closed his eyes and nodded. "I see your point."

"Now as to you and Ophelia—"

"There is no me and Ophelia. Despite Nathan as evidence to the contrary, there never was, really."

"I wish that made me feel better, Adam." She retreated inside, went to her son and picked him up. "Relationships and parenting are hard enough without having to cope with this kind of thing."

"This kind of thing? You mean the whole identical-twins, secret-baby-of-prominent-local-lineage, fathered-by-returning-ne'er-do-well-son thing?" Adam followed her inside, chuckling. "You actually know other people who have to cope with *that* in their relationships?"

"Well-l-l-l." Josie rocked from side to side with Nathan on her hip before rolling her eyes and conceding with a shy laugh. "Well, no relationship is perfect!"

"I guess not." Adam laughed, too. "So, how do you suppose that, year after year, generation after generation of imperfect people have managed to fall in love, make a commitment, establish homes, raise families and grow old together?"

Josie fell very quiet. "A lot of them haven't managed those things."

"But those who have, what do you suppose a lot of them relied upon to help them get through it all?"

"God," she said softly.

"Then let's me and you do that, too, Josie." Adam held his hand out to her.

"You want…to *pray*…with me?"

"It surprises me a little, too, but these past few days I've thought a lot about my new role and what I need to do, about businesses based on Biblical principles and…about us. I think it's the right thing to do, don't you?"

She did. So she slipped her hand into his.

Adam took her hand and bowed his head. For a long moment he said nothing. Or perhaps he prayed in silence. Josie didn't know exactly what to do, so she used the moment to gather her thoughts, to humble herself before the Lord and to praise him and thank him.

She had so much to be grateful for, she realized, even in the midst of all her doubts. For Nathan. For Mt. Knott. For her work. For her baking talent. For Adam.

And for this day. This chance to know how it felt to be a part of a real family.

She drew a deep breath and held it. That's when she realized that Adam had begun to speak.

"I am a lost sheep, Lord, returned to the fold, and yet not even sure he belongs *in* that fold. I did not come in humility and hope, but bearing pride and a grudge. I am flawed and fearful that I am unfit for the task You have set before me, to be a father to Nathan and a friend to Josie."

"Friend," she whispered before she could stop herself.

"Because of all the demands on any relationship, but most of all of those between a man and a woman raising a child together, the bonds of friendship are necessary to endure one another's faults and missteps with laughter and goodwill. Thank You for bringing Josie into my life and into the life of our son, Nathan. Help us to face this and every day with faith in You and trust in each other."

He squeezed her hand, which Josie recognized as his way of asking her if she had something to add.

"Bless all those who gather today." She choked

back her emotions. So many things she wanted to say. So many things she simply could not express except to say, "We submit to Your will and praise Your holy name."

"Amen," Adam murmured.

"Amen," Josie agreed.

He released one of her hands but clung to the other long enough to coax her to look up and meet his gaze.

"You ready for this?"

*For what?* she wanted to ask. *For you and I to begin our "friendship"? Or for the responsibility of transporting and serving enough pie to fill up the considerable bellies of every hungry person in Mt. Knott?*

"I'm, uh, I'm not sure."

"Neither am I." He laughed softly, almost not a laugh at all. "But ready or not, here we go."

## Chapter Thirteen

Adam would have loved more time alone with Josie, but knew it was for the best that Jed and Warren showed up honking their horns and hollering to their "Sweetie Pie" that they had come to fill up their trucks. Of course, as soon as they peered inside the bakery truck they agreed it was a much better mode of pie transportation.

They happily helped Adam load up the supplies while Josie ran around with the phone glued to her ear, frantically reorganizing her moms-with-mini-vans, answering last-minute questions and checking on the lopsided status of salads versus sides. And each time the three men saw her, she had on a different outfit.

Finally one of the moms arrived in her triple-car-seat and double-bumper-sticker brand-new mini-van. With much persuasion she loaded up Nathan and pledged to look after him until Josie and Adam got there.

Josie waved goodbye to the happy toddler, then rushed inside her house, shouting as she did, "I'll be ready in a sec, Adam. Just let me get a change of clothes."

"You have a whole pile of clothes that you've changed into and out of already on your bedroom floor," Adam reminded her.

"I know, but I just remembered something I have in the back of my closet," she called back.

"You look—"

Warren cut him off with a somber shake of his head. "Don't even try to finish that sentence, son. Not if you hope to get rolling toward the Crumble in the next twenty minutes."

Jed stood on the front-porch steps. "Warren's right."

Warren cupped his hand to his ear and grinned. "Say that again."

"On this *one* occasion." Jed drove home the point by placing his hand alongside his mouth and shouting it for all to hear, before he dropped both the hand and his voice and grumbled, "Warren is right."

Warren chuckled, then turned to Adam, motioning for him to follow along as the older men went to their trucks. "It's one of them, what you call, no-win situations."

"A trap." Jed nodded.

Adam paused on the lawn. "A trap?"

"Uh-huh. Not a bear-trap type of thing, though. More one of those woven-finger-puzzle deals." Jed touched the ends of both his index fingers together and Adam could picture exactly what he was talking about.

"If you start trying to reason with a woman about how she looks in some kind of outfit you will never be able to extricate yourself."

Adam thought of the red-white-and-blue shirt that looked sort of sailorish, and the white jeans she had been wearing. "I was just going to say she looks fine."

Jed sucked air between his teeth.

Warren winced. "Fine? You actually intended to use that word? Fine?"

"But she does. She looks—"

"Shhhh." Jed put his finger to his lips.

"Don't say it again." Warren opened the driver's-side door on his sun-faded blue truck. He hopped in and gunned the engine. "We'll meet you down at the Home Cookin' Kitchen to help load up the pies."

Jed got into his green truck and gave a wave. "You can thank us later."

Adam didn't know if the men meant he should thank them for stopping him from getting into a no-win situation with Josie or for loading the pies. Either way it made him a bit uneasy to feel he was in any man's debt.

That thought kept him quiet on the whole trip to Josie's Home Cookin' Kitchen to collect the baked goods, and as he and the other men passed one another taking pie after pie to the big, waiting bakery truck.

He had come back to Mt. Knott to square away old debts, as it were, to tie up loose ends and be done with the place once and for all. He stood on the sidewalk and watched the comings and goings of Josie's friends and neighbors, so happy to pitch in and make this barbecue a success for everyone involved.

Mt. Knott, he decided, was not a place you could just be done with all that easily. Each new day, each new association, brought with it a responsibility to others, a connection, an opportunity to be a part of something good and productive and hopeful. How had he lived here so long and not seen that? How had he worked among these people and still managed to lose his way?

He only had to think of the benefactor of today's picnic to find the answer to that question. Adam set his jaw. As soon as they finished loading the pies he would be going out to the Crumble for the biggest showdown of his life so far. He would face his father, not as a black sheep or somebody else's baby, but as an equal. Or perhaps, depending on Dora's recommendation, as his boss.

Why didn't Adam feel better about that?

"That's the last of them." Jed slapped Adam on

the back. "You be careful with that precious cargo now, you hear?"

"Don't worry." Adam shook off the sting between his shoulder blades. "Not a single piece of crust will be broken."

"I ain't worried about the pie, you just get our girl there in one piece."

"Okay, let's do this." Josie stood before him, all smiles and softness.

Something was different about her, but he couldn't put his finger on it. Of course, if he tried to put his finger on anything to do with Josie, Adam knew she'd slap it away and tell him what for. He smiled at the thought and hurried to open the door of the bakery truck for her.

"Thank you." She bowed her head, started to climb in, then stepped back and asked, "By the way, how do I look?"

*It's a trap.* He could hear Jed growling out a warning.

*A no-win situation.* And Warren, too.

Adam shut his eyes and kissed her so lightly on the temple that he wasn't sure he hadn't simply kissed a wayward curl. Then he whispered, "You always look perfect to me, Josie."

"That's so sweet." She glanced a featherlight kiss of her own off his jaw then got into the truck. "Let's go out to the Crumble, then."

*The Crumble.* How many times had Adam snickered cynically over the aptness of that tag for the place he intended to bring down once and for all? Now it sounded like one of the sweetest places on earth.

He drove down the town's tree-lined street waving as he did to the people bustling out to their cars. They carried blankets and baskets, folding chairs and portable playpens, outdoor games for the kids and at least one wheelchair for an elderly member of the family. This was a big day in Mt. Knott. The Burdetts were finally giving something back, and no one wanted to be left out.

He rolled through the streets of Mt. Knott, past the post office with the American flag—the largest of many that hung from the handful of businesses still operating in the old downtown area—fluttering overhead.

Bingo pulled up on the sidewalk alongside Adam's truck, waved from his scooter and hollered out, "I'll be out to the Crumble soon as I finish up my route. Don't let Jed and Warren eat all the choice cuts and leave me with nothing but bones and gristle!"

"Jed and Warren *are* nothing but bones and gristle," Adam joked. Still, he hated to think about the kind of trouble he'd bring down on himself if he actually tried to get between Josie's best patrons and the buffet table. "So you'd better kick that scooter into high gear and don't waste any time getting out there yourself."

"Will do!" Bingo gave a salute with the packet of mail in his hand then, true to his word, zoomed off down the sidewalk at top speed leaving Adam in his proverbial dust.

"Admit it."

"What?" Adam scowled.

"This place is starting to get to you."

"What? I've lived in Mt. Knott all my life."

"No, you never lived in Mt. Knott, not really. And now that you've got a taste of it, it's gotten to you. You're starting to care about these people."

"Some more than others," he said almost under his breath.

She leaned back against the gray-and-brown upholstery and looked out the side window. "I'll tell Bingo you said so."

Adam barked out a laugh.

Josie shifted her shoulders so that her upper body faced him, and she smiled, clearly pleased with herself.

But over what? The joke or because she thought she had him figured out? Had the people of Mt. Knott "gotten" to him all that much? How could that be when he had known them, or known of them, or known they existed at least, all his life? "I want to go on record as not accepting that I haven't lived in Mt. Knott all my life. Except for college I've been right here."

"You have that right. You said so yourself, you

spent most of your life right here." She made an open-handed gesture toward the slightly rusted sign proclaiming, Carolina Crumble Pattie Way. "On this road, at the Crumble or at the big ol' Burdett mansion."

"It's hardly a mansion."

"Compared to most of the houses around town?" She waved at some kids who had twisted around and were making faces from the back window of the car in front of them. "It's a mansion."

He tucked his chin down and squinted at her a bit sideways, so as not to take his eyes completely off the road. "You've been there?"

"Well, no. I just always *imagined.*"

"It's not a mansion," he insisted. "It's a home. *My home.*"

He had never thought of it that way, not even as a kid, but suddenly it was the only way he could see the large craftsman-style residence with secondary ranch- and cottage-style houses for the brothers on adjoining lots. *Home.*

Josie had never been there, and he wanted to take her.

"It's more of a compound, actually. You know, a big piece of land with one big house and some smaller ones. Burke has a ranch-style. Jason has a smaller version of the big house. Cody and Carol have a bungalow, or, uh, is it a cottage? Do you know the difference?"

She shook her head.

"Neither do I," he admitted.

"And where did you live when you were out there? The barn?"

Actually he had a log house. Strong and sturdy and set apart from the rest, but lacking anything to make it personal inside, anything to give him a reason to have gone there to stay or even visit on this trip back. "Yeah. Me and the other lost sheep, we bunked out in the barn. Baaa-aaah."

"Except you're not lost anymore," she reminded him. "You found your way home."

Adam started to refute that, or maybe ask Josie what role she had played in bringing it about, but just then he realized they were at their destination.

"Stop." She held her hand up flat. "I'm going to get out and go on ahead. See that big white tent over there?"

"Sure." How could he miss it?

"You make your way to that and I'll figure out the best place for you to park to unload."

"Can't you just ride over with me?"

She frowned at the slowly moving line of cars ahead of them. "Adam, I'm supposed to be in charge here. I can't do that from the back of the crowd."

"Okay."

"See you in a minute." And out she got.

Cautiously he made his way through the old rutted parking lot toward the open area where the barbecue would be held. Partly because he didn't want to arrive with a single one of Josie's pies damaged and partly because he wanted to savor every moment leading up to…

Well, that was it, wasn't it? He had no real idea what he was going to find at the Crumble. No idea what recommendation Dora might have for him. No idea how his brothers would react to his suddenly showing up. No explanation for how his father could be so welcoming to him after a lifetime of treating Adam like an outsider and then more than a year of Adam *behaving* like an outsider.

Josie's warning to know what he wanted rang in his ears.

When he had arrived in Mt. Knott he thought he'd had such clear goals. He had planned everything, step by step. First step, get out from under his family once and for all. Second step, make anyone who had wronged him pay for not accepting him, not believing in him, by taking over the Crumble and making everyone accountable to him. Third step…

He really hadn't gotten beyond the second step. Two steps then nothing? Now *there* was a surefire way to get nowhere.

He supposed he could still make a run for it.

Then he saw Josie with the baby in her arms, standing by the large white tent.

The instant she saw him, her face lit up. With her hair that wild knot of curls, her cheeks red and a crowd surrounding her demanding her attention, she looked frazzled but happy. She pointed to a parking spot just the right size for the bakery truck and gave a weary but grateful smile.

Adam wasn't going anywhere but right where she needed him to be.

He parked, hopped out of the truck and went straight to her.

It was perfect outside, as if the weather itself were connected to the mood in Adam's heart. Bright and sunny, but not blazing. Breezy enough to keep the bugs away but not strong enough to fan barbecue smoke into everyone's eyes and effect the taste of all the food.

And Josie looked perfect, as well. Fair as the day and just as gentle, but with just enough energy and bluster to keep him on his toes. Adam reached out and took Nathan from her, bending as he did to place a kiss on her cheek. It seemed the most natural thing in the world. His way of both thanking her for doing all this and of reassuring her that he would be there for her should it start to overwhelm her.

It wasn't until he heard the subtle gasps and chuckles from the crowd around them that he realized the larger implications of what he'd done.

"What?" He looked around them, challenge in his tone, his posture and his words. "Just my way of thanking Josie for doing such a good job with the pies and all."

"Oh? Is that how it's done?" Jed moseyed up to the forefront with Warren at his side. "Here me and Warren been rubbing our bellies, saying 'Mmm-Mmm' and leaving generous tips when we pay our bills."

"Didn't know we could accomplish as much with a Yankee dime."

Adam scowled at the old expression. The way he understood it a Yankee dime was a stolen kiss that meant nothing to the one doing the kissing. He didn't like the implication. A week ago he'd have glared at the old guys and told them just what he thought.

A week ago he'd been a "Stray Dawg" who had both bark and bite. Now?

Now he knew how to play the game.

"Hey, I was just following orders." He raised his shoulders and dropped them.

"Someone give you orders to go slopping sugar on our Sweetie Pie?" Warren studied the crowd as if the guilty party might just step forward and save him the trouble of having to sniff him out.

"Yeah." Adam folded his arms over his chest. "You did."

"Me?"

"You told me to take special care of my precious cargo. I did just that. And here she is, signed, sealed and delivered."

"You said that, Warren?"

And if he needed more proof that he was, indeed, a stray in this town no longer, Adam brought the joke home. "He did. But then he also said that I shouldn't tell you that you look fi-*i*-ne in that outfit."

It wasn't a lie. But Adam did feel a twinge of guilt that drawing out the word *fine* like that did give it a bit of a different spin, implying he thought she looked great instead of merely suitable.

"You don't like this outfit?" She turned on Warren.

"No. I never said—"

"No?" She pulled out the fluff of pink holding her hair up on top of her head. "I knew I shouldn't have changed out of the patriotic one."

"No, I meant yes."

"Trap," Jed muttered.

"Yes?" Josie worked her fingers through her hair trying to get it to…well, no telling what she wanted it to do. What it *was* doing was falling around her shoulders and sticking to her cheeks. "Yes what? That I should have changed?"

"No." Warren shot Adam a look that would have melted butter.

It didn't affect Adam, of course, especially when he caught a glimpse of a short black haircut darting through the clusters of picnickers at Dora Hoag speed. "If y'all will excuse me, I'll be right back."

With that he took off after the woman, trying his best not to appear to have just taken off after anyone, least of all a woman. Didn't want to give the town anything to gab about tonight over pie.

He glanced back over his shoulder at Josie, who kept bobbing up and down on her toes, trying to peer over people to find him.

Correction. He didn't want to give the town anything *else* to gab about over pie and coffee tonight.

"Ms. Hoag?" Somehow he managed to shout out her name without getting his voice beyond a stage whisper.

It must have worked because the woman whirled around just as he came up to her and practically jumped out of her skin. "Burdett. You're here."

"Of course I'm here. I'm the guest of, um, honor."

"Not to hear your brother tell it." She smiled slow and sly.

Adam had no idea his boss was capable of that kind of smile, or of making a joke. Or dressing as if she truly belonged at a Carolina barbecue. "You look, uh…"

"Hold the small talk, Burdett." She flashed her palm outward to keep him from making a fool of himself trying to keep his compliment businesslike. "I know what you want."

"You do?" Adam snorted out a hard laugh. "Wish you had told me that months ago. Would have saved me a whole world of heartache."

"What? I don't…"

Adam dropped the jest and became all business again. "You're talking about your recommendation, of course."

"Yes, I've... I've gone over the preliminaries and—"

"Maybe we should go somewhere more private for this." He looked around them. They stood in the shade of a tree that Adam had remembered being big enough for climbing even when he was a kid. It was huge now, but somehow it seemed smaller than it did back then. And while it offered cool, pleasant shade, the soothing rustle of thick leaves and the smell of earth and bark mingled with the tangy smoke from the barbecue, it also seemed too casual a place to hear this kind of news. Besides, between the tree and the passing knots of family and friends, it seemed too out in the open. A place where they could be too easily spotted, too easily overheard.

"We don't need to go anywhere."

"But—"

"Because I am meeting your brother here any minute and because there is nowhere on these grounds that are going to make this any easier to say."

Adam's heart leaped. What was the expression, one man's trash is another man's treasure? Dora Hoag thought she was delivering bad news but that "bad news" was exactly what Adam had been hoping for. "You are going to recommend Global pass on the Carolina Crumble Pattie, lock, stock and lousy building."

"Just the opposite."

Adam froze halfway to high-fiving his very proper boss. "What?"

"I am going to recommend that Global buy the Carolina Crumble Pattie lock, stock and lousy building. Then tear it down."

"Tear it…what?"

"Down. To the ground." She jabbed one finger in the direction of the roots of the old tree. "Take the recipe and put it in a vault and leave it there while we try to come up with a cost-effective alternative. And in a few years, when people get nostalgic for the old snack cake, we will bring it back with a fanfare and sell it internationally."

"Cost effective? Meaning inferior?"

"We can't go on using the best ingredients, Burdett. If we did, we'd have to charge as much for a single patty as we normally charge for a whole box of snack cakes."

"Have you ever tasted a Carolina Crumble Pattie? They are worth a dozen boxes of those flavorless globs of chemicals Wholesome Hearth calls snacks."

"I know." She shifted her feet, twisted her hands together, then craned her neck, all signs she wished Burke would show up and rescue her from having to talk to Adam about this. "That's why I'm saying we have to vault the recipe and give it some time before we come out with our version."

"Under the Carolina Crumble Pattie name?" Adam kept his gaze trained in hers even though out of the corner of his eyes he could see his oldest brother approaching.

"Of course. We need to own the name. It has thirty years of great marketing behind it."

"It has a lot more than marketing behind it, and that's the part you can't buy or keep in a vault."

"A family's life work? A product made with care, the pride of a whole community? A standard of excellence?"

"And more," Adam said.

"We don't want those things." Dora batted her eyes and waved her hand. "We just want the perception of having those things. And that's what we get by buying your family out and using their reputation and product branding."

Adam sighed. He'd been through this before with other products and had always convinced himself that, as Dora had often reminded him, it wasn't personal.

But this? This *was* personal. "What about modernizing the facilities? Adding new snack lines? Giving stock to employees? Given enough time, work and money, I could make the Carolina Crumble Pattie an international moneymaker."

"Of that I have no doubt."

"But?"

"But you don't work for Carolina Crumble Pattie, Burdett. You work for the Wholesome Hearth Country Fresh Bakery."

"I'd gladly step down and take on a different position in order to oversee this project."

"You would?" She tipped her head to one side, clearly not sure what to make of that.

"You would?" Burke rounded the old tree. His tone was far more disbelieving than that of Adam's boss.

"Yes, I would." Even Adam hadn't known he was going to say that until it was out of his mouth. But now that it was out there… "Gladly."

Dora acknowledged Burke's arrival with nothing more than a shift of her head. Her focus remained on Adam. "That's all well and good and perhaps even leans slightly to the noble, Burdett."

"Thank you." Adam puffed his chest up a bit.

She put her hands on her slender hips. "But we don't need nobility at Global."

"What?" He exhaled and leaned against the tree.

"We need you. We need your sharklike instincts. We need you to ferret out small places like this so we can move in and do whatever we have to do to help keep Wholesome Hearth at the top of Global's international food chain."

Adam replayed that message in his head once, then twice, each time gleaning new bits of information that led him to conclude, "First I'm a shark. Then I'm a weasel. Finally I'm just something at the bottom of the food chain?"

"Up to you." Dora shrugged. "You can be who-ever you want to be."

Be whoever he wanted to be? In his whole life no one had ever believed that of him.

From somewhere in the crowd he heard Josie's laughter.

His whole life no one had ever believed he could be whoever he wanted to be: that he could be more than a stray dog; that he could be a better Christian; a better businessman; a better citizen; and Nathan's daddy.

*Except...*

"There's just one thing I have to ask you, Dora."

She arched a pencil-thin eyebrow, though Adam didn't know if the subtle but slightly spooky affecta-tion was in reaction to his demand to ask her some-thing or to his using her first name so casually.

"I'm listening," she said, finally.

"When we first came out here, you said business is nothing personal."

"Uh-huh."

"But then you also let it be known that you didn't think it wasn't such a bad thing for a business to be based on Biblical principles."

"I don't know what you're getting at."

"I want to know which method you used to ar-rive at your recommendation? The nothing personal or the Biblical?"

She smiled slowly. "I did what Global pays me to do."

"And Global was founded on Biblical principles?"

"*Was* founded. Global has changed."

He thought as much. If she had said she had come to this decision through prayer and an understanding of guiding principles, he would have needed to hear more. But given this information, he knew what he had to say and what he had to do. "Global *has* changed. But then, so have I."

"Which means?"

"I quit."

## Chapter Fourteen

"**Y**ou what?" Josie tried to make the words Adam had just spoken make sense.

"Quit."

"Quit what?" She darted her gaze to the people and things surrounding them. "Quit your family? Quit the barbecue? Quit...on me?"

"No. No." He took her by the upper arms and bent slightly to put them in a direct line of vision. "I would never quit on you, Josie."

"Then...?"

"I quit my job."

"Your factory job?"

"My..." He didn't have to say another word for Josie to know how wrong the speculation that he had blown his inheritance and had to take a job in a rival food factory.

"You don't have a factory job, do you?"

"Not unless Global moved the office of vice president of acquisitions and mergers for Wholesome Hearth Country Fresh Bakery into the factory, no, I don't."

"Vice president?"

"It's not as big a deal as you might think. Global has VPs by the dozens."

"But now they have one less?"

"Yeah. Now they have one less." He practically beamed with the news.

"Why?"

"Because I just quit."

"Why did you quit?"

"Oh." His whole expression fell.

Josie had been too busy to eat today and yet she suddenly felt as if her stomach was filled with stones. "Adam?"

He groaned and rubbed the bridge of his nose with his thumb and forefinger. He scrunched his eyes shut tight. His usually smooth skin creased into faint crow's feet. His shoulders went rigid.

It made her think of the image Conner Burdett had spoken of, of the little boy with his hands perpetually in fists. She ventured a touch on his forearm, trying to encourage him to unclench and trust her, though she wasn't sure he would. He had never come to trust his father, why would she be any different. "Adam?"

"Josie, I've…I've kept so much from you."

"I've kept something from you, as well."

"What?"

"My secret ingredient." She knew it was not on the same scale. Whatever Adam had kept from her, and probably others in town and in his family, had led him to a point where he found relief and pride in having quit a very high-powered and fancy-titled job. She had said it, though, to try to lighten the mood. And, to try to shore up the connection between them, she quickly added, "Remember when you said you'd tell me your secret if I'd tell you mine?"

He dropped his hand to his side, and the creases in his face relaxed, just a little. He even managed a hint of a smile, but only a hint. And he looked as if it could thin out to a scowl without much provocation. "I remember."

"Well then, I'll make it easier for you to tell me what's going on with you." She curled her fingers into the soft fabric of his orange-and-blue striped baseball shirt and stepped close enough to shut the people around them out. "I'll tell you my secret ingredient, then you can tell me about your secret, um, life."

"Doesn't sound like a fair exchange." He gazed deeply into her eyes, his gratitude at the way she had taken all this evident.

"Are you kidding? You've tasted my pies. I've seen the mess you have made in your life. Who do you really think is getting the bigger secret here?"

She laughed. It rang a bit hollow, but not phony. "Are you ready?"

"Anytime," he whispered.

"My secret ingredient is…"

She actually felt people inching close to them as she spoke those words. She gave them a backward glance, her eyes narrowed in warning.

Not a person retreated.

She cleared her throat and went up on tiptoe, cupping her hand to shield her mouth as she leaned close and whispered in Adam's ear. "I pulverize a Carolina Crumble Pattie into the mix for the top crust, then brush it with butter and my own mix of spices the last few minutes of browning."

Adam pulled back, his face a blank.

Suddenly Josie felt those stones she had imagined in her stomach grow ice cold and begin to tumble around.

"So if the Crumble closed…" Adam said.

"The Crumble is closing?" A man standing near them asked in a voice that carried across the gathering.

Adam shook his head. He held up his hand. "No!"

"Stray Dawg says the Crumble is closing," the man repeated louder this time.

"I knew his coming here was suspicious," Elvie chimed in straight away. "You know he works for a competitor, don't you? I heard he and his brother are in on this—courting an exec from Wholesome Hearth—"

"Please. Stop. Wait. Listen. Burke is not a part of this." Adam tried to take it back, to stop the remark from turning into a wild rumor that would spread like fire through the closely knit community.

And who knew who would get singed by the flames?

Josie could already feel the heat. "If the Crumble closes, Adam? You want to know what would happen to me? I'd not just be out of an ingredient, I would be out of my livelihood."

"Josie—"

The murmuring around them grew louder and louder.

"Belly-up and bankrupt because I'd have no way to pay back my small-business loan." Josie swallowed to keep the cold lump of fear from rising and strangling her. "So, you see, you have to do everything you can to make sure that does not happen."

"It's not. It won't." He gave her a shake and a look that said he meant that with all his heart. "Not if I can do anything to stop it, it won't."

"Those words would mean a bit more if you weren't the one that started the ball rolling on this whole thing." Adam's older brother loomed behind him, seeming to have shown up from out of nowhere.

"You? You are the one responsible for closing the Crumble?" Josie still could not make it all fit together. She searched Adam's face, but found no comfort in his pinched and pained expression.

"Ya-ya-ya." From a few feet away she heard her baby babbling. She whipped around to find him in Jed's arms, blissfully alternating between chewing on a cookie and slobbering on Jed's shirt. The older man didn't even seem to notice as he smiled at her and nodded.

Warren stood beside him, and Warren's wife. She took her husband's hand and all of them smiled at her as if to tell her that they were there to support her no matter what.

That's when it hit Josie. No matter what happened with the factory or the town, she had the thing she had always wished for. She had a family. Not in the conventional sense but a very real one nonetheless. She had people who cared for her and her son. She had a place to go in a time of need. She had the love of the Lord and she had hope. She always had hope.

"The Crumble is not closing," Adam said, drawing her attention back to him.

"You don't have any say in that anymore," Burke reminded his brother.

"Stray Dawg is the one closing the place down," Elvie announced to the people who had shown up late.

"I knowed there was something sneaky about his coming back to town," one of the newcomers yelled.

"Don't go talking about my big brother Adam like

that." Jason, Lucky Dawg, came forward and took his place beside Burke. "He's not sneaky. He's right here in the open."

"Would everybody calm down here? This is all rumor and speculation. Nothing productive can come from that." Cody joined his other brothers, hand in hand with his wife, Carol. "Now, I know all of you folks and I minister to a good deal of you. I'm not saying you don't have a right to your feelings. I'm just here to say that Adam is not just my brother but he's yours as well. A brother in the Lord. We need to think about that before we go throwing stones."

"If the Crumble does close, I want you all to know, it won't be my doing." Adam snagged Josie by the wrist. "I did not foresee this. I did not want it."

"You still don't get it, do you?" Burke planted his feet shoulder-width apart and crossed his arms. His very stance spoke of holding his ground and challenging his brother. "You think Dad is throwing you this shindig because he suddenly cares about all these people? Because you coming back made him a new man and helped him see the error of his ways?"

"I, uh…" Adam glanced at Josie, then at the faces of the crowd. Finally he cleared his throat and said, "Maybe not because of me, no, but I do think people can change."

"Amen, brother," Cody said, moving around so that he and Carol seemed to be on Adam's side now.

"People change, but Conner Burdett?" Burke scoffed.

"Hey. Show some respect," Jason barked. "You may be Top Dawg in the wolf pack but he is still our daddy."

"Yeah, well, our *daddy* is throwing this big deal, inviting out the town for the first and last time, to celebrate what you've done for him."

"Given him a grandson?" Adam asked.

"Brought Global here with an offer to buy out the Crumble. He doesn't know the offer will close us down and maybe be an end to the Carolina Crumble Pattie forever, but I don't think that would matter to him one bit. The old man plans to sell out first chance he gets and retire."

"That offer hasn't been formally extended." Adam went toe-to-toe with his older brother, but because of their heights it did not bring them eye to eye, literally or figuratively. "It's just one person's recommendation. The old man doesn't know for sure how it will all play out."

"He doesn't have to know how it will all play out. He knows Global is prepared to come in with a lot of money, and if it's not enough, he is prepared to ask for what he wants. He knows they want to make some kind of deal and what it could mean for us."

"Us?" Adam motioned to the people surrounding them. "Or us?" He gestured to Jason, Cody, Carol, himself then Burke, but not Josie or Nathan. She tried not to take that as a sign of his feelings.

"What it could mean to the family," he said.

*Mt. Knott is my family,* Josie tried to remind herself. Still, it hurt a bit to have been so obviously excluded. Whatever comfort she found in her friends and neighbors, she still longed for something more.

"What it could mean to *him,*" Burke clarified.

"What about Mt. Knott?" a man in the crowd demanded.

While another raised his voice to ask, "What about the people who still have work at the factory?"

Burke just shook his head.

"Now, wait one minute here. When I started all this I never intended…" Adam cut himself off. Again he looked at the faces of those around him, this time ending with Josie. He reached out and took her by the hand. "Actually, I never thought it through that far. I expected to blow in and out of town and not really even know the results of my efforts until I was safely back in my office."

"But you *expected* the best, right?" With her eyes, Josie begged him to confirm it. She wanted something more, both as a family and from Adam, and that had to be built on knowing that deep down, he was a good, caring man.

"I guess *best* is a relative term," he said softly.

"Not when you're talking about my relatives," Burke chimed in and not softly at all.

A few people laughed.

Josie was not one of them. "Adam, you said that after this picnic I might not want you to kiss me, but you wouldn't say why."

"Maybe he planned on putting a lot of onions on his burger." Jed's attempt to throw a little levity into the tense situation only made things worse.

People murmured.

Feet shifted in the dry grass.

Burke cocked his head and hooked his thumbs in his belt loops. To Josie it had all the earmarks of a man deciding if he wanted to take a swing at another man.

"Adam, I have to ask this." Josie took a step forward, placing herself alone with Adam in the circle created by the bystanders. "Did you want to hurt your father and family so badly that you cooked up a plan that would take down the Crumble and Mt. Knott in the process?"

"No."

"Huh." Burke's shoulders eased slightly.

"I believe you," she said.

"You do?" More than one person around them asked it out loud, but it was Adam's hoarse whisper that she answered.

"I believe that you had acted on high emotion and out of old anger and fear, and did not think through the consequences of your actions. It's not the first time you've done that."

"Ya-ya-ya."

Adam lifted his chin and narrowed his eyes in Nathan's direction.

Josie put her hand on his cheek and turned him to face her again. "That's what stray dogs do. They growl and snap at anything that seems a threat to them. And everything seems a threat to them."

He lowered his gaze and nodded.

"But you are not a stray dog."

Burke opened his mouth.

Josie glared at him.

He shut it.

"You are a man who has come to take his place in the community and be a father to his son." Josie stroked her hand along the side of his face, feeling the beginnings of late-afternoon bristle on her palm. "And no matter what happens with this business or any other in town, I know you have found your place. You have come home."

"Home." He could hardly get the word out.

"Sure. He's going to have a home no matter what. But that don't necessarily apply to the rest of us here today," came a gruff voice from the back of the crowd.

Adam looked at Burke. "I never meant for it to go this way."

"I know. And to be honest, well, it was only a matter of time until some big corporation moved in and made an offer, or came up with a competitive product that would run us out of the market, or even just waited until we put ourselves out of business." Burked took a step forward, his hand extended to his younger brother. "At least this way we may come away with enough bankroll money and what's left of our reputation to get the ball rolling on some new project."

Adam took his brother's hand, shook it once, then used it to yank the larger man off balance and into a bear hug.

"Hey, wait a minute. I'm the hug-your-fellow-man preacher-type. Quit horning in on my territory." And with that Cody joined his brothers in the embrace.

Jason stood back a moment.

"Well, what you waiting for?" A grouchy old man's voice asked what everyone was thinking.

At first Josie thought it was Jed but when she looked, Nathan had shoved the cookie in Jed's mouth. He couldn't make a sound.

That meant…

"Get your tail in there and act like a brother, not some snarling dog." Conner slapped his next-to-youngest son on the back.

"Dad?" Jason stumbled forward, then laughed and threw his arms around the rest of the pack.

Conner came forward and did likewise.

Josie laughed with delight at the picture they made, but even as she did some small part of her ached. All her life she had yearned to be a part of a family like this, and all she had gotten was…

"Ophelia?" She squinted into the crowd right into a face that was identical to hers.

## Chapter Fifteen

In two or three hurried steps, Josie reached Jed and Warren. She took Nathan in her arms. If Adam noticed, she didn't know. Her attention remained on her twin sister and the rising anxiety in her own chest.

Ophelia circled through the crowd, seemingly to give the Burdetts—and Adam—a wide berth. She had clearly spotted them all, but had she seen Josie? Had she been seeking out and found the baby that she had left in Josie's care?

"Is that…?" someone asked.

"What's *she* doing here?" Warren wanted to know.

Josie wrapped Nathan deeper into the protection of her motherly embrace. "I don't know," she managed to whisper, though her throat had gone bone dry.

"Does it matter *why* she's come?" Jed stood shoulder to shoulder with his regular counter-companion.

Warren shook his head. "Pardon me for saying it, Josie, but in all the years we've known you, that little boy is the only good ever come from one of your sister's visits."

The baby hid his face in her shoulder and she cradled the back of his head with one hand.

"Run, Josie," someone close by hollered.

"We can detain her," Jed suggested, though from the look on his face, tangling with Ophelia was the last thing he wanted to have to do. "Run if you feel you have to."

*Run?* Grab her son and get out of the crowd, out of Mt. Knott? She could even lie low for a while, knowing that Ophelia would never have the patience or resources to wait her out.

*Run.* If the roles were reversed and she had shown up unannounced before the adoption were finalized that's exactly what Ophelia would have done. Assume the worst and protect herself.

That's the way they had both been raised. Take what you want and run with it, no matter who you have to leave in your wake, no matter who it hurts. Only it had never hurt just the ones left behind. Josie knew Ophelia still bore the scars of the times she had put instant gratification above all else.

*Run?* Where to? And *from* what? Josie knew that Ophelia had probably chosen this very public event for her surprise visit, because anywhere else she expected her sister would have evaded her. That she'd have done everything possible to keep Ophelia and Nathan apart. Here, with so many people around and on the outskirts of town with no friendly home or business to duck into, Ophelia thought she would have the advantage over Josie.

But Josie knew she had the advantage. Surrounded by people Josie loved and who loved both her and her son, and with Nathan's father close at hand, her son would be all right. That's all that mattered. And besides, by allowing her to be a part of how Adam had changed and grown these past few days, the Lord had prepared Josie for this exact thing.

*Does it matter why she's come?* Jed's question rang again in her ears.

Josie thought of the prodigal's return that had so been on her mind of late. She remembered the stories of lost lambs and Josie had her answer.

She raised her head to see the Burdetts still talking among themselves, hugging, laughing, unaware of the small drama building on the fringes of the onlookers.

Josie knew how to respond when the lost lamb returned to the fold.

She *did* run. With Nathan in her arms she ran straight toward Ophelia.

"Phellie!" She used the special nickname she alone used for her sister. "Over here!"

"Pheenie?" Ophelia sputtered. Her expression was

a clash of emotions, surprise, apprehension, defensiveness, disbelief.

Josie stopped with barely a foot between them. Her fears reared up and made her question if she had done the right thing.

Nathan squirmed in her arms.

Josie gave him a kiss. He was safe. He was hers. And her hurting and once-lost sister had come back. If she were truly the woman of faith she wanted to be, now was the time to set her childhood fears aside and trust the Lord.

She reached out her trembling hand to Ophelia at last. "Welcome home."

Ophelia glanced down, hesitated, then took it.

The second their fingers touched Josie felt a rush of warmth and love she had not known since they were little girls together.

Ophelia must have felt it, too, as tears filled her usually cold and calculating eyes.

And just that fast they were hugging one another, Nathan between them, wriggling and giggling.

A murmur went up around them, something between a gasp of surprise and an approving cheer.

"Okay, okay. Let's get this over with—what are you doing here? How did you find us out here? And would you like to hold the baby?" Josie laughed and pulled away, facing her sister and the future at last. She sniffled and wiped away a tear from her sister's cheek, then stood back, giving her a once over. "And why are you wearing my clothes?"

Ophelia tugged at the sailor-style shirt then at the waistband of the white jeans that Josie had slipped out of, preferring the pink-and-green outfit she had on now. "I tore mine breaking into that Home Cookin' place of yours. Found these on the counter and just…"

"You broke into my business?" She tried to remember if she had put the money away properly when she had closed up last. She recalled leaving the drawer out when Adam had been there, but nothing else. "Why?"

"Because it was locked," Ophelia said as if Josie had just asked the stupidest question possible.

Josie did feel stupid. And naive. And…

"As for your other questions," Ophelia went on. "I am in town because I have a lot of unfinished business here. There are flyers about this party all over the place, and yes." She stepped forward and put her hands under Nathan's arms to lift him away from Josie. "I would very much like to hold the baby."

"Want I should call law about that break-in, Sweetie Pie?" Warren asked.

"Sweetie Pie?" Ophelia gave Warren a suspicious look. She tugged Nathan free and curled him close to her, then asked Josie, "This is your…sweetie?"

"No, that is *my* sweetie." Warren's wife stepped forward, her experience handling rude teens at the bowling alley coming in mighty handy as she met Ophelia eye to eye. "Everyone calls Josie 'Sweetie Pie' because she means so much to us and we wouldn't want to see her hurt."

Josie wanted to tell them all that her sister would never do anything to hurt her. But she couldn't do it. She swallowed to wash back the acid sickness at the back of her throat as she studied the woman holding her—Josie's...and Ophelia's...son.

For the first time in maybe five years Ophelia did not look like an older sister to Josie. Her face was scrubbed clean and her complexion rivaled Josie's for color in her cheeks and freckles on her nose. She did not have on her usual layers of makeup, nor did she reek of cigarette smoke. She wore her hair natural again, just as Josie did. The curls falling around her shoulders, clean and free of streaks of blue, pink or wine-red. She wore no jewelry, no studs in her eyebrows or biker symbols around her neck. No black nail polish. She was not sneering.

Josie closed her eyes, waited one second, then opened again, half expecting to see something of the old Ophelia there that she had not noticed before. But no.

Not since they were kids and they had played "trick the teacher" by swapping places in the classroom had these identical twins looked so...identical.

It seemed to fascinate Nathan, who wound his

chubby fingers in Ophelia's hair and singsonged his contented "Ya-ya-ya."

"Ya-ya-ya," Josie murmured, her eyes fixed on her child and hoping this would not be the time he finally formed the word *Mama*. She didn't know if she could take that. She drew a deep breath, aware of the collective breathing of the people around her. She heard some commotion, but blocked it out in order to ask what she had to ask. "What *unfinished business* do you have here?"

"Maybe we should go someplace a little more private?" Ophelia rubbed her hand over Nathan's plump leg.

Private. Josie tried to think what to do. Tried to ask the Lord for guidance, but her heart was beating so hard and her head ached. All she could think about was taking Nathan back and…

"Josie, do you want me to go get—" Warren began.

His wife interrupted with a statement aimed Ophelia's way. "Maybe everyone should stay right here while I go get the sheriff."

"No one needs to call the sheriff." Adam pushed through the ring of people, his face grim but filled with a peace that had not been there before he reconciled and accepted the forgiveness of his father and family.

For a split second relief washed over Josie. Then it dawned on her. With Ophelia's new look and with her wearing Josie's clothes, Adam might not be able to tell them apart. Even when they were separated by time and space and all sorts of experiences, Josie had worried that Adam's feelings for her were tangled up and colored by his feelings for Ophelia. Or at least by his sense of responsibility and natural concern for the woman who had carried and given life to his baby boy.

If Ophelia demanded Nathan back, it only stood to reason Adam's attention, perhaps even his affection would follow, right?

The anguish was almost too much to bear. Ophelia's return might cost her both Nathan and Adam. She would lose everything she held dear and Ophelia would be the one to have a family at last and Josie would have nothing.

But God had brought her to this point. He had prepared her. She knew that. She could not stand there silent and put Adam to some kind of childish test; she had to speak and face what was to come with faith and hope.

Josie opened her mouth to say something.

Ophelia did the same.

"I don't want to hear it." Adam put his hand up as he spoke to Ophelia. "I have a few things to say myself. But first let me get one thing straight."

He *spoke* to Ophelia. He *approached* Ophelia.

Josie's heart ached. It actually ached. He did not know the difference between Josie and...

"Ophelia, give me my son." He took Nathan gently from her. "He belongs with his real mother."

He turned and met Josie's eyes. In one step and without taking his gaze from hers, he brought the baby to Josie.

"You knew," she whispered as she cuddled her son close.

"Ya-ya-ya."

"Of course I knew." He ran his hand over Nathan's head, then rested it lightly on Josie's arm. "I told you that. I *know* you, Josie. The good and the bad, the sweet and the secret. I know you by the way you look at our son and by the way I feel when I look at you."

*How do you feel when you look at me?* She pressed her lips together to keep from blurting out the question.

Adam smiled at her, gave her arm a squeeze, then turned slightly to make eye contact with Josie's twin. "Sadly and to my own detriment, I only know Ophelia by her pain."

"Pain." Ophelia repeated the word quite softly. Not defiant and ugly as Josie expected. She nodded, her shoulders slouched slightly, as if she had slipped the word on like a yoke and was trying to decide what to do next. Finally she took off the yoke, humbled herself and said, "I didn't come to try to take Nathan away from you, Josie."

"You didn't?" Josie's own burden lifted. "I mean, I didn't think you had. I *hoped* you hadn't, but…"

"But I hadn't given you a lot of reasons to trust me up until now." Ophelia reached out and tugged on the lace of Nathan's shoe.

"I always wanted to…trust you, Phellie. I always wanted to."

"And now I want to be worthy of your trust, Pheenie. I came here now to make sure everything was all right."

"By breaking into my place of business?"

"I didn't know how to find your house. I'm not from here, remember?"

Josie thought of telling her that she could have just asked anyone, but then remembered that everyone, including Bingo and his little red scooter was out here.

"So I figured Josie's Home Cookin' Kitchen was the best place to wait for you."

"So you broke in?"

She shrugged. "Old habits die hard. And I did it for a good reason. I needed to see you."

"Yeah?" Josie tried keep her hope on a leash. Her sister had a way of making big deals out of nothing and acting as if the most important things were of no consequence whatsoever.

"See, that private eye you hired spoke to Mom, who tracked me down, set things in motion. Made me think. I'd done this one good thing, but hadn't really done it right." She pushed her hair back. She cocked one hip, then swept the back of her hand along Nathan's cheek. "I finally found where Adam had got to and tried to contact him to tell him about the baby. When I learned he'd gone back to Mt. Knott, I felt I had to come. I was afraid he'd try to take Nathan away from you."

"It did cross my mind," he admitted. "At first. Then I saw Nathan with Josie and…"

"Da-da!" Nathan yelled.

"And I knew that's where he belonged," Adam finished, never looking away from Josie.

Did she dare believe what she saw in his eyes? Or was the emotion of the moment coloring her perception? Josie struggled to keep her voice strong as she tore her gaze away from Adam's and spoke to her sister. "I thought when my letter to you came back returned…"

"I don't know about a letter, but I moved out of my old place. Too many temptations. I'm in a program now at a church."

"You've accepted Christ?" Josie took a joyous step toward her sister.

"I, uh, I'm opening up to it," was all Ophelia would say. "It's just a lot to do alone, you know? Stay sober. Overcome a lifetime of selfishness? How do you do that?"

"You started when you decided to have Nathan," Josie said.

"Something I feel I can never thank you enough for," Adam added, his head bowed slightly in a show of gratitude and humility. "Thank you, Ophelia, for not compounding *our* selfishness. For having Nathan *and* giving him to a person who would love him no matter where he came from, who would make a home for him, no matter what personal sacrifices she had to make."

Adam touched Josie's arm, pride and happiness shining from deep within his eyes. "Josie, I… You… Thank you. Not just for what you did for my son but what you've done for me. The things you've made me realize, the way you've helped me look at my world…I…"

Josie held her breath.

"My brain tells me it's too soon to say this, but it's really how I feel." Adam moved close to her and took one of her hands in both of his. "I love you, Josie."

"Wooo-hooo!" Jed led the cheer that went up through the crowd, when they all began to laugh afterward, even Ophelia joined in.

"Now, you say it back to him, Sweetie Pie," Warren prodded in a teasingly loud whisper.

Josie wanted to say it, but her voice failed her, so she mouthed it instead. *I love you, too.*

Another whoop.

Adam broke into laughter and pulled her into his arms, kissing her temple, her cheek, then lightly, her lips.

The crowd showed their approval with applause this time.

Adam kissed her again, this time on the forehead; then he kissed Nathan on the head, as well, before he took a deep breath and looked at Ophelia. His expression changed to guarded kindness. "I have something more to ask you, Ophelia."

Ophelia dropped her gaze downward. She spoke softly, guessing, "Why didn't I tell you about Nathan sooner?"

"No." He shook his head and stepped away from Josie to face Ophelia fully, sincerely, humbly. "Can you ever forgive me?"

"What?"

He reached out and took her by the hand. "I'm asking for your forgiveness."

Josie's heart swelled.

"But...but why?" Ophelia looked past the man and found Josie and Nathan.

"Because it's what families do," Josie explained, choking back a sob. "It's what happens when the lost lamb returns to the fold. We try to make things so they don't stray again. God loves us and forgives us and so we—we do the same for others."

Ophelia's face went blank, no doubt as she tried to process it all.

Josie marveled that she, herself, did not burst into tears. *A family.* An unconventional one, to be sure, but if Ophelia forgave Adam and was open to talking to the two of them, a family they would be.

Adam cleared his throat, which by his standards

was probably close to a total emotional breakdown, she suspected.

"Oh, forgive him already! I couldn't stand it if you didn't." Jed scrunched up his whole face, trying to look annoyed, but was unable to hide his emotional investment in it all.

Warren pulled out the red hankie and blew his nose, good and noisy.

Josie laughed. She couldn't help herself. Adam loved her! He'd made amends with his family. Nathan was going to be hers legally. Ophelia had returned and was open to trying a new way of life.

Sure, the Crumble might still close. Her business might fall as a result. She and Adam might not work out or have a long-term relationship beyond their connection to Nathan, but Josie had the thing she had longed for all her life….

"What do you have to be so happy about?" Ophelia asked.

Josie threw her arms around her sister and gave her a hug, with Nathan still in her arms. "Because I have family. And for the first time I can recall I feel like nothing is going to take that away from me."

# *Chapter Sixteen*

By the first week of November all the leaves had changed to brilliant orange, yellow and red. Some had begun to fall, making a trip down a winding mountain road feel like a trip through a confetti-strewn parade route.

Why not? Josie felt she had so much to celebrate.

She strolled to the front door of the Home Cookin' Kitchen, then turned to look at the prayer list on the wall.

Among the requests for health and job security now read the words Josie never thought she'd see:

"Pray for the Burdett family as they make their big decision." Warren had been the first to sign that one. Jed next. Then Josie. The list grew and grew and even included Elvie Maloney and Micah Applebee, only two of the most high-profile of the Burdetts' detractors.

Adam had come last night with his camera phone and taken a photo of the wall scrawled floor to ceiling with names.

"I want to carry this into the meeting," he had told Josie with a kiss to her cheek.

Josie had returned it with a kiss to his lips. She thought that was a completely acceptable way to send her sweetie off to the meeting that would determine the fate of the family business. Global had done something called a "due diligence." Conner complained they'd come in and pulled records and files and snooped around everything except their medicine cabinets. Today they would present their offer to the board. Adam was just sitting in as a guest and advisor, but with so much at stake they were all anxious.

The sky had gotten overcast throughout the morning. It threatened to drizzle any minute now. The wind kicked up, and Josie watched a few leaves tumble down from the nearest tree.

Bingo beeped, and she went out to meet him, shivering as she did.

"Sorry, Sweetie Pie, bills mostly but there is one here from your sister."

"Thanks, Bingo."

"Hope it's good news."

"Me, too." Josie would save that letter for later. Ophelia had had a setback, but after spending a lot of time with Carol and Cody Burdett, had gone into a residential Christian rehab program.

She thumbed through the rest of the envelopes.

Bingo peered over her shoulder, probably hoping she would read her sister's letter and share all the news.

"Nothing new on the adoption," he told her. "Not that I read your mail, you know, but I got to—"

"I know, read the outsides to know what to deliver." Josie laughed, thanked him and hurried back inside to get out of the autumn chill.

The lack of information did not worry her. The adoption process was well underway and Adam…

Josie looked at the phone and held her breath. This had been one of the longest mornings of her life. The coffee commuters had already come and gone, and she'd even had time to clear away their mess and count up the proceeds. For once the amount not only covered her costs, it gave her enough left over to buy herself a cup of coffee—and not one of her own, the fancy kind in a city coffee shop.

She had counted that twice, then taken some fresh pies out of the oven and served them to the regulars, who gobbled them up, each making comments about her secret ingredient. They'd noticed it this time because Josie had been leaving it out. Or experimenting with different things trying to come up with a substitute. But today, with the Crumble on the line, it only seemed right she'd make her pies with the Carolina Crumble Pattie mixed into the top crust.

Adam should have called with some news by now.

"You ever tell anyone that secret?" Jed poked the last bite of his pie into his mouth.

"What secret?" Warren scraped up the last of the cherry filling on his plate with the side of his fork. "Only secret she's keeping is when she's going to wise up, toss over that Burdett and run off and marry me."

"You old fool. Who in their right mind would toss over a strapping young fellow with a great big inheritance burning a hole in his pocket, just waiting to get reinvested right here in Mt. Knott, for a broken-down ol' pie hog like you?" Jed laughed.

"He really going to invest in Mt. Knott no matter which way the vote goes at the Crumble, Miss Josie?" Warren wiped his mouth then took a sip of coffee.

"That's what he says," she confirmed.

"Good for him."

"Good for us," Jed threw in. "'Cuz if the Crumble goes…"

If the Crumble went—meaning the Burdetts sold out and Global shut them down and restricted them using the recipe ever again—then it didn't matter how much money Adam invested in the town, Josie's pies would never be the same. And she couldn't help wondering what would become of other parts of her life?

*R-rr-rr-ring!*

Josie jumped.

"That might be the call." Warren slapped his hand on the counter.

"You think so, Captain Obvious?" Jed nudged him with his elbow.

"Hello?" Josie held her breath, expecting to hear Adam on the other end. "Oh," was all she could muster when she heard the voice of the paper-goods rep on the other end, wanting to know if she needed to place an order. "Nope. Sorry, I still have a bit left over from the barbecue."

"Not him?" Jed asked.

"Now who's Captain Obvious?" Warren wanted to know, before he added to cheer Josie up, "Won't be long now."

"Can't draw it out forever," Jed agreed.

"How long can it take to plan out the future of one family and a whole townful of fine folks?"

"Adam!" It was as if a light had been flicked on and her whole day had turned bright just to see him standing there. She ran to him and threw her arms around his neck. "What do you know? What did they decide? What happened? Tell me the good news first, okay, sweetie?"

"Yeah, sweetie, tell us the good news first," Jed and Warren chimed in unison.

"The good news?" Adam's dark eyes sparkled. He touched Josie's hair, stroked his thumb along her jaw, then placed a kiss on the tip of her nose. "Well, I was going to save this for a more-private time, but if you want the good news first…"

"Hurry up!" she demanded, knowing he was toying with her.

"Okay." He nodded then dropped to one knee before her.

"What?" She looked down at him, confused and more than a little excited. "What are you—"

"Shhh. You asked me to tell you the good news first, right?"

"Right."

"The good news is that I plan to take care of you and Nathan for the rest of your lives, no matter what happens at the Crumble or with our extended families. And toward that end—" he reached inside his black leather jacket and pulled free a small red velvet box "—Josie Redmond, will you marry me?"

Josie held her breath. She had imagined him coming in here and telling her everything from they had saved the business to telling her he had to ride off on his Harley, never to return. But this?

"M-marry you?"

"You know what this means, don't you?" Jed asked his counter mate.

"Yup. That she is never ever going to wise up and marry me." Warren sulked, then brightened. "Although, my wife will probably appreciate that news to no end."

"No, you fool, it means that them Burdetts sold out the Crumble. If they didn't, he wouldn't want to propose first, he'd have told her the good news up front."

Josie put her hand to her throat. "Is that an accurate assessment of things?"

"Has anything those guys come up with ever been accurate?" Adam's smile grew, slowly at first, then spread wide until he couldn't contain a roll of joyous laughter. "We did it, Josie."

"We...did?"

"The family turned down the buyout."

"Yee-hooo!" Jed hollered.

"Well, I'll be!" Warren shook his head.

"But why? How? What's to keep the place from bottoming out and going bankrupt?"

"New blood."

She winced. "What?"

He took both her hands in his. "We have a third party, new investor. Came in at the eleventh hour with some great ideas for restructuring, starting some new product lines and running the business based on Biblical principles."

"Biblical?" Josie had heard Adam and the brothers discussing that before. "And this new investor..."

"Wants to partner with the family. One member of the family more than others, I suspect."

She shook her head. Nothing he had said since the proposal had really sunk in. "I don't..."

"Dora Hoag. My old boss."

"Oh!" Josie laughed at last.

"*That* made sense to you?"

"Love always makes sense to me." She put her arms around his neck.

"Then you are a wiser person than I am, Josie, because love has had me baffled until I met you."

She went up on tiptoe and kissed him.

"Does that mean she's accepting his proposal?" Jed asked.

"Yep. Get out your Sunday best, you old fool, looks like you and me are going to be flower girls."

And they were.

Not flower girls, but they did have the responsibility of bringing Nathan down the aisle and holding him there to bear witness to the marriage of his parents.

Everyone they loved was there, Ophelia, Conner, Burke, Jason, Cody and Carol. And Bingo. And even Dora came.

And when the minister pronounced them man and wife, Nathan wasn't afraid to put in his two cents. "Dada! Mama! Ya-ya-ya!"

\* \* \* \* \*

Dear Reader,

As a parent, I have long understood the father's rejoicing at the return of the prodigal son. As a former air force "brat" who grew up to be a social worker, I've always tried to work hard, respect others, consider the greater good and be a team player. I've seen people who did none of the above rise to the top and reap what seemed like abundant rewards, while I worked away unnoticed in the background. Because of that, I definitely see the point of the brother who had remained with his father, working and being obedient.

But as I grew older, I began to think about the nature of forgiveness and family and wondered what it must feel like to be the one on the receiving end of that rejoicing and forgiveness. I know how it feels to accept and be grateful for these good gifts from the Lord, of course. But given human nature, I suspected it was a much different feeling coming from another human, especially one as close as a family member, where there are so many issues built into the relationship.

And so came the story of *Somebody's Baby*. A

story of family and forgiveness and the hope and joy that comes when a lamb is returned to the fold. I hope you enjoy it.

*Annie Jones*

## QUESTIONS FOR DISCUSSION

1. Josie had to deal with coming from a family that did not support her faith. How can Christians deal with loved ones who reject their faith?

2. How can Christians reach out to those who have no family support to help them in their walk with the Lord?

3. Adam took his inheritance and his share of the family business and, in a manner of speaking, reinvented himself. If you were to receive a windfall, what would you do with it?

4. Would you like to live in a small town like Mt. Knott? Why or why not?

5. Josie was known for her special pie crust. Do you have a recipe that you are known for? Do you keep it a secret? Whom would you share it with?

6. Do you know any twins? How do you tell them apart? What makes them different from each other?

7. When his mother died, Adam felt he lost the

one person who truly accepted him. Have you ever felt all alone in the world? How did you overcome that?

8. Mt. Knott is a tight-knit community. Does your community offer you prayer and encouragement? Are there ways that you could offer that to others?

9. In the end, several characters have to ask for and also give forgiveness for their behavior. Many times we do not get to speak directly to those we forgive or they to us when we need to be forgiven. Do you think that asking for and openly giving forgiveness changes the nature of the act? Makes it harder or easier to follow through on?

10. Do you think it's more difficult to accept human forgiveness than divine forgiveness? Why or why not?

She will give birth to a son, and you are to give him the name Jesus, because he will save his people from their sins.

—*Matthew* 1:21

# SOMEBODY'S SANTA

To my family far and wide (yeah, the older we get the wider we are!): For all the merry Christmases past and all the joyous new years to come, thank you and God bless!

# Chapter One

Burke Burdett had lost himself.

The man he had always believed himself to be had vanished. Nobody needed him anymore. Nobody wanted him. Nobody even realized that he had gone.

It had happened so quickly he still didn't know where he fit into the grand scheme of his company, his family or even his own life. But he did know this—years ago he had made a promise and now he had to see that promise through, even if it meant he had to go someplace he swore he'd never go to ask help of someone he swore he'd never see again. Even if it meant that he had to trade in his image of Top Dawg, the eldest and leader of the pack of Burdett brothers, to become somebody that nobody in Mt. Knott, South Carolina, would ever have imagined. If Burke ever hoped to find himself again, he was going to have to become Santa Claus.

Fat, wet snowflakes powdered the gray-white Carolina sky. Dried stalks of grass and weeds poked through the threadbare blanket of white. Everything seemed swathed in peace and quiet solitude.

Winter weather was not unheard of in this part of South Carolina, but Burke Burdett had rarely seen it come this early in the year, nor had he ever considered it the answer to somebody's prayer. His prayer.

He looked to the heavens and muttered—mostly to himself but not caring if the God of all creation, maker of the sky, and mountains and gentle nudges in the form of frozen precipitation, overheard— "And on Thanksgiving Day of all times."

It had to be Thanksgiving, of course, one of the few days when Burke took the time to actually offer a prayer much beyond a mumbled appeal for help or guidance.

This time he had asked for a little of each and added to the mix a heartfelt plea, "Please, prepare my heart for what I am about to undertake. Give it meaning by giving me purpose."

If he were another kind of man, he could have waxed eloquent about love and honor and humbling himself in order to learn and grow from the experience. But he wasn't that kind of man. He was the kind of man who wanted to feel productive and useful. There were worse ambitions than asking to be useful to the Lord, he believed.

So he had left his prayer as it was and waited for

something to stir in him. It had stirred outside instead. Snow. In November.

The whole family had ooohed and ahhhed over it, and for an instant, Burke recalled how it felt to be a kid. And just as quickly he excused himself and drove awry from the family compound of homes.

Now in the vacant parking lot of the old building that housed his family's business, the Carolina Crumble Pattie Factory, Burke did not feel the cold. Only a dull, deepening sense of loneliness that had dogged him after spending a day surrounded by his family. In years past that family had consisted of his mom and dad, Conner and Maggie Burdett, his three brothers, Adam, Jason and Cody, and maybe a random cousin or two in from Charleston. This year two sisters-in-law and a nephew had been added. But it was the losses that Burke simply could not shake.

Age and grief had ravaged the tough old bird who had once been the strong, proud Conner Burdett, left him thin and a little stooped, worn around the eyes and unexpectedly sentimental.

Sentiment was not the Burdett way and seeing it in his father made Burke think of weakness and vulnerability. Not his father's but his own.

Burke clenched and unclenched his jaw and squinted at the low yellow-and-tan building where he had worked since he'd been old enough to ride his bicycle there after school. It did not help that the realities of the changing market had their business by the throat and had all but choked the life out of what had once been the mainstay of employment for much of the town of Mt. Knott, South Carolina.

They had made a plan to deal with that, or rather, his brother Adam had. He had gone out into the global marketplace, learned new techniques and made powerful allies. He was the one, the family had concluded by an almost unanimous vote, who needed to take the reins now. That plan had come at a cost. Burke, who had always carried the title Top Dawg in the pack of Burdett boys, had been asked to step aside.

Step aside or be forced out. By his own family.

In doing so Burke had lost his place not just in the family but, he thought, in the whole wide world. Not that they had fired him outright. They had asked him to stay on in a different capacity, but they must have known he'd never do it. After all, who had ever heard of Upper Middle Management Dawg?

So he had tendered his resignation and never returned, not even to collect his belongings. Until now.

Adam was to take on the job that Burke had held, for all intents and purposes, for a decade now. Adam, with his expertise in international corporate business dealings. Adam, with his new ideas for marketing and distribution. Adam, with the one thing that made him the most honored in the eyes of Conner Burdett, the thing that would assure them all that their name and reputation and even their business would go on—a son.

Burke didn't even have a girlfriend. How was he supposed to compete with that?

He wasn't, of course. To know that, Burke only had to think about Adam and Josie and their son, Nathan, how happy they had looked today seated at the massive Burdett dinner table together. Love and joy and wanting the best for those you care about, *doing* your best for them, that was what mattered. Winning?

Winning, Burke decided as he let out a long, labored sigh, was for losers.

And for the first time in his life, Burke felt like a loser. Not because of the loss of his position with the company or the unlikelihood that he would become a husband and father anytime soon, but because he had failed at that one thing that really mattered in life.

Burke shuddered. The wind whipped at the collar of his brown suede coat. He pushed his gray Stetson down low, as much to hide the dark blond hair that everyone in town would recognize as to protect his head and ears from the cold. Today, Thanksgiving Day, he felt the cutting ache of the loss of his mother down to his very bones. She had died two years ago, come Christmas Eve. *Two years.*

Yet it felt so fresh that he could still feel the heft of her coffin as he led the procession of pallbearers that day. He flexed his hand as if to chase away the memory of the icy brass handle he had clutched to take his mother to her final resting place. But it had been too long.

He had let too much time go past and now he had to face the truth.

Until this year the running of "the crumble," as everyone in Mt. Knott affectionately called the business, had kept him busy. It had occupied his time, his thoughts, his energy. He hadn't even had time for dating, much less a real relationship, for seeing friends or making a real home for himself or any of the niceties most people his age took for granted. He certainly didn't have time to take on some silly pet cause of his mother's. One he didn't understand, didn't approve of and had only learned about when she was on her deathbed. Even if it was the one thing she had asked that Burke and Burke alone, of all the brothers, undertake. Her dying wish.

He swiped a knuckle across his forehead to nudge back his hat, ignoring the sudden sting of a flake that swirled beneath his Stetson to land on his cheek.

His finger brushed over the faint old scar that jagged across his eyebrow.

Conner had given it to him—the scar, not the business. The Crumble he had had to fight for in every sense of the word. He'd used the law, his family's consensus and finally even his fists to win his birthright as oldest of the four Burdett sons. His birthright—his place as head of the Burdett household and CEO of the family's already foundering enterprise.

Burke had gotten that scar the night he'd taken over as head of the family business. He'd been running it behind the scenes while his mother was sick, without much input at all from the rest of the family, but Conner's name had always remained painted in gold on the glass of the door to the big office. Until that night. That night everything had shifted, like a great jutting up of land along a fault line. They had all known it would come one day but had done little to prepare for it.

That night Adam had cashed out his share of the Crumble factory, taken the inheritance his mother had left and run away. And Conner and Burke had pushed their always contentious relationship to the edge.

He hung his head. Even after all these years, even though he and his father had made their peace, Burke felt a pang of regret that it had gone so far. But his father's grief over losing Maggie had driven them to the brink of bankruptcy. Adam's actions had sealed the deal.

It was either challenge his father and take over or lose everything that they had worked to achieve.

Burke stroked the memento of that fateful night. Two things had happened then that would forever shape the rest of his life. First, he'd become a man, the leader of his family, the one they would all depend on. And second, he had decided, as he saw his father sobbing in misery over the remnants of what had once been a proud life, that Burke would never let himself need another person the way his father had needed his mother. It was a man's choice, as he saw it. You cannot love one person that much and still have enough left to serve the many who depend on you.

He'd been true to his word on both counts. He'd applied the ruthless business tactics that his father had taught him, slashed jobs, cut the budget to the bone, stripped away bonus plans and reduced salaries, starting with his own. It wasn't enough.

And as for needing anyone?

Need was some other person's weakness. Not his. Ever. Except…

There was his mother's dying wish.

A wish too long ignored.

A job that no one in Mt. Knott could know about, much less help him with.

He *needed* to take care of that.

Christmas was only five weeks away. Time was running out.

He'd looked at his predicament from every possible angle. In order to preserve everything his mother had worked so hard to keep secret for so many years, he would require a certain type of person. Someone from out of town. Someone who would work hard, collect her sizable paycheck and then go away before December twenty-fourth to leave his family and his town to celebrate the sacred holiday, without so much as a backward glance. Someone who shared his beliefs that business is not a personal thing, that sentiment breeds weakness, and that needing someone is not the cornerstone of a good life but a roadblock on the way to the top.

He forced his hat back down low on his head and made his way toward the building at last. He would duck inside and grab the box that had been waiting there for him ever since he had cleared out of his office to make way for Adam. In it he'd find a phone number on a business card. Tomorrow morning, he'd have to make the trek to Atlanta.

# Chapter Two

"Working on the day after Thanksgiving, Ms. Hoag? I thought you'd be out shopping with the rest of the country."

*"Shopping?"* It took Dora Hoag a moment to grasp the concept. "Oh, *shopping! Christmas* shopping. As in gifts and glad tidings and ho-ho-ho and 'Hark! the Herald Angels...'"

Dora let out a low sigh.

She glanced up from the paperwork on her enormous desk at the salt-and-pepper-haired man, Zach Bridges, owner of the company who cleaned their office building. She knew him, just as she knew everyone on his cleaning crew, the night security guards, the lunch cart girls, everyone at the nearest all-night coffee shop and the company maintenance staff. Dora knew pretty much anyone who, like her, was still working long after others had gone off to...

well, do whatever it was people who did not work *all* the time did when they were *not* working. She knew them, but they didn't know her, not really.

Granted, each year she took off most of the month of December, using up some of the vacation days she hadn't taken during the year. After seven years she thought ol' Zach might have figured out that she did not need more time to go caroling, wrap packages or bake cookies. She was hiding.

Hiding from the hurt the most joyous time of year always had meant to her. After all, what happiness is there in the season of giving when you have no one to give to?

Dora supported all the charities, of course. She'd worked at missions serving food and dropped a mountain of coins in little red buckets. She went to the candlelight service at her church, and her heart filled with love as they sang the hymns about the baby born in the manger. But when the last parishioners had called out their goodbyes, Dora had always been alone. Like the last gift under the tree that nobody claimed.

"Let me guess. You're the type who has all her shopping done before the stores even put up the first display. Oh, say, long about the end of September." Zach's smile stretched beyond the clipped edges of his mustache. "That way you don't have to face the rush this time of year."

Dora would have loved a reason to brave the

throng and chaos this time of year to find just the right thing to express how she felt, to make someone smile, to give them…well, just to give from her heart. Instead she had work to do, and if she hoped to take her yearly sabbatical starting next week, she had to get back to it.

She flipped over a piece of paper in the file and narrowed her eyes at the long column of numbers. "I'm shopping all right. I just have a different idea of what constitutes a bargain."

"Looking for a couple of small businesses to snatch up and use as stocking stuffers, eh?"

"Snatch up? You make me sound like a bird of prey swooping down for the kill."

"Eat like a bird," he said, emptying the day's trash—an apple core, a picked-over salad in a plastic container, half a sandwich with just the crusts nibbled away. "And you're always flitting around, never perching anyplace for long."

"I've been based in this office for seven years, now, Zach."

"Seven years, and I'm still dusting the same office chair. Ain't ever in it long enough to wear it out and requisition a new one."

"Point taken." She laughed. For a moment she considered quizzing the man on what else he had concluded about her over the years, but a flashing light and a buzz from her phone system stopped her.

"Ms.…." The barely audible voice cut out, followed by another buzz then, "This is…" Silence, another buzz. "…says that…" A longer silence, a buzz, then nothing, not even static.

She frowned.

Zach chuckled and gave a shrug. "Security. Brought in extra help for the holidays and made the new ones work this weekend."

"Not like you, huh, Zach? You let your staff have the time off and came in yourself." She admired that. It showed the character to put others before your own desires and the integrity to make sure you still meet your promised goals.

"Just the way I roll, I reckon," Zach said matter-of-factly. Then he nodded his head toward the bin beneath her paper shredder, his way of asking if she wanted him to take the zillion cross-cut strips of paper away with the rest of the trash.

She shook her head. Nobody got a glimpse of her business, not even in bits and pieces. She glanced down at the pad on her desk and the silly little doodle of a very Zach-like elf pushing a candy-cane broom and suppressed a smile. It was only business, she admitted to herself as she tore off the page and slid it into the middle of the pile of papers waiting for the shredder. The man might come to some conclusions about her on his own, but she wouldn't supply any confirmation. That was the way *she* rolled.

Never show your soft side. Never reveal all your talents, even the more whimsical ones. Never let anyone get a peek at what you think of them. Never share your dreams. Never act on anything in blind trust, not even your own feelings.

And most importantly, never let your hopes or your heart do the work that is the rightful domain of your history and your head.

She'd learned that lesson the hard way and not all that long ago.

She looked at the nest of shredded paper and blinked. Tears blurred her vision. The tip of her nose stung.

For an instant she was in South Carolina on a lovely summer day at a family barbeque. Not *her* family, but one in which she had thought she might one day find a place.

*Dora Burdett.* How many times had she doodled that name like some young girl in middle school with her first crush? *Crush.* What an apt word for what had happened to that dream.

She cleared her throat, spread her hands wide over the open file before her and anchored herself firmly in the present. "If you'll excuse me, I have to get back to my work."

"Always wheelin' and dealin', huh, Ms. Hoag?"

"I head acquisitions and mergers, Zach." She raised her head and stared at the massive logo for GrimExCynergetic GlobalCom Limited on the green marble wall beyond her open door, where professional decorators had already begun hanging greenery with Global gold-and-silver ornaments. "It's my job to find the best deals before anyone else does."

"One step ahead of all those poor saps who took the long weekend off to get a jump on the holidays, right?"

"Yeah," she said, her voice barely above a whisper. "Those poor saps."

*How she so wanted to be one of them.*

All her life that was what she had wanted most of all—to have somebody recognize what she had to give, and to accept it and her. Not as an obligation or duty or in hopes of currying favor but because… she mattered.

Dora had never truly felt that she mattered. She, the things she did, the things she thought, her hopes, her dreams, *her*. Not in that way when someone loves you despite your shortcomings. When someone not only wants the best for you but feels you are the best for them, that you bring out the best in each other. She did not grow up in a home like that.

Her mother died when she was born. Her overwhelmed father left his newborn in the care of a childless and already middle-aged aunt and uncle while he went away to "find himself" and "get his head on straight," as people said in the seventies.

Apparently he never did either thing, because he never returned for Dora. Sometimes when Dora thought about him she imagined a man wandering about with his head facing backward, asking total strangers if they had seen his lost self.

Aunt Enid and Uncle Taylor did their best to care for her as their own. They started this by naming her Dora, which already put her at a disadvantage among peers with names like Summer, Montana and Jessica. So she kept to herself and worked hard, trying to make her foster parents proud. And for her effort she drew the attention of teachers and administrators. They called her "the little adult" and made jokes about her being "ten going on forty" and tried to get her to lighten up a little. But whenever they needed something done—from choosing a child to represent the school at a leadership conference to helping out in the office or being in charge of the cash box at the pep club bake sale—they tapped Dora.

She learned quickly that hard work and efficiency opened doors. It wasn't the same as fitting in or mattering to someone but it came a close second. About as good as Dora thought she'd ever see.

Still, she couldn't help wondering how different her life might be if just once someone had reached out and asked her to come through the doors her drive had created.

A small thing.

A shouted invitation to join a crowded lunch table.

A remembered birthday.

An explanation of why a certain blond-haired,

South Carolina gentleman had slammed the door in her face when she had only wanted to…

"I'm dreaming of a…"

"Please, no Christmas songs, Zach."

"Too early in the season for you?" the man asked, as he tossed his dust rag on top of his cart and began to back the cart out of the room.

"Something like that." Especially when her mind had just flashed back to last summer and that family barbeque when she had thought that finally she had done something so caring and constructive that it would change her entire life. That the man she had offered to help, she dared hope, would change her life.

*Dora Burdett.*

She pressed her eyes closed.

Zach cleared his throat.

A twinge of guilt tightened her shoulders and made her sit upright, look the man in the eyes and produce a conciliatory smile. "Oh, don't get me wrong. I'm not one of those who wants to do away with merry Christmas or any of the wonderful trappings of the season. I just…"

She put her hand over her forehead, as if that would warm up the old thought process and help her find the right words to explain her feelings. Except, it wasn't her brain that was frozen against all the joyous possibilities Christmas represented to so many. She loved the Lord, and observed His birth in her own way. "I love going to church for the candlelight service on Christmas Eve. I love singing the hymns and all, but…."

"But after that you don't have no one to go home to and share it all with," Zach said softly.

"How did you know that?" The observation left her feeling so exposed she could hardly breathe.

"You don't dust around folks's knicknacks and gewgaws or throw out their calendar's pages or run into them working on the day after Thanksgiving year upon year without learning a thing or two about those folks."

The answer humbled her even if it didn't bring her much relief. "I'll bet."

"Anyway, don't think it's my place to say—or sing—anything more, but I hate to leave without at least…" He scratched his head, worked his mouth side to side a couple of times then finally sighed. "I'll just offer this thought."

Dora braced herself, pressing her lips together to keep from blurting out that she didn't need his thoughts or sympathy or songs. Because, deep down, she sort of hoped that whatever he had to say might help.

He lifted his spray bottle of disinfectant cleaner the way someone else might have raised a glass to make a toast. "Here's to hoping this year is different."

It didn't help.

But Dora smiled. At least she thought she smiled.

She felt her face move, but really it could have been anything from a fleeting grin to that wince she tended to make when forcing her feet into narrow-toed high heels. Just as quickly she fixed her attention on the papers in front of her and busied herself with shuffling them about. "Thanks. Now I need to get back to work. Can't make a deal on merely hoping things will improve, can I?"

"On the contrary." The challenge came from the tall blond man who placed himself squarely in her office doorway. "I'd say that hope is at the very core of every deal."

Burke Burdett! Questions blew through Dora's mind more quickly than those fictional eight tiny reindeer pulling a flying sleigh. But the words came out of her mouth fast and furious and from the very rock bottom of her own reality. "How dare you show your face to me."

"Show my face? The view don't get any better from the other side, Dora," he drawled in his low, lazy Carolina accent.

Zach, who had worked the cleaning cart into the hallway by now, laughed.

Dora opened her mouth to remind him it wasn't part of his job description to make assumptions about her or eavesdrop on her and her guests. The squeak, rattle, squeak of the cart told her Zach had already moved on, though. She was alone in her office with Burke Burdett.

But not for long.

She reached out for a button on her phone, hesitated, then raised her eyes to meet those of her visitor.

He had good eyes. Clear and set in a tanned face with just enough lines to make him look thoughtful but still rugged. But if one looked beyond those eyes, those so-called character lines, there was a hard set to his lips and a wariness in his stance.

"Give me one reason not to call security to come up here and escort you out," she said.

"Well, for starters, I don't think the poor kid you've got posted at the front desk knows how to find the intercom button to hear you, much less where your office is." He dropped into the leather wingback directly across from her. Years ago an old hand had taught Dora that standing was the best way to keep command of an exchange. *Stand. Move. Hold their attention and you hold the reins of the situation.*

Burke had just broken that cardinal rule. And made things worse when he stretched his legs out in front of him, crossed his boots at the ankle to create a picture of ease. He scanned the room, saying, "Besides, he was the one who let me in."

Dora wasn't the only one who noticed and befriended the people everyone else looked right past. "And what did you use to convince that so-green-he's-in-danger-of-being-mistaken-for-a-sprig-of-holly security guard to get him to do that?"

"Use? Me? Why, nothing but the power of my dazzling personality and charm."

"I've been on the receiving end of your charm, Mr. Burdett. It's more drizzle than dazzle." She'd meant it as a joke. A tease, really. Under other circumstances, with another man, maybe even a flirtation.

Burke clearly knew that. All of it. He responded in kind with the softest and deepest of chuckles.

And Dora found herself charmed indeed.

"So the security kid is already sort of on my side in this deal," he summed up.

"Deal?" She stood so quickly that her chair went reeling back into the wall behind her desk. She did not acknowledge the clatter it made. "There is no deal. You made that very clear to me when you cut me out of your family's plans to save the Crumble and get things there back on track."

Last summer, after working his way quickly up the corporate ladder at Global, Adam Burdett had returned to Mt. Knott with a scheme to buy out Carolina Crumble Pattie and get some satisfaction for all the perceived wrongs done against him by his adoptive father. It had all seemed a bit soap operaish to Dora, but as a good businesswoman she knew those were exactly the elements that put other people at a disadvantage in forging a business contract. Emotions. Family. Old hurts. They could push things either way.

In this case, they had eventually gone against Global's proposed buyout. And in favor of Adam Burdett, and by extension, Dora. Together they had the wherewithal to save the company and the desire to do so. It wasn't what either of them had planned, but then love had a way of changing even the most determined minds. Adam's love for Josie—now his wife—his son, his family. And Dora's for the town of Mt. Knott, its way of life, the thrill of a new venture based on the same kind of Biblical principles that had once motivated Global a few dozen mergers ago. And her love for Burke.

She hadn't loved him right away but by the end of the summer, she thought she did love him. And she thought he loved her back.

Only she hadn't been thinking. She had been feeling and acting on those feelings. Which had brought her full circle, only then she had become the one at a disadvantage in the contract negotiations. Dora was out. Adam was in. Burke had been nowhere to be found.

Burke glanced her way, then went right on surveying their surroundings. "This is a *new* deal that I've come to talk to you about today."

"New deal? Why would I talk to you about a new deal? Or that old deal? You didn't talk to me about that then and I don't want to talk to you about..."

"Look, I'm here now, dazzling or not, with a new deal to discuss. The past is past. I can't change it.

Isn't there anything more important for us to talk about than that?"

Only about a million things. Yet given the chance to bring up any of them all Dora could come up with was, "I can't imagine what we'd have to say to one another."

"I can. At least, I have some things I want to say to you."

Her whole insides melted. Not defrosted like an icicle, dripping in rivulets until it had dwindled to nothing but a nub, but more like a piece of milk chocolate where the thumb and finger grasp it—just enough to make a mess of everything.

"You have something to say to me?" She bent her knees to sit, realized her chair was a few feet away and moved around the desk instead to lean back against it. "Like what, for instance?"

"Like…" He tilted his head back. He narrowed his eyes at her. He rested his elbows on the arms of the chair.

The leather crunched softly, putting her in mind of a cowboy shifting into readiness in the saddle. Readiness for what, though?

She held her breath.

He leaned forward as if every decision thereafter depended on her answer, asking softly and with the hint of his smile infusing his words, "Like, what do you want for Christmas?"

She almost slid off the edge of the desk. "I…uh…"

*What did she want for Christmas?* "After six months of not so much as a phone message, you drove all the way from South Carolina to Atlanta to ask me what I want for Christmas?" She stood up to retake control of what was clearly a conversation with no real purpose or direction. "Are you kidding me? Who does that?"

He could not answer her. Or maybe he could answer but didn't want to. He just sat there.

And sat there.

She could hear him breathing. Slow and steady. See his eyes flicker with some deep emotion but nothing she could define without looking long and hard into them. And she was not likely to do that.

She cleared her throat. She could wait him out. She had waited him out, in fact. He had been the one who had come to her, not the other way around. Even though early on there had been plenty of long, lonely nights when she had wanted nothing more than to hop in her car, or in the company jet or hitch a ride on a passing Carolina Crumble delivery truck to get herself back to South Carolina to confront him. Or kiss him.

Or both.

She wanted to do both. Even now. Which made it imperative that she do something else all together. So she plunked down on the edge of the desk again and said the only thing that made any sense at all to her, given the circumstances. "What I want is for you to go back to Mt. Knott and just leave me in peace."

"Peace. Yes." His slow, steady nod gave the impression of a man who longed for the very same gift—but doubted he'd ever find it. "That I can't promise you. That's better a request for the One who sent his Son."

"Nice save," she whispered, thinking of how deftly he'd avoided her demand for him to leave.

"Best save ever made, if you think about it."

She looked out into the hallway at the Christmas decorations going up. Global would not have a nativity scene, or any reference to the birth of Christ, and yet they covered the place in greenery, the symbol of life everlasting. All around her this time of year, the world came alive with symbols of hope. They rang in the ears, they delighted the eye, they touched the heart. It was such a special time, a time when one could believe not just in the wonder of God's Son but also in the possibilities for all people of goodwill.

Maybe even for a person like Burke.

Maybe he *had* really come here because he wanted to know what she wanted. Maybe he needed to know that she could still want him, to tell her that he had made a mistake, to tell her that she...

He shifted forward again, clasping his hands. "As for me..."

*As for me.* He had asked what she wanted, ignored

her reply and went straight for his real purpose in coming. *Me.*

*Himself.*

He didn't want to know about her, he wanted to ask her to do something for him.

The moment passed and Dora stood again. She had to get him out of here. She had to keep him from saying another word that might endear him to her, that might give her reason to hope....

"As for you, Mr. Burdett." She moved to the door and made a curt jerk of her thumb to show him the way he should exit. "I don't really care what you want for Christmas."

"Not even if what I want, only you can give me?"

# Chapter Three

Burke had broken the first rule of negotiation. He had let his counterpart know the strength of her position. He had been upfront and told her that he wanted to make a deal and she was the only one he wanted to deal with. He might as well have handed her a blank check.

And he would have done just that if he had thought it would work.

It wouldn't. Not with a woman like Dora. So he had done the next best thing, given her all the power in the situation. Now that, that was something she had to find compelling. Right?

Burke swallowed to push down the lump in his throat. He was not accustomed to anyone questioning his judgment and actions. Even when they included his limited charm, fumbling coyness and... Christmas cutesiness.

*Who does that?* Dora's earlier question echoed in his thoughts. Who drives all the way from South Carolina to Atlanta to ask a grown woman—one who clearly hates his guts—what she wants for Christmas?

Certainly not Top Dawg, the alpha male of the Burdett wolf pack. Certainly not him. And yet, that's exactly what he'd done.

And he had no idea whom to blame for it.

"What do you want, Burke?" She folded her arms over her compact body, narrowed her dark eyes and pursed her lips, a look only Dora could pull off. A look that probably set countless underlings and more than a few superiors shaking in their boots. A look that made Burke want to take her by the shoulders and find the nearest mistletoe. "What could I possibly do for you?"

He forced the obvious and inappropriate answers aside and started at the beginning.

"It's a long story. Goes back to my mom." He squirmed in the fancy wingback. He tried to make himself comfortable but the back was too stiff, the seat too short, the leather too slick. Not to mention that his trying to pin his actions on his late mother, too flimsy.

He wasn't a man who needed to assign blame, it was just that something had brought him to this point and he sure wished he knew what it was.

"Your, um, your *mother?*" Dora did not flinch

but her no-nonsense squint did soften as she prodded him to say more.

He jerked his head up and their eyes met. He hadn't planned on that happening. Hadn't prepared for it—hadn't steeled himself against the accusations he saw aimed like a hundred arrows right at him.

How could he have prepared a defense for those? He'd earned each and every one of those unforgiving, poisonous points. She had every right to hate him, or at least not to want to see him and to turn down his proposal outright. "Uh, yeah. My mother. Thing is she started this…it all started a long time ago, really. Long time before she was my mom or met my dad or had any idea that her life would turn out, well, the way it did."

Dora looked away from him at last. Her shoulders sagged, but she kept her chin angled up, in that way she had that she thought made her seem brave and sophisticated.

Seeing her like that made Burke want to push himself up to his feet and take her in his arms and hold her close. To lay his cheek against her soft, black hair and tell her that when she acted that way he could see right through to the scared, lonely little girl he had seen in her since the first time she powered her way into the Crumble to try to buy it out.

She sounded the part, too, quiet with a tiny quiver that she forced to be still more and more with each word. "None of us knows the way our lives will turn out."

"My mom did." He matched her tone, without the tremor. "Or she thought she did."

"That's the kicker, isn't it? When things don't turn out the way you thought they would?" Try as she might to come off all cool and in control, his showing up like this had obviously thrown her off balance. "When you start down a path. You make plans. You pray about it and feel you've finally..."

She glanced out the door.

He uncrossed his ankles and set his feet flat, just in case he decided to up and bolt from the room. It wasn't his style to do that kind of thing, but then again, neither was the way he had treated Dora earlier this year. Something about her made him do things he'd never thought himself capable of.

"Things just don't..." She shuffled the files on her desk.

He looked down. He should have worn his new boots. Dora deserved for him to put his best foot forward, literally and figuratively.

Dora cleared her throat.

He crossed his ankles again, his way of making it harder to give up on his quest and hightail it back to Mt. Knott.

"Like you said," she murmured at last, "...the way you thought."

"Yeah," he said. "That's the kicker. When things don't turn out the way you wished they would."

She'd said *thought*.

He'd said *wished*.

He wondered if she would correct him and in doing so bluntly and unashamedly confirm that they were talking about their own failed plans. If only she would and they could get it out into the open.

Burke was an out-in-the-open kind of man. Always had been—except when the good faith of a woman who didn't have sense enough to give up on him was at stake. That's how he'd gotten into this predicament in the first place.

He'd wanted to be upfront with Dora from the get-go, but the underhanded way in which his brothers had cut him from his spot as top dog of the family business left him hurt, humiliated and wanting to tuck his tail between his legs and hide. He knew that about himself. Knew that what he'd done, dumping her by pretending the only thing between them had been a business deal, was wrong. If she would only call him on it maybe they could sort it out and then…then *what?*

He shook his head. "You see, my mom, she had this plan for her life."

Dora held her tongue.

He felt he had to forge ahead.

Fill the silence.

State his case for coming here after all this time.

And if he got what was coming to him in the bargain? He'd take it like he took every blow and disappointment he'd suffered in life, without flinching and letting anyone see his pain.

"College, travel, adventure. Mom had the brains, the courage and the means to do it all. Something I know you can relate…" Too soon. One look into her eyes and he could see he had tried to get her to invest in this on a personal level much too soon.

"Yes?"

No, not too soon. He'd read her all wrong.

He'd spent hour upon hour with her. They'd discussed everything from business to barbeque sauce. He'd even sat by her side and mapped out a future that would forever intertwine them, if only on their corporate income tax papers.

The things unsaid had promised more, and he knew it. Their laughter, their shared beliefs, their dedication to their work. Those things made it easy to be around Dora, something he'd never felt with another woman. They also made it easy to let go of her when their business deal fell through.

*Fell through.* Pretty words for having been kicked out by your own family and finding yourself left with nothing more to offer anyone, least of all a woman like Dora.

No position. No power. No purpose.

Burke knew that Dora needed those things for herself and from anyone involved with her. After the

family had put those—position, power, purpose—
out of reach for him, a personal relationship with
Dora had become impossible for him.

He pressed on with his pitch. "My mother changed
her life plans completely so that she could give her
all to her family and the new dreams we would create together."

Dora would never have done the same.

"So your mother made her choice," she said.
"Most women do. We tell ourselves we can have it
all, and maybe we can but most of us know we can't
have it all and give our all, all the time. So we all
make choices. That *is* something I can relate to."

There was an eagerness in Dora's eyes, an intensity. Did he dare call it hope? Or merely an open-
ness to hope? It was so slim, so faint. He doubted
she even knew she was revealing it. It embarrassed
him a little and humbled him that he should have this
advantage, no, this blessing. That he should get this
tiny glimpse into something so personal, the best
part of this woman he admired so much.

Not until this moment did he realize that while
Dora Hoag might be living the life his mother had
never realized, it was not by her own choosing.

That changed everything—save for the fact that
he still couldn't pull off any of this without someone's help. Dora's help. But now instead of wheel-
ing and dealing to get it, he knew he had to win her

over, make her want to do it as much as he wanted her to do it.

Without giving her any warning, he stood and held his open hand toward her. "Let's get out of here."

She looked at his outstretched palm then at the door. "You go first."

"Stop playing games, Dora."

"At the risk of sounding repetitive—you first."

"I don't play games." He dropped his hand.

"I know." She folded her arms again. "And you don't make a trip to tell someone something face-to-face that could easily be said on the phone or by email."

He acknowledged that with a dip of his head.

"So just say what you came here to say and then kindly get out," she said quite unkindly.

"You're right. I did come to tell you something. And ask you something. But first I have to show you." He reached into his inside coat pocket.

Her arms loosened slightly. Her shoulders lifted. "If you were any other man, I'd expect you to pull out a small velvet box after a statement like that."

"Small? Velvet?" His fingers curled shut inside his coat. "Oh!"

She tilted her head and gave him a smile that was light but a bit sad. "I don't play games, either."

"I'll say you don't." He shook his head. She'd gotten him. He'd come here thinking he knew what he was walking into and how to maintain control of it and she'd gotten him. To his surprise, he didn't mind. In fact, he kind of liked it. He liked this feisty side of her. "But you sure do a have an overactive imagination, lady."

"Overactive? Because I once thought of you as a man of his word?"

Suddenly he liked that feistiness a little less. "Hey, let's not go there, Dora."

"Where else would you like to go, Burke? You seem to be up for a lot of travel all of a sudden. Coming here. Wanting me to go someplace with you. Maybe we should add a little trip down memory lane to your itinerary."

"Memory lane?" He smirked.

"What?" Lines formed in her usually smooth forehead. She pursed her lips and waited for him to say more.

"Just a pretty old-fashioned term, don't you think? I'd have gone for a play on time travel." He was trying to lighten the mood.

She wasn't having any part of it. "I was raised in a pretty old-fashioned home by my great-aunt and uncle. It's the way they talked, I guess. It's not so unusual. You knew the meaning."

The meaning he knew. The tidbit about her upbringing he hadn't known. Did it make any difference? Probably not to his plan, but it did explain a few things about her outlook on the world and the world's outlook on her. Nobody got her, not really. Nobody knew her.

Try as he could to stop it, Burke found that she was bringing out the protective nature of his Top Dawg personality again. To keep from caving into that or allowing her to rehash how badly he had handled things between them last summer, he stepped forward. He pulled the business card he had gone to retrieve from the Crumble out of his pocket. He gazed at the off-white rectangle with raised black lettering atop brightly colored shapes for only a moment before he handed it to her.

"What's that?"

"That's where I want to take you."

"To a doctor's office?"

"A pediatrician's office."

"Why?"

He moved to the doorway. "Come with me and I'll explain everything."

She did not budge. "So far, you haven't explained anything. You haven't answered a single one of my questions. Why should I let you show me this place?"

"Showing is simple." He held out his hand again. "Answers are complicated."

She ignored his gesture and raised one arched, dark eyebrow. "Then uncomplicate them."

Uncomplicate a lifetime of mischief, hope, happiness, tough choices and intricate clandestine arrangements? Couldn't be done.

*Rattle. Squeak. Rattle.*

Zach and his cleaning cart went wobbling by the open door.

Burke grinned. Maybe he couldn't just hand her the whys and wherefores of his situation, but if Dora wanted answers he could at least give her one. "You asked me who comes all the way from South Carolina to Atlanta to ask someone what they want for Christmas. It's not so hard to figure out, really, if you think about it."

Zach's raspy voice rang out in a Christmas carol about Santa Claus.

Dora frowned.

Burke jerked his head toward the open door. "Go ahead. Say it. You know you want to. Who makes a trip to ask someone what they want for Christmas?"

"S-Santa Claus?" she whispered, as Zach rounded the corner and his song faded.

Burke gave a small nod of his head, then looked up to catch her eye and winked. "That's me. And if there is going to be Christmas in Mt. Knott this year, I am going to need your help."

## *Chapter Four*

"Okay, we've been driving for fifteen minutes."
Dora glanced out the window of his shiny silver
truck. Her, tooling around Atlanta in a pick up with
a South Carolina snack cake cowboy Santa-wannabe
at the wheel—listening to country music's finest,
crooning Christmas carols on the radio. What happened to her policy of not trusting anyone, especially
anyone named Burdett, again? What happened to her
plan of ditching Christmas again this year by making herself scarce before sundown? What happened
to this place that Burke had promised to show her,
the one that would give her a reason to forgo the not
trusting and the ditching and make her want to…

The lyrics to a song she'd heard moments before—
"I Saw Mommy Kissing Santa Claus"—popped into
her head. Burke Burdett? *Santa?* Difficult to imagine. Kissing him? Hardly the kind of thing a seri-

ous businesswoman, an angry almost-girlfriend or a woman of good Christian character ought to be dwelling on! She stole a peek at his rugged profile and noted the way he seemed to fill up the cab of the truck and yet still leave a place for her to sit comfortably beside him.

"Burke?"

"Hmm?" He didn't look at her and yet the casualness of his reply gave her a sense of familiarity no quick cast-off glance in a truck cab ever could.

She flexed her fingers on the padded car door handle and forced herself to study their surroundings as she counted off their recent itinerary. "I've seen the art gallery where some lady from Mt. Knott had her first show. The jeweler's where your mother used to have special ornaments engraved. And the building of the accounting firm that employs the valedictorian of your graduating class."

She hoped she hadn't missed anything. He'd told her it would all make sense in time so, ever the bright, obedient girl, she had tried to make mental notes as they drove along.

"Yeah?" He seemed engrossed in reading the street signs.

If he didn't know where they were going then why had he brought her along? And why had she come? She squeezed her eyes shut to put her thoughts back on track.

She crossed her arms and tipped up her chin. "So

far you haven't really shown me anything that supports your claim of needing me to help you play the jolly fat guy."

"Hey." He tapped the brake lightly and stole a sly, amused glimpse her way at last. "Is that any way to talk to Santa?"

"*You* are not Santa."

"Maybe not," he conceded, with an expression that was neither jeering nor jovial but somewhere in between. Then he made a sharp turn, and used the momentum of their shifting center of gravity to lean over and whisper, just beside her ear, "But I'm on his team."

"Oh, right." She shivered at his nearness. "Team Santa. I suppose you have the T-shirt and matching ball cap?"

"No can do. Team Santa is strictly a hush-hush kind of deal." He sat upright behind the wheel again and fixed his eyes straight ahead. "Not that I would look devastatingly cute in said hat and shirt."

He would. He'd be downright adorable, with his suntanned skin and deep set eyes that twinkled when he knew he had the best of a person in a given situation—and Burke always had the best of everyone in any situation. He knew it and so did she.

She couldn't take her eyes off him now. So strong, so confident, so manly but with just a hint of boyish excitement over this odd adventure he insisted on dragging her into. This was the Burke she had known last summer. The one she had wanted so much to give her heart to, right up until his last quick, cutting phone call when he'd ended their professional and, by extension, personal relationship based on the results of the family meeting. Correction: the Carolina Crumble Pattie board of directors meeting, a board made up of the members of the Burdett family. This Burke and the man who had torn her dreams to shreds with a soft-spoken and deceptively simple, "nothing personal, just business," seemed to be two entirely different people.

A man like that…he was not to be trusted.

That reminder made it easier for her to sit back and create a little verbal distance. "I suppose next you will try to tell me that you're an elf?"

"Why do you think I let my hair get this shaggy?" He tapped the side of his head. "To hide my pointed little ears."

"Really?" She did not look his way. "I thought you let your hair grow out for the same reason I keep mine short."

"Because it makes you look like a little girl all dressed up in grown-up clothes?"

"No." She crinkled up her nose at his way-off-base guess. "Because…um, does it?"

She put her hand to the back of her head. If anyone else on earth had said that she'd have given them what for, but coming from Burke, it had a sweetness that took her by surprise. She had always suspected that he could see the young Dora, the frightened, lonely and longing-to-belong child who lurked just beneath her polished surface. The notion warmed her heart. And chilled her to the core.

"That's not…that is…the point is, we both keep our hair the length we do for the same reason."

"I hope not. My hair is long but I hope not long enough to make me look like a little girl!"

"I like your hair." It wasn't all that long, really, just grown out enough to add to the overall appeal of this man who was rough-hewn, unfettered by convention and free from any kind of vanity or fussiness.

"Do you?" he asked softly.

"Yeah," she said, more softly. Almost childlike, almost flirty. The CD had stopped playing a few minutes earlier and she didn't have to compete with sleigh bells and steel guitars to be heard.

He looked into her eyes for only a moment before he squared his broad shoulders and stuck out his chest. "Then I guess I'll cancel my regular appointment with the barber."

"You don't keep any regular appointments with a barber, Burke. Just like I never *miss* mine." She sat in the truck with posture so perfect that only the small of her back made contact with the upholstery. "I wear my hair short for the same reason you don't bother to keep yours trimmed. I'm too busy with my work to bother with upkeep and style."

He did not dispute that, just turned the wheel and

took them down a quiet residential street in a part of town Dora had never seen before.

They fell silent.

The air went still around them.

Dora should have let it go. Let him make the next move, the next comment. He had brought her here to prove something, after all. She didn't need to ramble on, cajoling and teasing and then retreating, hoping he would follow. That phase between them had passed. Now it really was just business.

*Nothing personal. Just business.*

No, not even business.

Once he had shown her the last of these places—he seemed to think they would add up to something that would somehow affect her—and shared this story of his, she'd probably never see him again. If she were smart she'd just keep her mouth zipped and wait it out until he dropped her off back at her office building.

"So if your hair hides your ears then I guess you wear that cowboy hat of yours all the time to hide your pointed little head?" So much for keeping her mouth shut.

"Elves don't have pointed heads." He frowned. Actually *frowned* as if he had to think that over and make the point quite clear.

She gulped in a breath so she could launch into an explanation that she had meant it as a joke.

He beat her to it by adding, with a wink, "It's just our pointy little hats make it look that way."

She laughed at the very idea of Burke in a pointed hat. "Someone sure is aiming to get on the naughty list."

"Aww, you haven't been that bad. Lots of people make cracks about elves and helpers and Santa's weight issues."

"I wasn't talking about me. I was talking about you, for fibbing about wearing a pointed hat."

"I'm not fibbing." He looked quite serious, but couldn't hold it and broke into a big grin. "And I have the photo to prove it."

"Then prove it."

"Uh, I, uh, I don't have the photo with me."

She shook her head. "For a second there, you almost had me believing you."

He went quiet then. Not silent, not still, but quiet with all the power, control and even reverence that implied. She could hear the tires on the road, the squeak of the seat cushions, the beating of their two battered hearts.

Her skin tingled. Her throat went dry.

For only a moment it was like that, then Burke turned to her, his intense, serious eyes framed by playful laugh lines as he whispered, "Believe me, Dora."

Oh, how she wanted to—to believe him about the

hat, his being Santa and, most of all, that he needed her in a way that he needed no one else in the world.

But life had taught her that those kinds of beliefs only led to disappointment. So she kept it light, played along. "You in an elf hat?"

His eyes twinkled. "With red and green stripes, a plump pom-pom and a brass jingle bell on the end."

"What are you going to tell me next?"

"That this is what I wanted you to see." He pulled into a parking lot, slid the truck into a space and cut the engine. "This is why I need you."

"To go to a pediatrician? What? You need me to hold your hand while the doctor holds your tongue down with a Popsicle stick and makes you say 'ahh'?" What was he trying to pull?

"No. Not to go to the doctor, to see what she's doing."

"What? Seeing patients?"

"On the Friday after Thanksgiving." He nodded, his gaze scanning the lot.

Dora took a moment to follow his line of vision. It did not take long for her to come to a conclusion. "This is some kind of clinic?"

"Every Friday, even holidays—except Christmas and when the Fourth of July falls on Friday." He watched as a little boy scurried ahead of a young woman carrying a baby and then held the door to the office open. "A clinic for people who have jobs but no insurance. Just the doc's way of giving back because once upon a time somebody did something nice for her."

"And what does that have to do with Santa Claus coming to Mt. Knott, South Carolina?"

He hesitated a moment, gripping then repositioning his large, lean hands on the steering wheel. He started to speak, held back, then took a deep breath. Finally, he worked his broad shoulders around so that they pressed against the window and his upper body faced her. His brow furrowed. His eyes fixed on her then shifted toward the children. He kept his voice low as if he thought one of them might hear. "Do you know the story of the first Santa, the real Saint Nicholas?"

She kept her backbone pressed to the seat and her cool gaze on the man. "I think the real question here is, do you know how to answer a question directly when it's put to you?"

"Humor me," he said with grim sobriety just before he broke into a crooked grin.

It was the grin that got her. She sighed. "The real Saint Nicholas? Hmm. Turkish? Skinny fellow, too, not the bowlful of jelly Clement Moore described. Or the ho-ho-hokey, soda pop–swilling, round-cheeked invention of American advertising."

"Right. The Bishop of Turkey. He surreptitiously gave bags of gold to girls who otherwise would not have had a dowry so they wouldn't be pressed into servitude or prostitution."

Now she moved around in the seat, impressed. Suspicious but definitely impressed. "You said that like a kid reading off a plaque in a museum."

"Close. Only the museum is my mom's office in the attic of our family home, and the plaque is a caption under an old print from a book she has framed there."

"Really?"

"Really."

"I'd like...".*...to see it someday.* The rest of the sentence went unfinished. She had no business inviting herself, not only into the home where Burke had grown up, but into his late mother's office. "I'd like to know how that relates to this pediatrician's office in Atlanta?"

"Easy. The original saint gave money to girls in order to give them the power to make better lives for themselves, and by extension better lives for their families and their communities."

"And this doctor is doing the same?"

"Because?"

"Because she..." Dora looked at the office once again. On the sign with the doctor's name was the symbol of a gold coin with a wreath encircling a Christmas stocking. "Because once upon a time that doctor got a visit from Saint Nick?"

"Who is?"

"You."

"My mom." His gaze dropped for a moment and

the grief seemed so real and still so fresh in him that Dora did not know how to respond. She didn't have the chance, as he quickly recovered and met her gaze with his sad and solemn eyes. "From the time she decided to stay in Mt. Knott and raise a family instead of traveling the world, my mother gave out grants and scholarships to deserving girls and young women who otherwise would not have had the opportunity to make better lives for themselves."

"Wow. She paid for their college?"

"She helped. And not just college. Private high schools. Vocational training. Trips. Conferences. Art supplies."

"Art…oh, art supplies. So the artist, the jeweler, the accountant were all…"

"Just the artist and accountant. The jeweler is where she has the gold medallions engraved that she gave the recipients to let them know they were chosen."

"She didn't present them in some kind of ceremony?"

"She kept it quiet. The jeweler sent them from here so no one would ever know who they came from."

"People suspected the Burdetts, though. They'd have to."

"If they did, no one ever said."

Dora studied the coin with new eyes and understanding. "There's writing around the edge."

"'We give to others because God first gave Christ to us,'" he said, without even looking at the sign or the coin he had just quoted.

"And no one knows about your mother's good works? Really?"

"Only the accountant who manages the financial side of things, me and now you."

"Not even your brothers? Or your dad?"

"It's a secret Mom entrusted with me alone on her deathbed."

"Oh, Burke." She reached out to touch his face, to lend support and comfort.

"But me alone? I don't think I'm up for the job."

*Job. Only business.* She curled her fingers closed and put her fist to her chest.

"That's why I need your help. I need someone who isn't from Mt. Knott to help me pull this off. Because as a Burdett I can't do anything in Mt. Knott in secret."

"Including taking me out there to manage this for you," she reminded him, switching swiftly into organizational problem-solving mode. "How would you ever explain that?"

"Oh. Yeah." He scowled. "Unless…"

"Yes?" She needed him to come up with this solution, not because she didn't have one to offer, but because it was his project. She had no intention of investing in it emotionally or even mentally unless he could find a way to win her over to it. Which meant she wasn't getting involved.

"Well, you were out there all last summer and no one questioned that."

"I was in negotiations to buy into your business then." She folded her arms and clamped them down tight. "I don't suppose you want to revisit that?"

"There's a lot about last summer I'd like to revisit."

And a lot of memories she wanted to send packing. She shut her eyes. "Burke, I…"

"Just come out and stay at the family compound, Dora."

"What?"

"We won't have to say why you're there. People probably wouldn't believe anything we told them anyway."

"I can't just leave work." It was the first thing that came to her mind. Not a lie or a means of deceiving him but just a gut reaction, telling the man the kind of thing he'd expect her to say.

The crooked grin returned. He shook his head slowly. "You save up all your vacation time all year and take it in December."

"How did you know that? Did Zach tell you?"

"Who?"

"Zach, the…" The closet thing she had to an old friend. She sighed. "Never mind. Just tell me how you knew that."

"Because you told me."

"I did?"

"One night when we talked about the future. You said if you ever got married you'd want it to be in December."

Her cheeks grew hot. She found it hard to swallow. Marriage? The future? She remembered that night, but not the things they had said—just the way it felt to be near Burke, to sit out on the porch beneath a blanket of stars. Had she really let her guard down so completely? "Was I under the influence of Carolina Crumble Patties?"

"Maybe."

"Sugary foods get to me, you know. Make me say things I don't necessarily mean." As did certain men.

"You meant this."

"You said a lot of things I thought you meant, Burke."

He did not say a word in his own defense.

He couldn't, she realized. And just that quickly she also understood that she could not help him, even with this worthy cause. She could not allow herself to be that vulnerable again, especially not at Christmas.

She looked out at the doctor's office building again. "Just because I don't go into my office most of December doesn't mean I don't have things to do."

"Yeah. Right." He nodded, his eyes downcast. "Everybody has things to do. We live in a busy, busy world. So busy doing the things we have to do we often let go of the things we should do."

That stung. It was true of course, which was probably *why* it stung. "Burke, I—"

"Oh, I don't mean you specifically, Dora." He looked at her, then at the pediatrician's sign, his face stormy with emotion. "Over the years my mom has given out a lot of time and money, and none of those people have ever tried to find out who their benefactor was so they could offer support."

"But this is good," she held her hand out to indicate the clinic taking place right before their eyes.

"Yeah, this is good, but I can't help thinking."

"What?"

"We have kids in Mt. Knott, too."

"What?"

"Everyone always says, why doesn't the Crumble factory do more? Why don't the Burdetts help out the town more? But how many of them ask, what more can I do?"

"I'm not from Mt. Knott," she felt compelled to remind him. She did not owe the town or its inhabitants anything. But then, who was she indebted to? Beyond her aunt and uncle and the unseen powers-that-be at Global? No one. No one needed her on a personal level.

"People don't seem to see that every doctor who goes someplace else to practice, every young person who goes off to college and never comes home, every citizen who gets his gas, does the grocery shopping or sets up business outside of Mt. Knott takes something vital away from the community. The Crumble and the Burdetts can't counteract all that."

"I know."

"We shouldn't have to try."

"I know."

"I just keep thinking that at some point somebody is going to step up."

"That's why you keep the Santa gifts a secret, isn't it?"

"Huh?"

"You're a big softie, admit it."

"Well, thank you for that much."

"But you could put some stipulations on the gifts. Say the recipients have to give something back to Mt. Knott, serve the town a certain amount of time."

"I couldn't do that. Mom never did and I want to carry on her tradition."

"Tradition shcmadition. You do it because you have faith."

"I'm a man of faith, yes, but—"

"Faith in your fellow man. And woman, for that matter."

"I don't know what you mean."

"'We give to others because God first gave Christ to us.'" She read the words from the coin on the sign. "You want to keep this all a big secret because you are hoping that one day one of these girls who are gifted will turn around and do the right thing and give back to the town because they want to, not because they have to."

He didn't deny it but he didn't jump on her claim and praise her for seeing right into his thought process, either.

"Or, at the very least, that the town's people, knowing somebody among them has done these good things, will want to do something for the town, too."

"Is that a crazy thing to hope for?"

"That you hope to inspire people and make it easier for them to give to others?" It was all she had ever wanted. And the very thing she had worked so hard to keep herself from doing. Until now. "No, I think it's wonderful, especially at Christmastime."

"I can't do it alone."

"You don't have to, Burke."

"You mean?"

"I hope you saved that hat you said you had." She could not believe she was saying this but…well, she had known he would have to sell her on the idea to get her to join in. She also knew that the best sales were made by a person who truly believed in what he was selling. Burke, in his own raggedy, begrudging way, believed in Christmas and in his mother's dream. It was within Dora's power to help him realize that dream—a gift only she could give him. How could she refuse? "I may have to borrow it if I plan on becoming this year's Santa's helper."

# Chapter Five

Monday was soon enough to get started. Too soon, really, for Burke's tastes. Yet, by his mother's standards, they were already eleven months behind schedule. For her, the undertaking she called the Forgotten Stocking Project was not a special holiday event but a year-round commitment.

If he had let Dora have her way they would have gone to work the day she accepted the position as his assistant. Why not? It's not like she had a bunch of family hovering around for the weekend wondering why she wasn't there diving into the leftovers with the rest of them. Or asking a lot of questions that they considered to show concern but really hinted that she needed to be doing something different with her life.

So, when will you be bringing someone special home for the holidays?

Don't you get lonely in that big house all by yourself?

Now that you aren't working at the Crumble practically twenty-four/seven why don't you start something new? Like, say a family of your own?

He didn't know whether to pity Dora or envy her for not having to endure that. He looked around at the people gathered in Josie's Home Cookin' Kitchen, at the people he had known most of his life chatting with friends and loved ones, then at his sister-in-law, *the* Josie of the Home Cookin' in the restaurant's name, and decided, in his grudging curmudgeonly way, that he did not envy Dora. Pity might have gone too far, but he did wish that Dora didn't seem so very alone in this world.

She'd mentioned her father. Gone off to find himself when she was still quite young. He wondered why with all her resources she hadn't tried to locate him.

She had probably weighed the risks against the potential gains and had come to the most practical conclusion. Dora was first and foremost a businesswoman, after all. Right?

Of all the people who knew Dora Hoag, Burke suspected he above all knew better than that. Dora was so much more than a businesswoman. She was the child she had been and the friend she could be, a good listener, smart, funny, a thoughtful Christian and a…a woman.

Dora was a woman, with all the faults and every fine quality that came with being one. But she had no person to share her joy with and no trusted friend to lean on when things did not go well.

Except she did. She had both, in him. Only maybe she didn't see it that way.

Burke settled onto a stool at the counter. He pulled out a menu, even though he'd had breakfast a few hours earlier and it wasn't quite time for lunch. He'd arrived only a few minutes before the hour he and Dora had agreed to meet. He'd planned that so he wouldn't have time for a lot of chitchat with the patrons, but it also meant he wouldn't have time for a piece of pie. If Dora would be anything—and to his way of thinking, Dora Hoag could be many, many things—she would be prompt.

"Coffee?" Josie lifted up a sturdy white cup turned upside down on a matching saucer.

Burke watched her, thinking how blessed his brother Adam was to have found someone like Josie.

"Sure." He nodded then slid the menu back in place, glad not to have to order something as a cover for hanging around the place. "Surprised to see you here today."

"Why?" Josie paused, his coffee cup still in her hand, to take money from a customer.

Ching. The cash register rang out. Its drawer popped open.

Josie tucked the exact change away then thanked the customer with a radiant smile and a soft word.

Burke squinted as he tried to figure her out. "Thought you'd given up all this to be a full-time mom."

"A *what?*"

"A, uh, a full-time mom?" Burke usually didn't have that much trouble making himself heard or understood.

"That's what I thought you said." *Whomp.* She sent the cash drawer slamming shut with a swing of her hip.

"Uh-oh," Warren, one of two older fellows who occupied the stools at the diner almost every morning of the week, ducked his head.

Burke sat perfectly still, unsure what was headed his way.

"Burke Burdett!" Josie set the cup down firmly enough to make it clatter against the saucer. "Every mother is a full-time mother!"

With a flare of authority that made it clear she thought she had given the final answer on that, Josie spun around and nabbed the coffeepot.

He frowned. He should have let it go. He'd said what he'd said, she'd said what she said and…and she'd gotten the last word. Being Top Dawg, he just couldn't drop that bone. "I thought some of them were working mothers."

"What?" Josie held the coffeepot back as if she

had half a mind not to serve him at all after that remark.

"Oooh. Should have just said 'yes ma'am' and quit while you was ahead," muttered Jed, Warren's cohort in café commentary. "You ain't getting no pie, after a remark like that, no sir."

"Yup. That boy's definitely going on the no-pie list," Warren confirmed, his head shaking forlornly.

"I mean, uh, *every* mother is a working mother?" Burke tried to slip back into his sister-in-law's favor by saying what he thought she wanted to hear. What did he know about this motherhood business, anyway? He'd always sort of thought that he'd raised himself, looked after himself. He hadn't really needed his mom for much. What was the big deal?

"That's better." Josie exhaled and took a second to regain her composure.

"Whew." Burke pretended to wipe his brow for the benefit of Jed and Warren, his counter-mates.

They chuckled.

"And I'm down here today because the place still has my name on it and I intend to keep a hand in running it. Also, I had to come to oversee the end-of-the-month paperwork." Josie approached the counter again. "Your turn."

"Huh?" Burke dragged the saucer and cup closer in front of him on the counter and flipped the cup over.

"I could say the same about being surprised to

see you here." Josie held the pot up. The dark brew sloshed, sending its warm, rich aroma wafting his way. "The way you took off the day after Thanksgiving we all half expected not to see or hear from you again until we got a postcard from you halfway around the world."

"Saying I'd joined some far-off army rather than spend the coming holidays with y'all?" He chuckled, though now that he thought of it maybe that wasn't a bad alternative, once this whole Santa mess got worked out.

"That's what the guys thought. The girls…" She dipped her head and the curls of her ponytail fell over her shoulder as if every part of her had to move in close to get in on this tidbit. "The girls thought maybe it would say you'd run off and eloped and were on an extended honeymoon."

He jerked his head up to meet her gaze. "Married? I don't even have a girlfriend."

"You don't have to have a girlfriend to get married, Burke." Josie laughed. "No one ever thought of me as Adam's girlfriend. I was his baby's adoptive mother, then I was a thorn in his paw, the next thing anyone knew, I was his wife."

Wife? Burke winced. Had he given anyone reason to think that he and…the one woman on the planet he had allowed to become the thorn in his paw…had ever considered…

"Who is getting married?" Warren wanted to know.

"Why do you care, you old coot? Ain't like they plan to invite you along on that fancy honeymoon." Jed gave his companion a nudge in the shoulder. "Way I hear it your wife wasn't too keen on you tagging along on your own honeymoon."

Jed laughed.

Warren joined in, grumbling something that sounded partly like a complaint about his friend's sense of humor and just a little bit like agreement with his assessment.

Burke tensed. He'd spent so much time with his head buried in the business of late that he had forgotten how easily gossip got started in this town.

Gossip? About his supersecret project involving his mother's dying wish and his…his…Dora?

Josie had already gone all demure and amused, looking down as if the task of pouring coffee, something she did a hundred times a day, required her utmost attention. She lifted the pot.

"On second thought…" Burke stuck his hand over the cup.

Too late.

Josie pulled up but not before a stream of steaming hot liquid splashed over his knuckles.

"I'm so sorry." Josie winced.

He yanked his hand away and, knowing every eye and, more importantly, ear in the place had suddenly fixed on him, gritted his teeth and merely said, "My fault."

He slid from the stool and wiped his hand on a paper napkin from the dispenser on the counter.

"Come back into the kitchen and run that under some cool water." She motioned toward the open door a few steps behind her.

"No, I'm not staying." He wadded the napkin up and, realizing the large trash bin was across the room, stuffed it into his pocket rather than prolong his time there. "I can't stay."

What a bad idea to meet Dora here. He had to get out before she came strolling through that door and fueled who knew how many rumors, spreading from this point like wheel spokes in every direction, to every home and family and inquiring mind in Mt. Knott. Ex-business partner, thorn in his paw, soon to be wife. The town would have them married before they finished their Christmas shopping!

He checked his watch. She was already a few minutes late. Not like Dora. He didn't have any time to...

"Sorry, I'm late." Dora stood in the open front door with a space-aged looking gizmo attached to one ear, her hair an uncharacteristic mess. Fresh but still formidable. Without her power pumps to give her height or her tailored business suit to give her substance, she looked like a cross between a waif arriving at the gates of an infamous orphanage and one of those bright-eyed girls with big dreams getting off the bus in the big city. She wore a black fuzzy sweater, a single strand of pearls, some black-and-white checked pants and black shoes. With bows.

It was the bows that got to Burke. He didn't think he'd ever before seen her wear anything so out of character and yet so perfect.

She clutched her expensive leather briefcase to her chest, blinked those big, brown eyes and blew away a piece of straw that had tangled in the soft curl of black hair alongside her cheek. "I'd blame traffic but, well, is getting behind a slow-moving tractor hauling hay considered traffic around here?"

"Dora?" Josie, still standing close to the kitchen door, cocked her head. "*Dora Hoag?* Talk about being surprised to see somebody in here!"

A murmur moved through the room.

It had the effect of a bucket of cold water on Burke's head—a most unpleasant wake-up call but one that got the job done and quick.

Think fast, Burke warned himself. No. Act fast. That's what this situation called for. To act fast, talk fast and think about what he had done later.

"Yeah! What a surprise to see you come walking through that door today at, uh…" Another glance at his watch. "…Ten minutes after ten in the morning."

"What? Did we get our wires crossed? Is this the wrong day? Wrong place? Wrong…what's wrong, Burke?" Dora spoke softly as though he were the only person in the room.

He liked that feeling.

Liked it a lot.

Too much.

He cleared his throat and took her by the upper arm, turning to, in essence, present her to the room and to emphasize to her that they were not alone. Then he leaned down and whispered for her ears only, "Play along, please."

"Play? Burke, what's going on?" she managed to ask, barely moving her lips.

Cool trick but not one a bulldog of a man like him, accustomed to barking out orders meant to be heard and carried out, could pull off. So he faked a cough and used his fist to hide his mouth as he said, "For the sake of secrecy. We can't be seen planning in a public place like this."

"No lies," she commanded, under the cover of slapping him on the back in a show of helping him with his sudden coughing fit.

Slapped him a bit harder than the pretense called for, he thought, but then maybe she felt she deserved the indulgence for the way his family had treated her. The way he had treated her. The way he was treating her right now.

"Okay, no lies." Even though lying would have been the easiest way to go. But it was Christmas and he was supposed to be a better man this time of year, right? "Not that I make lying a way of life, you know."

She shot him a look that suggested she did not know that.

It hurt but he understood her position.

"So, what are you doing in town?" Josie had made her way around the counter now and had her hand out to Dora, the woman who had been her husband's boss at Global not so long ago.

"Me? I, um, I have some time off," Dora blurted out.

"So you invited her here for the holidays?" Josie took Dora's hand but her eyes focused on Burke.

"No!" That was the truth. He fully expected Dora to be gone before the holidays rolled around. Once she'd finished her part in the vetting and selection process, he expected her to hightail it out of town to leave him, the town and his nosy, matchmaking family to tolerate, um, *celebrate* Christmas as usual.

He glanced down at Dora.

Usual? How could he carry on as usual knowing she was alone in the world during the season when so many, like it or not, came together with their loved ones?

"That is, I didn't invite her to spend the holidays with us but—"

"He told me about Mt. Knott this time of year and I wanted to come and see it for myself." Dora released Josie's hand then looked up into Burke's eyes, her expression reassuring him that she would not insinuate herself on him or his family. "I came of my own volition. I'll only stay as long as I feel welcome."

Burke felt like a jerk. Probably because he was one, from the way he had roped her into helping him, to the way he was treating her this moment. Then and there he vowed he would do something to make it up to her. Somehow. Someday.

"Well, as far as I'm concerned you are welcome to stay the whole season." Josie beamed. "Ring in the New Year with us, if you like."

"The New Year?" Burke scowled. Jerk or not he had no intention of having Dora Hoag all but move into this town—this very small, very up-in-everybody's-business town.

"Oh, I plan to be back at work the day after Christmas. I always am," she said, before Burke had the chance to say something awful that would hurt or embarrass her. "Like I said, I just came for, well, because Burke had said…it just seemed right to, well, you know. You all know your little town better than I do, surely you understand why I came."

*Get the other guy to tell you his strengths and in doing so, you will discover where you need to be stronger.* Burke recognized that Dora had the finely honed people-assessing skills of a seasoned CEO or sales executive. If the folks around them asserted that she had surely come here for the fresh air, she'd need to make sure they saw her soaking up plenty of it. If they discerned she must be trying to buy out the Burdetts again, then by simply spending time around the Crumble every day she would fuel that rumor and throw everyone off the scent of her real objective. And if anyone guessed the real reason? Ha! Who in this town would guess she had come to Mt. Knott to play Santa's helper?

It was an old negotiating technique that Dora had, after a few false starts, fallen back on. She was clever, he'd give her that. And sharp witted. And—

He gazed down at her, smiling right at the two men sitting at the counter even as her knuckles went white on the handle of her briefcase.

And adorable. Dora was adorable.

"So?" she prodded. "Y'all know why I'm here, right?"

Another murmur went through the room.

Josie frowned.

A woman in a booth started to say something then thought better of it and shook her head.

Finally Warren sputtered in disgust, "Oh, c'mon, y'all," and slapped his leg. "Ain't it obvious? She come to participate in our fabulous downtown hoedown, all around, by the pound, glory bound.... Stop me, Jed, I can't seem to get to the end of this thing!"

"You got the name wrong, you old goat." Jed nudged his friend to show he'd have none of his tomfoolery. "It's Homemade Holidays Down on the Homefront."

"Down Home Holidays Downtown," Josie jumped

in to correct them both. Then she turned to Dora. "We thought, to generate some interest in people coming into town to eat and shop, we'd have a big kick-off celebration with a parade, street vendors and that evening a lighting ceremony and sing-along and maybe carriage rides through the street."

"That's what she's talking about," Jed proclaimed. "That's what she came for. Couldn't be nothing else, could it, Top Dawg?"

Burke cleared his throat. No lies. This did give them a position of strength. A reason for Dora to hang around. And he wanted her to hang around. For the work. Again he cleared his throat then nodded in her direction. "You really should stay. Give you a feel for the place like nothing else could."

Everyone looked at Dora as if her approval could make or break the whole event.

"I'd love to," Dora said, her eyes bright and her whole demeanor so light that Burke wanted to glance down to see if her feet had lifted off the ground.

"Great!" Josie approached as though she suddenly felt Dora were her personal guest. "Do you have a room at the motel or would you like to come out to the compound?"

*The compound?* Burke had asked her here to get a feel for the town, not to move in on his home turf. He frowned at her and maybe even shook his head, she wasn't sure.

Dora's shoulders slumped slightly, he thought,

then rebounded and her standard straight arrow all-business poise returned.

"You didn't let me finish," she said. "I'd love to attend your Down Home Holidays Downtown."

She got it exactly right after hearing it only once. She would, of course, but it still impressed Burke and reminded him why she was the perfect person for the job.

"But I can't really stay around Mt. Knott indefinitely."

"Well, there's nothing indefinite about this, young lady," Jed noted.

"It's tomorrow night." Josie took her by the arm and began to lead her farther into the restaurant.

"A Tuesday?" Dora followed, her feet dragging slightly.

"No other time for it." Warren swung around to face the counter again.

"The Chamber of Commerce thought having it before Thanksgiving was rushing things a bit." Josie pointed to a seat at the counter for Dora.

Dora looked at Burke.

He smiled, though he suspected it wasn't a warm smile. If she wanted more, like some kind of affirmation that this was all a great idea, she wouldn't find it from him. Burke knew very little about any of this, seeing as he no longer played a role in the Chamber of Commerce, or in much of anything these days. He clenched his fingers and his jaw tightened at the reminder of all he had lost—all he no longer had to offer.

"And this past weekend, with people traveling to be with family and all, no sense in holding it then." Josie pulled a piece of green paper from beside the cash register and handed it to Dora.

"Not to mention that most any given Saturday half the town empties out, people heading elsewhere for shopping and entertainment and such." Jed stretched his neck out to peer over Dora's shoulder at the flyer with all the information about the event printed on it.

"Sunday is the Lord's day. Monday is get-back-to-work-and-already-realize-you're-a-day-behind day." Josie hurried to fetch another saucer and coffee cup. "Wednesday it's back to church for the goodly lot of us."

"Shouldn't that be the Godly lot of us?" Warren pondered aloud.

"Thursday's middle school football—we're in the play-offs." Josie set the saucer down and flipped the cup deftly. She nabbed the coffeepot and held it up to ask silently if Dora wanted any.

Dora nodded.

Josie poured. "Friday—high school football. That's an all-day and way into the night deal, what with pep rallies before and bonfires after."

"Then there we are back at Saturday and the great exodus." Jed nudged his own cup forward as if it were a reluctant volunteer that needed coaxing to step up and claim its refill.

"So Tuesday really was the only practical time to have it." Josie filled the cups, one right after another, with all the precision of a machine at the Crumble factory and a lot more grace and goodwill. She also saw to it that Jed and Warren each got another slice of pie, something no machine, or expense-conscious businesswoman, would ever have done.

"I see. Yes. I am interested in this." Dora waved the paper around in a way that made Burke think that if it had been on white paper instead of green it would have looked like she intended to signal her complete surrender to the persistent and wonderful citizens of his hometown.

That thought made his hand freeze with his steaming cup of java halfway to his lips. Dora giving in to Mt. Knott? He never considered a thing like that could happen, but seeing her like this, all sweet expressions and hay in her hair, laughing at Jed and Warren's cornpone jokes?

"You know, if Ms. Hoag says she can't stay until the big event tomorrow night, we should probably just—"

"Do you suppose they have a vacancy at the hotel where I stayed last summer?" Dora pressed her lips tight and those big eyes of her went flinty and fixed on Burke's face. She crossed her arms and tipped her sweet, slightly pointed chin up.

He supposed that look had scared many a brave man, but it just made Burke want to grin. The woman had fire in her, he had to admit that.

"Then you'll stay for it." Josie clapped her hands.

But Burke had been burned too often and much too recently to dare to play with fire. "I'm sure Ms. Hoag is much too busy to…."

"I wasn't asking, Burke, I was insisting." And just that quickly Josie had Dora by the arm again, this time guiding her to the best booth in the place.

A booth. Not a seat at the counter. A seat at the counter said you were in a hurry, either that or you were Jed or Warren. But a booth? A booth said you were settling in for a spell.

Burke watched the women, then realized that everyone else was watching him watch them. Some curious, the rest sort of smug about seeing him overruled by his own sister-in-law.

Jed and Warren grinned.

"You are in big trouble now, boy," Jed muttered, swiveling around to go back to eating his pie.

"Half the town already got you married to that gal in their minds." Warren shook his head.

Burke knew they were right. Dora had walked in here a woman alone in the world and less than an hour later she was practically his fiancée. Only he didn't have a fiancée and wasn't looking for one.

This, he thought, mostly to himself but also a little bit as a plea for help to the Lord of all creation, this could be a problem.

## Chapter Six

Dora's head was spinning. She couldn't figure this guy out. First, he hadn't wanted her to stay for Mt. Knott's Christmas kickoff. He'd asked her to come here but now he did not want her to stay. Why?

Dora glanced over her shoulder at the man standing with one hand on the lunch counter and the other raised to his forehead. A strand of blond hair fell across his knuckles, and he shook it off.

Jed or Warren—even though she'd spent many hours in this place last summer, Dora never had gotten straight which one was which—said something. Both men laughed. Burke's expression turned icy.

Dora plunked down in the seat and cradled her coffee in both hands, though that did nothing to warm the chill she felt coming from Burke's blue eyes.

The man, Jed or Warren, had probably said something personal. Burke did not do personal.

But Mt. Knott and its residents? Nothing but personal. Too personal.

And personable.

They had taken Dora in today as if she had never left after last summer. They treated her like one of their very own. An old friend. No different from anyone, not even the town's Top Dawg.

To be treated like one of the crowd had to drive a man like Burke, a man who defined himself by his position, his accomplishments, crazy.

Dora smiled to herself. Mt. Knott might drive Burke crazy but she was just crazy about the place, and the people. She couldn't think of a nicer, warmer, sweeter place to be during the Christmas season, and she looked forward to the townwide event tomorrow night.

No, Burke did not want her here at all but here she was. She sighed.

She put her shoulders back against the seat and drew in a deep breath, savoring the familiar smell of Josie's hearty fare.

Dora had eaten lunch at Josie's Home Cookin' Kitchen almost every day last summer. Sometimes dinner. Now and again breakfast. And coffee. Lots and lots of coffee at all hours of the day and night while she and Adam Burdett and Burke had pored over the details of the business, discussing what they should do, what they could do and what they would never want to do with it.

The thing they had never wanted to do was to let it slip out of family hands. Dora probably read too much into that, right up until the moment Burke had let her know she was never going to be a member of their family or their future business plans.

If it were possible, she felt even more unwanted by Burke now than she had sitting alone in her office on the day after Thanksgiving. What had she gotten herself into? And how did she get out?

She twisted around in the seat to look at the front door and the chalkboard wall caught her eye. Josie had painted almost an entire wall of the one-room restaurant with chalkboard paint to give the little ones something to occupy them while their parents visited with friends and ordered dessert.

Dora had to admire the younger woman's initiative and creativity. And, looking at how a portion of the wall had come to be used, she also had to admire Josie's heart. She'd allowed the townspeople to use the board to send messages, not just to each other, but in a special place sectioned off by vines and scrolled lettering, for prayer requests.

That section had been full last summer when many people had concerns about job security, the need for rain, the future of the Crumble. Dora fixed her gaze on the list now and shook her head.

The seasons had changed and, of course, the circumstances, but the things that people laid before the Lord varied little. Most people wanted the same things, after all, didn't they?

The sound of Burke's boots moving across the floor made her breath catch, but she kept on reading.

Prayers for health, well-being, peace of mind.

Prayers for prosperity.

Prayers for the people whom they loved.

People wanted to have a purpose, to have enough to sustain them in that purpose and to love and be loved.

That's all Dora wanted, when you boiled it all down. Same as the folks in Mt. Knott. Same as everyone, even those who thought they were above all that mushy stuff.

The footsteps stopped.

Dora swung her head around at last and looked up at the king of the mushy-stuff haters. She smiled, even as the promise of tears bathed her eyes. "I can see why you chose here to start on the proj—"

"Pie." Burke interrupted with a stiffly cheerful insistence. He shifted his eyes, reminding her that they did not have the privacy here they would have had in a café in Atlanta. "Yeah, Josie makes great pie. Mind if I join you and we order ourselves some?"

"Yes, I…"

"You mind?" He actually looked disappointed.

"I mean, yes, I'd like some pie, and no, I don't mind if you join me." She motioned to the bench across from her in the booth. "But aren't you worried you're keeping me, since you seem to think I'm so busy I can't stick around until tomorrow night?"

"Yeah, about that, Dora." He dropped into the seat. "No hard feelings."

"Of course not. Nothing personal. Just business."

"Exactly." He nodded slowly then slumped back in the seat as though a great weight had been lifted from his shoulders. His broad shoulders strained at the denim of his work shirt, shoulders that looked like they could carry the weight of the world as easily as lift a small child to see tomorrow's Christmas parade. "Just business. I'm glad you said it and not me."

*But you did say it!* Had he forgotten already? Dora would never forget last summer, his hushed, hoarse voice, the clipped formality of his words, even the way he paused between one phrase and the next. *Nothing personal...just business.*

As if—well, she had never quite figured out why he had done that. Probably weighing his words so that he wouldn't give her anything to throw back at him.

Just like now. He'd let her use it as a justification for his actions, and how could she ever deride him for it? But it still hurt.

She tried to convey the message with her eyes and with the tension in her body. With the silence she left hanging uncomfortably between them and finally by jabbing the toe of her shoe into his shin.

Which he did not even feel through his jeans and cowboy boots.

"As long as we're clear on that…." He jerked his chin up and looked toward the counter, searching.

"You thought I wasn't clear on that?" She batted her eyes, doling out a measure of unspoken sarcasm to go with her, well, big ol' dose of spoken sarcasm. Another message the big galoot did not pick up on.

"No, not you. I know you, Dora. You are all business."

Now there was a kick she couldn't ignore. She opened her mouth to protest that claim.

"Not…not all business." He made a face like a kid trying to fit together a complex model kit or do long division in his head. He brushed his hair back from where it touched the scar cutting across his darker blond eyebrow. "I know that. But as far as this business between us is concerned, you are. All business."

"Tell me once again about how you dazzle people with your charm?" She pursed her lips but couldn't hold it and broke into a subtle smile to let him know she was teasing.

He chuckled and caught Josie's attention and called out for two slices of her freshest pie.

"Going to take one out of the oven in a sec. Give it fifteen minutes to cool, and I'll have it right to you."

"Thanks." He checked his watch.

"Waiting for pie? Sounds like a good enough excuse for you to sit here, and I won't have to rush off back to my busy, busy life."

He had the good form to wince a little at his own behavior. But not much. "I said all that just now because I didn't want to appear too eager to have you here."

Dora's turn to wince. "Wow, thanks."

"You're welcome."

"How do you do that?"

"What?"

"Only hear what you want to hear."

"I wish. If I could do that I'd…" He looked into her eyes. He shook his head and looked away and said no more.

Unlike Burke, Dora had a knack for hearing both things said and those unsaid. It had come in handy in her line of work, but now it made her feel a bit too vulnerable. She did not know how she could keep things between her and Burke merely professional if he kept telling her so much about himself by not telling her anything.

She reached her hand out across the table. "You actually care what people here think of you?"

He looked down at the place where her hand rested near his. "No. Not so much. As the head of the town's biggest business, I couldn't let that kind of thing get to me."

She touched his wrist lightly with her fingertips.

"I don't care what anyone thinks." He withdrew

and dropped his hand into his lap, shifting back in his seat. "But I do care about what people *say.*"

"Spoken more like a VP of marketing, not a CEO," she teased. "But I thought there was no such thing as bad publicity."

He squinted, looked left then right, then focused in on her. "Dora, you don't know how people get ahold of an idea in a small town and run with it."

Now Dora took a look around them, her eyes wide open. She observed the friendships all around them, the sense of community, the way that people wanted not only the best for themselves but for one another, too. She shook her head just a little and fixed her gaze on Burke again. "Actually, I suspect you are the one who doesn't know that, Burke."

"What do you mean?'

"Let's just say I don't think you are giving the people of Mt. Knott the credit they deserve."

"Yeah? Well, thanks to me and my lousy handling of the Crumble no one will give them the credit they deserve." He sat back, hearing what he wanted to hear all over again. "Going to be a bleak Christmas for a lot of folks around here, Dora."

"Money isn't the only thing that makes a merry Christmas, Burke," she said quite softly, since she doubted he'd listen.

He cast his eyes downward and nodded. "Yeah, but money is what I've got to give, thanks to my mom's life mission. Now you and I have to decide who to give it to."

"I can't help do that if you don't want me to stay here in Mt. Knott."

"I didn't mean for you to not actually stay, Dora. I only felt I had to put up some resistance to your hanging around town."

She nodded. "To protect yourself."

"To protect you."

From what? *Humiliation,* he would have said and she knew it. Knew it because she had already lived through it once.

"Fair enough," she conceded. "You don't want people to know about, um, about our *business* or thinking they know too much about our personal lives."

"Yeah."

"Then why meet me here? Your sister-in-law's place is the social hub of the whole town."

"Nowhere else much to go on weekdays if you're retired or work second shift or are a farmer who doesn't have much to do this time of year."

Or are out of work because the Crumble laid you off, or a business dependent on people laid off by the Crumble closed. He didn't say it, but Dora only had to read the prayer requests on the chalkboard wall to know the thought had occurred to him.

"That and there's pie."

He smiled the most genuine smile she'd seen on him all day. "And there's pie."

"Good choice then." She pulled out a pad and pen and began to write. "Not to mention that the wall alone gives me enough information to keep me busy for days."

Burke's hand closed over hers. "What are you doing?"

"Making notes."

"You can't be seen doing that."

"Then how do I collect the information?"

He scowled and glanced around them. "You have a camera phone?"

She tapped the earpiece attached to the side of her head.

He studied her Bluetooth a moment. "Can you read them off, like into voice mail or something?"

"Or *you* could."

"What?"

"Pie!" Josie set down two plates in front of them with practiced stealth. "Won't bother you. If you need anything else, holler."

And she backed away. Didn't turn and walk away. Oh, no, backed away with her eyes on them the whole distance back to the counter.

Dora tried to hide a chuckle. Maybe Burke could control the things he said, but he had no sway over his friends and family. They would think what they liked and say what they thought.

Good for them.

Even if it would make her job—and maybe her holiday—a bit tougher.

"Where were we?" Burke asked, steadfastly ignoring the cherry pie filling that dripped from his raised fork.

"You were going to call and read the names to me so I wouldn't be caught writing them down."

He set the bite of pie down on the plate, his silverware clattering.

"Well, it makes sense, doesn't it? To me they are just names and a brief request," she said. "You should be able to give me more background."

From the look on his face, she realized he didn't think he could do that.

"Well, if you can give me anything more to go on, that would help." A sentence she had longed to say to this man time and time again over their brief courtship and at least a time or two since they had parted ways. *Give me something more to go on, help me to understand this.* Dora sighed. "If we want to keep up the appearance of my having come to town just to look around—"

"Which you did."

"Which I did." She took a bite of pie. It was as good as she remembered it. No, better. Maybe that was because she was enjoying the company. Or maybe because she was enjoying getting the best of that company. If Burke had wanted to call all the shots on this project he shouldn't have called in a corporate hotshot. "Then I should go and look. Poke around a bit. Maybe start with some churches, the library, the newspaper."

"And do what?"

She outlined the list, touching her fingers to count down the tasks she had in mind as she did. "Ask at the churches if there is anyone in need I could consider for a donation. Read up on the town as a whole and its history. Then, at the newspaper, maybe look up stories on past recipients."

He clasped his hand over her raised fingers to cut her off. "Those I have in my mom's files."

She cocked her head and smiled. She did not slip her hand away from his. "Are you inviting me out to the Burdett compound to look them over?"

He let go of her hand. "No."

"Of course not." *Business. All business.* "Just as well, because I need you to stay here."

"Here?" He went for another bite of pie.

She gave him a look meant to scream, *you really do just hear what you want to hear,* and said, in a crisp, hushed voice, "To call me up and leave the names from the wall on my voice mail."

He wolfed down the bite. "Won't that look odd?"

"I thought you didn't care how you looked to other people?" Which was a shame because he looked terrific. Except for that... "You've got a..." She waved her hand over the side of her mouth. "Just a little..."

He frowned at her, confused.

"A…" Another wave of her hand. "Oh, here."

She stretched up from her seat, reached over the table and dabbed away a blob of bright red cherry filling from the corner of his mouth.

"Thanks." He laughed and swiped the pad of his thumb over the same spot. "Of course, now everyone in this diner is going to talk about this."

"About what a sloppy eater you are?" She sat back down.

"About how you and I shared some pie and how you found a reason to touch my face, to make it your business to look after me."

*To make it your business to look after me.* The thought made Dora sad and wistful all at once. "All the more reason for you to stay here and make the call. It will look better than the two of us heading out of here together."

"Good point. You certainly don't let anything slip by, Dora."

"Hey, what's a good little helper for?"

He looked at her a moment but said nothing.

A good helper. A helpmate. The thing she had always wanted so much to be for one man. For this man, she had once thought. Now she had her chance, even though it could not last.

"Hey, Josie, can I get a refill on coffee?" he called out, as if to remind Dora that in his world he had plenty of helpers. They were his employees, servers and beneficiaries. Though she had taken on this job strictly as a volunteer, he did not see her any differently.

"Anyway—" She started to slide out of the booth.

"Stay." He did not reach for her with anything but the most sincere look deep in his eyes.

Her heart stopped. She did not move.

"Wait until Josie gets over here, then we'll make our goodbyes. If we do it in the open like that it gives people less reason to try to guess what we said or why we said it."

She sat and felt her whole body sag a bit. "Funny, sometimes you can be right here hearing every word and still be left wondering those things."

"Hmm?"

"Eat your pie," she said. "We have a lot of work yet to do."

# Chapter Seven

Burke could not read a single name on the list without stopping to wonder about the story behind the request. He knew some of them, but far too many held no larger meaning than they would for a stranger passing through town.

Conner Burdett had had a rule about knowing too much about the people who worked for him. He was against it. In much the same way kids learned in 4-H never to name the animals they later might have to sell for slaughter, the old man thought it best not to have any personal connection to a worker, because you might have to fire him later.

Adam, Josie's husband, the second Burdett son, had followed that edict to the letter. Made him a better manager, some said. Most must have said it, Burke decided, since he was the man in change of the whole shebang now.

But Burke wasn't made that way. Despite being the adopted son, Adam was Conner all over. And Burke was his mother, in conscience, in commitment to a calling and by her design, now in Christmas spirit.

So where he had initially intended to pick and chose only the people most in need of some kind of grant, he ended up reading the entire list into the phone, each with a notation, a personal observation or bit of encouragement.

"The Sykes family asks for prayer for their daughter, Jenny, who is serving in the army overseas. Would be nice to do something for someone in the military."

And.

"The cheerleaders need to raise money to go to a competition this spring. It's not exactly what Mom had in mind, but I think it would give the whole town something to get behind. They need that. They deserve it."

And later:

"The Pennbreits simply say they are praying for everyone because it's all they can do right now. There's a story that would break your heart, Dora. I don't know if they have sons or daughters, though. Does it matter?"

He didn't think so but he trusted that Dora had the wherewithal and the detachment to make the right call on that. Still, he felt compelled to reminder her,

"They're good folks. They're all good folks, Dora. I wish I had the means to help them all."

*I know, but maybe you aren't meant to help them all, Burke,* he could hear her soft words in her head. He could imagine her soft reply clearly in his mind. *Did you ever stop to think—*

"I am thinking, Dora. Can't help but think." He said out loud he'd meant that just as he had meant the last thing he said before flipping the phone shut and leaving the Home Cookin' Kitchen. "Guess sometimes you don't realize how blessed you are until you stop dwelling on all the wrongs you think have been done to you and look around at what other people are dealing with, and ask yourself, what can I do to make things better?"

What he had decided to do was head home. Yes, *home,* not the house, as he had taken to calling it since his mother had died.

Home. The place where he had grown up and where he had returned to live after his mother's death, for Conner's sake. As the oldest son and the one who had unseated the old man from his position as CEO of the company he had founded, it was Burke's duty to move back in. His place both as a son and as a brother. The only place he still retained now that Adam had taken over at the Crumble.

He sat in his truck and gazed at the house at the center of the Burdett compound. Five structures, each indicative of their owner.

Stray Dawg, the second son, the loner tamed by love who now had a wife, son and the reins of the business, had an upscale log cabin on a wooded two-acre lot. Jason, dubbed Lucky Dawg because he was born after Conner and Maggie had given up ever having another child and for never having broken a bone, despite a love of extreme sports, had designed an Irish cottage, complete with a meandering stone path and hunter-green shutters. While Cody, the youngest of the bunch, still called Hound Dawg despite having answered a call to the ministry, lived with his wife, Carol, in an old-fashioned-style farmhouse complete with wraparound front porch, like something right out of *The Andy Griffith Show.*

Burke's house, a small, simple ranch style, looked more like a guesthouse than a place where a man would want to spend his free time or one day raise his family. Dora had stayed there last year when she had been in negotiations to buy into the family business.

Burke had not even crossed its threshold since she had left. Not that they had happy memories there. She had always come over to the main house to avoid even the appearance of impropriety. But still, just knowing she had eaten breakfast at their table caught his imagination. She had rested her head on the pillows and dreamed who knows what dreams, about being his partner in life as well as business, he supposed. They had never discussed that eventuality outright but it had been an unspoken possibility that had woven itself through their every moment last summer. She had lived in his family's home, learned the ropes of his work, spent her days with his family. She had even attended Cody's church with him.

Home, work, family, church. She'd seen all the sides of the man that mattered and hadn't run off—until he had chased her off. It had humbled him then to think of a woman like Dora even considering caring for a man like him. Now? Well, now he wasn't that man anymore.

She must be counting her blessings today that she had escaped ending up with him. Here in South Carolina without a job or any real plans for the future.

Burke had invested his all in the company, in his place there and among his brothers, and his own family had sized him up and found him unworthy. Still, he had tried to fight for her. He had championed her cause of allowing her to buy into the Carolina Crumble Pattie Factory and he had failed. He had been determined to get for Dora whatever she wanted one way or another, but in the end he had failed to get her a place in the business. The whole house of cards—home, work, family and all their unspoken possibilities—had caved in.

He gripped the steering wheel and gritted his teeth. By now she surely understood that she was better off without him.

He got out of the truck and stood, trying to decide

whether to go to the main house where he had taken up residence—if by residence one meant that he had been sleeping on the pull-out sofa in his father's old office—or to finally return to his old house. The house he had once moved away from with a sure conviction of his station in life. The house that Dora had probably imagined the two of them would one day share.

He looked skyward for a moment, not seeking guidance from above, but just to find some respite from the choices laid out so plainly before him.

Following the brief flurries of Thanksgiving Day the temperature had warmed considerably. The clouds had cleared away. In fact, the sun shone so brightly that by nine in the morning people could shed their lightweight jackets. Everyone needed a baseball cap or dark glasses to shade their eyes, and here and there the summery sound of flip-flops could be heard along the sidewalks of Mt. Knott. In other words, the weather matched Burke's mood—totally inappropriate for the approaching holiday and the task that lay ahead for him.

There was only one way to change his mood. Something that he had to do, that he had promised Dora he would do. Something he had put off doing for two years now. He had to go to Santaland.

That made the choice of houses for him. In a matter of moments he was outside the locked doors of the attic office that no one had entered since his mother's death. Before that, only she had been allowed through those doors. Her office. Her sanctuary. Her domain. Right up until the night she had given him the key, told him what she had been doing all these years and to go and see it for himself.

He put his hand on the doorknob. He took a deep breath. Dust assaulted his nostrils. He sneezed. Once. Twice. Three times. Silly him, he half expected to hear his mother's voice from the other side of the door call out, "God bless you, baby."

In the deafening silence that greeted him instead he thought better of the plan to come here. He turned, started to tuck the key away then paused. He sniffed, lightly this time, cautiously. What was that smell?

Pine. Probably from some scented candle that his mom had had on her desk to keep her in the holiday mood all year round. He imagined it, deep green in a large glass jar sitting right where she had placed it before she got too sick to climb the stairs.

It seemed to draw him back.

He had to do this.

For his mom.

For all the good folks of Mt. Knott.

For Dora.

"Dora," he said softly. He pulled his phone from his pocket, flipped it open and pressed the button to show his last placed call. If he were the kind to go in for a lot of heavy self-analysis, he'd say wanting to leave a message on Dora's voice mail at this precise moment was his way of not facing his memories and concerns all alone.

Instead he said out loud as he pushed Call, "I'll map the place out as I go so if she needs to get to files or anything I won't have to come back with her."

A soft electronic purring ring filled his ear.

He cranked the doorknob to the right and gave a nudge with the toe of his boot just above the threshold where age and weather had swollen the wood and made it stick.

Another ring.

The door swung open.

R-r-r-ring.

He flipped on the light.

Correction: lights. Hundreds of them. Maybe thousands. Not just the two large overhead low-watt bulbs that glowed dimly from their frosted fixture-coverings, but string upon string of tiny twinklers strung from every rafter, framing every window and running along every surface. They even outlined the huge old desk painted gleaming black with bright gold scrollwork accents, in the same style as an old sleigh Burke's mother had purchased years ago and restored to perfection.

Guilt tugged at Burke over that. They had always stored the sleigh in the barn where they housed a couple of horses and countless cats. Each year when his mother had announced it was time to get the sleigh out and go caroling, Burke had been the one to go get it, hitch up the horse and bring it around.

That last year, the year his mother died, she had asked him to bring the sleigh out for her. "I want to give you boys one last happy memory."

"We don't want a memory, Mom. We want you to get better. You can't get better if you go out in the cold night air."

"Burke, I'm not going to get better. I certainly won't be well enough to go Christmas shopping this year. Memories are all I can give you this year."

Burke had refused.

Refused to fetch the sleigh. Refused to accept the memory-making experience. So a few days later when his mother had asked for another favor?

He glanced around him. From every nook and cranny statues, dolls and likenesses of Saint Nicholas peered out from under a robed hood, a red and white fur cap or even, in a couple instances, a cowboy hat.

"Take over my legacy, son. Continue the good work. Don't be afraid to change someone's life for the better."

When his mother had asked him to do this, he could not refuse.

Rr-r-r-r-ing.

The tone drew him into the present again. In a moment Dora's voice mail would pick up.

His gaze fell on the credenza behind the desk and

all the framed photographs of the girls his mother's charity had helped over all these years.

All those stories. All those fresh starts and new opportunities. All those changed lives. How had she chosen? How had she known who was deserving and how had she dealt with the disappointment that so few had given back to the cause?

That hadn't bothered her, he knew. She'd told him even at the end of her life that her responsibility was to be a cheerful giver and to act in the name of the Lord. She couldn't control what the receiver did after that. If they squandered their gifts or used them for ill, that would be between those receivers and God.

The lack of appreciation and failure to give back to the town was his issue. And one of the reasons he felt so inadequate to take this all on.

Maggie Burdett.

Saint Nicholas?

Top Dawg?

"Uh-uh." He pulled the phone away from his ear. There was one name he knew did not belong on that list and it was…

"Burke? Burke Burdett? Is that you?"

"Dora?"

"Don't sound so surprised. You called me."

"I thought I'd get your voice mail."

"You want me to hang up? You can call back and let my voice mail pick up."

Yes. That was exactly what he wanted. Oddly

enough, it was also the one thing that he did not want—to lose contact with Dora. "That's kind of silly, isn't it?"

She didn't confirm or deny it.

"Yeah." He cleared his throat. "Okay. Well, I've got you now. That is, we have each other…on the line."

"Good. I actually found out a lot today and have some good leads. One thing I need your input on, though, is when to call the jeweler."

"The jeweler? Why?"

"It's the Christmas season, Burke, maybe not where you are but for the rest of us—"

"Oh, it's Christmas where I am." He shifted to take in the full panoramic view and chuckled. "Definitely Christmas."

"That's a busy time for a jeweler. We need to get our order in so he can have the charms ready and engraved with everything but the names of the recipients. I bet your mom had records about when she ordered them and all the specs on them."

"I'm sure she did." From the looks of it, his mom had never thrown anything away.

"Great. If you can just read them off to me?"

"Hold on. I'll just look over…here." He tried to maneuver without tipping over tiny trees or stomping on delicate glass baubles. He yanked open a drawer only to find a small snow scene made from a mirror and cotton batting where file folders should have

hung. "I'll tell you what. Why don't I handle everything with the jeweler?"

"Are you sure? I'll be headed back to Atlanta soon
anyway."

"You will?" He shut the drawer with the snow
scene in it and a puff of glitter sprayed up onto his
hand. "Why?"

"Because that's where I live," she said, and left
it at that.

Burke didn't need the lecture that could have followed. He thought she showed great restraint and
good manners by not pointing out that he had left
her little choice by not providing her a place to stay.
"You can stay as long as you need to and bill your
room at the motel to me, of course."

"What? I would never ask you to pay for that."

"You expect Global to pick up the tab when you
travel. This is no different from that." He opened
another drawer and then another searching for the
information about the jeweler, or about his mother's selection system, or at least a tissue or hankie
to clean the glitter from his hand. A dozen boxes of
old-fashioned icicles tossed in with a ledger for the
project, from a decade ago. Some tin noisemakers.
The template for the letter she must have once meant
to send with the coins but never finished. A sheet of
self-adhesive gift tags. "Just a business expense. You
may not take a salary for your time, but I can't let you
pay out of your own pocket to help me do my job."

"Don't you mean your mission?"

"Do I?" He paused to give that a moment's thought.

"Or maybe a calling?"

Mission? Calling? The terms exuded a higher purpose than trying to assuage his guilt over his many failings. Burke couldn't own up to that. If he were to chose a word he'd pick *obligation. Responsibility.* An expectation that came with being born a Burdett. "No, *job* is the right word."

"Well, then I guess you're one of the lucky ones in Mt. Knott. Asking around all day I've heard that unless you work for the Crumble, there aren't any jobs to be had around here."

"How do you think I'd do at crumb cake inspecting?" The next drawer he tried stuck after opening only an inch. Were those files inside?

"I suspect you've known a few crumbs in your life," she shot back.

She didn't name names but he got the idea she meant him and felt it an unfair categorization. Instead of telling her so, though, he channeled his annoyance into freeing the stuck drawer and with one mighty tug.

"Christmas cards?" And not new ones that someone could use, either. But old ones, from people they hadn't known for years if they had known them at all, probably saved for the pretty pictures. "And speaking of pictures…"

"Were we speaking of pictures?"

Burke stared at the faded color photograph of him dressed as an elf for a kindergarten play. He chuckled under his breath. "Yeah. Yeah, we did speak about pictures. The one in my hand in particular."

"The…not the…the elf?"

He laughed at the unabashed delight in her voice. It was a sound he had heard almost daily during their summer together. He'd missed it. He'd missed her.

"Oh, this I have to see," she said. "Of course, I suspect to do that, I'd have to slide down the chimney by night and rifle through the house until I found it for myself."

"Actually—" He looked around, then at his hand, then at the boxes of junk and cabinets, also filled with junk. "You may be right."

"What? I, uh, Burke, I may be thin but I don't think I can actually fit down a chimney."

He chuckled.

"And as for rifling through a house? Not my bailiwick, buddy. Legal history, financial documents, tax records, ask me to find my way around those and I won't quit rummaging until I found out who owned the land the house sits on before Carolina was a state."

"That would be a Burdett," he informed her, half wondering if he might turn up an ancestor or two in the dust and mayhem of his mother's office. "And that would be exactly the kind of dedication this situation calls for."

"Burdett dedication?"

"Dora dedication." He picked up a receipt for hundreds of dollars' worth of school supplies paperclipped to a pamphlet of illustrated Christmas carols. "The only way to get the information we need fast is to get someone to come to the house and organize my mother's things."

"I would be proud to help with that, Burke. All you have to do is—"

Ask. His mind went instantly to all those things left unsaid between them and he knew that if he did this, he had to be clear about what he wanted from her from the very start.

"You couldn't just come in and work up here in the office. No one else knows about this place. It's just a small space across the hall from where they think my mother used to spend her days." He wondered how anyone could have known his mother and believed that she could ever get anything done in the tidy yellow decoy room with the white furniture across the hall from her actual "office." "Whoever came in would have to pitch in and get the downstairs in order by day then work up here after hours when everyone thinks they have gone to bed."

Dora cleared her throat. "Is that a job offer, Mr. Burdett?"

"Well, it's not as glamorous a job as crumb inspector."

"Why would anyone believe I'd do that kind of thing—putting your mother's things in order—for you?"

"You wouldn't be doing it for *me,* really."

"No one would believe I was doing it for my health, now would they?"

"We'll tell them the truth. We needed an objective person to go through Mom's things but we also wanted someone familiar with the family. All we have to do is throw those two ideas out—a person who knows the Burdetts and can still be objective about us, and the list suddenly gets very narrow."

She hesitated.

He knew if he said anything more, asked her from his heart, gave just the tiniest insight into how much this meant to him, into what she meant to him, she would do it in an instant. And be hurt all the more when their work ended and she realized that he had nothing more to offer a woman like her. He remained silent.

She said nothing.

As negotiating tactics went, this was one of the oldest of the bunch. It went back to children in the school yard. First one to blink loses.

Finally, after what seemed forever, Dora sighed. "When do I start work?"

Burke tried not to sound too pleased with himself. "I'll move from the main house back into my old place in the morning. You can move in here anytime after noon tomorrow."

"Move in? I didn't really bring enough stuff to move in, Burke."

"You know what I mean."

"No, I don't. How long do you anticipate me staying?"

"Until the job's done."

"The job. Yes. Of course. Just business, huh?"

"Just business," he echoed. "Is there anything else?"

*Tell me. Tell me, Dora, that there is something else.*

She held her tongue for so long that he almost wondered if they had lost their connection. When she finally spoke he realized that their connection had been lost long before today, as she said in a quiet voice just before ending the call, "No, Burke. I guess there is nothing else. I guess maybe there never was."

## Chapter Eight

Dora's heartbeat kicked up a notch. She'd come for the day, thinking she'd spend a few hours discussing things with Burke, gather what information she could then head back to Atlanta to sort through things. But here she was, already more than a day later, standing before the main house of the Burdett compound—moving in!

"Just visiting," she murmured firmly to keep that particular little flight of fancy in check. "No different than whatever five-star hotel I'd pick to spend the holidays in these last few years."

She gripped her purse and briefcase—she never went anywhere without it—in both hands, took a deep breath and marched up the front steps. She paused in front of the large door with its glass inset, looked down and saw four sets of footprints stenciled onto the painted floor. Hound Dawg's, the smallest, showed the treads of tennis shoes. Lucky Dawg, the name under the next set of prints preserved by a tough protective finish, had the feet positioned in such a way that Dora could almost see that brother's cocky stance. Adam, Stray Dawg's, prints faced toward the steps and the last set.

She moved to the full-sized boot prints, pointed directly at the door, of a man who knew where he belonged and had no intention of budging.

Dora looked around a moment. She wet her lips. She held her breath. This was it. Crossing the threshold back into the world she had once hoped would be hers meant…she didn't know what it meant, really, only that once she did this she couldn't undo it. Just like this past summer when she worked so closely with them—with Burke—she could only move through what happened next. No turning back.

If she were smart or, rather, wise, she'd run. She exhaled at last, looked straight ahead then stepped inside Burke's footprints.

They made her shoes look almost childlike. And though the footprints were only made of paint and many years old, she felt as though, through them, she had made a small connection to the man.

She put her hand on the doorknob and a shiver shot through her body.

Who was she kidding? No different than a five-star hotel? This was the Burdett family home.

The place where the man she had once hoped to

have a future with was raised. Where he had lived
these past two years. Where the people who had
first invited her into their midst and into the middle of their business, then later tossed her out without so much as an explanation, met over deals and
meals alike.

Dora reached out to touch two fingers to the or-
nate *B* etched in the glass of the oval inset on the
dark green door.

"Five stars?" She looked at the grime on her fingertips then at the chipped paint around the broken brass and plastic doorbell, then at the footprints
strangely preserved against the faded blue-gray of
the weathered porch. "I don't think this place would
even rate a lone star." She peered through the glass to
the darkened rooms beyond. "A falling star, maybe."

At least at a hotel she got the hustle and bustle of
holiday activity and a beautiful tree to gaze upon.
Not to mention she usually enjoyed a roaring fire
without having to go outside in the elements to gather
wood. That and the lights and excitement of the city
cheered her up.

Where were the Burdetts' decorations? The tree?
The lights? What was there here to offer her a sense
of warmth, of hope, of excitement?

The door swung open.

"Welcome to my home. It's good to have you
here." Burke stepped up to the threshold, his hand
extended.

Dora's arm trembled as her palm met his. Trembled! She had shaken hands with some of the most powerful people in her industry and never let her nerves get the better of her. Why couldn't she get control of herself now?

Burke's expression was an odd mix that Dora couldn't quite call delight but wouldn't deny held a certain amount of pleased relief. He was nervous, too. "I was beginning to think you'd changed your mind about coming."

She had changed her mind. Multiple times. Yet somehow it always got changed back and so here she was. Standing in Burke's shadow and in his footsteps. Giving up her usual holiday activities to give other people a Christmas while in return she would have—

She lost her train of thought as the smell of turkey and gravy, pumpkin pie and coffee filled the air.

"Dora's here!" Burke called over his shoulder.

"Don't make her stand outside, bring her in, we're waiting for her!" Josie peeked at her from the wide arching doorway that led to the dining room.

A cheer went up from the entire Burdett family.

She would give up her usual holiday and in return she would have the best shot at a real Christmas she'd ever known.

Dora came inside and before she could even thank them for welcoming her, Burke had taken her briefcase and someone else had scooped up the plastic bag of personal items she'd picked up at the one store in town, a chain discount, general mercantile type of place.

"Can we eat now?" Jason, the third of the dog pack, howled.

"Ain't fitting. T' have company like this fine lady come here and not provide her with a proper spread." Conner Burdett, who had probably once stood almost as tall as Burke, pushed his way past his sons and daughters-in-law. Rail thin and aged by grief, he still had a hard edge to him that said he wouldn't be taken advantage of.

Or fooled.

Or even charmed by anyone.

The grip of his handshake told Dora he recognized her as not just anyone. He knew who she was, what she did for a living and that in another place and time she would have been a powerful ally—or opponent—in business.

"Though I admit I find myself perplexed as to why you are here, Ms. Hoag. Why you would *want* to be here," he amended, his tone and demeanor changed from when he had barked at his wolf pack of a family.

Message received. Conner didn't want her here.

The old man turned and walked toward the arched doorway.

Dora shifted her gaze from one face to the next, ending with Burke. He prodded her to move with a nod of his head. Dora understood this as her cue to follow Conner and she did so.

"It's just leftovers, buffet style with these mangy mutts, nothing fancy," Burke warned her. "I hope that's okay."

"Okay?" Here was her out. She could simply say she thought she should find other accommodations, that an old house and Mt. Knott, South Carolina, simply did not meet her standards. Except…

She took a second to study those accommodations. The smiles, the smells, the light in the family's eyes and Burke, trying to smooth her way, and once again her mind changed.

"There a problem?" Conner demanded, turning slowly. "What's good enough for my kin not good enough for you, young woman?"

Dora eased out a long breath, brushed a glance Burke's way then met Conner's unyielding stance. "It's better than good enough, Mr. Burdett. Your home is grander and more agreeable than any five-star hotel in any exotic city in any corner of the world."

"What?" Conner turned and fixed a hard, squinty-eyed gaze on her. "What did you say?"

A lot of people would have been intimidated by the strange look on the old man's face and the energy with which he asked his question. Both seemed determined to push her back a step, knock her off balance, challenge her.

Obviously the man had not considered his target. If she did not know how to stand her ground, keep her equilibrium and rise to a challenge, she certainly would never have spent a day in the company of Burke Burdett. And she sure wouldn't be standing in his home now.

She raised her chin, trying to make herself an imposing figure, and smiled, because, well, the old man looked like he needed a kind smile. "I have traveled all over the world. Paris, Rome, Tokyo, I've stayed in fancy hotels and even a palace or two and I have to say, Mr. Burdett, your home has them all beat."

"You, little girl…" He stabbed a bony finger directly at her face.

She braced herself for a tirade, not sure if he would go into detail about everything he found lacking in her or merely call her a liar, which she wasn't.

Burke stepped up and put his arm around her shoulders. "Mind your manners, old man."

"No, you mind yours. I'll remind you not to go grabbing on our honored guests like a crate of Crumble Patties ready for loading on a bakery truck." Conner plucked Burke's hand from Dora and batted it away.

"What?" Burke stepped back, his hands up, clearly more from surprise than from sheer obedience.

"Honored guest?" Dora asked.

"Why, yes." Conner beamed down at her and put

his arm where Burke's had been moments before. "Such a perceptive, wise and well-spoken young lady, you are welcome in my home anytime."

"B-but don't you want to know why I'm here?"

"Yeah, you've come to put my house in order." Conner came off gruff but his pale eyes shone with gratitude and more than a little grief. That quickly shifted to something more like accusation as his attention went to Burke, then to impish sweetness as he turned to her and added, "And I couldn't think of another person on earth I would want to do it."

That shut Dora up.

At least long enough to try to take it all in.

"Seems a waste of a powerful executive." Adam, who had once worked under Dora's tutelage at Global and now ran the whole operation at the Crumble, eyed her cautiously.

Her cheeks burned. She had been so focused on her feelings about Burke that she hadn't thought about having to play the humble servant to people who had treated her so shabbily.

"But Burke said you volunteered," Adam went on. "He said you were the cheerful little helper type."

"Volun—? Cheerful little helper?" She shouldn't have been peeved by that and if it were just the two of them, she'd probably laugh off the whole elf connotation, but to let everyone think she'd pushed her way into this with such a flimsy excuse as being a helper type? This whole deal was Burke's doing and he needed to own up to some part in it. "I'd have never presumed to offer, of course, if Burke hadn't—"

"You know, I never even asked if you wanted to put your things away and clean up before we eat, Dora." Burke grabbed her by the elbow and pulled her gently against his chest.

At his touch, her anger faded more quickly than she would have liked. Anger, after all, had often proved a reliable ally in protecting her from people getting too close, and from any weakness on her part for trusting too much, too soon, too… "I'd like that."

As soon as they were out of earshot, she dug deep and tried to rekindle her initial feelings of embarrassment. "I volunteered?"

"What's wrong with that? Volunteering is nice."

"It makes me seem like I couldn't wait to worm my way back into…" Your heart. She struggled to take her eyes off him and tear her mind away from thoughts of what might have been between them. Maybe she shouldn't have come away alone with him, even just a flight of stairs or two. Even if it was all only a business proposition. That thought snapped her back to the reality of the situation. "It made me seem far too anxious to worm my way back into your family's good graces."

"Trust me, they would never even consider that was what you were doing."

"Because they see me as a serious professional?"

"Because…" He turned and winked at her over his shoulder. "My family is worm proof."

She opened her mouth to make a cutting remark about this not being the time for joking, then it dawned on her that he probably was not making a joke so much as a painful private observation and covering the truth of it with a joke. The Burdetts had shut him out as well as her, and it had to have left its mark on him. That concession was the most personal glimpse he'd given her into what was really going on with him these days. She accepted it, and his offering of closeness by opening up, with a gracious nod of her head.

He led her on upstairs, took her luggage and set it outside the door then beckoned her to a narrow doorway. It opened to a secluded stairway.

"Besides, I had to let them think it was your idea to see to my mother's things and that meant helping my father deal with her estate, because I couldn't very well tell them that this is why you had to come." He flipped on the light.

Dora gasped. No wonder they didn't have any exterior decorations. They were all here.

"Oh, Burke. You really are…"

"Don't call me that name."

"Name?"

"Jolly old you know who." He pressed one finger to her lips. "Please don't call me that. I'm just me.

A flawed man without a clue how to accomplish the task before him."

His first concession about his family had been more than she expected from him. This uncustomary humility, this way of telling her how much he needed her without really telling her how much he needed her, this was a precious gift, indeed.

She closed her eyes and whispered, "No, you're not, you're the Top Dawg," placing her fingertips on his hand as he swept it along her cheek.

"Not anymore." He shook his head. His hand fell away. "You saw it yourself. We're in my father's house. My brother speaks for the family and runs the Crumble. This is all I have."

"This seems quite enough, Burke. If you do the right things with it all." After a moment measured by no less than a heartbeat, it dawned on her she had said that while looking into his eyes.

He held her gaze for just one fleeting second, then looked through the door, his jaw clenched. "It is what it is."

Just business. He did not say it, but he did say it, in his posture, in his grim expression even as he fixed his attention on the wonderful landscape of the office before them.

She flushed, cleared her throat then hastily flung her arm out toward the glittering space. "It's a great, um, jumping-off point."

"It's just a mishmash of an inheritance, not by

my own doing. Plus I have to hide it away, which is not my style."

"Oh, I don't know. You seem a very private person to me." From *me,* she might have said instead but decided not to push it here and now. With her trust issues and all the things she had yet to say to him or his family about the way they had ended things, she was hardly one to throw stones.

"Yeah. I guess. But guarding your privacy and actually hiding things from people that matter to you? Very different. Doesn't feel right and yet…." He held his arms out to indicate the cluttered, covert office.

"Not your style."

He met her gaze and with an expression that admitted he was only half kidding asked, "You think it's too late to change my nickname to Lost Dawg?"

"You're not lost. You can't be. You've always got someone to guide you." She reached down and picked up a multipointed silver star meant for the top of a Christmas tree.

He nodded then looked around at all the clutter of Christmas items overwhelming the small space. He rubbed his eyes and groaned. "I'm sorry I got you into this."

She set the star down and came to stand beside him. "I'm not."

His hands dropped from his face and he bent his head to look down into her eyes. "You're not?"

"I really do like it here," she whispered. She

started to step back, literally moved by her own surprise at her confession, but Burke stopped her, taking her by the shoulders. She stilled and murmured, "I really, really like it."

"I like having you here."

"I'll try to be here every evening."

"What?" He cocked his head.

"In this office." She peered beyond him into the room. "I said I liked it here. You said you liked having me here. You did mean in the office, right?"

"No, Dora." He inched in closer.

"No?"

"I mean in my arms." He placed his crooked knuckles beneath her chin and nudged it up into just the right position to place a kiss on her waiting lips.

She wanted to tell him she couldn't allow that kind of overture. They were business associates, after all, nothing more. But in Burke's arms, kissing him, all that fell away. For the briefest measure of time, and despite the sparkle of Christmas ornaments and lights all around them, it was summer again. Anything was possible and—

"Dora? Burke? We went ahead and blessed the food. Served ourselves and now Jason wants to know if he can start on seconds or if he has to wait for you?" Adam's voice carried up the stairs and sliced between them as effectively as if he had pushed them apart and sent them to neutral corners.

Only Dora could not imagine a place in this

house, in this town, in her heart or mind, where she would feel neutral about this man. That scared her.

A lot.

But fear alone could not account for the rabbit-quick beating of her heart.

"Sorry about that." He tipped his head to one side to make clear that he meant the interruption. "Hope having all these people around while you try to get things done doesn't drive you crazy."

"Are you kidding?" Dora embraced the chance to talk about anything that took the spotlight of awkwardness off what had just happened. "Spending time around your family is one of the reasons I came here. This will be the first Christmas in a very long time that I won't feel utterly alone in the world."

Quick thinking! Take the spotlight off how *readily you gave into his* kiss and put it right on the humiliating reminder that you have not a soul in the world who cares enough about you to share the most wonderful time of the year with you.

"Dora…"

He pitied her. She could tell. And she hated it.

Her whole life she had just wanted to give from her heart and find someone who would take what she had to offer gladly. People didn't take anything from those they pitied. They became objects of sympathy and charity, not wellsprings from which to draw love and support.

Suddenly Dora realized that this might be the loneliest Christmas she'd ever known.

"We should go." Dora stepped backward and fussed with her hair.

"Yeah." Burke cleared his throat and jerked his thumb toward the open door. "By the way, I'll do whatever I can to help go through my mom's belongings downstairs for you."

"With me," she clarified, her head held high. "Expecting others to do the work I have committed to as mine is not my style."

Her clipped, driven business persona rose to the surface again.

"I know. That's why Global values you so much."

"Global? Values?" She tried to piece those words together so that they made sense to her but she just couldn't do it. Global was a huge corporation that thought of her as a cog in the machine. As long as she kept on churning and the wheels kept going round and round she had a job. The second she stopped? She harrumphed. "Where did you get the idea that Global cares anything about me?"

"You said they had been founded on Biblical principles." He repeated something she had told them when they had still been in discussions about the Carolina Crumble Pattie operation selling out to the megacorporation.

"Yes, a long, long time ago. They've grown.

They've changed. They're no longer a family business, like yours."

"Hey, from where I'm standing mine's not strictly a family business anymore, either." He grumbled then he opened the door and held his hand out to allow her to go first.

The sounds of laughter, of plates clattering, of conversation wafted up from the lower story.

They washed over her, each one pricking at her raw emotions.

"That—" she pointed out the door, "—is not something I would ever hear at Global. Global is just a big, faceless and heartless corporation."

"That may be, but at least your heartless corporation hasn't kicked you to the curb. You don't see the faces at Global every time you get up in the morning and find you have nowhere to go. You still have a job."

Dora found it hard to feel sorry for Burke, who had so much, in contrast to her. She had, well, a job to do. "Speaking of jobs, when can I get back into this office?"

"My dad usually is asleep by nine."

"I can pitch in going through your mom's estate by day then, and come up here by night."

"I'd appreciate it. If you can make some sense out of her system that would help me next year and the year after and the year, when—"

"I get it." She cut him off because she did not want to hear the rest of that sentence.

"When you won't be around to help me anymore." He said it anyway.

"You just won't take a hint on a silver platter, will you?" She hurried past him and out into the hallway.

"Hmm? Hint? You mean—" He shut the door, turned the key in the lock then spun around and in one fluid movement snagged her arm and pulled her close. "This?"

"This is not a hint, Burke," she whispered, finding it hard to breathe. "This is either the real thing or nothing at all. It's not a game."

"Do I look like a man who plays games, Dora?"

"No." *Then kiss me again and make it mean something,* she wanted to demand. Of course, she didn't. She wouldn't. A kiss like that from Burke was something he would have to give, his gift to her. And something he had to be willing to receive in return from her with the commitment that their kiss would mean more than a fleeting physical connection.

They had once had a future together, or more accurately, the promise of a future. That had changed and Dora did not completely understand why. But she was willing to try again. If he was.

He gazed deeply into her eyes.

She held her breath. Her heart pounded. She had no idea what he would do next.

"You're right." He let her arm go and moved away.

"We can't let ourselves get distracted from the work ahead."

"Work," she said softly as she followed him down the stairs. "That *is* all there is between us, I guess."

"Did you say something?" he asked over his shoulder.

"I, um, I—" *If you can make some sense out of her system that would help me next year and the year after and the year, when you won't be around to help me anymore.* Burke had made his choice. She had to accept it.

They went down the stairs and headed for the dining room.

She should never have expected more. "I knew what I was getting into, Burke. I don't think you have to worry about me getting distracted again."

# Chapter Nine

*...This will be the first Christmas in a very long time that I won't feel utterly alone in the world.*

Dora's words had kept coming back to him as they ate their meal, cleaned up afterwards, then all hurried off to the heart of Mt. Knott to join with the community to welcome in the coming season of goodwill.

"You know if it hadn't warmed up the way it has, I'd say drag out the old sleigh and ride into town," Jason announced, as they all headed for their cars outside their family home.

"Oh, I wish we could have." Carol turned to Cody, clapping her hands. "I only got to ride in it that one time. Of course, I'll never forget what happened that night."

"What happened that night?" Dora leaned in to whisper to Burke. "Did they get in an accident?"

Jason, who was passing by them at that very moment, barked out a laugh and promptly broke into the chorus of "Jingle Bells."

"Worse." Burke tried to maintain a proper scowl as he swung open the passenger door of his truck for his guest.

Dora put one hand on the door but did not climb up and into the cab right away, instead stopping to challenge him. He found that awfully charming, her fearlessness to stand up to him about the smallest things, even as a joke. "Worse?"

She clucked her tongue, shook her head and acted shocked to even imagine what could be worse.

"They got engaged," Burke answered, adding a jerk of his head to prod her to get into the car so they could get going and put this conversation behind them. He was not looking forward to having to spend his evening with the entire town of Mt. Knott, including a whole lot of people he had personally had to lay off from the Crumble. All of them acting as cheerful as possible. Trying to make it through the best they could. With him feeling guilty, both that he would be snooping around to decide which of them had the most pitiful circumstances, and that he could not simply help them all.

"Getting engaged is worse than getting into an accident?" she asked as he hurried her along.

"Doing anything that showy, like proposing in a sleigh, is worse because if you don't get it right or she turns you down, you will never hear the end of it."

"I can see that, especially in a small town like this where people are liable to talk," she agreed, joining in his jest.

"What do you two plan to get up to, to get people talking?" Cody asked, using his very most serious look of keeping an eye out for trouble, as any good preacher should.

"Nothing. Honest." Burke held his hands up like a kid who had been caught rattling the lid to the cookie jar. Then, for good measure, he gave Dora a quick wink. "We're on our best behavior."

"That's too bad," Conner grumbled, as he made his way slowly down the steps of the house, too proud to allow anyone to help him. "Don't know how this family is ever going to have any more grandkids with that kind of attitude."

Dora looked at Burke, a bit shocked.

"I'm not sure he actually heard what I said," Burke explained.

"Then again I'm not sure he didn't hear every syllable," Cody warned. Carol and Cody laughed, apparently having heard the old fellow's views about abandoning good sense and reason now and then in order to add a few new branches to the Burdett tree.

"Don't mind them. Sometimes they forget how to talk to people who aren't beholden to the Burdetts for their bread and butter." Burke stuck his hand out this time, trying to hurry her into the truck at last.

"I don't mind." She slipped her hand in his then

paused for a moment. "I enjoyed sharing bread and butter with the Burdetts, so I guess I can stand it. In fact, I find it all endearing, the stories, the teasing and the bickering."

"I like her," Cody said, flashing the dimple that so many young women had sighed over that it had earned him the nickname Hound Dawg.

How could you argue with a woman who found your family's senseless babbling endearing? Went back to having spent so many holidays alone, he figured. Only explanation for finding charm in the Burdett clan. If only she had her own clan, her own relatives to laugh and bicker with.

"Anyway, it's not so bad getting talked about, you know." Cody gave Burke a playful punch in the arm.

Burke considered striking back, not hard but firmly enough to tell his baby brother he did not want a lecture on what he should do regarding Dora.

"After all," Cody went on, even before he dropped his fisted hand to his side. "Jesus was the talk of the town a time or too if you recall."

"Still is," Dora noted.

"So right," Cody nodded to her then gave Burke a no-nonsense look that suggested he thought his big brother should not let this woman go. "I'm telling ya, man, I like her."

"Maybe they should stay behind and rig up the sleigh." Carol whispered in her husband's ear loud enough for all to hear. She then wriggled the fingers of her left hand so that her diamond ring flashed in the light from the open truck cab. "Cody proposed to me in that sleigh on a winter's night three years ago."

"How romantic!" Dora folded her hands high on her chest and spoke directly to Cody. "Your idea?"

Cody pressed his lips tight and rolled his eyes in just the right way to silently rat out his older brother.

"You?" Dora looked at Burke with undisguised awe and surprise.

"Yeah. Well. I just—"

"Had to come from him." Conner passed his oldest son, clapping him hard on the shoulder as he did. "It's his sleigh. His mama bought it for him when he was a little tyke, before any of these other mangy mutts even came along."

Suddenly it dawned on him that his mother had been planning his taking over for her for a very long time. He'd certainly let her down these past two years.

Well, why not? Hadn't he let down everyone he cared about, as well as plenty of people he didn't even really know, these last two years?

"Your sleigh?" Dora cocked an eyebrow at Burke. "You own an actual sleigh? Is it red with gold trim and silver bells?"

He had cut her off before she could ask him where he kept his reindeer or make some other joke about the irony of the man who would rather not be Santa owning that particular kind of conveyance. "No. It's black and gold, just like—" Then he realized he had to cut himself off before he gave away where she would have seen the desk with the same high-gloss black paint and gold filigree. "Just like in an old Currier and Ives print."

"Oh, I'd love to see it sometime."

"Out in the barn." Cody helpfully pointed the way. "Though I can't for the life of me think of a reason he'd want to find an excuse to get you off alone in a dark, secluded place like that."

"I did ask if he'd put the wheels on it so we could take it into town tonight, maybe give some rides up and down Main Street and around the courthouse like the other people with wagons are doing," Josie chided, as she tucked her son into his car seat in the minivan parked next to Burke's truck.

"Guess he was too busy for that." Conner climbed into the seat beside his beloved grandson.

"I don't know doing what. Ain't like he had to get up and go to a job like the rest of us." Adam tossed his car keys up and caught them again in the same hand.

"Maybe *busy* isn't the right word. *Distracted.* That's more like it." Cody, ever the peacemaker, rushed in to verbally separate the two older brothers, who seemed to have forever been warring with each other since Maggie and Conner had adopted Adam. Burke had seen him as not just a rival but a replacement.

"Right." Adam did not relent. He never did. He was like the old man that way, except he knew when to pick his battles. Adam didn't push the things that didn't need pushing. It was what made him the ideal candidate to run the newly reorganized business and made Burke want to grab him by the scruff of the neck and tell him to back off when Adam concluded, "Guess the man was too distracted by *something* to do the few things we depended on him to do."

In the past, Burke would have put his brothers in their places, or at least stood his ground to defend the scraps of his place in the family. Not today. Today, he had to try to digest the fact that his mother had been quietly asking him to take on this job his whole life and he had failed her. He had failed Josie with her simple request. Just as he had already failed Dora by not securing her investment in the Crumble— just as he'd surely fail her again if he let down his guard around her.

He caught a glimpse of Dora's face and the joy the exchange brought to her. He had failed her, but he would not do it again, starting here and now. These fleeting moments were all he could give her, after all.

"Yeah, yeah. You guys are just jealous because Mom bought you a car or a motorcycle, which none of you still owns, by the way, and she gave me a truly classic and classy mode of transportation."

"Because she knew you'd need it," Dora whispered.

He could not give her a home—his had been empty the last two years. Or a real job, the kind equal to her achievements. He had no idea what he would be doing once he'd fulfilled his obligation to follow through on his mother's pet project.

"At least once a year," she went on.

Beyond that…

There was no beyond that for them. Only the work before them. "Only this one Christmas," he reminded her.

"Then we should make it a memorable one," she murmured.

…*the first Christmas in a very long time that I won't feel utterly alone in the world.*

Burke understood how Dora felt. It was a cliché, Burke knew, that old saying about feeling alone in a crowd, but that didn't keep it from resonating deep within him.

A few minutes later, he looked out, mostly over the heads of the people milling around on the sidewalks of downtown Mt. Knott. People he had known his entire life, his family, his former employees, even his fifth-grade teacher, and yet Burke felt completely alone.

His gaze fell on Dora's sweet face.

Well, not completely.

What could he do to make this time memorable for her? To keep her from feeling the way he did now, deserted and misplaced, when her work here ended and she had to return to Atlanta alone for Christmas? Now that she'd heard about the sleigh-ride proposal—two things not on his agenda, marriage and sleigh rides—every small effort he might make would fall short.

"I don't think I've ever been to anything like this." She stood on tiptoe and made a sweeping search of the scene as if she feared missing something.

"Sure you have." He squinted at the clusters of people representing churches, schools, clubs and causes in town. The booths left over from the Fourth of July, done up in greenery and plastic red ribbon and candy canes, did seem a bit shabby and worn. "Well, maybe not *just* like this."

His mind went to the great decorations stored in the barn with the sleigh. He had worked a lot of hours organizing the outdoor lights with a system so that he could put them up single-handedly, because his brothers never seemed to be around when that kind of chore popped up. Of course, the best thing was the huge nativity scene, the kind usually seen in front of a church.

The figures were plaster casting that stood about three-quarters of a person's size. His mom had repainted their robes in vibrant colors to reflect the joy she felt for the occasion. It had always seemed gaudy to his tastes but people seemed to like to visit it set up on the courthouse lawn, until the year the town council got "nervous" about it and asked her to move it to the Crumble.

Instead she put it in crates in the barn and left it there. They hadn't been opened in ten years or more and now sat beneath tacky pink-and-blue-and-white sparkly fake fiber-optic trees, and three-foot-tall figures of Victorian carolers that rang bells when the right switch was flipped. He should have volunteered some of those things, not the nativity but other things to make this downtown festival a little brighter.

"So you did stick around, Miss Dora. Glad to have ya." Jed raised his whole arm and swung it back and forth in a greeting from across the way. "Too bad you couldn't get a handsomer date!"

"Someone's trying to get our attention." Dora gave a small wave back.

"That what he's doing?" Burke didn't mind that Jed found him unattractive, but the man did not have to go shouting things that made the whole town think he was Dora's date. "I thought maybe he was signaling to bring a small aircraft in for a landing."

"Small aircraft? Oh, you mean like a flying sleigh full of—*oof!*"

The gathering crowd pushed them closer together.

She put out her hand to brace herself from going face-first into his chest.

"Yeah, a sleigh full of *oof* and Saint Nicholas, too," he teased her softly, then bent his head and met her gaze. Just for a moment he knew they shared the same thought, the same memory—of the kiss that they shared.

*Just this one Christmas*. They should make it memorable.

She looked deeply into his eyes then broke contact and used her hand to steady herself. She smiled briefly then stepped away again.

They were wise not to follow through on another kiss. Still looking down at her now, he couldn't say the urge to pull her close had subsided so much as it had been subdued. It would be wrong, of course, to pursue a relationship with Dora at this point in his life. And he could not delude himself. If he kissed Dora again, with their already fragile history, he was as good as making a promise. A foundation from which the rest of their lives would be built.

It would imply trust and hope, things Dora clearly did not take lightly. Things that Burke would not offer lightly.

He fought the temptation to move still closer to her, to smell her hair, touch her face and see the light glow of a blush work across her cheeks. Then to lower his head and…

"Dunk the elf and win a prize!"

Burke blinked then looked around them again. The whole while he had been lost in Dora's eyes they had moved along with the cluster of people around them to the small midway of games and food booths.

All around them people laughed and greeted one another.

Overly loud Christmas music poured out of poorly placed speakers, crackling, crooning, then crackling again.

Adam and Josie had gone on into the Home Cookin' Kitchen leaving Conner to parade baby Nathan around, making sure nobody had any doubt as to the kid's lineage.

Carol and Cody met up with their youth group to check on proceedings at their Dunk the Elf booth. Some of the larger boys tried to convince Cody he should take a turn on the board above the murky tank of water.

"No one would dare dunk you, Preacher," someone called out.

"Ought to be *one* Burdett who'd step up and do it," came another observation.

"No," Burke said, before Dora could even open her mouth to volunteer him.

"I was going to suggest Adam," she shot back.

"Adam?" It should not have hurt his pride to hear that. But it did.

"He's the CEO. He's the guy they will take the most delight in soaking to raise money for the needy folks in town."

"Yeah, only he isn't the one who made them needy." He scanned the crowd knowing full well that this threadbare, makeshift gathering was going to be the highlight of more than one family's holiday, especially now that the Burdett party at the Crumble was a thing of the past. "I did that."

"No, your father did that. You tried to keep as many people employed as possible."

He looked at her, not sure whether to be impressed or wary.

"You have to know," she continued, "that I did plenty of research before I ever even considered investing in your company."

"Sure." He did know and just then it dawned on him that Adam probably had known, too. And Conner and the others. Could that have been behind the huge risk of not allowing Dora to buy in? She knew them too well, and she might have too readily stood with him against them.

Not that he saw his family as wicked or scheming. They had just come to one conclusion while Burke, and maybe Dora, had come to another. The other Burdetts were doing what they thought best, protecting the business they all loved just as much as he did.

It was one of those no-win situations, Burke thought. Only not winning had cost Dora and the townspeople more than it had any one of the Burdetts. Burke felt worse than ever now.

"Combing over the data, I believe your plan for the Crumble was working." Dora did not look at him as she spoke but strained her neck to get a good look at the goings-on in the church youth group booth.

"Slowly. However, with a fresh infusion of cash things would have turned around soon."

"*Your* cash?"

She shrugged, still avoiding eye contact.

"I wish it had worked out that way," he said,

"So do I."

"Yeah?" He couldn't help smiling to think of her on his side.

At last she turned to him, her smile coy and a bit crooked. Her eyes glittered in the mix of streetlights and bright Christmas decorations. "If you had stayed in the top spot, it would be you on the board about to take the plunge right now."

For a split second Burke considered doing it, if just to show her he could take his lumps.

But before he could volunteer, Adam climbed into the seat and donned the baseball cap with the pointy ears that the kids had provided for him.

"Sure it wasn't your brother in that elf picture I've heard so much about? He looks awfully cute."

"I'm sure," Burke growled.

Carol took the first pitch and missed by a mile.

Cute? She thought Adam was cute? And for what? Doing the job Burke had done long before he got a shot at it? Taking the place in the business and in the dunking both that was rightfully Burke's? Dressing like an elf? Burke had done *that* long before Adam as well. "No. It's not Adam. It was my job long before he even came into the picture."

The crowd shouted for Carol to try again.

Adam laughed, put his thumbs in his ears, wiggled his hands and stuck out his tongue.

"What was your job?" Dora asked.

Carol cocked her arm back, placing the softball in perfect position—for Burke to take it.

"To be Top Dawg," Burke came back. He threw the ball with all his might at the small target.

*Wham!* The ball hit the mark.

Adam went down into the tank with a *yeowl,* his hat flying up in the air.

Some people whooped and started a chant, "Top Dawg! Top Dawg!"

Everybody laughed, even Adam.

Well, almost everybody. Burke couldn't shake Dora's assessment. It should have been him in that tank.

Not that he would have ever gotten in it.

He stared at his younger brother who rose from the water, dripping wet. He bent to pick up the cap he'd tossed to safety earlier and waved it to egg on the crowd.

Josie, standing ready with a towel, leaned in to kiss Adam and found herself in a big, damp hug. She laughed, too.

The townspeople cheered some more.

Dora clapped.

For a fleeting moment everybody seemed content with their lives, happy even, and Burke had the odd sensation that maybe things were exactly as they should be.

Adam as the head of the business. The new leader of the Dawg pack.

"Isn't this a hoot?" Dora applauded Adam as he walked by, waving and enjoying the appreciation of the crowd.

"Oh yeah," Burke droned even as he found it in himself to give her a lopsided grin. "It's a regular hoot and a half."

"Be nice," she whispered.

"I am nice," he protested.

She narrowed her eyes, more flirting than challenging, and opened her mouth as if she had every intention of refuting his claim.

"Okay. You win a prize, Burke." Carol strolled up to them with a plastic mug with the church's name on it in one hand and a trio of glow-in-the-dark necklaces in other. "What do you want?"

He looked at Dora.

She mouthed the word *necklace* and, while he stored that preference away for future reference, he shook his head. "I want…"

Maybe it was the way he drawled it out. Or the fact that he spoke a bit too loud. That he stood a good five inches above the tallest person there. Or maybe, just maybe, it was because even after everything that had happened he really was still the Top Dawg—but everybody seemed to pause and listen.

"I want..." Burke nearly closed one eye and drew a bead on his younger brother. He pointed his finger. "I want his hat."

People whooped.

Dora beamed her approval.

"The hat isn't one of the prizes," Carol whispered.

Burke reached around to his back jeans pocket, tugged out his wallet, withdrew every last bit of cash he had on hand, tucked it all into the plastic mug in Carol's hand and said, "It is now."

"Give the man that hat, tank boy!" Cody demanded.

Adam obliged. Or rather, Josie obliged for him, giving it to Burke with a curtsy and a giggle.

Burke accepted it with a nod of his head then turned and presented it to Dora.

"This should come in handy," she said, giving it the once-over.

"I hope you don't already have one," he said, enjoying the look of excitement on her face. He helped her tuck her hair behind her ears and settle the hat on her head.

"How's it look?" She posed and batted her eyes for him.

"I don't know," he said softly.

She stopped still. "You don't know how my hat looks? Why not?"

"Because he's not looking at the hat," Jed called out.

And he wasn't.

He wanted now more than ever to kiss her. To make that promise.

"Okay, enough of this! Who's brave enough to go next?" Cody barked out.

Dora gave Burke a weak smile.

The younger brother pressed his hand to Burke's back to thank him for the donation and dunking Adam, and to prod him to take his obvious flirtation with Dora out of the church parking lot.

Burke moved on before Jed could make a bad marriage pun about him and Dora taking the plunge.

"So, do you like that hat or not?" she asked again, clearly making nervous small talk.

"I like it." He wished now that he'd put that childhood picture of himself in his pocket and brought it to show her. "Reminds me of somebody I've seen a photo of lately."

"Don't see how it could." She walked ahead a few steps then turned to look at him over her shoulder. "I don't *have* anybody."

*...the first Christmas in a very long time that I won't feel utterly alone in the world.*

He couldn't give her much. Not a home or a position in the business or a future. But this? With a little help, maybe he could give her the one thing that would end her lonely Christmases from this year on.

# Chapter Ten

The next week flew by faster for Dora than the final countdown of "The Twelve Days of Christmas" sung by a bunch of third-graders who knew that as soon as they finished the last *e-ee-e-eeee* of the partridge in a pear tree they'd be excused for cookies and punch.

During the daylight hours, Dora kept to the downstairs part of the family home, sifting through the remnants of Maggie Burdett's life. After a quiet dinner with Conner and sometimes Burke she would excuse herself and head upstairs, where she tried to sort out the remarkable woman's more private and encompassing legacy.

There was so much to learn about the town and its people. So many angles Dora could imagine taking to bring order to the eclectic mangle of a system Maggie had developed over the years. Should she consider granting the coins on merit or need or both? What about potential? Or doing the maximum good for the most people?

Would eight smaller gifts accomplish the goal? Or did it have to be one spectacular award to do Maggie Burdett justice? The only thing even resembling a mission statement Dora had found was what Burke had told her early on: *We give to others because God first gave Christ to us*.

All the while the days went whirling by. Those geese were a-layin', those swans a-swimmin' and those lords, Dora could practically feel those fancy-footed dudes doing a number on her poor aching head.

For the most part, Burke gave her no input. He always seemed to have mysterious work to do elsewhere or he just kept to himself in his ranch-style house sitting a half-acre away on the compound grounds. And yet everywhere that Dora looked she saw him, or something of him. And more often than not it gave her a glimpse into the man that his real and guarded presence never had.

She dragged her thoughts away from the man who had involved her in the project and then conveniently disappeared as she fixed on the task at hand.

"This single place setting doesn't seem to go with anything, Mr. Burdett." On her knees on the dining room floor, Dora held up a piece of china in a regal black-and-red pattern with gilded edging. With it she brandished a gold-plated knife, fork and spoon with clean, modern lines and a bold letter *B* engraved on the handles.

She carefully catalogued them on a yellow legal pad to leave a record so the often-squabbling siblings would know everything they came across and what had become of it. Often, while Conner Burdett told her the story of this thing or that, she doodled a quick sketch of an object or how she imagined it was used.

She flipped back to the first page of the pad to peek at the doodle there, a big shaggy dog wearing a Santa hat and elf ears. She considered drawing a Bad Dog sign beside the pooch and held back her smile as she turned again to the list and that troublesome lone place setting. "Should I box these up or put them with the things to give away?"

"Oh, no. No, no, no." Conner had dragged everything out of the linen closet and into the room, which was large enough to accommodate a long, dark table, eight straight-backed chairs, a buffet, a china cabinet and still leave room for a person to move all the way around with a serving cart. He held his hand up. "Don't go and do either of those things."

Dora took a deep breath and braced herself to hear what Conner had said about every scrap of paper, piece of clothing or useless nicknack she had held up—"There's a story behind that." Which he would then proceed to tell her.

At length.

In detail.

Twice.

"No, no, no." He shook his head, squinting. "Put those back in the china cabinet where you found them."

Dora waited for more.

Conner went back to shuffling through a stack of tablecloths.

Maybe he hadn't understood her question. Or perhaps in the dim light from the dingy, aging crystal chandelier, he hadn't actually seen what she had held up. "Mr. Burdett?"

"Now how many times have I asked you to call me Conner?" He gave her a sly smile and then a wink. "Mr. Burdett is my firstborn."

Dora had to chuckle at that, even though she completely understood and agreed with the comment. "Conner, then. I…"

"Look here." He yanked up a crisp pink, white and olive-green cloth with a motif of funky Santas and Christmas greetings in odd-size text. "Maggie got this the very first Christmas after we began keeping company." Conner, sitting in the chair at the head of the table, unfolded one corner then practically caressed the cloth with the palm of his weathered hand. "Before we were married, or even engaged yet."

"For her hope chest?" Dora wondered aloud. Her great-aunt had had one of those and tried to start one for Dora, who had told her that none of the other girls Dora's age had one. The truth was that Dora would have loved one but the last thing she needed was yet another thing to single her out, make her seem out of touch.

"Hope chest?" Conner scratched his head. "No. Not for my Maggie. Her hopes ran in an entirely different direction than tablecloths and putting away things for home and hearth. That's why when she showed me this, I knew."

Dora leaned in to get a closer look. "Knew what?"

"That she was going to be my wife."

Upon closer inspection the tablecloth made her almost laugh out loud. She couldn't imagine old sour Burke growing up eating Christmas dinner off this.

"I had just about given up the whole idea that Maggie would want to settle down and stay here in Mt. Knott with me. But this tablecloth changed all that. Perfect fit for this table, which had belonged to my parents."

"Let's keep it out, then." She accepted the cloth from his hands as though it were made of spun gold. "I'll launder and press it and we can put it on the table for Christmas in honor of your marriage and your Maggie."

"Thank you, Dora, for doing this with me." His eyes got misty, for only a second, then he cleared his throat. "You're the only person in these past two years would have trusted with the task."

"Me? But Mr., um, Conner, you really hardly know me and what you do know, well, I got the impression, no, actually, the legal notice of failure to complete a contract that made it pretty clear your family didn't really have much use for me."

That was the sore spot. All her life Dora had found her niche in being useful. To be told she wasn't?

"That were the case you wouldn't be here now, would you?" He scoffed and went back to sorting through the other tablecloths, hardly able to hide the tears welling in his eyes with each memory they brought.

"I see," she murmured, humbled at the freshness of the man's grief even now.

There was so much sadness in this house, so much gone unsaid between family members that might have healed it, or lessened it. It made Dora's heart ache for them. Was it really so hard, she wondered, this relationship between parent and child?

She shook her head and went back to the work at hand. "But this? Why would you want to keep a single place setting?"

"It's Burke's."

"Burke's?" She held it up. It was hardly big enough to serve a slice of Josie's pie and had no companion pieces. "Burke has a china pattern?"

"It was his when he was a baby."

"Baby? But it's fine china."

"Nothing but the best for my son."

"So they each have one?" She looked up and tried to find three more plates with utensils.

"No. Just Burke. Just our little prince."

"Your Top Dawg," she said softly.

"From the day he was born," Conner confirmed. "By the time we adopted Adam we had figured out how impractical it was, feeding boys off fancy plates."

"Guess Burke taught you a thing or two." She smiled.

"In his own way, yes."

"And what way was that?" she asked.

"The hard way, my dear." He said with a gleam in his eye and unabashed pride in his voice. "Always the hard way."

Dora laughed, but not from the heart. Her thoughts went back to trying to teach herself how to run the Forgotten Stocking Project and her head throbbed anew. "I'm surprised this plate survived intact."

"I ain't rightly sure he ever used it." The older man reached out and took the plate for his own inspection. "But, oh, the plans we had for that boy when we bought it and then...."

"Then you realized he had plans of his own," she said softly. Suddenly the parent/child conflict became clearer in her mind. What, she wondered, had Conner expected of Burke that he could not give?

Giving, she realized in that instant, was not Burke's strong suit. And giving was the only thing a parent would want, that a child not act grudgingly or out of teeth-gritting obedience but to submit freely and from the heart. Yes. She could imagine the conflict between father and son now, and had a new insight into the reasons the Bible often taught about the relationship with God in terms of a loving Father wanting the best for His children.

*"For I know the plans I have laid for you,"* declares the Lord, *"plans to prosper you and not harm you, plans to give you hope and a future."* Being a lifelong planner who always feared for her own future, Jeremiah 29, verse 11 had always held a special appeal for Dora.

"That's nice." Conner folded his hands and gazed at the plate again. "That's all I ever wanted for my sons. For them to prosper. For them to have hope and a good future."

"You provided for that, Conner, when you built up the family business."

"Exactly why I did it." He nodded, still not making eye contact with her. "And exactly why I didn't think—don't think—all of my boys should carry on in it."

*Wow.* What an odd and yet profound statement. The kind of thing Dora suspected the old man might never have said to anyone else. The kind of thing she wanted to hear more about. "Are you saying—"

"I'm saying this work won't do itself." He clapped his hands. "We still got a week's worth of work ahead, and that's not taking into account the barn or the upstairs."

"Week? Barn? Upstairs?" She didn't know which to worry about first. She had planned to head back to Atlanta in a couple of days. She hoped that distance and her own surroundings would help her gain perspective on the best approach for the project. "I don't think I can stay out here doing this for that long. I have things that need my attention."

He trained a beady eye on her. "You were a jiggler, weren't you?"

"A—" Dora didn't know whether to be insulted or charmed. "What?"

"When you were little. I bet you were the one who crept in under the cover of darkness, laid on your belly under the Christmas tree and gave each and every one of your presents a little—" He raised both hands as if holding a package then demonstrated as he said, "—a jiggle."

Dora laughed and hoped it didn't come off too awkward and iffy. "No, Mr. Bur—"

"Eh, eh, eh."

"Conner. I was not then nor have I ever been a jiggler."

"Of course not." Burke leaned in, plucked up the yellow legal pad and began glancing over it as he said, "Way too unreliable a means of checking inventory for our Dora."

"How long have you been standing there—" She turned away from Burke, leaning against the doorframe with a heart-melting smile on his lips, to his father as she shared an inside joke with the older of the two men, *"Mr. Burdett?"*

Another of the brothers would have naturally protested that Mr. Burdett was their father. Given the old man his props, as it were.

Not Burke. Not Mr. Business. Not the real *Mr. Burdett*.

He wasn't going to give anybody anything. Not even a direct answer.

"Where you been?" Conner wanted to know.

"I had things to do," he said cryptically.

"Apparently you didn't get them all done." Conner dove back into the work before him.

"What makes you say that?" Burke asked.

"You forgot to pick up dinner."

Every evening since she had gotten here Burke had shown up about this time with "to go" boxes from Josie's restaurant. The food was good and plentiful and Dora hadn't minded one bit not having to add cooking to her list of duties. But she had felt a bit strange that it probably looked to Conner as if she were too snobby to pitch in and pull together a simple meal.

"I'll go back to town in a minute," Burke said. "How are things going here?"

"We found your baby plate."

"Can't say you ever ate off it." Conner gazed at it and whispered, "But, oh what plans we had...."

"I don't see any use in keeping it." Burke handed

her the legal pad, pointing to the plate listing, as if to order her to move it off the list of keepers.

Dora took a breath but did not take the pad, not just yet. Taking it implied agreeing with him and she couldn't do that as long as Burke would not even give his father a moment of sentimentality. She wanted to—well, never mind what she wanted, she decided, reining in the temptation to lose her temper or to cross the line between personal and professional behavior. Burke wouldn't give anything, including a hoot about what his father was really saying to him.

"Bad dog," she muttered under her breath.

"What?" Burke pushed the pad toward her again and when he did the pages flipped to reveal the drawing on the front.

He paused, studied the blatant representation of himself with elf ears and finally chuckled softly before handing it to her again. "I'll go back to town to pick up dinner now. Is the special okay with everyone?"

This time she did take the pad. Maybe the man wasn't so bad.

Dora had already given plenty, but then she had come here looking for a way to give as much of herself as possible. Maybe that meant she needed to set an example and give a little more. "How about I do the cooking tonight?"

She worked her way over toward Conner on her

knees, intent on using the arm of his chair to climb to her feet.

As she wriggled by, Burke nabbed her by the arm and helped her up, peering down into her eyes with a hint of doubt as he asked, "You cook?"

"I sure do." She freed her arm from his grasp and tipped up her nose. "When there's a fridge full of Josie's wonderful leftovers to throw together into a casserole or hash."

"Oh. Yeah? Well, in that case, I cook, too," he shot back with a grin, showing a glimpse of the man who had assured her that he was actually this nice at the downtown holiday event.

"Then maybe you should give us all a break and do the honors tonight," she teased. Only she wasn't completely teasing. She honestly thought it would serve this man well—this high-born prince of snack-cake bakers, this sometimes very bad dog—to do some good for others instead of deciding for them or directing them or even dogging them.

Of course, that was the part he picked up on. The kernel of truth beneath the jest. Dora should have seen that coming. It's exactly what she would have done, only she liked to think she'd arrive at a more accurate reason to have taken offense at the remark.

"I should cook because I'm the only one who hasn't been working?" Burke still had her hand in his, and his hurt and anger held her attention as though they were alone in the room. "Is that what you're saying?"

"No." *Well, sort of.* She had, if she confessed, been aiming to change him, because she thought he could do more, be more. She had no business prodding him that way, of course.

Because the only thing between them *was* business.

"Just laying out the terms of the contract, Mr. Burdett. You know, always ask for more than you think the other guy will ever give when you begin negotiations." A smart tactic usually but since Burke wasn't about to give anything, just opening her mouth had blown the whole deal at the onset. "We have leftovers and both of us are equally capable of—"

"I submit that capability in cooking is a pretty subjective thing, Ms. Hoag," he shifted quite easily into CEO mode.

Something that did not put her off one bit. "I gladly accept your submission, Mr. Burdett, and I—"

"Knock it off, the pair of you!" Conner moved the table linens from his lap to the floor, signaling the end of his task and his patience. "You both know how to cook. The kitchen is thataway. I'm hungry."

Burke and Dora exchanged a brief look. In a boardroom, they probably would have shaken hands as a sign that they had reached an agreement. Instead they started off in the direction Conner had just pointed.

"Good. Go. About time you two turned up the heat." Conner waved them away, calling after them. "And while you're at it, make some dinner, too!"

"I'm sorry about him," Burke said as he ushered her into the kitchen.

"Don't be. I like him." She went to the fridge and started pulling out the remnants of earlier meals.

"Well, he likes you, too."

"You say that like you think we both have bad taste in the company we keep."

"Did I?" He frowned but she wasn't sure that it was a comment on how she had read him, or because the food in the container he had just opened had gone bad.

So she went on, getting out a big ceramic casserole dish and pulling salt and pepper from the overhead cabinet. She knew where it all was, having gone through this room cataloging every gadget and gewgaw.

As she worked she made the kind of small talk she usually heard other people making in the break room. A question couched as a thought. A tidbit of information thrown out for comment without the formality of requesting a comment or opinion. "Um, your dad thinks we have a week's worth of work left but I think I should go back to Atlanta for a few days."

"I agree." He threw the box he'd just sniffed into the trash can.

"With what?" This was why she never engaged

in that break room chitchat. She wasn't any good at it. And, of course, everyone at work was so afraid of her they usually emptied the room before she could attempt to join the conversation. "Staying for another week or going back to Atlanta?"

"Atlanta." He scanned the boxes and picked up another one. A quick peek inside then he handed it to her. "Start with this."

She took the box and peered inside, too, feeling more like part of a production line than a participant in a conversation or creative endeavor. "Okay. Then what?"

"Then you tell me where I can meet you there."

She'd meant *then what do I add to the mix of leftovers?* not *then what happens with you and me?* "You and me? In Atlanta? At the same time?"

"Sure."

She clutched a wooden spoon in her hand until her knuckles went white. Maybe she had read him all wrong. Maybe he was more giving than she thought and right now he was giving her a chance to make something more of their relationship. "In Atlanta?"

"If that's where you'll be, then that's where I need to be."

She stopped filling a casserole dish with macaroni and cheese from the box Burke had passed to her. How long had she waited to hear him say just that? She took a step toward him.

"Yeah. Makes sense doesn't it?" Another box, this

time set aside. "Down there we don't have to have any secrets."

"Secrets? About the project?"

"About the... Oh! Yes, the project. Yes. That's right. How could I forget the project? It's the reason I'm here. I do have a lot to talk to you about." She flipped the last of the boxes open and studied the contents. "We need something to hold all this together."

"The project?"

"The food, you know, some canned cream-of-anything soup?" Dora jerked her head up. Actually, yes, that was exactly what they needed for the project, something to hold it, and them, together long enough to see it through. "Now that you mention it, though, we do need something to make this project cohesive. It's all over the place now. I can't seem to find any formula for how your mom made her choices. If we—"

"Save it." He plunked down a can with a pull-top lid then made a stirring motion with one hand to ask her to hand him the spoon. "In Atlanta we can meet someplace, you can give me your report and answer any questions I have then."

"Ok," she murmured, as the glop from the can fell on top of the noodles with a slurpy plop. She had come here because she thought she had something to give, but in reality what she had given had always been his to begin with, his to take and his to reject if he so desired.

She slapped the spoon into his palm, not angrily but more like a nurse handing a surgeon a scalpel. They would be in Atlanta just what they were here and now, a couple of professionals with a deadline on a job they had both committed to see through. "Then after that I can go over things with the accountant and get an order in with the jeweler."

"I'll do that." He stepped in and took over the construction of the casserole as well.

"I don't mind." She held her hands up, feeling absolutely useless. Her least favorite feeling in the world.

She watched him a moment and realized that he had already begun to pull away from her, the way one does when a collaboration nears conclusion. *Correction,* she thought, *feeling useless is my* second *least favorite feeling in the world.*

He churned the food in the dish and added salt and pepper, never once turning to acknowledge her. "Dealing with the other team members, that's my place, Dora."

And she had just been put in hers.

"Besides, if you and I are both gone at the same time then we both return at the same time, people will talk." He yanked open a cabinet, pulled out a half-empty bag of potato chips and sprinkled some on top of the mix. "I won't have that."

She leaned back against the counter, trying to get some satisfaction from the fact that he had taken over the meal-prep duties after all. "Protecting your reputation, eh?"

"Protecting yours."

"Gallant but unnecessary." Just how she felt about him taking charge of the kitchen instead of offering to do it out of kindness and generosity. "I don't care what people think of me if I know my actions are honorable and right."

"Yes, but you're working in my home. And though people don't know it, on my mother's project. I can't have that compromised."

Right. Business. It always came back to that with him. Everything did. She suspected that after the Christmas festival he had made his brother write out a charitable donation receipt with a notation at the bottom: for elf employment.

"So, Atlanta?" he asked.

"Atlanta." She nodded then suggested a place for them to meet.

"I'll put it on my calendar." He slid the casserole into the oven and set the timer.

"Me, too," she said, watching him walk away, leaving her with the less glam job of cleaning up the small mess they had made.

She looked around her. She was spending her yearly vacation in an old house in Mt. Knott, South Carolina, playing helper to the world's surliest Santa.

This was her gift, not to Burke, but to the town, and now to dear, still-grieving Conner Burdett and to Maggie. They deserved her best.

Come to think of it, *she* deserved her best.

She was going to do this the way she would if it were her project from the get-go. Then she would find a way to bring it all together and when they met in Atlanta she would give her all to Burke with no strings, no expectations and, like that fellow who sent the rings, the hens, the drummers, dancers and maids a-milking, a strict no-givebacks policy.

# Chapter Eleven

"Job hunting? That was your story?" Dora slid into the back booth in the small coffee shop at the address she had given him to meet her. "You told your family you were off job hunting?"

"Sure? Why not?" And by that Burke meant, *why not do a little job hunting* as much as, *why not tell the family that's what I'm doing?* He took the other side of the booth, making the table wobble with every inch he scooted along the shiny-red vinyl and gray duct tape–patched bench. "Nice place you picked to meet, by the way."

"I like it." Dora pulled her laptop from its case, flipped it open. "It's quiet, out of the way."

He checked out the clientele, more of a "can't never tell" lot, it seemed to him. A couple of bleary-eyed types with one hand affixed to a computer and a coffee cup in the other. And in the corner a fellow who clearly felt invisible to the world, and liked it that way. "Yeah, the place is practically abandoned."

"Hey, it has ambiance." She connected her Wi-Fi service with the push of a button.

"Good. I think people who eat here sometimes *need* an ambulance."

"Ambiance. Atmosphere. It's cozy. Quaint. A piece of Americana. One of those, what's the word?"

"A dive?"

"A mom-and-pop operation," she corrected with a hint of a smile and a steely-eyed glower.

Mom-and-pop. Suddenly he understood the appeal it had for a woman who had neither. So he tried to find something positive to say about the place where Dora had practically set up an office away from, well, her office. "I see they have a bottomless cup of coffee."

He pointed to a sign, smiling, trying to make nice.

She barely took her eyes off the computer screen.

Forget nice, he wanted to see the fire in her eyes. "Of course they don't say if that means they keep refilling your drink, or if the coffee is so strong it eats the bottom right out of the cup."

That did it. She gave him the look, all flash and polish and a touch of little girl ready to defend her corner of the playground.

"I like their coffee," she said.

*I like you,* Burke wanted to say. Instead he just sighed and shook his head, grinning like a fool.

That softened her up a bit and she conceded, "So the place is a bit of a greasy spoon."

"I don't think the grease is limited to the spoons, Dora." He picked up his water glass and held it up so that the fluorescent light shone through, highlighting the smudges.

"Enough of that. So, it's no Josie's Home Cookin' Kitchen—"

"Or Dora's home cooking for that matter." He meant that as a jab at his having come all the way to Atlanta to meet with her and her not inviting him to her home, but she didn't seem to pick up on that.

"But it's got big tables where they won't chase you off if you sit for a while, a Wi-Fi hotspot and the coffee keeps coming."

Or maybe she had brought him to the place where she spent more time than home. "Spoken like a woman who comes here often."

"Not *that* often."

"Hey, Dora. The usual?" A chubby-cheeked waitress in a bib apron with the strings wrapped around her thick middle and tied in front—which gave her a soft, lumpy look that seemed to say "hey, the food's great here"—offered up a half-empty coffeepot.

"No, thanks." Dora put her hand over the top of her coffee cup and glanced nervously at the waitress. "I, uh, think I'll have hot chocolate."

"Hot chocolate? Really? This early in the—"

"No time of day too early for hot chocolate." Dora beamed.

"—Season," the waitress finished. "I mean you don't normally switch to the sweet stuff until the week before Christmas."

"What can I say? I'm in a holiday mood," Dora droned, her beam decidedly bummed.

"Last year you held off right up until Christmas Eve. Or was it two years ago?"

Dora blanched.

Burke loved it.

And hated it.

Loved seeing her squirm like this, getting this tiny glimpse into her secret indulgence of hot chocolate around the holidays, but hated, hated, hated the thought of this bright-eyed, brilliant woman spending Christmas Eve in this greasy spoon. Granted, he could see what drew her to the mom-and-pop operation but he couldn't help thinking that even Mom and Pop found something better to do on December twenty-fourth than hang around here.

"And for you, sir? Hot chocolate as well? It's good. I can highly recommend it."

Burke scowled. "I don't usually go for the—"

"He's already so sweet as it is," Dora needled.

"I was going to say I don't usually go for the rich stuff."

"He rich enough as it is?" The waitress didn't so

much as smirk to apologize for the directness of her question.

"As a matter of fact…" Dora gave him a look.

"I'll take the hot chocolate," he said.

"With a shot of Dairy Dream on top?" she asked, pointing to a laminated picture clipped to the menu of a frothy whipped-creamlike substance floating on a cup.

Dora opened her mouth but Burke cut her off. Much as he'd love to hear her say out loud that he was, indeed, *dreamy* enough already, he actually wanted the stuff in his drink. "That would be fine. Thank you."

The waitress snapped a very professional "Yes sir" and scooted off, calling out after herself, "I'll bring your whipped cream in a dish on the side, Dora, just like always."

"Don't come here that often, eh?"

Dora bit her lower lip and raised her shoulders sheepishly as she gave Burke a guilty glance.

He would have gloated at being proven right so eloquently, so unarguably, so…deliciously, except that seeing her like this he didn't feel like gloating.

"Shall we get down to work? Or do you have to rush off and put in your application someplace?" She whipped her head around toward the front door. "Hey, you know, I think I might have seen a Now Hiring sign in the window here. If you want I can put in a good word for you."

He shifted awkwardly and the cushion beneath him sighed and groaned. "Yeah, I want to talk to you about that."

"About the work we need to do or about your claim that you are job hunting?"

"Can't I do both?"

"Oh, Burke, really. You have such a noble cause to tend to." She sat up all prim and proper in her navy-blue business suit and gleaming but simple gold jewelry.

Suddenly he wished he had chosen the glow-in-the-dark necklaces as his prize at the church dunking-booth. He'd have loved to see her in those, and the elf hat, and…. "Excuse me, did you say noble cause?"

"Your mother's legacy." She rolled her eyes, something he figured she'd never do in a bona fide business meeting, and pressed on, "I don't believe for one second you want to do anything, especially anything as demanding as job hunting, to distract you from that right now. Or ever."

"Ever? A man has to work, Dora."

"And there is plenty of work to be done with this, Burke." She slapped down a stack of file folders onto the table even as her eyes fixed on the computer screen. "I can see why your mother worked on it year-round. It's a full-time job in its own right. Or could be. If you did it right."

If you did it right. The reminder that he had not

done it, or much of anything, right stung. Suddenly the thought of asking her to put in a good word for him at Global seemed pointless. Silly, even. Besides, Adam had worked at Global. Burke was looking to blaze his own trail once again, as he always had, not to follow in his younger brother's footsteps. But the job interview he'd had there this afternoon had gone so well, and the position they had open sounded like a perfect fit for him.

His teeth were on edge. He wanted to defend his work ethic and record to her on one hand, but, on the other, she had offered him the single best hope for doing something meaningful with his life since his family had so lightly dismissed him. Between a rock and a hard place. Only there was nothing hard about Dora, though many people thought of her as tough as nails. He saw right through that to the little girl all alone in the world, and to that scared and lonely child all he could say was, "I'm listening."

"I've been thinking a lot about this." She scooted forward, her eyes lit with enthusiasm. "You could create a foundation to build on your mother's dream."

"I think my mother has already laid a pretty good foundation, Dora."

"Not that kind of foundation, Burke. This kind." She pressed a button on her keyboard and spun her laptop around.

There, on the screen was a logo, a hand-sketched image of the coin that his mother had made at the jewelers in Atlanta with a glimmer of light bouncing off the rim. Below it, in simple but elegant script, the words *The Forgotten Stocking Foundation*.

He pointed to it. "What's this?"

"Just a rough example. I toyed with the idea of a stocking or a something more, oh, you know, Santa-ish, but then I thought it was a better idea to honor the One who moved the original Saint Nicholas and us to action." She stroked her fingertip over the upper right curve of the coin on the screen.

Burke blinked and when his eyes focused in he realized what he had taken to be a flash to show the shine of the gold was really the image of the cross at the center of a star of Bethlehem.

He nodded slowly. He liked it. "But I don't really understand it."

"Your mom accomplished so much, Burke, but in a way that only a person who lived and worked and listened and learned about the goings-on and needs of a small community could."

The waitress brought their hot chocolates and clunked them down, the cups clattering against the saucers, the saucers thumping against the table. She opened her mouth to say something but Burke spoke first.

"Go on." He'd meant to encourage Dora to keep talking but the waitress must have taken it as a direct command, and she hurried off.

"Maggie did so much."

"You said that."

"But—" She wet her lips.

"I thought so." He sat back. "She did so much but what? She didn't do enough?"

"I'm not criticizing her, Burke. I'm not trying to downplay any of the work she did."

"But?"

"Just looking over the records I have been able to pull together, I am in awe of her." She placed her hand on a thick file folder. "She helped so many people, created the recipe and the logo for the Carolina Crumble Pattie and raised four very competent and compassionate sons."

"But?" He was a Dawg with a bone.

"But I think we could do more. Much more."

*We?* She had no right to include herself in his family business. No more place in it than he did. And he guessed, in a funny way, that did make them a *we*. "What makes you think *we* need to do more?"

"See for yourself." She worked a second file from beneath the first one and slid it across the table toward him.

"More rough examples?"

"No. More harsh realities."

He frowned then flipped open the file folder to see a name along with a page full of neatly typed notes on the person's situation. He picked that up and beneath it found another name, another summation.

And under that another and another. He raised his gaze to meet Dora's.

She sighed and tugged a piece of paper from the pile. "Look here. A budding scientist who can't go away to college because her mother died last year and there are two younger siblings to care for."

"I know them."

"A talented painter who just needs a little space for a studio."

He nodded at the name on the page. "She's good."

"A family who—"

He put his hand down over the page she was peering at. "Dora. I know all this. I know there are a lot of worthy folks in need, that's why I hired you to sort them out."

"Sort them how, Burke? By depth of desperation? By the most potential good to be seen, and if that, whose good and over how long? Does someone who can be a doctor take precedence over someone who wants to go to a technical school and be at work in six months? Does the scientist get a coin while the artist gets an empty stocking?"

He looked again at the papers lying side by side and shook his head. "Maybe we could do both."

"Maybe so but we can't do all of them."

Now he got it. Now he saw her quandary. "Let me guess, you want to help all of them, don't you, Dora?"

She didn't say yes, but she didn't have to because

it shone in her kind eyes and the way she pressed her lips tightly together to keep from blurting out something totally unprofessional.

"Dora, I don't see how—"

"I thought you'd never ask."

With that she launched into what Burke could only call a high-powered, take-no-prisoners, this-was-why-Global-paid-her-the-big-bucks-and-gave-her-a-company-car, smokin' sales pitch for the establishment of the Maggie Burdett Forgotten Stocking Foundation.

It sounded great.

Correction. Her voice sounded great.

"This year we make the announcement and give small grants with multiple recipients. What we can't do we ask locals to pitch in and help with. Someone probably has empty space for that studio, and surely someone can help with day care for those kids if we pay for reliable transportation so the college-bound girl can come back and forth on weekends."

Her *enthusiasm* sounded great.

"Then the real work begins. First we set up the means to raise money to serve just the immediate region. In a year or so the whole state. Eventually we should be able to reach anywhere they know the name Carolina Crumble Pattie."

Even the way she paused and took the tiniest sip of hot chocolate then smacked her lips ever so slightly sounded great. The pitch? Burke really wasn't listening.

He didn't have to listen.

"It sounds good, Dora."

"I'm so glad you think so. When can we—"

"Never."

"Never?"

His brothers and father had displaced him, and he did not owe them anything. The town had all but forgotten his years of dedication and sacrifice in favor of the promise of a new start with Adam, while they themselves made no effort to invest in Mt. Knott or one another. He owed them even less. He had made promises to Dora and to his mother—those he would honor but even they had their limits. Or, rather, he had his limits. He did not have it in him to do what Dora was asking. "Just this one Christmas, Dora. That's all I committed to. That's all I have in me."

"But why? You sat right here a few minutes ago and told me you were ready to take on a new job."

"I am." He flipped the file folder in front of him closed. "I plan to take a job, too. I feel that I have a lot to give if someone would have me."

*I'll have you.*

She'd never say it. She didn't want him any more than anyone did, he supposed, but he would give her ample opportunity to prove him wrong. When she sat there, her eyes narrowed and her lips pressed tight, he went on. "As soon as this one Christmas is past,

I will be back hard at work again, but not as Santa Claus to the entire South."

"So you're rejecting this out of hand?"

"No, I'm rejecting it out of common sense."

Her face went pale. Her lower lip quivered so slightly he doubted anyone else would have noticed it. Then she rallied and raised her chin. The disappointment in her eyes cleared. She nodded. "I see."

"Look, Dora, it's not personal. It's just—"

She held her hand up. "As an early Christmas present to me, I'm going to ask that you not finish that sentence."

He shut his mouth. Nodded once.

She nodded, too. Then forced a mild, tense smile and nodded again.

For a few minutes he felt that they might sit there like that for the rest of the night, like two silent bobble-head dolls. Nodding and smiling. Nodding and smiling.

In his capacity as CEO, this was the point where he would have stood up, shaken her hand and thanked her for her time before walking away. Nice and tidy. But today he was acting as a person, talking with another person, dealing with feelings and history and… and nothing about it was nice or tidy.

Well, last summer had been nice right up until the part when his whole world fell apart. He flexed his hands around the mug of hot chocolate and tried to think what more he could say. "So, how do you plan to spend the rest of the day?"

"Foundation or not, the job isn't done."

He reached for the files. "I can take it from here."

"I mean the job I'm doing for your father. I owe it to him to see that through until the end."

"You're going to Mt. Knott?" He hadn't expected that.

"Don't worry. I'll try to finish up before you get back." She clicked her laptop shut, tucked it in the case and slid out of the booth. "That will be my Christmas present to you."

## Chapter Twelve

Dora stood in the dining room of the main Burdett house, trying to look inconspicuous while three brothers and two wives finally faced the mountain of memories left by their mother. Burke had not returned from Atlanta nor had they seen one another after their tiff in the coffee shop.

She'd given it her best shot and been turned down. Only business, she reminded herself, nothing personal.

Her part was over. In reality she probably should have excused herself and gone upstairs to finish up there. But she really didn't think she could manage that without drawing attention to Maggie's secret office and the project that she had kept hidden from the family her whole marriage.

*Families.* Dora didn't know what to think of them.

Of this one, at least. Her own, she had always be-lieved was the exception to all the rules.

"What was Christmas like when the boys were young, Conner?" She asked a unifying question to try to make herself useful.

"A lot of grabbing and arguing and pushing and pulling, and a lot of laughter and love. Basically just like every other day around here."

"Hey! That's mine." The next to the youngest brother, Jason, lunged for an old tin box, the kind Boy Scouts used to sell filled with peanut brittle or log candy at fund-raiser time. Dora had found a whole stash of the things in the back of a closet, most of them empty but a few holding the kinds of treasures young boys might have stowed inside— marbles, rocks, four-leaf clovers.

"No, yours was red." Cody held the box up high, just out of reach from the brother a scant year older, but a full four inches shorter. "This one, the blue one, is mine."

"You're both wrong." Adam, the eldest, and short-est, of the three, leapt up and whisked the box away from the grasping fingers of his younger siblings. "That's mine. I know because I left a dent in the un-derside of it when I banged Burke over the head with it when he said it was his."

"Ha! That proves it can't be yours. If this metal had ever met with Burke's hard head it would be dented beyond repair," Jason observed.

To which the other brothers paused, shared a look, then broke into laugher.

Adam turned the box over in his hands. "Bet Burke still has his tin squirreled away someplace. Man, you can't get that dog to turn loose of anything."

He'd turned lose of her pretty easily, Dora thought before it dawned on her. Maybe he never really had ahold of her—maybe the connection she felt last summer had come from her alone?

"Hey, like we don't know that." Jason eyed the tin as if he weren't quite sure he was ready to let Adam keep it. "Hasn't forgiven us yet for ousting him from the Crumble."

"I still feel pretty lousy about that," Cody confessed.

Dora tensed. She wondered if she should excuse herself, or start humming Christmas carols really loudly to remind them they had an interloper in the midst. Except, she really wanted to hear this.

"Don't none of you try to carry the burden for that decision." Conner pulled himself up to his full height for the first time since Dora had been here. He set his jaw in grim determination, but kindness and care flickered in his eyes. "That was strictly my doing."

"Yours?" It slipped out before Dora's decorum could lock it inside her.

"Yes, young lady. Me and that firstborn of mine been at odds since long before I decided he ought to eat off fine china."

She looked once again to the plate.

"He's the one you thought shouldn't follow you into the family business?"

Conner's mouth twitched. He gave his other sons a once-over then he turned to her. "Too much of his mother in him. Too much of the little prince we expected him to be. Both those things always at war inside him."

That's why the old man kept that place setting. It wasn't just a reminder of the plans he had for Burke but of how he had tried to shape his son into something he wasn't meant to be and the price they had both paid. The conflict between them, the things he felt he had robbed his son of doing.

"So you corrected that by kicking him out of the business?" she asked.

"We had words. We had legal battles. We even came to blows at one point. But in the end I bested him with the one thing I knew he'd have to accept—good business."

Dora tried to take all that in. "Is that why you turned my investment down?"

"Didn't seem right to invite you into the family just when we kicked Burke out." Cody gave a sympathetic shrug.

"Personally, I was all for that." Adam threw his hands up to show he had no part in her rejection. "You would be way more nice to sit across from in board meetings."

"Prettier, too," Jason agreed.

Dora had to smile at that even while she had no idea what to do with the rest of the information. "Have you ever told Burke any of this?"

"Did she suggest trying to reason with Top Dawg?" Adam asked, laughing.

"Reason he'd go for, like telling him we were doing it for his own good? He'd pull an Adam just to prove us wrong." Cody gave his older brother, the one who had run off with his inheritance and taken a job with Global to try to run the family out of business, a jab in the ribs with his elbow.

"Neither the business nor the family could have withstood that," Conner told her.

"Hate to contradict you, sir." She folded her arms and looked at the lot of them. "But I've gone over your business with a fine-tooth comb and seen the inner workings of your family and I have to say both are far stronger than you are giving them credit for."

"Flattery ain't going to change our minds," Adam tossed the tin in his hand up a few inches and caught it again.

"Yeah, if you want to be a part of the business or the family, you're going to have to do it the old-fashioned way," Cody warned.

"Hostile takeover?" she asked, one eyebrow cocked.

"Some might call it that." Conner chuckled. "But

we were thinking if you want to be one of this pack, you're going to have to marry into it."

With that they all dove back into the once neatly stacked piles of things that Dora had spent days going through and organizing to see what they wanted to keep, store away for future generations or give away.

*Marry?* It wasn't even within the realm of possibility. Dora knew that, but why ruin this shot at making a lasting memory with something so impermanent as reality?

Boxes got shuffled from hand to hand. Papers avalanched onto the floor. Grown men whooped like children at coming across some long forgotten memento.

"Some things never change." Conner chuckled softly.

"Some things have changed, though. A lot." Dora moved her gaze away from the undoing of all her hard work to the closet where she had relegated box upon box of Christmas decorations, filling the small storage closet from floor to ceiling. "I take it you once went all out with the decorations."

Conner followed her line of vision. "We haven't had any of that stuff up since we lost our sweet Maggie. She passed at Christmastime, you know."

"I know." Dora put her hand on the old man's arm. "It must be hard for you to see all those things. If you'd like I'll just shut the door and leave them for you to deal with another time."

"But?" He stopped her in her tracks.

She inhaled and held it, then let it out with a soft chuckle. "Did anyone ever tell you that you sound a lot like Burke?"

The man's forehead wrinkled in confusion.

Dora laughed.

"I guess maybe the real issue is that the men of this family have no difficulty reading me like a book. They don't just hear what I say, they listen to what I am *not* saying." Dora looked from Conner to Adam then to the single place setting she had carefully, some might say lovingly, placed front and center in the china cabinet, the one that had been for Burke. "And unlike the people who work for me, they have the gumption to call me on it."

Conner had seen through her lame attempt to suggest that it was time to return to their old family traditions. Adam had stayed ahead of her in business negotiations and sent her packing before she had known what hit her. And Burke?

Being a master of not having to say much to speak volumes, Burke had seen through the razzle-dazzle of her Forgotten Stocking Foundation to the heart of the matter. She had tried to horn in on his territory. To make herself a part of his work, his family and his life.

Dora wet her lips. "Okay, you got me. I could close that closet door and leave it all for you to deal with at some later date. To let another Christmas go by without a tree or any lights or even a manger scene that I suspect your wife would have set up in a prominent place year after year."

"You know about that? We haven't set that thing up in more than a decade."

"You haven't had a crèche in your home for that long?"

"A crèche? Oh, no. I thought you meant the near life-size one we used to set up for the whole town."

"You have a nearly life-size nativity scene?" She whipped around to look at the boxes, sure she wouldn't have missed *that*.

"We did. Not too sure what became of it after Maggie had a meltdown over the town council kicking the holy family off the courthouse lawn, though. Burke might know. His mama always went to him to deal with things like that."

Dora chose not to respond to that, out of respect for Maggie and the objective of keeping secret what Maggie had asked Burke to deal with.

"There is a smaller crèche in there someplace though. She picked it up on some island. Can't recall which—" His face contorted with the strain of trying to remember.

"Fiji? Hawaii? Crete?"

"Long!" He snapped his fingers.

"Long Island?"

"Got it at a dime store. Little plastic thing." He made a frame with his hands to indicate the size.

"Got it before she even met me and said she always dreamt of starting a collection of nativities from everyplace she traveled. Wanted a whole roomful but then she met me and ended up with just the two—the big one and that plastic thing. Not enough to even fill a box."

"What she ended up with could not be contained by even this one house," Dora reminded him, and with a hand on his shoulder, drew his attention back to Adam and Josie with their son, Nathan, to Cody, Carol and Jason, all talking at once, holding up objects and sharing their fondest feelings about their mom.

Conner smiled at last. "I reckon you think it's time to let some of what she loved spill out again?"

"I do."

"What do you have in mind?"

She hadn't actually gotten Burke a Christmas gift besides her promise to leave before he returned. Which she still planned to do but somehow, after all they had shared, she felt she should do more. No, it was more than that.

She still saw so much good in Burke. So much, well, as much as she had tried to avoid the emotion her whole life, *hope*. He had so much to give if he would only let go of it. So much to share. Not with her, she understood that. He felt undone by the loss of his job, his lifelong work, his place at the top. He associated her with that loss, and she, of all people, understood that.

But he had brought her here to give something that only she could. She had yet to do that. The work on the project? He could have hired someone else, someone who had no contact at all with the town or the workers at the Crumble or his family, to compile all that and even make recommendations for him. What he could not appoint anyone else in the world to do was to tell him the truth.

She owed that to him. And he owed her...one memorable Christmas.

"Well, we have all these things and the house is so drab...."

And just like that Dora found herself in the middle of a family. Not an outsider. Not an observer. A member.

They heard her out then flew into a decorating frenzy. The sisters-in-law worked on the inside of the house, hanging swags of faux pine with red-and-gold ribbon over the fireplace and around the banister and filling every empty space with knicknacks and baubles. The brothers tackled the outside. That didn't take as long as Dora had expected since a whole system of hooks and latches that were hardly visible during the year had been installed and the lights, which had all been stored in neat rolls with tags showing where they went, fit right into them.

She and Conner took on setting up the large artificial, pre-lit tree and had just finished putting the star on the top when the doorbell rang.

Dora gasped. "I didn't think Burke would come back for another hour or more."

"Burke? Since when does he ring the doorbell?" Josie asked, even as she hurried to answer it.

"We three kings…" the three Burdett brothers belted out their own version of the old song, this one extolling their hard work and success at outdoor holiday lighting.

The women laughed.

Conner joined them. They stepped out onto the porch and, as the final note of the song warbled through the rafters, Adam flipped a switch.

"Oh!"

"Wow!"

"You did all this?"

A thousand white lights twinkled around them, warming the dusky late-afternoon sky like candles lighting the way on an overcast day. Framed by a semicircle of glittering pastel trees set of Victorian-style carolers stood, some moving mechanically from left to right, others lowering and raising songbooks and all of them opening and closing their mouths silently.

Cody pointed to them and laughed, sheepishly. "We couldn't find the music but Burke just drove up so we can ask—"

"Who did this?"

"Burke?" Dora stepped from behind Conner, her heart pounding. She had wanted to do this for him and be gone, to leave him with this wonderful sight and never see him again. But here he was.

Here *she* was.

And here was her heart, laid out and exposed in this small token she had wanted Burke to have— his family Christmas restored to him. "I planned to leave before now but it all took a little longer than I expected."

"So this was your doing?" he responded in quick, barely controlled anger.

Indifference. Mild amusement. Even gratitude, those she might have anticipated. But anger? Why anger?

The old Dora, the woman she had been before spending these last two weeks going over other people's troubles, thinking of ways to be of service, acting in a small way as a part of a family and a community, would have seen this coming. That Dora knew to never let your heart or your hopes do the work of your history or your head. "It was my idea, yes, but I only wanted to help."

He shook his head and anger faded to something else. Pain? Embarrassment? "If I need help, I hire it."

"You hired me to help," she reminded him.

"Not anymore." He moved past her, then looked

back. Framed in the glow and flicker of thousands of lights, he fixed his eyes on her alone, angled his chin up and set his jaw as he said, quietly, "You're fired."

## Chapter Thirteen

"Fired? Fired? I'll tell you who is fired, mister. You. You are the one who is fired here. I should have known you wouldn't be up to the job."

"Burke was working for Dora?"

Dora and Burke both startled at hearing Adam's voice. They looked his way then at the rest of the family staring unashamedly at them.

"I am not working for anyone, least of all you, Adam. Or any Burdett. That means I don't owe a one of you an explanation." Burke nabbed Dora by the arm and pulled her, gently but firmly, into the house.

She cooperated and went with him but the second they crossed the threshold, she yanked her arm free.

The door fell shut.

Dora turned on Burke, her eyes flashing. "Unlike your family, I may not have the power to actually fire you from the work we're doing, Burke, but somebody should. Someone as stubborn and prideful as you has no business setting himself up as some kind of icon of giving during the most joyous season of the year."

He stepped back. He'd come home thinking he'd find things much as he had left them, without decorations and without Dora. Instead he had returned to find all the people who had shirked the duty of decorating the house for their mother standing around congratulating themselves on a job well done—using his system. And now Dora was standing here telling him he didn't belong in the only role he had left?

Actually, that he sort of agreed with, in principle, if not in the personal emotional toll it would take. "Hey, I never wanted that job in the first place."

"Good, it doesn't suit you." She snapped. This time when her lower lip quivered she did not control it well. Tears glittered in her eyes. The little girl who he had always known lurked just beneath the surface of her unflappable, businesslike exterior came out of hiding and in full temper-tantrum mode to boot. "In fact, you'd look pretty silly in the suit that comes with the job, anyway."

That hurt. It shouldn't have. After all, what she'd told him was he couldn't pull off the jolly old elf look in red, fur and jingle bells. No rosy cheeks. No snowy white beard. No belly like a bowlful of jelly for him, no sir. In a way it was a compliment.

Only Dora didn't mean it as a compliment.

And that bugged him.

The fact that it bugged him, well, that scared him. Because it meant that deep down he wanted Dora to—no, not see him as Santa Claus—but to think that maybe he had some of the same stuff as the Saint who had worked so hard and risked so much to give others a better life. He wanted Dora to believe in him.

But he knew she was right not to. Nobody else had, why should she? "I'm not Santa Claus. I never was."

She folded her arms, pure defiance. "That's not what you told me in my office the day you recruited me to come here and help you."

He opened his mouth to deny her claim, then realized she was right. Not that he'd ever tell her so. She was right. He was wrong. All wrong.

He shut his eyes for a moment and bowed his head. Not to pray, as he really should have, but to hide. To stall. To give himself a moment to gather his thoughts so that he could say something tender, profound, healing.

"I, uh, you know you're not really fired, right?" he stammered at last. Was that the best he could do? Maybe his family had a point when they ousted him from the office of CEO. "Of course. You know you're not fired because you were volunteering your services but…."

"You don't have to tell me that." She waved away his response then turned and faced the front room.

"But I'd appreciate it if you'd share that with your family."

"My family?" For the first time he realized the decorating hadn't been limited to the outdoors. His gaze brushed over pine boughs and ribbons and the little plastic nativity scene his mother had treasured for so long, and the Christmas tree, with a tinfoil star on the top.

"Yes. Please tell your family you did not really just fire me." She frowned, cast her eyes down, then exhaled as if to say *moving on now.* Only she didn't move on. "It may seem like small thing to you but I care what they think of me. And, well, I've never been fired from anything in my life."

"I have." His gaze moved slowly again to that star. A knot tightened in the pit of his stomach. "Let me tell you, it's not fun."

She softened a little then, her shoulders shifted. She ran her delicate fingers through the fringes of her dark hair, which now touched her earlobes and fell over her eyebrows. "A lot of really powerful and successful people have been."

"Fun?"

She smiled, though not a cheerful or genuinely amused smile. "Fired."

"Oh, yeah. Yeah. You hear that all the time but when it's happening to you it's not as inspiring as people think it will be." He tore his gaze from the tree, whisked it back over the room, then shut his eyes and rubbed his temple in defeat. "Maybe it's because for every person who rebuilds and goes on to bigger and better things after a failure there are a lot who don't ever rebound wholly."

"Being fired is not necessarily a sign of failure."

Eyes still tightly shut, he rubbed the bridge of his nose, his forehead, as if somehow he could erase the whole scene from his mind. "Says the women who does not want any one in my family to think it had happened to her."

"Just tell them at some point, okay? I won't stick around for it. I should have left already so you could get back to—"

"No, Dora." He looked up at last. "There is no going back."

"What?"

He wished he could just leave it at that but he knew she'd find out sooner or later. "I got a job offer when I was in Atlanta, and I think I am going to take it."

"You'll be working in Atlanta?"

"The company is headquartered in Atlanta but they have jobs all over the country. All over the globe, actually."

"You're going to work for Global?" Her expression brightened. Her gestures became lively as she shot off questions without giving him a chance to answer. "In what department? What's your job title?

Do you need me to show you around? Where will you be based?"

He didn't meet her gaze as he answered only her last question, "London."

"London?" She took a moment to process that. "London, England?"

"I don't think they have an office in London, Kentucky." He cocked his head and studied her. She looked different than she had in the coffee shop yesterday. Softer around the edges. Less angles to her. Less, business. "You haven't kept your hair appointment since you've been here."

"I, uh…" She tucked a c-shaped curl behind her ear.

"I like it," he said. "It will go nicely with the ball cap with the, um…" He made a motion with a couple of fingers toward the side of his head. Suddenly he wished he had shown her the picture of him as a kid, pointed hat and all. Too late for that now. Too late for so many things.

"With the elf ears," he finished.

This time her smile came freely. "So, London?"

"Yep."

"They're taking a second-generation Southern snack-cake business king and sending him to London?"

They weren't sending him. He had made it a stipulation of taking the job that they send him as far away

Mt. Knott as possible. "Yeah, their only concern was whether I could learn the language."

She did not laugh at his lame joke. "Isn't that a waste of a resource? You know the market *here*. The tastes of the South. This is where you have street cred."

"Street cred? As a guy who runs a snack-cake bakery? All I have from that is crumb cred." He chuckled with a tinge of bitterness.

"What about your family?" Dora pressed on. "How can you just leave them behind? What about..."

*Me.*

If she said that one word everything might change and Burke knew it. And so he prayed that she would not say it.

"What about the Christmas project?"

He had entered all of this with a prayer that God prepare him for what lay ahead. He had spent hours in Atlanta going over every step that had led him to this moment. He exhaled trying to shore up the unexpected ache in his heart that came with the reminder, *Careful what you pray for, you might get it.* "That's my concern now, Dora, not yours."

"Then, I *am* fired?"

"No. You've done your part. You're job is finished."

"But I was going to..." She shut her mouth and pressed her lips until they went white. Her eyes grew still and sad. Clearly she knew that what he'd said was true. Her part in all of this was done. "So the foundation—"

"There is no foundation." Again the double meaning of that stung. His own foundation had been kicked out from under him. He and Dora had no foundation for a relationship. He had no intention of turning this yearly whim into an obligation that he would commit to only to find himself unseated by a better man, or woman. "Dora. Give it up. It's over. I am letting you go."

"Letting me…go." She nodded. For a second her eyes shimmered with unshed tears. Then she rallied, raised her chin, squared her shoulders and smiled. "Well, I may not have any experience being fired but being let go? That's old hat to me by now. Everyone I ever cared about has let me go or let go of me. I've survived that, and I suppose I'll survive your doing it, too."

Burke opened his mouth to say something but couldn't find the right words.

Dora did not share this problem. "In fact, I may be the one getting the better end of this deal."

"What?"

"Because I didn't just get something for my trouble, I *gave* something. I'll leave a part of myself here in Mt. Knott, but I'll take a part of it with me, as well. Can you honestly say you will do the same?"

"What are you talking about? I have given practically my whole life to the people here, to the business and well-being of this community."

"But what have you let them give to you?"

"Huh?"

"You ever ask your family why they voted you out and Adam in, Burke?"

"I didn't have to ask. They liked his ideas. The direction he wanted to take things. I made my pitch. He made his. They voted. I was out. That simple."

"I have known your family for a few months and though I learned the most about them these last couple of weeks, you have known them all your life and you don't seem to know them at all."

"Huh?"

"When is anything simple with the Burdetts?"

She had a point.

"They voted you out because your dad never thought you should be there in the first place."

"Yeah. Yeah, that's the story of our lives. Me and Dad always locking horns. I should have figured he was the one who—"

"The one who wanted the best for you," she finished on his behalf.

"What? No. Dora, this, this gentle old frail figure of a man you've seen around here, that is not Conner Burdett. Not the one who raised me and founded the Carolina Crumble Pattie Factory. He was ruthless. He was hard and driven. He was a man of good business."

"A man of good business? Isn't that the way Dickens described Scrooge?"

He opened his mouth to refute it but said instead, "Close enough."

"And you were on your way to being just like him. When all along, your family could see that you should have been more like your mom."

He stared up at the star then at the plastic nativity. He thought of that picture of him helping his mom one Christmas long ago. Of the light system he had worked to perfect to make his mom happy and of the Forgotten Stocking Project she had entrusted to him alone. "Funny, I always thought I should have been more like myself."

"Well, there's something to be said for that." She tipped her head to acknowledge his thinking. "I've spent a lot of my time here trying to figure you out, Burke."

"Surely there were more interesting things to focus on." He shifted his weight, uncomfortable with the idea of Dora's fascination yet curious about what conclusions she had come to—and if she thought him completely beyond all hope.

She moved farther into the room. "I've seen your baby plate, gotten to know your family, gone through your mother's most prized and even private things and yet, I don't think I know you any better now than I did when you showed up in my office the day after Thanksgiving."

"I never planned to—"

"I know. You never planned for me to know you. But that day, I did. I saw the real man beneath the CEO, beneath the Top Dawg. I saw someone who wanted to make a difference in the world."

He did want to do that, he couldn't deny it. But how could he when he couldn't even make a difference at the Crumble or even in his family home? He focused on the star again.

"But you can't make a difference in a world that you won't fully participate in, that you set yourself above, even if you do it for what you consider all the right reasons."

"Is this lecture for my benefit or yours, Ms. Checks out of the world for the whole month of December and when she is in it, she's in her office, on the road for work or in a coffee shop at all hours doing business on her laptop?"

"Fair enough." She held her hand up. "But there is a difference between the two of us, Burke."

"There are several, actually, but my mama raised me too polite to point them all out." He smiled, hoping to break some of the tension.

She relented and chuckled, quietly. "The difference I was talking about is that we both started this out as people too busy to—"

"Be bothered by hair care?"

She looked up at him in a quick, startled motion then laughed. "You've been to the barber!"

He nodded and ran his fingers through the closely clipped hair along the side of his head. "I've had a little free time lately."

She nodded. "Me too. And I've put it to good use."

"You don't like my haircut?"

"I like it just fine."

"But?"

The single word made her look away, almost as though he had caught her staring at him too long.

"The difference I'm talking about is that during this season, this one Christmas that I will always remember, I have changed."

"How?"

"I guess I did what you said you should do."

He shook his head. "I don't know…"

"I took the time to become more like myself."

"Yeah, but when you do that, you become more like, well, somebody pretty terrific. If I would do that, who would I be like?"

"I suppose you should try to be like someone who is at the very center of Christmas."

"Saint Nicholas?"

"Christ."

"Oh." He hung his head. He should have thought of that. "Is that what has happened for you, Dora? Has your time here strengthened your faith?"

"In ways I hadn't expected, yes. While I was here I gave my time and attention and in return I was given kindness and a glimpse into another way of life." She moved to the tree, touching the tips of the branches so that the lights bounced and set the ornaments sparkling. "And stories. Wonderful stories. Some that touched my heart and others that will have me laughing every time I think of them."

He looked around him. "I know a lot of stories."

"And people. And pie. And memories. I've only been around this town a couple of weeks this time and I've gotten all that." She stood at the far side of the tree so that he could not see her whole face and she looked at him. "And you?"

*Yes. You've got me. If you want me.* The problem was, of course, the thing that kept him from blurting that out—nobody wanted him. At least not as he was. And he was too old to change, wasn't he?

"Burke, you complained about people not doing their part for the town. About them not shopping here, not setting up businesses and medical practices here, but this town already had its primary business, yours. Maybe no one ever felt the town was big enough for anything else."

"Hey, it's a Top Dawg's instinct to bark and snarl and chase off any threats to his, um…"

"Top doggishness?"

He grinned.

"Only you are not a dog, Burke. No one here was ever any real threat to your position in the community and in the end, what did all your snarling and snapping get you?"

"Nothing, I guess. But then, I never wanted—"

"Anything from anyone. That's it." She stepped out from behind the tree. Her dark eyes had grown wide and somber but shone with a warmth and kindness that Burke did not know how to take. "I thought for a time you didn't know how to give. Then I thought you didn't know how to share."

"You really thought those things about me?" That hurt even more than saying he'd look bad in a Santa suit. "People think those things about me?"

"No." She shook her head. "People know you are capable of those things and so much more."

"People?" He wanted a definition. He wanted names.

She did not offer them. Instead she turned and moved to the mantel where the plastic manger scene sat. "Everyone talks about this being the season of giving. There's more to it than that, Burke. Giving is nothing if no one is there to receive what is offered. The baby Jesus came for all of us, but for those who turn away and do not accept the gift of salvation, it's just a story. It's a package wrapped in pretty paper that is never opened."

He wasn't sure what she was trying to tell him.

"You have the power to open you life, Burke. To not just give but to welcome what's given to you."

"*What* has been *given* to me, Dora? Nothing. I worked for everything I have and even so have seen it all taken away from me, from my position at the

Crumble to having a chance to decorate the Christmas tree with my own family."

"Burke, that's just not…" She launched into a denial but cut herself short. She stood there, blinking for a moment. She looked down. She shook her head. "Oh, Burke. I never thought of you wanting to help decorate."

"I used to always put the star on top of the tree for my mom. You know, just because I was the oldest, and the tallest, so I had to do it."

"Sure," she said, as if she really bought his premise that he had acted solely from a sense of duty.

"Not that I won't take you words to heart but…."

"Do. Please. Because…"

*Because I love you.*

That's what he wanted to hear her say. Careful what you pray for, he warned himself.

She had already turned to walk away and as she reached for the doorknob she added, "Merry Christmas, Burke. And happy New Year—in London. Maybe you will finally find what you're looking for there."

## Chapter Fourteen

"You better not cry, you better not...Ms. Hoag? Are you...are you crying?"

Dora sniffled and began hastily reshuffling files on her desk. "It's the day before Christmas Eve, Zach. I didn't think you'd show for work today." With Christmas falling on a Wednesday this year, the building would be pretty deserted all week long. "Nobody else is."

"That's why I am here, ma'am." He came into her office, leaving his pushcart of cleaning supplies in the hallway. "So nobody else on my crew has to be."

"You're a good employer, Zach."

"Rest assured I'll be out of the building like a reindeer with its tail on fire the minute I finish up my rounds. Won't see my sorry old face again around here until the second of January, either."

"I think it's a nice face." She slid the files marked

Personal into her briefcase then met his eyes and smiled.

"You all right, Ms. Hoag."

"I'm…" She paused to think about that question for a moment, to really think about it. "I'm better than all right, Zach. And please, we've known each other for so long, please call me Dora."

"Won't that raise some corporate eyebrows? The head of a janitorial service and a big boss lady on a first-name basis?"

"Corporations don't have eyebrows, Zach. They are not human. They don't have faces, which they like because if they did they'd have eyes and have to actually see what they do to people. No facial expressions, either, because they have no emotions. Nothing is personal with them, it's all business." She stood at last. "And I am going out of business."

"No! You? Say it ain't so. Global would never turn loose of a big-time team player like you."

"Global did not turn loose of me, I turned loose of them." For once she had been the one to let go, to stop trying so hard to win approval, and it felt *wonderful*.

Wonderful and just a little bit scary. Burke had called it though, no turning back. Her time in Mt. Knott with the Burdetts had changed her.

"I recently came to understand I was wasting my gifts and decided I need to do something more meaningful. I don't want to be part of Global's team any-more, Zach. I'm getting in a whole new league."

His neatly clipped silver mustache twitched, hint-ing that he wanted to break into a broad grin or let out a celebratory whoop. His eyes twinkled. "I know how you feel."

"You do?"

"Yep. Was on the fast track myself for a lot of years. Corner office, stock options, racked up enough frequent flyer miles to jet to the moon and back. Then one day, ffftttt."

*"Fffttt?"*

"Company downsized and I was gone."

"So you became a…" She pointed to the dust rag thrown over his shoulder and the cart waiting in the hall.

"Independent contractor?" He chuckled. "Well, made sense. I knew offices. I knew what the sixty-hour-a-week crowd expected. Started my own busi-ness. Became my own boss. Twenty-three years later, I have a nice home, a thriving business and time to play with my grandkids."

"Sounds great." She sniffled again. "I wish I'd known your story earlier. I know someone who might have benefited from hearing it."

He shrugged. "It's nothing special."

"I disagree, Zach. You're special. So is every-one who puts in a full day of work, does their best and still finds time to make the world around them a little better."

"I do that?"

"You always make me feel better when our paths cross. Oh, that reminds me!" She yanked open a drawer and pulled out a red envelope and handed it to him. "It's a Christmas card. I don't think in all these years I ever gave you one before."

"Why, thank you, Dora, dear." He poked his thumb under the flap.

"Oh, don't open it here—"

Too late.

His eyes went practically buggy at the check inside the card with the Star of Bethlehem on the front. "Oh, Ms. Hoag, I couldn't…"

"Dora, please."

"Dora, I can't accept—"

"But you have to accept, pal," came a deep masculine voice from the doorway. "It's a gift. Like life. You have to welcome what's given, then it's up to you to make the most of it."

"Burke!" Dora plunked down into her chair with a thud. She hadn't realized she was doing that until the wheels rattled and she suddenly found herself looking up at the two astounded faces of the men standing just inside her office.

"Hello, Dora." He stood there in his suede coat buttoned up to the neck, new jeans and a gray cowboy hat. "Did I come at a bad time?"

"No," she said softly, when what she wanted to say was: it depends on *why* you came.

"I better get back to work." Zach touched the corner of the envelope to his eyebrow in salute. "Thank you, Dora. If I don't see you again, merry Christmas and my hopes for the very best in the coming New Year."

Burke moved into the office to let Zach out. He tipped his hat.

Zach shot him a warning look then took up his pushcart again. "He knows if you've been bad or good so be good for goodness' sake! Oh…"

Burke chuckled as he turned around. "You sure it's not a bad time?"

She shut the drawer she had taken Zach's card from and gave her desktop a final scan. "If you'd shown up a few minutes from now, I'd have already left."

"Starting your holiday early?"

"I'm leaving Global." She stood again, this time taking up her briefcase.

"When? Why?"

"When? Now. Why? Because it's long overdue." She came around the desk, trying to look brave and serene when she felt scared and shaky. And more than a little heartbroken. She wanted to demand of him: What are you doing here? Haven't you hurt me enough? Instead she said, "If you like, you can walk with me to the door."

"Maybe we could head over to your favorite coffee shop, then?" He stepped quickly to the coatrack and lifted her long black wool coat from the hook, holding it open as she approached. "You'll want to bundle up. It's turned cold finally."

"I know." She reached out to take the wrap away from him but with one elegant move he slid the sleeve over her outstretched arm.

This brought him so close that she found her face shaded by the brim of his hat, creating a private world where it was just the two of them gazing into each other's eyes.

"They were predicting snow in Mt. Knott when I left this morning. A white Christmas for sure."

"A white Christmas in Mt. Knott? Sounds…" Romantic and lovely and a wrenching reminder of how, despite giving her all, she was going to spend another Christmas all alone.

"I got the sleigh all prepped." He held up the other shoulder of the coat for her.

"Oh." She fidgeted with transferring her briefcase so that she could put her arm through the sleeve.

"Hoping to take it out tomorrow." He helped her with her coat then left his hand on her shoulder.

She couldn't help smiling, just a tiny smile, then she met his eyes again. "Why are you here, Burke? Surely you didn't drive all the way from South Carolina to tell me that you are planning a sleigh ride on Christmas Eve. Who does that?"

"Gonna find out whose naughty and nice," bellowed Zach from a couple of offices away.

Burke laughed and gave a jerk of his head in Zach's direction. "You know who does that."

"So, now you're back to claiming you are Santa Claus?" She fussed with the collar of the coat.

"No." Burke lifted her hair from where it pressed against her neck and arranged it over the back of her collar. "But I am on his team, remember?"

She pursed her lips, not sure of what she would say to that but feeling she had to say something.

Then he produced a small, square photo of himself, in full elf regalia.

"You found it!" Dora took the picture and studied it with sheer delight, her anger and hurt over the man's actions forgotten momentarily.

"You were adorable."

"What do you mean *were?*"

"And your mom was so proud." She ran her fingertip over the image of Maggie Burdett standing off to one side.

"No. My mom was tickled at seeing me like that. I didn't give her cause to be proud for a long, long time." He took the photo back from Dora's hand. "I plan to change all that now."

Her pulse raced. What was he trying to tell her? "You…what do you…have you selected a…"

"Let's go to the coffee shop. I have a lot to tell you."

"Tell me here." She stepped over and shut the door. "I'm in a hurry."

"You leaving town?"

"No, I have some last-minute Christmas shopping to do."

"Oh?"

"You say that like you don't believe me. What? You don't think I have anyone in the world to give to?"

"I think you give to everyone you know, Dora." He took her hand. "Only some of us were too stubborn to see what amazing gifts you were offering."

"What do you mean *were*?" She threw his own earlier question back at him with a more cautious tone. Okay hopeful. She did not say it cautiously, she said it with hope. Lots and lots of hope.

"I've changed, Dora." He took a deep breath, then cocked his head and amended, "I'm trying to change. I want to."

"That's something."

He laughed. "I can't do it, though, Dora, without help. I can't do any of the things I want to do, that I feel called to do, without accepting the guidance, the hard work, the...love of a some very good people."

"You're truly blessed, then." She cleared her throat trying to banish the quiver and hoarseness from her voice. "Because you have a lot of good people in your life."

"Yeah." He took her hand. "More than I deserve."

"Burke—"

"Dora, I have a confession. I didn't come all the way to Atlanta to tell you about the sleigh and the snow."

"I thought as much." There was that sliver of hope in her voice again.

"I had to come, you know, to go to the jeweler's and to stop by the accountant's to set a few things up before—" He cut himself off, his expression concerned.

That *hope*. It did her in every time. She clenched her hand around the handle of her briefcase. "Before you take that job in—"

"I'm not taking that job."

"What?"

"London? Are you kidding me? You know what they call Santa Claus in London?"

"Father Christmas."

"Father Christmas!" he said a half beat behind her. Then he laughed. "No thank you. I am definitely not ready to be a father."

She laughed because it was the polite thing to do, and because if she thought about that statement too long, it would haunt her the whole Christmas holiday and beyond.

"'Course that doesn't mean I'm not ready." He reached into his coat pocket and went down on one knee.

"Burke? What are you—"

"Oh." He reached up and whisked the hat off his head. Only to reveal another hat there, a striped one with elf ears.

Dora burst out laughing, at the hat and in the sheer joy of what was happening. Or what she *hoped* was happening.

"Dora, I don't have a ring. The jeweler told me I would be a fool to just go and buy one without accepting some input from you."

"I wouldn't have minded," she said, surprised she could speak at all.

"*Now* you tell me." He frowned and shook his head, sending the tip of his elf hat wobbling.

Dora laughed in earnest then drew in a deep breath. "Um, I think you were about to ask me something?"

"No, I wasn't."

"You weren't?"

"Nope." He pulled a flat velvet box from his pocket. "I was going to *tell* you something."

"Oh." Her joy subsided. She could hardly breathe.

"Dora, I decided who I am going to give the Forgotten Stocking coin to this year." He adjusted his body, shifting the knee he was balanced on. Then he lifted the lid of the box and held it out. "It's you."

"Me?" She stared at the marvelous golden coin which, unlike any she had seen before, was on a slender gold chain. Above the image the words, "We give to others because God first gave Christ to us," and below it, "The Forgotten Stocking Foundation."

"Foundation? Burke, do you mean…"

"Yeah. This year I am giving this coin to someone who can set things up so that anyone who wants to can be on the Saint Nicholas team. I have some other coins, too, and I hope you will come back with me to Mt. Knott to distribute them."

"Oh Burke!" She threw her arms around him and hugged him close, asking, "I won't have to wear these ears will I?"

"Not if you don't feel like it." He wrapped her in a tight embrace and laughed. "Oh, and one other thing."

"What?" she pulled away just enough so that she could look into his eyes.

"Will you marry me?"

"Yes! Yes! Yes!" She kissed his cheek, his temple, his jaw, then paused, her lips just inches from his, "On one condition."

## Chapter Fifteen

"I can't believe you made me go Christmas shopping before you'd pick out an engagement ring," Burke muttered to his bride-to-be as he hitched the horses up to his very own shiny black sleigh.

It had snowed yesterday and then again this morning. It had stopped an hour earlier but stayed cold enough that they could use the sleigh over the fluffy white covering on the ground.

"How else was I supposed to carry all those gifts?" She settled into the seat, arranging an old family quilt over her legs. "What is the use in marrying a gigantic elf if you cannot use him to haul your Christmas loot?"

"It wasn't *your* loot." He finished up then checked the time on his cell phone. "I think you bought something for everyone in town."

"Not everyone. Just the people I came across for

the project. And the people on the prayer list. And your family. And a few extra things in case I left anyone out."

"Don't forget those gaudy ties for Warren and Jed." He went around to the back of the sleigh where they had stored the gifts they were about to take into town.

"Hey, with those blues and reds and purples and yellows, they can spill virtually any kind of pie Josie makes on those ties and no one will ever know!"

"I wish we'd come up with a way to buy replacement nativity figures." He looked back where his brothers were hard at work loading the best and the least busted-up figures from his mom's long stored-away nativity scene into his truck bed.

"I was so sorry to see what bad shape they were in. We'll work on getting the whole scene completed for next year."

"Don't we have enough to do with starting a charitable foundation, planning a wedding, getting married, going on a honeymoon, extending the honeymoon..."

She laughed shyly.

Her laughter sounded sweeter than bells, even Christmas bells.

"Oh, please, organize, delegate, take charge, we can do all that in a flash and standing on our heads." She snapped her fingers then paused, and rushed to say before he made a questionable joke, "Except the honeymoon, of course."

He cupped his hand beneath her chin and brought his lips to hers.

*"Whooo-hooo!"*

"I cry foul! They don't even have mistletoe!"

"He sees you when you're smooching…"

Adam, Jason and Cody began to holler and tease.

She kissed his lips lightly again. "You have given me hope again and restored my trust, Burke."

He glanced over his shoulder at the brothers carrying out the last of the statuary to the truck. He raised his hand and pointed. "Nope, not me. Not my job description. Not even within my means. But I do suspect who had a hand in that."

She looked at the Burdett dog pack, minus the Top Dawg, carefully lowering the figure of the baby Jesus into the truck and wrapping it to keep it safe. They had to add extra padding because so few of the pieces had survived the years intact.

Adam jumped down and shoved the tailgate into place with a wham. "Sure won't be much of a display this year."

"I had no idea that belonged to y'all. Always thought it was owned by the town and, when they stopped setting it up, that it was gone for good." Carol tugged her gloves on as she hurried toward the minivan to ride with Josie and Adam to the Crumble.

"Remember how everyone in town used to look forward to visiting it?"

"Noticed none of them fought for it when the council wanted it removed." Jason made one last safety check then strode to the truck cab where he would be entrusted with driving the precious cargo to town behind the sleigh.

"Hey! Mom never gave anyone a chance to fight for it. Just stashed the whole set away and never even told folks we had it. I think that was the wrong way to go about things. This is a town full of good folks who want the best for one another. Mom never let them prove that. None of us Burdetts have had enough faith in our community that they would pitch in and help us do what is good for us all." Burke couldn't believe those words had come out of his mouth. But he believed them and he was going to stick to them. "And I think maybe it's high time we corrected that."

"How we going to do that?" one of the brothers called.

Burke only had to think a moment before he reached down to the floorboard at Dora's feet and raised the elegant burgundy shopping bag from the Atlanta jeweler. It contained six boxed coins with the recognizable logo on them, but no names, as he'd never been able to narrow it down to the most deserving. His plan had been to give them out this evening as he was moved to do so.

And at this moment, he was so moved.

"All of us Burdetts have been so very blessed." He kept the bag aloft as he spoke. "Not just with money and opportunities but also with health and common sense—"

"Don't forget good looks," Jason called out.

Everyone shared a laugh.

"Yeah, with *devastating* good looks," Burke embellished. "And with faith and with, though we often take it for granted, the blessing of each other."

"Hear, hear!" Conner bellowed, and each brother and wife and wife-to-be echoed softly in agreement.

"And with the wonderful gift of having known or benefited from the love of an amazing woman— Maggie Burdett."

Conner again raised his hand but he could not speak to lead a cheer. His sons did that for him, with joy and gusto. "Hear, hear!"

"With these blessings comes the responsibility to give to others. We have always given to our community as we were able. It is my proposal, my wish, my *gift* to you that you share our blessings in a way only the Burdetts can in Mt. Knott, this year."

The men shifted in their boots.

The women leaned in, listening.

Adam, Mr. Get-Down-to-Business, was the one who asked, "What is this about?"

Burke told them about their mother's secret and about his decision to start a foundation, then he laid out his own plan, the one inspired by Dora's assessment of him. "Give this coin to someone you trust and ask that they pass it along to the people they think need their Christmas wish answered the most." With that he handed out the coins.

Everyone murmured and oohed and aahed over them as the boxes came open.

Burke took Dora by the hand, gazed out on the newest members of Team Santa and said, "I say, let's give our friends and neighbors the gift of being able to give of themselves."

## Chapter Sixteen

After taking a moment to run inside and make some phone calls, Adam and Burke and Jason had led the caravan through town. The truck and minivan had stopped every few houses to pick something up or to explain what they had in mind while Burke and Dora had gone along ahead in the sleigh distributing presents.

The kids loved their toys, even though they were small. And the families in need appreciated the gift baskets of necessities paid for from the Forgotten Stocking Project funds.

"I hope you don't mind I've been showing off my necklace and going on about the plans for the foundation more than I've been talking about our engagement," Dora whispered, snuggling close to Burke as they pulled up in front of Josie's Home Cookin' Kitchen.

"I'm just amazed at how many people always knew the coins were my mom's doing." He made a shushing noise and the horses stilled. He got out first then helped Dora down.

She ran around and picked out the packages for the regulars. Travel mugs for the commuters. Some soft fuzzy slippers for "Bingo Barnes," the mailman with the aching feet. And those ties for Jed and Warren.

Inside they found the counter piled high with cakes, cookies and candy.

"Folks 'round here may not have much, but long as somebody's got the fixin' nobody will go hungry," Jed observed.

Dora had never seen anything like it. "Let's check the prayer list and see if we missed anyone."

But there were no names there this happy day. In their place someone had written simply and in beautiful lettering: Peace.

And everyone who had come in seemed to have added his or her name.

"That's so awesome," Dora had said, then turning to the man she loved, added quietly, "I wish they hadn't erased the whole board, though, because—"

"Don't worry. I got it." He pulled out his phone and showed her the picture he had taken of the chalk drawing of a shaggy dog wearing a Santa hat. "When I saw it on the prayer list I knew you still had hope for me. I didn't give you hope, Dora, you always had it in you. You always had all this love and trust in you just waiting to give."

Tears welled in her eyes.

He gave her a hug and a kiss on the nose then hustled her off.

By dusk all the gifts had been handed out, the cakes and cookies and candies shared, anyone who wanted to had taken a ride in a genuine open sleigh and the townsfolk began to gather in the parking lot of the Crumble for the big display.

No matter how many new, handcrafted, specially-made, carved or even gilded figures they brought to Mt. Knott for future nativity displays, none of them would ever come near the sheer wonder and joy and beauty the haphazard, disorganized, motley, messed-up jumble of mayhem that was this year's pageant.

Four-H-ers brought live animals. Plastic blow-mold wise men knelt in awe around the original plaster holy family. Plywood palm trees from the high school theater department swayed in snowy gusts alongside a cluster of children from Cody and Carol's church meant to represent an angel choir.

"This has got to be the most ragtag group ever brought together," someone observed.

"Which is as it should be." Cody stepped forward, his hands out. "Because Jesus was born in a come-as-you-are kind of gathering not unlike this one. He was put in an impromptu bed and Mary and Joseph had to make do with what they had, but you and I know, friends, that they were given the most precious gift of all."

"Amen," someone shouted.

"The gift of that long-ago night is the gift we share to this day—the hope of eternal life through God's Son, the light of the world." Cody made a signal and Jason pushed a plug into an extension cord and the whole scene lit up.

Everyone oohed and aahed.

Then someone called out, "What about the Santa coins?"

"Yeah, what happened to them all?" Dora asked, going up on tiptoe and holding up the one she wore around her neck as if anyone in that town didn't know what they were talking about.

"I got one," the young artist called out.

"Me too," called the girl who had lost her mother and her hopes of attending college.

Burke and Dora shared a smile, feeling their own instincts on those grants had been validated until—

"And then I gave mine to the Sykes!" the artist concluded.

"I passed mine along to Mrs. Beck, the lunch lady at the high school," the would-be college-bound girl announced.

"I got one!" someone called.

"Me too!" someone else chimed in.

"Gave it to…" The first voice shouted out what had happened to their coin.

One by one everyone in town who had been given a gold coin told the story of the gift and how they had shared it with someone they thought more in need than themselves.

As far as anyone could tell the tokens were, in fact, still on the move throughout the county, spreading good cheer and hope and allowing everyone who touched them to share in the experience of giving.

"That's the way it is around here," Jed finally summed up. "Got to look out for one another. Always someone worse off than you if you think about it and count your blessings. Merry Christmas, everybody!"

The cheer went out, "Merry Christmas!"

Burke pulled Dora close, her back against his chest.

As they stood there enjoying the sight, she murmured, "You certainly made good on your promise. This is a Christmas I will never forget."

"Just the first of many," he assured her.

And she believed him.

Then someone began humming "Silent Night."

"God meets us where we are," Cody took center stage—well, left of center, for he knew he was not the real star of the evening. "Whether we are in a manger in Bethlehem or a bakery in South Carolina, He says, "'Behold! I bring you good tidings of great joy! For unto you is born this day in the city of David a Savior, which is Christ the Lord.'"

And the crowd began to sing.

The snow began to fall.

And Dora thanked the Lord that she had found a place in the world and that because of the baby in the manger, she had never really been alone at all.

* * * * *

Dear Reader,

I hope you enjoy a little glimpse at Mt. Knott, South Carolina, at Christmastime. It's such a blessed time of year that I couldn't resist it as a backdrop for a book. Since I had hinted at the romance for Burke in *Somebody's Baby,* it seemed likely that he would be the next of the wolf pack to find love. So what I felt he needed was something most *unlikely* to add a little fun in the mix. I looked at the grouchiest alpha male of the group and asked myself—who is he the least likely to be compared to? The answer was, of course, Santa Claus. Once I'd gotten him into that pickle, it was great fun to present him with an equally matched mate in Dora, who had so much to give if only somebody would look hard enough to see past her all-business exterior.

Throw in some colorful locals, a small-town atmosphere, a secret cause for my secret "Claus" and the story practically wrote itself. Well, not really, it took a lot of work, but at least I got to listen to Christmas music the whole time!

For that I am grateful (for the judicious use of headphones on my part, my family is grateful) as I am for each and every one of you. My hope for you all is a blessed season full of hope and wonder and rejoicing in the greatest gift of all, the birth of Jesus.

*Annie Jones*

# QUESTIONS FOR DISCUSSION

1. Burke begins the story feeling alienated and displaced by his own family. He feels he has not lived up to their expectations and they have not lived up to his. Do you think this is a common situation, even among Christian families?

2. Dora feels her upbringing by much older foster parents made her out of step with her peers. Do you think this is a bad thing? Do you think she might have been less driven if she had been raised to be more social?

3. Dora realizes that the man who cleans her office knows her better than almost anyone. Are there people in your life you think you know well just from observing them, or being in close proximity with them, even though you don't often talk?

4. What do you think your office/personal space and work habits tell others about you? Is it an accurate picture?

5. Mt. Knott is portrayed as an idyllic small town, though it certainly has a lot of problems. Is it the kind of place where you would want to live? Why or why not?

6. Burke is having a hard time moving past his mother's death and celebrating her life. How do you think the loss of a parent, even as an adult, changes the life of a child left behind?

7. The Burdett family, prior to the matriarch's death, had many special Christmas traditions. Does your family have traditions that they have kept up for years, perhaps generations? Do you think traditions are important? Why or why not?

8. Burke is charged with deciding who should benefit from a Christmas coin that would help them realize their dreams. There are many programs for the needy at Christmas. Do you participate in any of these? On what grounds do you decide which programs you will support?

9. Burke has trouble dealing with feelings of having let his family down. Do you think his feelings are justified? Can you see his family's reasons for the choices they have made?

10. Dora has reached a point in her life where she cannot go on as she has before. She wants to be more than a high-powered workhorse. Do you think a person who has been as driven and successful as she has can actually reorder and simplify their life?

11. Burke's mother's reaction to having been told she could not put her Nativity set on town land was to stop putting it up altogether. She felt wronged and that more people should have stood up for the cause. This is happening more and more around the country, how do you think Christians should respond?

12. Dora is a woman who has so much to give, and Burke is a man who wants nothing from anyone. In the end she confronts him about the importance of accepting what others have to offer as a way of allowing them to shine, to grow and to realize their potential. Tell about a time when you were on both sides of the situation, as someone who wanted to give but was refused or accepted (and how that felt) and as someone who accepted what someone offered and how it affected you.

"Robin," Ethan said, just before his face appeared in the church belfry's open trapdoor, "come on up. It's perfectly safe."

He reached down a gloved hand as she put a foot on the bottom rung of the wrought-iron ladder.

"How does this thing work?"

"It's very simple. There's a tall pole with a hook on one end. I used it to slide open the trap and then pull down the ladder. When I'm done, I'll use it to push the ladder back up and lift it over the locking mechanism, then slide the trap closed."

"I see."

"Oh, you haven't seen anything yet," he told her, grasping her hand and all but lifting her up the last few rungs to stand next to him on a narrow metal platform. In their bulky coats, they had to stand pressed shoulder to shoulder. "Take a look at this." He swung his arm wide, encompassing the town, the valley beyond and the snow-capped mountains surrounding it all.

"Wow."

"Exactly," he said. "There's a part of Psalms 98 that says, 'Let the rivers clap their hands, let the mountains sing together for joy…' Seeing the view like this, you can almost feel it, can't you? The rivers and mountains praising their Creator."

"I never thought of rivers and mountains praising God," she admitted.

"Scripture speaks many times of nature praising God and testifying to His wonders."

"I can see why," she said reverently.

"So can I," he told her, smiling down at her with those warm brown eyes.

Her breath caught in her throat. But surely she was reading too much into that look. That wasn't appreciation she saw in his gaze. That was just her loneliness seeking connection. Wasn't it? Though she had never felt this sudden, electrical link before, as if something vital and masculine in him reached out and touched something fundamental and feminine in her. She had to be mistaken.

He was a man of God, after all.

Even if she couldn't help thinking of him as just a man.

*Will Robin and Ethan find love for Christmas,
or will her secrets stand in their way?
Find out in HER MONTANA CHRISTMAS
by Arlene James, available December 2014 wherever
Love Inspired® books and ebooks are sold.*

# An Amish Christmas Journey

by

## Patricia Davids

### Their Holiday Adventure

Toby Yoder promised to care for his orphaned little sister the rest of her life. After all, the tragedy that took their parents and left her injured was his fault. Now he must make a three-hundred-mile trip from the hospital to the Amish community where they'll settle down. But as they share a hired van with pretty Greta Barkman, an Amish woman with a similar harrowing past, Toby can't bear for the trip to end. Suddenly, there's joy, a rescued cat named Christmas and hope for their journey to continue together forever.

BRIDES OF
*Amish Country*

**Finding true love in the land of the Plain People**

*Available December 2014
wherever Love Inspired books
and ebooks are sold.*

LI87927

# *Love Inspired®*
# SUSPENSE

### RIVETING INSPIRATIONAL ROMANCE

# THE YULETIDE RESCUE

by

# MARGARET DALEY

## MISTLETOE AND MURDER

When Dr. Bree Mathison's plane plummets into the Alaskan wilderness at Christmastime, she is torn between grief and panic. With the pilot—her dear friend—dead and wolves circling, she struggles to survive. Search and Rescue leader David Stone fights his way through the elements to save her. David suspects the plane crash might not have been an accident, spurring Bree's sense that she's being watched. But why is someone after her? Suddenly Bree finds herself caught in the middle of a whirlwind of secrets during the holiday season. With everyone she cares about most in peril, Bree and her promised protector must battle the Alaskan tundra and vengeful criminals to make it to the New Year.

### ALASKAN
### + SEARCH RESCUE

### Risking their lives to save the day

*Available December 2014*
*wherever Love Inspired*
*books and ebooks are sold.*

Find us on Facebook at
www.Facebook.com/LoveInspiredBooks

LIS44637

*Big Sky Daddy*
by
# LINDA FORD

### FOR HIS SON'S SAKE

Caleb Craig will do anything for his son, even ask his
boss's enemy for help. Not only does Lilly Bell tend to his
son's injured puppy, but she offers to rehabilitate little
Teddy's leg. Caleb knows that getting Teddy to walk again is
all that really matters, yet he wonders if maybe Lilly can heal
his brooding heart, as well.

Precocious little Teddy—and his devoted father—steal
Lilly's heart and make her long for a child and husband of her
own. But Lilly learned long ago that trusting a man means
risking heartbreak. Happiness lies within reach—if she seizes
the chance for love and motherhood she never expected...

Montana
Marriages

**Three sisters discover a legacy of love beneath
the Western sky**

*Available December 2014
wherever Love Inspired books
and ebooks are sold.*